Praise

"Another amazing story line, very original. I could not put this book down. Very well written, and with a surprise ending!"

Sindy M.

"From the very first chapter, I could not put this book down. This novel is so much fun and the best piece of fiction I have read in a very long time. There is so much happening in this book, but it's so easy to read. Very well written. This would make a great movie!"

Steve

"This is the second novel I've read by these authors, and I LOVED it! The story started out strong, and, as before, the characters felt as if I'd known them my entire life. The thrills and turns had me on the edge of my seat wanting more. I highly recommend this book as a 'must read.'"

Linda Seder

"The beginning of a nice vacation with friends quickly turns into a nightmare no one could have imagined. The rest is a ride you would only experience on a roller coaster. With its ups and downs, you will enjoy every turn and be wary of the next corner. At times, it will take your breath away."

Sylvie

ALSO BY THE AUTHORS

SERPENTINE

MAJESTIC

HEADHUNTER

SKELETON

METROCAFE

sands press
Brockville, Ontario

METRO*CAFE*

Peter Parkin & Alison Darby

sands press

sands press

A Division of 10361976 Canada Inc.
300 Central Avenue West
Brockville, Ontario
K6V 5V2

Toll Free 1-800-563-0911 or 613-345-2687
http://www.sandspress.com

ISBN 978-1-988281-49-0

Cover Design by Kristine Barker and Wendy Treverton
Edited by Sparks Literary
Formatting by Renee Hare
Publisher Kristine Barker
Author Agent Sparks Literary Consultants

Publisher's Note

For information on bulk purchases of this book or any book published by Sands Press, please call 1-800-563-0911.

1st Printing September 2018

If you prick us do we not bleed? If you tickle us do we not laugh? If you poison us do we not die? And if you wrong us shall we not revenge?

-William Shakespeare

Chapter 1

Florida held a special meaning for Mike Baxter. It was, after all, where he and Cindy had honeymooned many moons ago, and almost as important—although he wouldn't admit it to Cindy—where he'd stroked his first "hole in one." Golf was the reason to be here right now as far as he and his buddies were concerned—middle of May, the cold of Canada left far behind, best friends together in the heat. Life didn't get much better than this.

It was 6:00 a.m., and Mike was standing on the front lawn of their Sarasota rental home, watching the sun rise in the east and the dew begin to evaporate off the grass. There was a light breeze in the air and the palm trees were swaying lazily. Mike lit a cigarette as he waited for his friends. He was always the first one ready to go when they went on these golf junkets, and sometimes his impatience got the better of him. But not today—it was too nice a day to be impatient. Java jolt in one hand, nicotine fix in the other, no worries except making their 7:00 tee time.

Jim was the next one to emerge from the sprawling ranch home. Tall, lanky and somewhat of a geek—but he was after all an accountant, so being geeky was pretty much mandatory. Behind him came Troy, all muscle and testosterone, wearing the loudest pink golf shirt that Mike had ever seen. Both of them sauntered down to where Mike was standing, and together they waited beside one of their two rental cars for their last friend. Gerry was always last.

Mike took out his Big Bertha driver and began taking some mock swings. They'd been out yesterday on their first round of the vacation, and he had felt a bit stiff. The winter rust had been piling up. He hoped today he'd score better. His two friends started swinging as well, and the three of them were soon hacking up some turf on the front boulevard. Still waiting for Gerry.

They heard the front door open and finally out he came with the four women in tow, each sleeping beauty still dressed in pajamas. Cindy, Carol, Amanda and Wendy, arms crossed against the morning breeze, slippers flopping on the pathway. The entourage came down to the car and gave each of their husbands a warm kiss. Mike figured this was just an attempt to make them feel better about the women's planned shopping spree today at St. Armand's Circle while the men were yukking it up on the golf course. Golf did indeed have a price—he'd been in the shops of St. Armand's Circle and that price was indeed steep. He shuddered as he returned Cindy's kiss.

"You boys have fun today, and behave yourselves," Cindy said to him with an admonishing look in her eyes.

"Well, you too." Mike said, with his arms wrapped around her waist. "Don't spend too much of our hard-earned money now."

"Considering your $200 apiece for a single round of golf, I think we women are entitled to a little pampering ourselves today, don't you?" Cindy smiled with that confident look in her eyes that Mike had become so accustomed to over their twelve years of wedded bliss. He had to admit she had a point about the green fees. They were outrageous, especially considering that he would, as usual, be struggling to just break a hundred.

Cindy looked gorgeous in her winter pajamas. They were in a hot climate, but each of the women had brought their winter nightclothes due to the constant hum of the air conditioning that the men always insisted upon. "Us guys are just so hot-blooded," they had pleaded. Mike squeezed Cindy around her nice round bottom and ruffled her auburn hair that had yet to be subjected to the usual morning routine. She still had the prettiest face of anyone he knew, and he was well aware that his buddies envied him. Mike liked that—the 'envy' part. It added extra meaning to the trash talk that they always threw at each other.

Cindy cupped his face in her hands. "You guys be careful out there. There's a storm warning out for this afternoon."

"We'll be finished by noon, so no need to fret. And if I had a dime for every time I've been warned not to golf in a storm, I'd be a rich man."

"You are a rich man," she retorted.

"Yeah, but not from golf!"

"Mike, I know you think I'm a nag, but sometimes you're just careless. Did you know that men get hit by lightning four times more often than women in an average year? And also, Florida has twice as many casualties from lightning storms than any other state. Did you know that?"

One thing about Cindy, she sure did her research and was an absolute fanatic about being careful with health matters. Mike found it irritating at times because he was more of a free spirit, but he knew she meant well so he loved her for it. It made her a great mom as well to their two little girls.

"Yes, dear, I hear you. You know I don't worry as much as you do, but I thank you for doing the worrying for me." Cindy just smiled in response and stretched up on her tiptoes to give him another kiss.

Gerry broke the tender moment and yelled out, "Time to hit the links! Let's go! Day's a wastin!"

"Aren't you the demanding one—the last one out of the house and you're trying to hurry us up," Jim taunted.

"Well, someone had to tend to the ladies. They do have their special morning needs, you know!" Gerry teased, as Troy punched him lightly on the shoulder.

Gerry was the flirt in the group, and he also had the most to flirt with. Well over six feet tall, and with looks that rivaled George Clooney, he knew he had the edge over the other three. But he was good-natured about it, and he was just as happily married as his friends. He just liked to tease them.

They had all been friends back in university, and their feelings for each other had endured since then. Many years after graduation, Mike, the entrepreneur in the group, had proposed a leveraged buyout of a property development company headquartered in Toronto. The market had suffered a downturn and they basically got the company cheap. It was an opportunity that Mike convinced his friends to follow him on.

They brought skills to the table that made the four-way marriage a good one, and each had owned a quarter interest in the company, renamed Baxter Development Corporation. Mike felt that using his last name was appropriate since it was, after all, his idea in the first place. No one argued, and they usually didn't with Mike.

Their individual share interests became diluted three years ago when they went public. They still held a significant thirty percent ownership between them but not enough proxies for controlling interest. However, each of them had become wealthy from the shares they sold on the TSX, so controlling interest wasn't such a hot button for them anymore. They could easily afford to buy their own second homes in Sarasota now— several of them for that matter and large ones at that.

Mike was a civil engineer, the sales oriented one in the group, and also the CEO of the company. Jim was an accountant, a CA in fact, and the CFO. Troy was a construction engineer and oversaw all construction projects and tendering. Gerry was a lawyer and handled virtually all of the deals on land purchases and development contracts. He was also general counsel for the company.

Jim, Troy and Gerry were subordinate to Mike as senior vice presidents, but in reality they all viewed themselves as equals. Mike seldom had to use his power as CEO to get things done, but his friends knew that he was not one to be toyed with. He was a powerful, charismatic man, crucial to the success of the firm and, truth be told, the reason for the wealth they all now had. His drive and vision had made it all happen, and the other three were realistic enough to know that they had him to thank. Baxter Development Corp. now had a market capitalization of well over five billion dollars, with assets throughout North America. The future looked bright for these forty-something executives, and their shareholders had a potential gem in their hands. Beyond North America, South America was beckoning due to some investments they had already made on that emerging continent. Mike had to give Gerry the credit for his acumen and initiative in scouting out that opportunity for them. By all accounts, it should pay off well over the next few years.

They bid their goodbyes to the ladies and piled into the rented Mercedes SUV. This monster had plenty of space for their clubs. The women would take the rented BMW for their shopping adventure, and the men were relieved that it had limited trunk space. Today they were golfing at the Coastal Club, a course with beautiful views of the waterways and bridges surrounding Sarasota. It was going to be a glorious day, if one was to judge just by the boyish smiles on the four eager faces.

*****

Mike drove his ball off the first tee, sending it flying about halfway down the 500 yard fairway. He looked over at his buddies with a cocky grin. "Try to beat that, boys." He was pleased to see that his first shot of the day had not strayed into the woods, or through a window of one of the swank homes that lined the course. That had happened to him far too many times. First tees were a pain in the ass, with everyone watching—from the practice green, the clubhouse, the patios—all snickering to themselves every time some poor slob made a fool of himself. Well, not today, thank you very much.

Jim hit next and he went somewhere off to the left where his vicious hook usually took him. Troy muscled his shot straight down the fairway, well past his much to Mike's chagrin. Gerry uncharacteristically shanked his into the woods.

They headed off in their power carts for a great day of golf. Nice to be off the first tee. Now they could really have some fun. Mike rode with Gerry. Jim and Troy teamed up in the other cart.

Hole after hole, they stayed close in their scores. Gerry seemed to have snapped out of his first tee jinx and was now a contender. They always had money on these games; made it more interesting. Winning cash didn't really matter to any of them anymore, not the way it did back when they were in university and didn't have any. It was more just a symbol of competition and victory now.

Mike thought back to how far they had come, starting off as students who had met each other in the university pub. They had been studying different disciplines, but made sure that they arranged time to hang out together. Those were fun days. After university they all went their separate ways as far as careers, but managed to keep their bond intact. It never wavered.

Then, Mike pulled them all back together again for the LBO and they never looked back. Now rich, living the good life, with very few cares. Sure, they still had the stresses of running a large company, but since they had gone public and hit the windfall known as the TSX, they didn't worry so much anymore. What was the worst that could happen? The board could fire them and bring in another team. Well, so what. They'd still be rich. They now had "fuck off" money. But, they each knew they were too young to retire, and they enjoyed seeing their company grow, still enjoyed the challenge. And it was still fun to be wheeling and dealing. The recent recession had been trying, but things seemed to be on the rebound. Real estate holdings were still depressed, but there was definitely light at the end of the tunnel. At least they had gone public before the recession hit and managed to get most of their personal wealth out of the company. Shares in Baxter had dropped dramatically since then but Mike was certain that he and his team could return their shareholders back to their IPO value, and then beyond. The beer cart made a return visit to them at the thirteenth hole, after having refreshed them previously on the tenth, seventh, and oh yes, the third too. They weren't feeling any pain now and the golf scores were looking good despite the suds.

They had one group in front of them who had just finished teeing off so they had a few minutes to wait before they could advance. Mike sat back on the golf cart under the canopy and sipped his beer. His three friends sat down on the grass and challenged each other to a chugging contest. Mike laughed to himself—not much had changed over the years. They were still students at heart, for a few hours a week at least.

Mike corrected himself slightly—Gerry had changed. He had noticed it over the last few years: more sullen, quiet, off in a different world. Mike knew that lawyers were a different breed and Gerry certainly had a lot of responsibility in the company with his large division. He oversaw 500 employees across the continent and had to worry about land deals, real estate market fluctuations, and how they impacted on the balance sheet. But he had always had those responsibilities since the four of them had bought the company fifteen years ago. Something was different, and Mike noticed that it seemed to start before their big IPO. There had been some family tragedies that Gerry had suffered in recent years, so Mike conceded those were probably a big part of the reason.

However, Gerry had been the only one of the four who was opposed to going public. He had needed extra convincing, and Mike called him into his office for many chats when that process was underway. He finally seemed to come around, which was good because Mike had wanted it to be unanimous amongst the four of them. But since then he wondered if Gerry had just agreed out of courtesy to the other three.

Gerry hadn't of course complained about how going public made him rich, but Mike had noticed that he didn't seem all that excited about it either. More just nonchalant...and preoccupied. It was a puzzle. However, Mike knew that Gerry was also a disciplined sort, having picked that up by flying fighter jets for the military after leaving university. He had also done a stint as a commercial pilot for one of the national airlines after his tenure in the military.

Too nice a day for psychoanalysis Mike decided. Everyone had the potential to behave differently in certain situations, and he had to respect that. But the gradual withdrawal of Gerry's closeness caused him more worry than Gerry's lack of excitement at the riches. He would have to sit down and talk to Gerry about that one of these days—maybe even on this holiday—just the two of them over a beer.

Troy's announcement that the coast was clear jarred Mike out of his daydreaming. He put his can of beer into the cup-holder, grabbed his Big Bertha out of the back of the cart, and started his climb up to the tee box for the thirteenth hole.

He noticed Gerry had already placed his ball on the tee, and was taking some practice swings.

Suddenly Mike noticed something else as well, and immediately felt his face drain of blood and the hairs bristle along his forearms.

Chapter 2

None of them had taken notice of the dark threatening clouds that had gradually crept over the thick stand of trees to the south of the tee box. Mike saw them first along with several eerie horizontal flashes between the thunderheads. The thick mass was right above them now.

He ran to the top of the mound and suddenly felt tingling from the top of his head to his toes. It felt like every hair on his body was erect. He knew what that meant. Static electricity was building quickly and a bolt was about to strike, very close.

He reached the tee box area and yelled to his friends, "Hit the ground! Get low!" Out of the corner of his eye he saw Jim and Troy drop to the ground and curl up into tight balls. They now saw the clouds too, and probably felt the same tingling. But Gerry kept swinging, strangely oblivious to the danger overhead. Off in the distance Mike could hear the warning siren from the direction of the clubhouse. A little late.

Mike ran towards Gerry as fast as his legs would carry him, and continued yelling. Gerry paused in mid-swing, club extended over his head, and looked back at Mike with a puzzled, almost annoyed look on his face. Mike kept going right toward him, keeping as low to the ground as he could. He knew Gerry wouldn't have time to react now, being more concerned with being disturbed by his friend than looking up to the danger in the sky.

Mike could feel the tingling getting stronger, exactly like touching a metal doorknob in a dry house, although in this case it was his entire body that was feeling it, not just his hand. For a split second he recalled the words of warning from Cindy, and for that same split second he felt stupid. He should have been checking the sky as they finished each hole. They had been too busy drinking and clowning around. Mike launched himself in a dive toward Gerry, toward that astonished face that had no idea what was going on. He tackled him in the back, at chest height, just as his eyes were almost blinded by a flash, a flash that seemed to start at the top of Gerry's extended golf club and snaked downward. Gerry lurched backward as the bolt connected, and the back of his head smashed into Mike's forehead. Mike felt the pain in his forehead for only a millisecond, as it was quickly dwarfed by a sharp knife lacing through his body, from his head to…everywhere. He could feel his tongue chomped by his clenching teeth followed by the familiar taste of blood. His eyes felt like they were going to explode out of their sockets. He knew he was now on the ground but he couldn't stand up; not that he tried, but he just knew that he couldn't.

Before everything went black, he felt a strange sense of relief as moisture began to spread inside the front and backside of his pants.

*****

Cindy was at the wheel as the BMW careened off Tamiami Trail into the Emergency entrance of Sarasota Memorial Hospital. She abandoned the car in a restricted area and threw the keys to a protesting parking monitor, as all four ladies raced into the lobby of the giant hospital. After shouting out some questions, they were directed down to the trauma waiting room, where they found Jim and Troy sitting forlornly with their heads in their hands.

Carol and Wendy knelt down beside their husbands and hugged them. Cindy and Amanda stood in front of them, both afraid to ask the question, but knowing one of them had to. Amanda spoke softly, "Have you heard anything yet?"

Troy looked up and shook his head slowly. "It's bad, really bad."

"Where are they now?" Cindy asked, voice trembling.

"The trauma team took them away—that's the last we saw of them," Jim replied. Cindy turned to Amanda and grabbed onto her. They squeezed each other tightly as the tears began to flow. Except for the sobbing, it was dead quiet in the waiting room; an ominous stillness that was eventually broken by official-sounding footsteps approaching along the antiseptic tile floor.

"Mrs. Upton and Mrs. Baxter?" Cindy and Amanda turned around and bravely faced the young doctor who was now standing there, mandatory stethoscope around his neck, clipboard in hand.

"Yes," Cindy replied, holding her head up high, bracing herself. "I'm Cindy Baxter, and this is Amanda Upton. Please, just tell us."

"I'm Dr. Fenton, the resident cardiologist. Do you want to come to my office to talk?"

"No, right here is fine—these are our friends." Amanda replied, as she leaned closer into Cindy.

Fenton took a noticeably deep breath—and then a second one. "Your husband has passed away, Mrs. Upton. We did all we could but his heart just couldn't survive the trauma. It was too severe. I'm so sorry."

Amanda went limp and collapsed in Cindy's arms, crying. The doctor reached out and helped Cindy get Amanda over to a chair. "I can give you something to help with the shock, a light sedative perhaps?"

"No, nothing," Amanda sobbed.

Cindy looked up at the doctor expectantly. "My husband?"

"He's stable right now. However, he did go into cardiac arrest and his heart is the main worry we have right now. He has some burns on his head and feet—the entry and exit points of the lightning bolt—but they will heal easily. It's the internal injuries we're worried about, as well as the possibility of brain damage. We won't know for a while yet. We'll need to keep him here for a few days."

Cindy brought both hands up to her mouth, and started to tremble. "Can I see him?"

"Yes, but only briefly. I can't emphasize enough how 'touch and go' this is for your husband right now. Follow me, please."

Cindy looked down at Amanda, who was being comforted now by Carol and Wendy. They both nodded reassuringly at Cindy and motioned for her to follow the doctor to her husband's side.

Dr. Fenton led Cindy down the hallway, through double doors to another hallway, then through to the Intensive Care section. He talked as he walked. Past a central nursing desk, to the private room numbered 207. Fenton stopped in front of the door and turned around to face Cindy. "Don't be shocked when you see him. We haven't had the chance to clean him up yet, and we really have to leave him untouched until a keraunopathy specialist has a look at him."

Cindy's scratched her head as she gazed at Fenton with a question in her eyes. "Sorry, Mrs. Baxter, I should explain. Keraunopathy is the study of the pathology of lightning, and only a few specialists in the world understand that mysterious field. We want the specialist to see how the lightning traveled down your husband's body. He'll examine the body of Mr. Upton also. You'll notice the deep burn mark on your husband's forehead, as well as the complete destruction of the soles of his shoes. He contracted the bolt through head contact with the head of Mr. Upton. It looks like they banged into each other."

Dr. Fenton paused to see if she was absorbing what he was saying. Cindy nodded and he continued. "Normal industrial electrocutions from man-made, high-voltage devices, produce a shock of no more than 60 kilovolts. However a lightning bolt can deliver up to 300 kilovolts. Most of the bolt slides over the surface of the body—a process called 'external flashover.' That's why you'll see his clothes singed in spots all the way down to his feet. The bolt we're mainly concerned with however is the smaller segment which went through his head, internally to his feet, and out; or vice versa. Only 20% of victims die from the immediate shock of the bolt. But the remaining 80% can have strange injuries and behaviors lasting sometimes for years, or life. These injuries are sometimes difficult to understand and treat. That's why the phenomena is being studied now as a separate specialty entirely—keraunopathy. It's new science that we're just starting to understand a bit."

Cindy looked at him with even more puzzlement now. The doctor squeezed her shoulder and said, "The good news is that your husband is in the 80% group that initially survive the bolt. So let's focus on thinking about that, okay?" She nodded. "We'll talk more later about some of the after-effects that may need treatment."

He opened the door to 207. Cindy paused in the doorway and saw her still handsome husband, hair singed, forehead burnt, oxygen mask attached to his face and monitors attached to his head and chest. He looked so helpless.

Dr. Fenton motioned her over to the bedside. She held Mike's hand and spoke softly to him.

Suddenly Mike opened his eyes, and Cindy lurched backward in shock. She looked at the doctor and he smiled knowingly. "He's awake, and he hears you. This is a good sign. I think he wants to talk to you."

Cindy looked down and could see her husband make a slight nod with his head. Dr. Fenton carefully removed the oxygen mask. "I'll take this off for just a couple of minutes. It will be good for him to interact with you, and good for me to observe how he does. His breathing isn't labored anymore so he may not even need this mask now. We'll see."

Cindy couldn't help but smile. The mask was off and she could see Mike's entire face, a face she was afraid she would never gaze at again. She leaned over and kissed his cheek, and he leaned slightly into her. He opened his mouth and started moving his lips but she could hear only a slight groaning sound. Dr. Fenton leaned over with a squirt bottle and sent a small stream of water into Mike's mouth.

Cindy kissed him lightly on the lips. "I love you, Mikey. Please be well, we need you so much," she said with tears in her eyes. She had hoped to not show her tears, to give Mike hope, not despair, to not make him think she knew something that he didn't. But she couldn't help herself.

Mike opened his mouth again and started to make some human sounds this time. Cindy knew he was trying to talk. She rubbed his cheek and leaned her ear close to his mouth.

"They…have…to change…my pants."

She looked into his eyes, thought for a second that he was trying to crack a joke like he usually did, then watched in horror as his eyeballs rolled up into his head. Dr. Fenton quickly put the mask back on, then checked the monitors and his vitals. Cindy backed up from the bed and put her hands over her eyes. She kept them there as she heard the words, "I think he's gone into coma."

Chapter 3

There were crucial things that needed to be done in Mike's absence. To begin with, Troy and Jim met with the head office staff as soon as they arrived back in Toronto, and then conducted videoconferences with the rest of their employees scattered across North America. They invited questions but only received a couple of tentative ones. People were stunned, pure and simple. One of the company's top executives was dead, and their CEO was in a coma.

After dealing with their employees, press releases had to be drafted and the company's PR agency dealt with that quickly and efficiently. These had to go out to the major media outlets in both Canada and the United States, and had to be worded such that confidence would be preserved and convey the message that Baxter Development Corp. was in good hands and would survive this setback, shocking as it was.

Troy convened an emergency meeting with the Board, which consisted of sixteen very anxious men and women from all major walks of life. They each had questions, more serious questions than the staff had, which was understandable considering the personal liabilities each of them faced as Board members. Change was always stressful but to have two executives disappear from action in one fell swoop was tough to swallow. The Board was worried.

Next Troy and Jim met with the rest of the executive staff, which consisted of ten vice presidents. They had to consider also that one of these executives would need to be promoted fairly soon to the senior ranks to replace Gerry in the Development Division. They couldn't wait until Mike was on his feet again—if he ever was on his feet again. Gerry's division was too important and too large to leave leaderless for long.

After all those ducks were in order, they met with senior representatives of the Ontario Securities Commission, which was the regulator that oversaw capital markets in Ontario. In essence, Baxter's presence on the Toronto Stock Exchange meant they were regulated by the OSC. This was an important meeting and it went well. The regulator seemed to sympathize with their dilemma and appreciated the speed at which the executives had responded with their communiqués and tactics to dismiss any nervousness. Disclosure was something that companies trading on the TSX had to practice like a religion, and they earned respect every time they demonstrated diligence to the regulator. In Baxter's favor, it had been a star pupil on the Exchange since being listed, and had observed every disclosure requirement in a timely fashion. It was disciplined and professional and the OSC liked that. There were too many other companies out there who required serious oversight, so Baxter looked comparatively angelic.

In between all this corporate stuff, Troy and Jim somehow found time to grieve for their friend Gerry, and worry themselves sick over their leader, Mike, still lying in a Florida hospital bed.

Troy spun his chair around and stared out at Lake Ontario from his fortieth floor window in the Harbor Square office complex. It was a wonderful view, but he couldn't enjoy it today. Spring had finally come to Toronto, a little late, but better late than never. It was, after all, the beginning of June and after a long punishing winter it was nice to finally feel and see the warmth again.

Thinking of warmth made Troy reflect back to just two weeks ago when they were all in Florida together. One of the reasons why they had planned their May getaway was the dismal winter they had suffered through in Toronto. It just wouldn't let up even well into the traditional spring months. So they just got together and went. Who could have known…

Troy had given the eulogy at Gerry's funeral, and the church was packed to standing room only. Gerry had had a lot of friends in the business community and they all showed up. Poor Amanda—she had been so upset, inconsolable. It wasn't just Gerry's death and knowing that her two boys would now miss out on their father's love, but it was the combined effect of numerous tragedies that had hit the Upton family over the last few years. Unbelievably coincidental and violent: Amanda's parents shot to death during a robbery at the store they ran, her brother killed in a hit and run, Gerry's two younger brothers gunned down as collateral damage in a drive-by shooting while on vacation in Puerto Vallarta. Now Gerry was gone. How much tragedy could happen to one family and how much could they take and stay sane?

Troy knew that the Board would not be patient for too long, and neither would their shareholders. He wondered how long it would take for them to pull the plug and start the search for a new CEO. Mike could be in that coma for a very long time. Troy hoped that he and Jim could hold off the wolves as long as possible. Mike was the creator and the driver, and he deserved the wait. The two of them were perfectly capable of keeping the ship steady for quite some time—and neither of them wanted Mike's job anyway, so the board would have to search outside the company. Which would not be a good thing. The culture would change and no doubt the senior staff would change. An unsettling thought to say the least.

Troy leaned over in his expensive leather chair in his plush corner office, clasped his hands together and mouthed a silent prayer. Troy hadn't prayed since he was an altar boy in the fifth grade.

*****

Cindy was sitting on the front porch of the Sarasota ranch house when she got the call. She had been doing nothing, the same activity she had been doing for the last two weeks. Her nails were chewed down to the fingertips, and her knuckles were swollen from excessive cracking. She hadn't been able to read or watch television, incapable of anything requiring concentration. Her only act of awareness was to call her parents in Toronto and ask them to watch their two daughters a little bit longer—maybe a lot longer.

She lurched at the ringing of the phone. She clumsily punched a couple of buttons until she hit the right one. Dr. Fenton was on the line, and she could tell he was excited as soon as he said hello. Cindy didn't have to ask. She just said, "I'm on my way." When she arrived at the hospital she ran down to room 207, which she could have easily found blindfolded by now. A nurse motioned to her to slow down but she just rushed right by, unseeing. Cindy's feet practically slid along the polished floor in through the open door. Then it felt like her heart stopped beating as she stared in stunned silence at her husband, sitting up in bed sipping a glass of juice through a straw.

Mike smiled at her between sips, and, picking his words carefully said, "I can see you've been sun tanning."

Cindy ran to his bedside and gave him the biggest kiss she had ever laid on him. He kissed her back and she was pleased to notice that he hadn't forgotten how to do that. She really hadn't known what to expect—she equated 'coma' with 'memory loss,' and the doctor had quickly corrected her on that. But she still didn't know what to believe. For the last two weeks she had been actually expecting the worst; that she'd have to transport him back to Toronto comatose and that he'd be in that vegetative state for the rest of his life.

Dr. Fenton had been standing in a corner of the room, and respectfully left for a while to let the two get re-acquainted. After some more kissing and hugging and discussions about the kids, Mike finally asked the questions that

Cindy had braced herself for.

"So, how long have I been like this?" Mike looked her squarely in the eyes.

"About two weeks now," Cindy said softly as she held his hand.

"Gerry?"

Cindy paused and squeezed his hand. "He didn't make it, Mike."

Mike pulled his hand away, looked down at his blanket and started twirling his fingers in the tassels. He didn't say anything at all, but Cindy noticed that his hands were trembling ever so slightly. He looked up at her and nodded as his eyes welled up with tears. "I need to be alone right now, hon. Okay?"

*****

A long week followed, with Cindy spending all day, every day, at the hospital with Mike. She was overjoyed at the progress he was making. By the end of the week with the help of speech and physical therapy, his walking had returned to normal and his formation of words was now accurate and back to their regular rate of speed—fast. Mike's appetite was ravenous despite the bland hospital food and his spirits seemed good, all things considered.

They didn't talk about the accident, not even once. Mike asked about Amanda and how she was holding up, but that was the only reference he made to the tragedy. And Cindy knew he only asked because he was well aware of the other tragedies that the Upton family had suffered over the last few years. He was probably worried that this might push Amanda over the edge.

At the end of the week, Cindy packed Mike's bag and they went to Dr. Fenton's office for a consult before heading back to Toronto. She just wanted to get Mike home, but this meeting was important. This is when the "incident" would be discussed and what they both had to be prepared for. She didn't think it was totally necessary—Mike seemed fine now, but she didn't want to have any regrets.

They sat in the doctor's modest office on comfortable leather chairs facing his desk. Mike seemed restless—his left leg was bouncing and he seemed anxious to go. She held onto his hand.

Fenton got right down to business. "You've had the shock of your life—pun intended. It's important for you to know what happened from an anatomy standpoint before you head back home. Your recovery has been wonderful, but I won't sugar-coat it; the worst could be ahead of you."

Cindy looked at Mike and could see his expression change. He was concentrating, but she could tell he didn't like Fenton's opening statement. She squeezed his hand a little bit harder for reassurance.

"Our keraunopathy specialist has examined you and Mr. Upton. I've also talked with your friends as to what they observed when the lightning bolt hit. It appears as if you were trying to tackle Mr. Upton to the ground to protect him. I know you remember that based on the discussions we've had together. Your two other friends report seeing a bright flash where your heads connected, and another one from the golf club upward."

Mike nodded.

"The bolt traveled through Mr. Upton's upright golf club, and slid sideways into his head. When the two of you banged heads, a secondary bolt went from his head into yours and out through your feet. Part of it went along the surface of your body as an 'external flashover.' That explains the burns in your clothing. By the way, as an aside, the reverse path could have just as likely been the case—it is thought by science that the main bolt usually originates from the ground and travels upward to the sky instead of from the top down. However, it doesn't really matter, the effects are still the same."

Mike just shrugged, indicating that he didn't care where the bolt came from.

Fenton got up from his chair and walked around to the front of the desk facing them directly. "It's a mysterious field, keraunopathy, and we don't completely understand yet why some people survive lightning strikes and others don't. We also can't predict the after-effects with any certainty. It's just not understood. The voltage from lightning is so powerful that the effects on the human body can be varied and unknown. Fortunately, and ironically unfortunately, it doesn't happen often enough for us to have a large enough data bank."

He walked over to his credenza. "Would either of you like some coffee?" They both shook their heads. Fenton poured himself a cup and continued.

"I want to share with you some of the after-effects that you might have to deal with. It's important that you see your family doctor as soon as you get home and report to him or her which of these happen to you, and any others that may be strange or different from what you're accustomed to. Don't leave anything out.

"Also, I would like your doctor to send regular reports to me here. E-mail, without your name mentioned, would be just fine. We'll give you a patient identity number on your way out. With your permission, I'll then pass your information along to Dr. Linoczek, our specialist, to be part of an overall study. It may help others who are struck by lightning."

Fenton looked at Mike and raised his eyebrows in a challenge. Mike just nodded in agreement once again.

"Fine, then. Here we go: chest pain, irregular heartbeat, loss of consciousness or blackouts, amnesia, anxiety and confusion, seizures, numbness and weakness in limbs, temporary or permanent paralysis, unexplained pains, shaking, sleep disorder, inability to concentrate, irritability, depression, headaches, fatigue, temporary or permanent deafness, partial blindness—and just general Post Traumatic Stress Disorder."

Fenton paused and waited for reactions.

Mike shifted in his chair. "Doc, I feel fine and I doubt that any of those things will happen to me. I just want to go home and put this behind us."

"I'm sure you do, but you need to know what may happen and that these conditions may occur without any warning, and possibly for the rest of your life. They could be minor, they could be major, or you may experience nothing at all. But you need to be on your guard; not just for your safety, but also the safety of others." Cindy blinked several times at Fenton's last statement.

Mike gave the doctor a wry smile. "Gotcha. If that's all then, we're out of here, okay? Thanks for everything you've done for me, and I mean that sincerely. But I'm sure I'm going to be just fine." Mike rose from his chair and put his hand in the small of Cindy's back, signaling her to do the same. They both shook hands with Dr. Fenton and bid their goodbyes. Cindy could see the worry in the doctor's eyes as he "examined" Mike for the last time.

She was silent as they rode the elevator down. The things Fenton told them had left a lump in her throat, but what really caused her silence was the feel of a gentle twitching in Mike's hand as she held onto it for dear life.

Chapter 4

"...so this brings us to the last item on the agenda today, which is a quick review by management of the foreign real estate holdings currently in play. Mike, do you wish to address, or would you prefer one of your executives to do that?"

Mike could feel the sweat dripping down his shirt, luckily covered up by his Saville Row suit. This was his first Board meeting since returning to work forty-five days after the lightning had laced through his body down in Florida. Forty-five days after one of his best friends had been killed almost instantly as their two heads connected in trauma. Sure, the paramedics had tried to revive him and so had the hospital, but the poor guy was probably gone before he hit the ground. At least he didn't suffer.

The Board had been sympathetic it seemed, but only during the coffee and muffin social before the meeting commenced. Then it was down to business except for the official "Welcome back Mike" from the chairman, Peter Botswait, who also dutifully led the Board and executive in a fifteen second prayer for the soul of Gerry Upton, who would be "sorely missed." This was all for the 'minute book' of course, and Mike always felt that there was nothing more insincere than a "sincerely" planned expression of grief and sadness for the minute book.

"Yes, I'll address the holdings, and my colleagues can jump in any time they feel they would like to add something." Mike glanced over at Troy Askew and Jim Belton, and they nodded back at him encouragingly. Mike felt a bit self-conscious—he knew his friends were fearful for him, hoping he would get through this first Board meeting in his usual fine style. They each wanted the Board to feel confident, and in turn the shareholders, that the company was still in good stable hands.

He began: "Our real estate holdings, as you all know, are substantial. Most of our tracts are in Canada and the U.S.A., but we do hold about forty million in undeveloped tracts in South America, and another twenty-five million in Mexico."

A director by the name of Guy Wilkins interrupted him. Mike knew him to be a senior partner with one of the largest law firms in Canada. "Mike, refresh my memory a bit here. How leveraged are we down there?"

"Those were cash transactions. Our lenders were apparently not too positive about allowing our lines of credit to be used beyond our domestic operations. And we were already leveraged pretty heavily here."

Guy nodded. "Where are we in South America?"

"Exclusively in Brazil. We felt the potential there outweighed any other South or Central American country. We own a large tract just outside the city centre of Rio de Janeiro, which is planned as a housing subdivision, and we purchased another large section in Angra dos Reis which is about 170 kilometers from Rio. That project will be a resort condo/hotel along a beautiful stretch of Juruba Beach."

"And in Mexico?"

"There we own land just outside Acapulco and also down in Huatulco. Both these areas are planned resort developments for us."

"Is that smart, Mike?" This from the chairman, Peter Botswait.

Mike looked down the table at Peter. "You're referring to the drug wars that are raging down there right now?"

"Yes, and the violence towards tourists."

"I admit, it's a concern, but we don't think it's enough to dampen our investment. Mexico remains a top tourist destination, easily accessible, and Huatulco is far enough south to be rather insulated. Most of the problems have been close to the U.S. border."

"True, but there have been attacks in the Acapulco area, have there not?" Guy posed this question.

"Yes, Guy, but we don't think those are necessarily going to persist over time."

"How long have we owned these properties in Mexico and Brazil?" Christine Masden, a chartered accountant from one of the "big five" jumped into the conversation.

"We've owned Mexico for about four years and Brazil for only two."

Peter got up for some coffee and glanced back from the side table. "When do you plan to begin development in these two countries?"

"Well, we've been holding off on both countries due to the economy. We thought it prudent to conduct new market strategies now as the old ones may have been rendered obsolete by the new economic realities. For example, instead of the high-end resorts catering to the rich, we may decide family resorts are more realistic now. As well, with the subdivision planned outside Rio, it may not be smart to develop an estate golf course community like we had originally planned."

"Wouldn't those revised plans corrupt your original 'return on investment' projections? Wouldn't that mean you might have overpaid for these properties?" Peter asked, between sips of coffee.

Mike had to partially agree. They were asking good questions, ones that he himself had been pondering.

"That could be the case, however higher density subdivisions do indeed retain ROE, and market demand for affordable family resorts could also increase turnover rates and occupancy rates. So in other words, it may be a 'wash.' That's why we need new studies and new proformas."

Christine leaned across the board table. "The sixty-five million you mentioned that was paid for the four properties, that would be book value, correct? In other words, have they been re-assessed yet for current market value? Have you made a provision in the balance sheet for unusual depreciation due to the recession and foreign instability issues?"

Mike looked over at Jim, his Chief Financial Officer.

Jim jumped in without hesitation. "No Christine, we haven't done that yet. We feel that the values have not been compromised and in fact may have actually increased if our plans become more realistic. We're holding off on re-valuation until our new strategic plans are finalized. We'll then test the values against those plans."

"So until then, it may be fair to say that some assets on our balance sheet could be overstated." Christine wanted the minutes to reflect her concern.

Mike took exception to this. He looked in Peter's direction. "Mr. Chairman, it's premature to make such a comment and I don't think it's helpful for the minutes to record such unwarranted speculation."

Peter nodded. "Agreed." He tapped his pen on the desk in front of the recording secretary. "Strike Ms. Masden's last statement from the minutes."

Peter took off his glasses and directed his next question back to Mike. "Have you personally seen these properties?"

Mike felt a lump in his throat. "No, I haven't. Gerry handled those transactions. He was in charge of all of our new developments."

Guy then stated the obvious. "Gerry's not here anymore, is he."

Mike didn't know what he could say to that, so he just nodded respectfully.

Peter raised his eyebrows and then closed his binder with an emphatic snap. "So, Mike, can we end this discussion by stating in the minutes that you will report to the Board on this matter at the next meeting, with updates on your revised studies?"

"Yes, that would be accurate. I'll address this again and make sure you are all up to date."

With that, the meeting was adjourned and the Board members hurried away to their next worries of the day. Troy and Jim patted Mike on the back, obviously proud of the way their boss had handled himself. Mike, however, wasn't so sure he deserved those pats. He had just been winging it.

*****

Back in his office, Mike asked his executive assistant, Stephanie, to bring him his usual lunch: sandwich and coffee. When it arrived he thanked her and closed his door. Putting his feet up on the credenza while looking out at the lake, he munched away on his egg salad sandwich and just enjoyed the quiet and privacy. Since getting back to work, he seemed to appreciate his alone time much more than before. Of course, he'd never been away from work that long before, so perhaps he had gotten used to not having the daily interactions. This was different, having his door closed. He had never closed his door before.

He had to admit that he was feeling pretty healthy considering what happened. He sure missed Gerry though. He regretted that he never did have the chance to sit down and chat with him like he'd planned to do. Now he would never know what had been troubling him over the last few years, and why they had begun to grow so distant.

Suddenly he felt a pang of guilt. Why was he thinking this was all about him? How selfish. Poor Gerry had suffered through the murders of Amanda's parents, the hit and run death of her brother, and the drive-by shooting deaths of his own brothers—all within the last five years. Of course that would change someone, dramatically. And here he was concerned that his relationship with Gerry had suffered. It wasn't about him, it was about the burdens Gerry had been carrying in his personal life. Yes, that had to be it, and would Mike have handled those tragedies himself any differently than Gerry had? Was he that devoid of emotion?

Mike finished his sandwich and sipped his coffee. Those questions from the Board today had been a bit mind-numbing, particularly since he knew they were legitimate concerns. And nagging away at him was the knowledge that he was a skillful delegator. Perhaps too skillful a delegator. As the CEO, he knew that he should have had more personal involvement with those projects in Mexico and Brazil. He felt sheepish having to admit to the Board that he'd never even seen the properties. But he had had unwavering trust in Gerry's ability to run his own division and of course his own management style was "hands off" unless something threatened to go off the rails.

Or was it because he and Gerry had been friends? Mike didn't really know. But what he did know was that he, Mike, was a gifted executive with great instincts. He was a visionary and dynamic. He made things happen, and he trusted others to follow his lead. But he seldom followed up on things. It had never really been necessary. Now that Gerry was gone, he felt vulnerable. There were things he just didn't know, and he had to correct that now. He felt that things were slightly off the rails and he had to now get more involved, "hands on."

*****

The phone rang and Mike lurched forward, spilling coffee down the front of his freshly-laundered shirt.

"Baxter here."

"Mike, are you alright?" It was Cindy, sounding concerned for some reason.

"Of course, hon. I just finished the board meeting and had a quiet lunch. But the phone jarred me a bit—now I've got coffee all over me!"

"The board meeting must have gone long today?"

"No, the same as usual. About four hours."

Cindy paused for a few seconds. Then, in almost a whisper, "Mike, it's 8:00 at night. Your board meeting was this morning. And you just finished your lunch now?" Mike finally took notice of the darkness that was enveloping the western sky. He glanced down at his watch and was shocked to see that Cindy was right. He frowned, and rubbed his eyes. Then he rubbed them again, just to make sure.

"Mike, are you still there? Are you going to come home?"

"I'm leaving right now, Cindy. The time just flew by on me today. I must be pretty drained from the board meeting. Keep my dinner warm, okay?"

He heard a sigh at the other end, and Cindy said, "Be careful. We should talk when you get home."

Mike slipped on his jacket, turned off his computer, locked his cabinet—and wondered where in hell the last seven hours had gone.

Chapter 5

"You know we promised Dr. Fenton that we would keep him posted, so that's why I emailed him. You shouldn't be surprised."

"I know, I know, but let's not make a mountain out of a molehill."

"Mike, seven lost hours is not a molehill!"

They were sitting at the kitchen table having an early breakfast. Cindy was trying hard to get his attention, but Mike was having a tough time accepting that this incident was a problem. She had whipped off an email to Fenton last night, right after he arrived home and admitted to her that he had no idea where the afternoon had gone. In hindsight Mike knew he should have stuck with the story that he had been so busy that the day had just flown by. When Cindy got her teeth into something, she was like a dog with a bone; a mighty cute dog, mind you, but still a dog.

"Keep your voice down Cindy; we don't want the girls to hear you and get all worried about me. They take after you that way."

"Well, somebody has to worry about you. You certainly don't. You've been through a major ordeal, and I've noticed the shaking in your hands. I know you've been trying to hide that, but I've seen it. Now you have just lost most of a complete day and you don't seem to care."

"I do care. But I also know that stress can just knock you out sometimes. I think that's what happened yesterday. It was my first board meeting since coming back, and I was obviously worried about it. And I had to deal with some uncomfortable questions. I think I just zoned out."

His wife got up from her chair and stomped over to the coffee machine, then whirled around and glared at him. "Zoning out is not normal, Michael, not at all! Not for seven consecutive hours!"

He hated it when she called him "Michael" because it usually meant only one thing—she was seriously pissed.

Cindy poured them both second cups of coffee just as their two little girls came down the stairs. Mike smiled as he saw them. They always had that effect on him; they were so adorable. Kristy was six and Diana was eight, and they were daddy's girls for sure. He jumped up from his chair, grabbed each of them in an arm, and swung them around in a complete circle.

They giggled as they usually did when Mike roughhoused with them. Diana, so mature for an eight year old, said, "Daddy, where were you last night? We had to go to bed without you tucking us in." Kristy nodded in agreement and tried to tickle her dad under the arms.

"I was at work girls. Sorry about that, but it was a busy day for me. I promise I'll be home for dinner tonight."

Mike looked over at Cindy and saw that she was allowing herself a smile, the first one of the morning so far. She knew he had a special bond with their daughters. She was a great mother, but dad was the fun one, the good-time guy. Cindy did most of the disciplining and attending to most of their physical needs, but dad got to do the fun stuff. But that was the way most families worked, and children needed that contrast. The girls loved both of them, but looked to each of them for different things. When they were sick, they wanted only their mom. When they scraped their knees, only mom could apply the Band-Aids. But when they wanted to feel grown-up, or have an adventure, they would look to their father.

"Okay girls, let's get your breakfast. And Mike, we'll talk some more when you get home tonight?"

"We will, and I'll be home on time. I promise." He reached down to give Kristy and Diana kisses and big hugs. They giggled again. Then he walked around the table and hugged Cindy, giving her an extra squeeze on the bum.

She looked up at him with a mischievous smile. "Okay, maybe I was making a mountain of a molehill."

Mike laughed, knowing she didn't really mean that, grabbed his briefcase and headed out the door.

*****

Today was one of the rare days that Mike was taking the subway. He didn't like to do it too often, but once in a while he just couldn't stomach the Toronto traffic and wanted someone else to do the work. Also, despite his protests to Cindy, he was indeed concerned about yesterday's "blackout," and didn't want to take a chance driving today. The subway station was close, about a five minute walk from their house. The Baxters lived in Rosedale, an "old money" neighborhood of mansions. While Mike's wealth wasn't exactly "old money," he didn't care whether or not the neighbors felt he qualified.

He just liked the neighborhood, had always dreamt of living there, and once he made it big he and Cindy decided to leave their modest home in Leaside and make the big splurge. The trees were huge, the security patrols were regular, and it was considered inner city so everything was convenient. And the investment was secure. People would drive through Rosedale just to ogle the monster character homes.

Their circa 1920s home, nestled high on a hill amongst towering maples, oozed eight thousand square feet of absolute charm. The gardens were gorgeous thanks to Cindy's green thumb and the kitchen was one that any gourmet chef would have an orgasm over. With Cindy's culinary talents, Mike felt that she deserved the best kitchen money could buy.

Sometimes Mike would just wander through their house soaking up the pride that he felt. He knew the place was "over the top," but he also knew that life was short. A fact that he was even more acutely aware of since Gerry's death.

He entered the Rosedale subway station, descended underground with all of the other morning commuters, dropped in his token, then headed downward again to the train platform. He purposely stood back from the edge, as he had heard of so many sad stories of people being shoved by drug-crazed maniacs onto the tracks. He wasn't going to take any chances.

Mike's suit-jacket flapped in the gush of wind as the silver train whooshed into the station. He shuffled his way towards the door along with about a dozen other miserable souls. As usual, the train was already jam-packed to standing room only, so once inside the car he had no choice but to just grab hold of one of the upper bars and sway along with the movement of the train as it resumed its journey through the tunnel.

The effect was almost hypnotic.

*****

The train pulled into Queen station and Mike was still holding onto the bar. A pregnant woman sitting in the seat in front of him rose to get off, but she paused in front of him first and said, "I can't thank you enough for what you did. That was so brave." Mike just stared at her, puzzled. He glanced around to see if she was addressing someone else.

A man standing next to him clapped him on the back. "This city needs more people like you. Punks like that have no respect for anyone these days. I wish I could be that brave. Maybe I will be from now on." The stranger gave Mike a manly embrace, then laughed sardonically. "When you threw them out the door at Dundas, I was hoping they'd fall onto the tracks!"

Mike looked at the woman and at the man, and just nodded. He had no idea what they were talking about. He looked around the car and saw several other people nodding and smiling at him. He felt as if he was in a glass cage at the zoo.

The pregnant woman said, "Please, take my seat." Mike sat down as she exited the train, and she looked back at him one more time and mouthed, "Thank you."

He thought that he must be dreaming, or that these people were crazy. The whole experience made him feel like he was in "Alice in Wonderland" and had just fallen through the looking glass. What the hell were they talking about? And why were all these strangers smiling at him? He could see heads craning their necks to get a look at him from farther down the car, and people talking in hushed tones and pointing at him.

There was a lady sitting next to him who suddenly reached her arms around him and hugged him. She opened her purse and pulled out some tissues and Band-Aids, and said, "Let me help you with your hand."

Mike looked down at his hand and saw that his knuckles were bleeding, badly. He nodded at her, not knowing what else to do. Then he noticed his briefcase had blood all over the bottom edges. What the hell had happened? He had either been involved in some kind of altercation and, amazingly, didn't remember it, or he was now in some kind of dream-state. He had no idea.

The lady finished wrapping his hand by the time they had passed through the King station, and in a couple of minutes he felt the train start to slow down again. He looked up and saw that he was at his stop, Union. Mike looked at her, smiled grimly, and thanked her. He rose from his seat and walked through the open door.

As he left the train, cheers and applause followed him out onto the platform.

*****

His in-box was overflowing with envelopes containing condolences that he knew he had to get to. But first he had to wipe the blood off his briefcase.

Mike couldn't remember anything that had happened between Rosedale and Dundas, but from the comments of the two passengers he deduced that he had somehow thwarted an attack on a pregnant woman and thrown some punks off the train at the Dundas station. How could he possibly have done that and not remember? He shook his head in frustration. And since when had he become someone who would step in and fight? That was not who he was. He had never been a coward, but he also couldn't recall any time he had stepped in to an altercation before. He usually won fights with words, not with his fists.

His secretary came into his office with his morning coffee. After putting his cup down on the coaster, she stood there and stared at his bandaged hand.

"It's nothing. Just a little accident this morning," Mike said nonchalantly. She nodded but gave him a curious look.

"Stephanie, could you ask Troy to join me here, please? As soon as he can?"

"Sure, I'll call him right away. He was in a meeting but I think it just wrapped up." Stephanie took one last glance at his hand as she left the room.

Troy made his appearance in less than five minutes. He frowned. "What did you do to your hand?"

"Nothing to worry about. Just a little accident at the house this morning."

Troy looked at him with feigned suspicion, and then laughed. "You didn't punch Cindy, did you?"

Mike laughed back. "You know me better than that."

"So, what's up boss? Why did you want to see me?"

"I want you to pull the files on those properties in Brazil and Mexico. You and I need to take a trip down there and start the revised strategic plan. As you know, the Board was concerned and rightfully so. I have to take a personal involvement in these projects and so do you. You're in charge of construction and these properties are dormant, producing no cash flow. We need to shit or get off the pot."

"Okay, I agree. But we don't want to rush to any judgments here. Gerry felt strongly about all four properties, and the development potential of each. He was only holding off due to the economy. We don't want to jump the gun on what could turn out to be wonderful future investments."

"I'm not going to jump the gun on anything, Troy. But I need to assess these for myself and so do you. The Board wants some assurance and I intend to give it to them."

"I'll pull the files. When do you want to go?"

"Arrange something for next week. We'll hop around to all four locations."

*****

Mike was tearing open envelope after envelope, reading through condolences from people that he knew, some he thought he knew, and some who he had no clue at all as to who they were. They all expressed their admiration for Gerry and how sad it was that he was no longer part of the executive team at Baxter Development Corporation. Each had their own agendas no doubt, and wanted to go on the record as expressing their grief. In reality, most of them probably didn't give a shit.

Then Mike got down to one extra-large envelope, adorned with flower stickers. He thought this one looked a bit odd, so he was extra curious. He tore the envelope open and pulled out a large sympathy card, with little puppy dogs on the front. Very odd. He read the message: " So sorry to hear about Gerry's death. I really enjoyed working with him over the years, and considered him my mentor. I would never have achieved the success I have today without his help. I will miss him. Perhaps you and I should do lunch sometime soon and reminisce. Yours faithfully, David Samson."

The name rang a bell. Mike frowned as he read the note again. There was something insincere about it, almost sarcastic. And the man's name was one he was familiar with. He was sure that someone named David Samson had worked for the company before, and there was some bad history. Baxter employed several thousand people, but what was it about this particular name?

Mike picked up his phone and dialed his CFO and buddy, Jim Belton. In addition to being in charge of financials, HR fell into Jim's responsibilities due to the close relationship of finance with benefits, pensions, and budgets.

Mike asked Jim to check personnel records for a David Samson. Within minutes Jim phoned him back. "Gerry fired a David Samson about five years ago. You recall: it was that suspected embezzlement with a purchase down in Chile."

A light bulb went off in Mike's brain. "Of course, how could I have forgotten? He purchased a property without proper due diligence! The property didn't even exist, right?"

"Right, exactly. Gerry fired him as soon as it was discovered. It involved about five million dollars; not a huge amount in the grand scheme, but enough for concern and certainly enough for dismissal with cause."

Mike was remembering back clearly now. "Didn't Gerry pursue criminal charges against this guy? Wasn't there some evidence of kickback to this Samson character?"

He could hear Jim leafing through pages in the file. "Uh, looks like Gerry dropped the complaint."

"What? Why did he do that?"

"The file doesn't say, Mike. Just says that the charges were dropped—

about four years ago."

"Do you have a phone number and address for David Samson?"

"Yes, could have changed by now but I'll email them to you. By the way, you should know that David Samson is not his original name. I just noticed that in the file."

Mike rubbed his bandaged hand. "How could we have hired someone with a phony name?"

"No, it wasn't phony. Looks like he legally changed it shortly before we hired him. His given name was 'Dawud Zamir.'" Another bell rang in Mike's brain at the mention of that Middle Eastern name. It was a very faint bell though, one of those that rings in the distance and you ignore it because it's too far away to care.

Chapter 6

"Mommy, Mommy, I just saw a man on TV who looks like Daddy!"

Cindy was tossing a salad for dinner, and looked up as little Kristy came running into the kitchen. She could see that her little girl was all excited and her cheeks were flushed.

"Don't listen to her, Mom. She's all mixed up. It was just some man beating up a couple of guys on the subway." Typical Diana, Cindy thought—always the voice of calm and reason. She was so mature for her age, and Cindy knew that sometimes it frustrated little Kristy who was enthusiastic about everything.

"It looked like Daddy, it did!"

"Did not!"

"Did so!"

Cindy could see that a shoving match was about to erupt. She put down her salad utensils, took off her apron, and knelt down to be at eye level with both girls. She gently rested her hands on their shoulders, and said in a soothing tone, "Why don't we watch it together and I'll give you my own opinion? What do you girls think of that idea?"

"You can't see it now anyway. It was just a little clip, and they said to tune in to the news at 6:00." Diana, as usual, paid attention to the details.

"Well then, we'll watch the news at 6:00. That's only about thirty minutes from now. But Kristy, it couldn't have been your father, you know. He hasn't taken the train since last week."

"I just said he looked like Daddy. I didn't say it was Daddy. Diana always takes the fun out of things. She knows he looks like Daddy, but she just won't say so because she likes to make me mad!" Kristy started to cry.

Cindy picked her up and cradled her for a few minutes. Kristy was six years old now but luckily still tiny for her age. Cindy could still hold her like a baby. She wanted her to stay that way as long as possible.

"Okay girls, you know what? We'll watch it anyway, and I'll tape it so

Daddy can see it too when he gets home. We can all have a good laugh together."

*****

"...and the breaking news tonight is about a Good Samaritan, caught on a camera phone. We reported on this incident last week. It occurred in a moving subway train during the morning rush hour and, according to witnesses, two hoodlums began harassing a young pregnant woman. They were trying to yank her out of her seat when a well-dressed businessman intervened and asked them to leave her alone. Apparently they ignored him and continued harassing the woman. The businessman then grabbed each of them... and... well, the video says it all. Film clarity could be better as the boy who took the footage was several yards away, but at least it gives our viewers a pretty good image of what happened."

Cindy and the girls were nestled together on the big reclining couch in the family room, watching closely as the footage began to roll. They saw two scummy men, perhaps about twenty years old, white, wearing black toques, ripped pants hanging down past the hint of their ass-cracks, leaning over a young woman and trying to drag her out of her seat. She looked terrified, and was frantically swinging at them with her hands.

Suddenly a man in a suit carrying a briefcase stepped forward, grabbed the collar of one of the men and threw him backward onto the floor. The other punk took a swing but missed. The businessman retaliated with a quick uppercut to the jaw. The young hoodlum went down. Then his buddy struggled to his feet and lunged at the businessman. He was met with the swing of a briefcase right smack in the face.

The train now rolled to a stop and the doors opened onto the station platform. The businessman dropped his briefcase and then, one by one, grabbed each of the guys by their shirt collars and ass-crack waistbands, and heaved them out the doorway as if they were useless pieces of luggage. The train door closed and the footage stopped.

The anchorman reappeared on the TV screen, with his eyebrows arched: *"Wow, thrilling footage, just thrilling. How heartwarming to see one of our citizens come to the aid of another. We are fortunate indeed that the boy came forward with his camera phone to share this with us, so we could in turn share it with you. Now we would like to know who this Good Samaritan is. He left the train at Union Station, apparently only uttering a 'thank you' to a woman who bandaged his bloodied hand. We do not know his name. We vaguely know what he looks like from this video footage. But it's not clear enough to accurately describe him. We're hoping that someone will recognize this person, or better yet, that this person comes forward himself. We'd like to talk to him and give him the praise and thanks he deserves. The police would also like to chat with him as a witness to the altercation and hopefully help the investigation with a good description of the thugs. I chatted with the Police Chief today, and he told me that this man would definitely be nominated for a heroism award, however the Chief urges the public to never take the law into their own hands because most instances, unlike this one, don't have happy endings."*

Cindy stopped recording and turned off the TV.

"See, Mommy? See what I mean? Didn't that hero man look like Daddy?"

Cindy hugged Kristy. "Honey, it wasn't that clear, and lots of people look like your Dad when they're all dressed up like that. But I can sure see why you thought that, I really can."

Diana glared at her mom and Kristy. "Well, I think you're both blind as bats! That wasn't Daddy." She got up from her chair and went down the hall to her room.

Cindy called after her. "We'll have dinner in about half an hour, Diana. Your Dad should be home by then." Cindy worried sometimes about Diana—she was such a serious little soul, and didn't let her imagination run loose like Kristy did. Kristy picked up one of her dolls and started grooming her. Cindy knew this would soothe her and help her forget about her sister's reaction.

She got up and walked back to the kitchen. Opened the liquor cabinet, poured herself a short whisky and chugged it. She knew that was Mike in the footage; she knew without a doubt. And she remembered his bandaged hand.

*****

Mike snuggled up next to his wife in bed, both with their books out and reading lights on. He enjoyed this time of the evening, just before falling off to sleep. It was a closeness that was comforting after a long day at the office. Cindy's body felt warm and he loved it when she swung her leg over his and pulled herself in tighter. It always aroused him. He looked over at her and admired her loveliness. Long auburn hair flowing down over her shoulders and chest, perfectly shaped breasts swelling under her nightie, legs exposed. She was still one sexy lady, and he was proud of her. At thirty-five, she was twelve years younger than him, but he was relieved to know that he still didn't look his age. He sometimes worried that their age difference would have an effect on their relationship once he was in his sixties, but that was thankfully still a long way off.

She caught him looking. "Are you horny or something?"

He rubbed his hand over her left breast. "Yeah, something like that."

"How's your hand?"

"Seems to have healed up nicely. It definitely won't affect my performance if that's what you're worried about." Mike flashed his best devilish smile.

Cindy leaned up on her elbow and looked directly into his eyes. "What did you think of that tape of the news footage tonight?"

"That was quite something. Nice to see people stepping up to the plate when others are in trouble. The girls sure had a good chuckle joking that it was me, eh? Especially Kristy."

"How'd you hurt your hand again, Mike? I forget."

Mike squirmed. "I tripped on the sidewalk and went down hard."

"Wouldn't you have scraped your palm, then—not the knuckles?"

"Not the way I fell."

Cindy sat straight up in bed and Mike saw that familiar look of challenge in her eyes. He braced himself.

"Why are you lying to me, Michael? What's going on? I know that was you in the video. Even with the images blurred, I can recognize my own husband, you know."

Mike pushed himself up into a sitting position, then suddenly began to feel faint. He tried to answer Cindy, but his mouth wouldn't work. Her face began to look distorted and the room was swirling. He brought his hands up to his forehead and covered his eyes. He could hear the muffled words "What's wrong?" but he wasn't sure who was saying them. He pulled his hands from his eyes and a bright light flashed in front of them, just for a second, but brilliant enough to momentarily blind him. Mike heard loud explosions going off in his head, and he thought he was going to pass out.

Then, in an instant, all became calm again. He could clearly see his pretty wife, with the short-cropped blonde hair sitting beside him on the bed, her face full of concern. He had to respond to her—what was that question again? Something about lying?

Mike leaned toward her and took her hand. "I would never lie to you, Mandy."

He had expected a gentle kiss, but was shocked to see the sudden horror in her eyes as she lurched away from him, tumbling not so gracefully over the side of the bed.

Chapter 7

Everyone loves a hero. Particularly an anonymous one. Such a fantasy always appeals to the masses, and provides a distraction to the rigors of everyday life. It gives hope that the 'good guys' are still out there, somewhere, and that once in a while they will swoop to the rescue and clean up the shit. Sort of like Batman or Spiderman.

The mass media know this phenomenon very well. Toronto television stations all picked up the hero story, and the subway video was being shown over and over again. They appealed to witnesses, as well as to people who might recognize the hero, to do their duty and come forward. And they appealed to the mystery man himself to proudly step to the front and assume his throne.

Predictably, the newspapers began a series of "subway violence" articles, digging into decades-old archives, chronicling the history of the Toronto Transit Commission (TTC) from suicides, accidents and blackouts, to murders, rapes and muggings. After reading these articles it was a wonder anyone ventured onto a subway again. There were the predictable calls in the editorial columns for increased police presence on the subway trains and platforms, and surveillance cameras in all of the train cars.

To Mike, all of this was unsettling. He knew now that he was the businessman in the train; he couldn't deny it any longer. And after watching the video, flashes of memory of what had happened came back to him. His brain had retrieved a vision of the incident, clearly seeing the thugs and seeing himself doing what he had seen on the video. But his memory included details that the video hadn't shown. So, in that respect he was relieved. It wasn't at all like the blackout he had experienced in his office. This time he could remember what he had done. The unsettling part was that he had needed the video to trigger the memory.

The Baxter's phone had been ringing off the hook as a result of the constant media barrage. People had recognized him, or at least thought they had. It didn't seem like it was going to let up. Mike was convinced the press would not surrender the story until they had pressured the anonymous hero to identify himself. They were relentless and over the top, as usual with any story with the least bit of sensationalism.

Friends, relatives and neighbors were calling and suggesting to Cindy that her husband was the hero. Even their eldest daughter Diana was getting calls from her friends. She was finally starting to give in to Kristy's assertions that their dad was the 'man of the hour.' Mike absolutely refused to answer the phone himself.

Diana had asked him several times now if he remembered anything at all. After all, Cindy had indeed warned Diana after Mike's lightning bolt accident that he might have periods of blackout. Cindy had decided not to talk to Kristy about this, as she was still too young and easily frightened. Diana however, was so mature for her age. But Mike didn't know what to say to Diana; he didn't want to confirm it, and didn't want to deny it. So he always just shrugged and left her in limbo. Not right, he knew, but he didn't know how to explain it to her because he didn't understand it himself. And she was still just a little girl, no matter how mature she was.

His first day back at the office after the first news telecast about the incident, made Mike feel very uncomfortable. Walking through the office amongst the staff, he could feel, if not see, heads lift up from their desks and follow him. He could sense their eyes boring into him as he passed and he could hear the whispers.

It reminded him of an unsettling experience he had had about twenty years ago when he had walked into a Burger King restaurant in downtown Toronto. This was around the time that the infamous Scarborough Rapist, AKA Paul Bernardo, was enjoying his reign of terror and the newspapers had published a sketch of the suspect. The sketch was posted in virtually every public place. Mike walked into the restaurant for lunch the first day the sketch had come out, and was stunned to see what looked like a drawing of himself on the wall behind the counter. Round face, blonde hair, boyish good looks—that was Mike in a nutshell when he was in his mid-twenties. All eyes in the restaurant were staring at him, or at least he thought they were. He noticed one of the employees nudge another worker, point at him, and then nod in the direction of the sketch. Mike felt so self-conscious that he turned right around and left without even ordering his Whopper.

The looks from the employees in his own office now brought that self-conscious feeling back, although admittedly it was significantly different this time. Twenty years ago he thought people suspected him of being a monster. Now people were pegging him as a hero.

It had been a tense few days at home since they had watched the video together. Cindy had insisted on talking about it the next morning, particularly the part where he had addressed her as 'Mandy.' Mike could only explain that away by saying that he had been thinking of Gerry and naturally had also been thinking about Amanda. Cindy had protested that the only one who had ever called Amanda 'Mandy' had been Gerry. It was his little term of endearment. So why had Mike called his very own wife 'Mandy?' Mike couldn't answer that, and didn't volunteer to her that she had actually looked like Amanda that night, at that weird moment. Sure, he remembered saying 'Mandy' and remembered seeing what he thought was Mandy right there in front of him on the bed, with her short blonde hair. Once Cindy reacted by falling off the bed in shock, it was like Mike was awakened from a trance.

He was now quite scared, and his imagination was starting to conjure up an unbelievable and crazy scenario.

Cindy had implored him to postpone his trip to Brazil and Mexico. Mike reluctantly agreed, and contacted Troy to change their travel plans to a couple of weeks later. Cindy made him promise that they would visit their family doctor together. Mike agreed to that as well. He knew he couldn't live in denial any longer about what was happening to him. He wanted this strange stuff to stop.

The good thing about their family doctor was that he was also a long-time family friend who just happened to have been a psychiatrist years ago before changing to family practice. He told them that he had switched because illnesses in the minds of his patients bothered him so much that he had had to go see a psychiatrist himself for depression. He now practiced family medicine, but only for a few close friends. He was semi-retired.

So because of their doctor's background, the psychological aspects of health issues could be addressed at the same time, something the Baxters had never availed themselves of before, and thankfully had never had to. Until now.

Mike and Cindy were sitting in the plush office of Dr. Bob Teskey, facing out onto busy Yonge Street. They were lounging on the mandatory comfy leather couch, when Bob entered the room with a smile on his face and a coffee in his hand. "Hey guys, haven't seen you since your Christmas party.

You should have popped by earlier than this though after that accident in Florida. Talking over the phone is not the same thing, you know."

Cindy jumped up from the couch and gave Bob a hug. Mike waited his turn and shook his hand. Bob Teskey was a tall, lanky fellow, with a thick mop of hair. He always wore the strangest glasses that seemed to have double-thick lenses, making his eyes appear quite bug-eyed. Mike thought that Bob looked like the stereotypical psychiatrist the way a casting agent would envision.

"I should have been in sooner, Bob, you're right. Cindy kept insisting and I kept delaying. But, better late than never, I guess."

"Okay, well, let's all sit down. Cindy has been keeping me informed on what type of symptoms you've been having, and I understand she's been e-mailing Fenton down in Sarasota—a good man by the way. I know him from a few conventions."

Mike jumped right to the core of the matter, anxious to get this uncomfortable process underway and over with. "Yeah, I've been having some blackouts—for relatively long periods of time during which I seem to be able to function: walk, talk, etc. Kind of what you'd expect from a sleepwalker, maybe. However, I seem to behave differently during those blackouts than I normally would, and I don't seem to have any memory at the time of what I've done—although a couple of times it has come back to me later."

"Mike, I have to tell you, you look just like that guy who's all over the news right now. The subway hero? Come clean with me—was that one of your little escapades?"

Mike was surprised by the blunt question, and the calm way in which it was asked. But then again, that's what this guy was trained to do. He looked over at Cindy and he could see in her eyes that she wanted him to be truthful, to get help for this.

"Yes, that was me alright. I didn't remember it until Cindy showed me the video."

"Are you going to go to the police?"

Mike crossed his arms over his chest. "I hadn't planned to, no. I really don't want the publicity."

"I didn't say go to the press. I said the 'police.' You probably have some descriptions of those two guys in your head right now that may help the authorities. And going forward with this may help you, knowing in your heart that you're doing the right thing. It's part of acceptance and closure."

Cindy was nodding her head in agreement. Mike looked over at her and smiled, nodding as well.

Bob continued. "That subway incident is several days old now. What prompted you both to come in to see me today? It must be something more recent?"

Mike went over to the side-stand to get some water for him and Cindy. "I think Cindy needs to tell you this part, Bob."

Cindy jumped in without hesitation, detailing to Bob the seven hour blackout that Mike had suffered in his office, the occasional trembling hands, and then what happened while they were sitting on the bed after viewing the subway video. Bob just nodded as he listened, while jotting down some notes.

He looked at Mike when Cindy had finished her story. "What was happening to you while you were sitting on the bed? Any physical or mental symptoms? Can you recall?"

"Yes, I can. A dizzy feeling, lights flashing, something like explosions in my head, stuff like that. Then it all went away and I saw Amanda, of all people, sitting in front of me on the bed. It seemed so normal and, well, it seemed right. I wasn't shocked or surprised to see Amanda's face. I could clearly see her short blonde hair. I wasn't looking at Cindy anymore. I was looking at Amanda. And it felt like she was my wife." Mike reached out and held onto Cindy's hand, squeezing it. She squeezed back and smiled at him, but he could see that all the color had left her face.

Bob nodded, got up from his seat and started pacing the office, his hand rubbing his chin. "What explanation do you think goes along with this behavior, Mike?"

"I honestly don't have a clue. However, I've been wondering, and this will sound really crazy, but is it possible that some brain activity of Gerry's connected with mine when our heads knocked, when the bolt hit?" Mike realized after asking the question, how stupid and supernatural it sounded. If Bob didn't think he was nuts before, he was probably convinced now.

"Well, there's no scientific evidence for that at all, although it's highly unusual for two people to knock heads at the exact instant a lightning bolt hits. So I doubt there are any precedents for this, because it has probably never happened before. I'll do some research on it though, crazy as it sounds. But scientifically, I don't think it's possible. The real question is: do you think it's possible? Because if you do that may explain a lot. The brain can play tricks on us if we believe something fervently enough. It can make fantasy reality, and make an irrational fear become real."

Mike shifted in his seat. He didn't know what he believed. "No, I'm not saying I believe that at all. I'm just throwing it out as a question. You're the scientist—you know what's possible and what isn't."

"Well, for example, Mike, if you lost yourself in a daydream or self-hypnosis about Gerry and began to believe Gerry was with you or in you, that might explain why in that dream-like state you saw Amanda instead of Cindy." Bob paused and then continued, slowly for impact, "But that wouldn't explain you turning into a ramrod hero on the subway. You've certainly never been a fighter, and I'm sure Gerry wasn't capable of running around beating people up on subways!" Bob laughed at the image he had created.

Mike rose from his chair. "C'mon Cindy, it's time for us to go."

Bob put his hand out in the stop symbol. "Whoa, I don't think we're finished yet. Don't be in such a hurry."

"I'll be back, Bob, don't worry. But I've had enough for today. This is all too unsettling for me."

Cindy opened the office door as they prepared to leave, but suddenly Mike turned around and faced Bob again. "That's just the thing Bob—Gerry was capable. He was a champion boxer during his university days and was even invited out to the Olympic team. He continued to develop his fighting skills while he was in the military. He could handle himself real well, trust me. He could have easily gone pro."

*****

The next day, Mike walked into the central police precinct and asked to see one of the detectives in the violent crime unit. He only had to wait about fifteen minutes before he was ushered into the office of a Sergeant Bert Stevens. Mike didn't waste any time. He told the detective that he was the businessman on the subway, but that he didn't want any publicity. Stevens promised him that he would keep him anonymous.

Mike filled out a report form that Stevens handed him, including his name and address. Then he gave a description of the two low-lifes he had beaten up and thrown off the subway. His description included nose rings, ear rings, studded lips and eyebrows, scars, tattoos, orange hair, and ass-cracks. He left nothing out—his memory of the details was remarkable considering he had been in basically a blackout state.

Stevens thanked him for coming in and promised again that he would not be identified. He asked Mike if he would agree to attend a private ceremony if he was nominated for a citizen bravery award. Mike said no. Stevens accepted his decision without protest; in fact Mike thought that he detected a look of respect in the man's eyes. He guessed it was probably a rare thing for citizens to do good deeds without expecting something in return, and maybe because of that the detective saw Mike as a breath of fresh air.

He shook Stevens' hand and left through the unit's outer office area, an area filled with clerical personnel. They were busy clicking away on their computers, no doubt trying to track down sordid histories on countless perpetrators.

Mike didn't notice the eyes following him; he was too intent on thinking about whether or not he had left anything out of his descriptions of the thugs. Nor did he notice the camera phone in the hand of one of the secretaries, extended above her cubicle wall, catching his full frontal image.

Chapter *8*

"Daddy, you lied to us. Why? You always tell *us* not to lie."

"Diana, I didn't really lie, I just didn't know how or what to tell you. I was ashamed of having you see me on TV beating people up. That's not how I wanted you to see your dad."

"See, Diana. I told you, I told you!" Kristy was pointing at her sister, and barely able to contain her enthusiasm. Mike could see she was clearly taking the news better than her sister.

Cindy intervened with her motherly touch. "Diana, your dad and I went to the doctor a few days ago and talked about this. Do you remember we told you when we got back from Florida that dad might have some blackouts and do things he wouldn't remember, due to the lightning bolt?" Diana nodded, but kept a stern unforgiving look on her face. "Well, that's exactly what happened here. I know it's hard to understand but your dad didn't remember, at first, doing what he did. Doctor Teskey is going to try to help us. After that visit we decided to tell you girls the truth."

Diana seemed to lighten up a bit. Cindy continued. "And, your dad has already gone to the police and told them what happened. He described the bad guys and hopefully now they'll be caught. The police even want to give your dad a heroism award. What do you think about that?"

Diana looked at her dad with the hint of a smile. "I am proud of you, Dad. I really am. I just wish I had known before I kept saying no about it to all my friends. You're a hero. That's really neat. Can you come to my school and talk to my class, maybe?"

"We'll see, Diana. I don't feel too much like a hero, because I still don't feel I was in my right mind when I did what I did. It was like I was unconscious. I feel like a phony hero. Does that make sense?"

Diana walked over and threw her arms around her dad's neck. Kristy, of course, had to do the same. Mike had both of them hanging on as he rose from his chair and swung them around. They laughed, and he got the feeling all was forgiven.

Cindy was coming back from retrieving the Saturday newspaper from the front porch. Mike heard her gasp. She stood frozen in the foyer with the paper unfolded to the front page.

"What's wrong, Cindy?"

"You don't want to see this. I don't want to see this." Her face was ashen. Mike rushed over to her and pulled the newspaper out of her hands.

A full image of him was splattered over the front page, accompanied by a smaller photo from the subway incident. The full image showed Mike, clear as day, walking through an office carrying his briefcase. The smaller subway photo caught him in full swing, briefcase striking a man in the face. The headline read: "The Briefcase Braveheart." Beneath the photos was a caption, identifying him as Michael Baxter of Rosedale, Toronto. There was a complete story as well, but Mike didn't want to read it. He just dropped the paper onto the floor and retreated to his study.

*****

Mike was driving, with not an inkling of where he was going. After reading the article in the paper he needed some space. Cindy and the girls hugged him more times than he could count, and they said all the right things. But none of it helped. The girls seemed very excited to have their dad plastered all over the front page. Cindy was horrified, and Mike was just angry.

He drove his black BMW 745i onto the 401, then veered north onto the 404. From there he exited off to the Aurora Sideroad and headed toward an enclave of expensive acreage homes, pulling into the driveway of one particularly palatial residence. He locked his car, walked up to the front door, and rang the doorbell. He knew whose house this was, but had no idea why he was here.

Amanda Upton answered the door, wearing yellow shorts and a pink halter-top. Her blonde hair had grown out quite a bit since the last time Mike had seen her. In fact, he hadn't seen her for several weeks, not since their vacation in Florida which had taken her husband's life.

For a split second she looked shocked to see him, but then broke into tears and threw her arms around him. She squeezed him so hard that he lost his balance and had to lean against the door frame.

"Mike, come in, come in. Where's Cindy?"

"She's at home. I'm just here by myself. I had to see you—it's been so long."

"It has. I haven't seen anyone since the…"

"I know…and we all understand, Amanda. I know the ladies have tried to get you out, but they know how tough it is. Just know that we're all here for you. Okay? We've been friends for a long time."

Amanda grabbed onto his arm and led him into the kitchen. "Coffee?"

"Yes, that would be great. I won't stay long. I just wanted to drop in on you for a few minutes."

Amanda poured two cups of coffee, and with her free hand she wiped away the tears from her cheeks. Even tear-streaked, her face looked adorable.

They sipped their coffees and talked. Amanda seemed glad to see him, kind of comforted, and poured her heart out about how empty her life had been over the last couple of months. Mike asked about her two boys, Charlie and Sam, who were fourteen and twelve respectively. She said they'd been adjusting to life without their father, but were still in a state of shock most of the time. Amanda was spending extra time with them, trying to do the sports things that Gerry used to do, but it wasn't the same for them. She knew they were embarrassed to be seen playing ball with their mother, but were too polite to tell her. She was confident it would just take time.

Mike brought her up to date on his life, and on Cindy and the girls, but avoided saying anything about the traumas he'd been experiencing. He knew she hadn't seen the newspaper or been watching TV very much, because she made no mention at all about 'The Briefcase Braveheart' story. He was relieved; he didn't feel much like talking about it with her.

"So, how did Sam like that new bike on his birthday?"

Amanda looked up from her coffee, a look of surprise in her eyes. "He… loved it," she said slowly. "His birthday was last month, and Gerry picked that bike out for him before he… Gerry must have told you?"

"Uh…yes…he did. Shiny red, a trail bike, right?"

"Yes, Sam's been riding it over every dirt road he can find! He's so happy with it, and he cried his little heart out when he saw it, knowing his dad bought it before…" Amanda choked up.

"Gerry would be happy. He loved his boys, and he thought the world of you, Mandy."

Amanda started to cry again, and in between her sobs, said, "You reminded me of Gerry there, just for a second. The way you said 'Mandy,' the same loving tone he used to use."

Mike walked around the table and gave his long-time friend a hug from behind. He nestled his cheek into her brilliant blonde hair and whispered in her ear, "Mandy, don't cry. Everything will be okay. I used to tell you that before our exams at U of T, remember? And you always aced them despite your fretting." Mike suddenly had the eerie feeling that he had no control over what he was saying. The words leaped out but he had no idea where they were coming from. And he couldn't stop them, almost as if he was suffering from some version of Tourette syndrome.

Amanda turned toward him with a puzzled look on her face then just shook her head as if to clear it, and quickly kissed his cheek. "I'm so glad you came by, Mike. It's been a comfort to me. But it's time for you to go, okay?" She jumped to her feet and smoothed out her hair. They walked to the front door together, Mike's long arm wrapped around her slender shoulders, Amanda with her arms by her side.

"Amanda, how's the alarm system? Is it functioning okay for you?"

Again, she looked at him with surprise. "Sure, it's definitely a secure feeling when I have it on at night."

"You can probably cancel that security patrol now, though. I doubt if you'll need it anymore." Again, Mike wondered where the words were coming from.

Amanda frowned and looked at him quizzically. "Gerry told you about that too? I was just thinking today of canceling it—you must be a mind reader! Gerry insisted on that patrol about three years ago, and it's been costing us an arm and a leg. They drive around the block every night and then just park near our house and watch until dawn. I don't know what Gerry expected them to be looking for, he wouldn't confide in me and neither would the security company. But, Gerry was worried about something and the fact that he was concerned always had me on edge."

Mike just nodded and opened the front door. Suddenly Amanda grabbed his arm.

"Wait! Why did you say I can now cancel it? Because Gerry's dead? Were we in some kind of danger while he was alive? Do you know something, Mike?"

Mike didn't know what he knew. He had just blurted it out, and now wished he could take it back. He gazed into Amanda's beautiful green eyes, and felt like he was going to melt. He also felt like he wanted to cry. He kissed her on the forehead, and walked down to his car.

Something made him turn around and look back at her. They gazed into each other's eyes for several moments, then Mike said softly, "There's nothing to worry about, Mandy. Not anymore."

*****

For the next three days, the scavenger journalists were camped out on the street outside the Baxter home, irritating the hell out of their older upper crust neighbors who all probably felt that the Baxters didn't belong there anyway. Cindy drove the girls to school each day, always honking her horn several times trying to make the morons with their video cameras move out of the way as she exited their four-car garage. Mike confronted the paparazzi only once, on the first day, and made it clear he wasn't going to make any statements to them either, other than "Fuck off, get out of my face, and off my street!"

At work, it wasn't much better. The newspaper article and subsequent news updates on the television networks, had bared his personal life to the world. Where he worked, the company that bore his name, how many children, where they went to school. The girls were thrilled with the publicity, Cindy was horrified, and Mike was trying to just take it in stride and say as little as possible. He knew, or at least hoped, that if he ignored the issue, it would gradually fade away.

Journalists tried to gain access to him at the office, but to no avail. When they realized they were getting nowhere, they managed to contact 'anonymous' employees or 'sources,' who readily gave interviews and insider information on Mike Baxter, his management style, his business success, and presumed wealth. One 'source' even gave details of the Florida lightning strike which had "claimed the life of one Baxter executive and left Mr. Baxter himself hospitalized for a period of time." This all added fodder for follow-up stories, which the press loved to do so they could drag something out for days and weeks.

Mike complained to Detective Stevens about breaking his promise to keep his name out of it. Stevens was apologetic but claimed that someone in the precinct must have sold the photo and Mike's identification to the press. He promised that he would find out who it was, and that employee would be fired as soon as he knew. Mike didn't care about that as it couldn't undo the damage.

Another follow-up story covered the arrest of two drug dealers who were the alleged subway attackers who were foiled by the 'Briefcase Braveheart.' Mike was summoned down to the precinct to confirm his description by identifying the suspects in a lineup. Indeed, they were the two slime balls who had attacked the pregnant woman. Other witnesses from the subway, including the pregnant woman, the gregarious man who had hugged him, and the bandage lady, were summoned as well. They all bumped into each other at the station, and enjoyed a brief but joyous reunion. Mike had just wanted to run, fast. His life was becoming far too complicated with this hero shit. And he felt unworthy. Because he knew it really wasn't he who had done that heroic thing. Not the conscious he anyway.

His executives and employees treated him like royalty. They had always shown him respect, but now it was ridiculous. He felt uncomfortable around them, as now they deferred to him completely. The adoration showed in their eyes, with everything he said, every step he took, every meeting he chaired. He could do no wrong in their eyes. He was hyped, he was a celebrity; but an accidental one.

Each board member had phoned him and congratulated him, commenting almost unanimously that this would bring great honor to the company to have a CEO at such a pinnacle of fame. Strangely enough, these insincere, opportunistic board members were right—Baxter stock had risen fifteen percent since Mike's face and story had been splashed all over the papers.

Following several days of fame and days of living with the nickname, 'Briefcase Braveheart,' Mike called Troy into his office. Troy was there in seconds, newspaper in hand, immediately drawing his attention to that day's editorial cartoon showing Mike's face and body adorned in animal skins, with long hair in braids, briefcase in one hand, a shield in the other. Troy bellowed with laughter; Mike managed a chuckle.

Then Troy read out loud the usually infamous 'Page Six' column, today sarcastically touting Mike as a viable candidate for leadership of the failing Liberal party.

"This is just a minor point, Troy, but wouldn't they be shocked to know that I'm a Conservative?"

Troy frowned. "I didn't even know that. For how long?"

Mike shook his head. "Never mind, not important. The reason I wanted to talk to you—have you made those flight reservations for our trip to Rio yet?"

"No, not yet. With all the publicity over the past couple of weeks, I figured you'd want to sit tight for a while."

"It's time. Book it for next week, okay? Rio first, then we'll drive from there to Angra dos Reis. Then back to Rio for a flight to Acapulco, then by car down to Huatulco." Mike had to get away and deal with something else. He needed a break from this craziness. Troy nodded, and strode to the door.

"Oh, and Troy."

Troy turned around. "Yeah?"

"Let's leave the golf clubs at home this time, agreed?"

Chapter 9

First Class was wonderful. Mike and Troy always flew this way, and it made their jobs just a little more bearable. Spending a good portion of their working lives in the air, it allowed them to arrive rested and well fed. It also made it possible to actually get some work done during those wasted hours above terra firma.

Their U. S. Airways flight left on time from Toronto, en route for their short two- hour trip to Charlotte, North Carolina. They would then have a ninety-minute wait for their connecting flight to Rio, a ten-hour marathon getting them into the *cidade maravilhosa*, or "marvelous city," at 9:10 a.m. Luckily, Rio was in the same time zone as Toronto so there wouldn't be a time change to worry about. They only had to worry about catching some shut-eye during the flight, which after a few scotches wouldn't be a problem. Yes, free scotch was another advantage to flying First Class.

Both of them were dressed in their worst blue jeans, and weather-worn T-shirts. Their shoes were tattered loafers, and their luggage consisted of one backpack each, stuffed to the drawstrings with as few clothes as possible. They were able to cram their backpacks into the storage bins so they wouldn't have to worry about checked bags. Mike noticed that the bins were getting mysteriously smaller every time he flew; pretty soon even his backpack wouldn't fit.

He looked around the First Class cabin, and saw half a dozen others dressed as shabbily as he and Troy. The others, in suits and fancy dresses, looked quite shocked that they had to share space with what appeared to be a bunch of bums. Mike smiled to himself and hoped that these preppies and prom queens, if they were connecting on to South America, wouldn't have to face the harsh reality of Brazilian life. He and Troy knew the score, as did probably the other six passengers who had wisely dressed like them. Kidnapping was a national sport in Brazil, second only to soccer in popularity. Like any other responsible company doing business in Mexico, Central, and South America, Baxter Development Corp. had arranged insurance for

Kidnap and Ransom. It covered up to ten million for any one kidnapping and protected any of their employees or executives while they were traveling on business. It also provided the built-in advantage of an international security company at their fingertips to deal with the negotiations and safe retrieval. Luckily, they had never had to call on the policy yet. The policy didn't cover family members though, so it was rare for Baxter employees to take their spouses or kids along.

*****

The captain was speaking over the intercom, announcing their approach to Rio de Janeiro. Mike jerked awake at the sound of the voice and for a moment couldn't remember where he was. Then it came back to him. The coffees at the Charlotte airport waiting for their connecting flight, three scotches and a meal early on in the Rio flight, then dreamland. He looked over at Troy who was still asleep and nudged him not too gently.

"We're approaching Rio, Troy. Thought you might like to catch a glimpse of the city from the air." Mike had been to Rio about a decade ago, but for Troy this was his first time. And morning had already broken, perfect for the eye candy that was Rio de Janeiro.

Troy grunted himself awake, and immediately turned his head to the window. Mike hoped Troy would remember that he'd been gracious enough to allow him the window seat and not waste the visual opportunity.

Most people were still under the impression that Rio was the capital of Brazil. However that had changed in 1960 when the city of Brasilia took over the role. Even though Rio lost the prestige of being the capital city, it retained its status as being the one and only true symbol of Brazil, the city that people envisioned immediately whenever they thought of the country. Sights such as Sugar Loaf Mountain, beaches like the Copacabana, and the breathtaking image of the *Cristo Redentor* statue—otherwise known to Anglos as "Christ The Redeemer"—were images that had captivated travelers for generations. And if those weren't enough for any tourist's appetite, there is the world-famous *Carnaval*, an annual festival that absolutely defines the concept of "Let's party!"

Most people who visit are also unaware that the Rio harbor area is one of the Seven Natural Wonders of the World. Or that Rio will be hosting the 2016 Summer Olympics after bidding for them four previous times over the past seventy-five years. It will be the first South American city to ever host an Olympics. And the citizens of Rio were excited to show the world their beautiful city; it was indeed one of the most stunning settings on the planet. While the citizens were busy getting excited, Olympic organizers fretted over security issues that were inherent to one of the most corrupt and crime-ridden cities imaginable. The paradox of Rio de Janeiro was undeniable.

Slums, known as *favelas*, existed throughout the city, mixed with middle-class housing on the picturesque mountain slopes. *Favelas* were the dens of drug lords and crime bosses, and the wealthier citizens of Rio accepted them as just a fact of life. These eyesores created the need for new housing, as the demand was high. The people who actually paid taxes wanted out, and desired neighbors who were more like them. This was the opportunity that Baxter Development Corp. wanted to capitalize on with its planned subdivision just outside the city.

The Olympics was one of the reasons the company had bought the two properties: land for housing on the outskirts of Rio, and beachfront property for a resort about one- hundred and seventy kilometers away in *Angra dos Reis* along *Juruba Beach.* Both projects could be completed well in advance of the Olympics. The timing was perfect, and Mike was excited about the prospects.

The plane landed softly on the runway and Mike could see that Troy was still being held spellbound by the sights he had seen on the approach. "Penny for your thoughts, Troy?"

"Christ, I've never seen anything like it! This is probably the most beautiful city I have ever laid eyes on!"

"Yes, it is. But, be warned. The underbelly of Rio is also one of the *ugliest* you'll ever lay eyes on."

"Even so, we won't be building in the underbellies. I can't tell you how excited I am to be here and to think that we'll be developing projects here shortly!"

"I agree. I think we've struck the mother lode with purchasing at just the right time down here. We now need to make sure we have the right plan in place, because we'll only get one shot at this and we can't afford to be wrong. It's nice to think of this as Gerry's legacy, as this was his brainchild from the beginning."

Troy nodded at this and Mike could see the melancholy in his eyes. They both felt the same way, as they began their quest to retrace Gerry's steps and finally get his show on the road.

After deplaning, getting the rental car was painless, quick and cheap. They chose a small and innocuous Nissan model that would draw next to no attention. That was exactly the way they wanted it. Normally when they traveled, the cars they rented were high-end, but not this time, not here in Brazil. They would be content to slum it for the sake of safety.

Neither Mike nor Troy spoke Portuguese, and substituting Spanish usually fell on deaf ears in Rio, so they planned to rely on hand signals primarily. Troy had a small Portuguese dictionary, which would help for the occasional word, but generally they would have no choice but to just wing it. They weren't worried. Both of them had traveled to so many countries and had encountered so many difficulties, that foreign cultures no longer intimidated them.

They had booked reservations in the *Centro* district of Rio, the area that contained the financial and business activities as well as most of the historic buildings. Not that they had much time to sightsee, but they wanted to blend in as best as possible and not be in the touristy sections if they could avoid it. Their hotel, located on the *Avenida Presidente Vargas*, was an absolute dive known as the *Alhambra*. Again, another deliberate tactic on their part. They would suffer through the filth to remain incognito.

Anyway, the *Alhambra* was just a place to sleep. Tomorrow, the exciting part of their trip would begin. Both of them would see, up close and personal, two of their prime properties for the first time and from there the planning could begin in earnest. Their visionary minds would be put once again to the test, which was a process that always charged the adrenaline for both executives. Mike and Troy knew that only moments like these were what motivated wealthy men like them to keep working.

Chapter *10*

Mike shielded his eyes from the sun and looked out along the wide expanse of property. The waves crashed against the shore several hundred feet behind them as he and Troy stood by the side of the road on *Av. Abelardo Bueno.* They had already located the numerous property markers for their fifty hectares of real estate, and had double- checked them twice already. Mike had his binoculars out as he scanned the boundaries. Troy had been fiddling with his hand-held GPS, punching in coordinates, erasing them, and re-punching them.

"No doubt about it. This is it, Mike. It's a swamp. A fucking swamp."

"No mistake on the GPS?"

"Nope. I've done it over and over again, and the property markers also match with the deed."

Mike scratched his head and raised his binoculars one last time, kidding himself into thinking he'd see some ray of hope. He felt sick to his stomach.

"Troy, we own one-hundred and twenty-three acres of swampland. We paid twenty-five million dollars for this unbuildable piece of shit!"

"Let's talk in hectares, Mike. Fifty hectares doesn't sound as bad as one hundred and twenty-three acres."

They had gotten an early start this morning, traveling the twenty miles southwest of the city centre to the famous and wealthy neighborhood of *Barra Da Tijuca.* This was considered to be the hottest new neighborhood of Rio, punctuated by picturesque rock formations, incredible Atlantic beaches, and wealth.

As they looked out over the expanse they could also see that the area was bisected by canals and lakes. There was no doubt that at one time almost all of this particular area had been swamp, and through painstaking dredging and filling, subdivisions had sprung up. Their "land" was one of the few areas that had yet to be dredged and reclaimed. It was obviously a leftover, and it was now all theirs.

Mike looked at Troy with some faint hope in his eyes. "What can you do with this? You're the construction engineer."

Troy's veins were bulging in his neck, matching the muscles flexing under his sweaty T-shirt. It was a hot day. He looked out over the swamp, and replied, "Nothing, Mike, nothing at all. The cost to dredge and fill this size of property would be ridiculous, not to mention the environmental impact requirements we would have to adhere to. In fact, due to wetlands, we may not even be allowed to build. I wonder if that was even investigated when Gerry bought this turkey. We might own a very expensive conservation area. Maybe we could just charge admission to birdwatchers."

"Troy, this isn't funny."

"No, it's not—but you have to admit, this does add a new twist to that old expression: '*I have some swampland in Florida to sell you.*' This global economy has apparently expanded that joke to Brazil."

Mike kicked some stones into the marsh, and sighed. "Okay, take whatever photos you need, and we'll get the fuck out of here. We have a three hour drive ahead of us to get down to *Angra dos Reis*, and quite honestly, I'm not looking forward to it."

*****

The drive down to *Angra* was a scenic one, not that either of them was taking any notice. They were cruising the little Nissan down the BR-101 highway, each lost in their own thoughts. Mike was at the wheel and he was still feeling sick to his stomach. He suddenly yelled, "Fuck!" and slammed his hands against the dashboard. "What the hell has Gerry done to us!"

Troy, despite his size, was usually the calm one under pressure. He just looked over at Mike and decided that at this very moment he should keep his mouth shut and let him vent.

Mike went silent again and began replaying in his mind the travel information he had read back in his hotel room about *Angra dos Reis*. He had to think of something other than the twenty-five million dollar swamp.

He remembered that the name of this area they were visiting meant "Bay of Kings" because it was discovered on January 6th, 1502, the day Catholics celebrate the Epiphany—the day the Three Kings visited the baby Jesus. The area was noted for its crystal-clear waters—a diver's paradise—and 365 islands to explore, one for every day of the year. He recalled that the area had several five-star resorts along the beach, and numerous Brazilian celebrities had summer homes there. New Year's day was apparently extra special, with a parade of brilliantly decorated boats entertaining the tourists and locals along the shoreline.

Mike sensed that this would be an excellent spot to launch a luxury resort, which was their plan for the twenty-five hectares of land Baxter Development had purchased for fifteen million dollars. Mike shuddered.

They pulled off the highway and drove along the top of a ridge, revealing the city of *Angra* down below. They both gulped. Ugly piers lined the shore with what appeared to be several ships under construction. If that wasn't bad enough, over the city horizon they could see the unmistakable shapes of two nuclear reactor domes, and what looked to be one more under construction. Mike and Troy glanced at each other without saying anything. Their silence said it all. Mike just kept driving, and tried his best to produce some saliva in his dry mouth..

Once they reached the bottom of the hill and into the city centre, their spirits rose. The opening into the harbor area revealed an incredible sight of mountains and tree- covered hills dotting the islands and shoreline. As long as they didn't look at the ship- building piers or the nuclear power plant, they could see why this area was deemed a paradise and why world-class resorts had been built here.

Troy pulled out his GPS and keyed in the coordinates for the tract of land they owned. The screen remained blank. He tried again. Still blank.

Mike pulled over into a parking spot along the city's main drag. "I see a tourist information office just down the street, Troy. Let's pop in there for some low-tech guidance."

They strolled down the quaint street, past the usual T-shirt shops and outdoor bars. The tourist information office was brightly adorned on the outside with painted flowers and palm trees. It had a nice colorful awning providing shade over some chairs and tables, next to bookcases stacked with travel booklets for the taking. They walked inside, relieved to get out of the oppressive heat for a few minutes.

A petite lady with excellent English greeted them the instant they stepped inside. She was standing at the counter, and graciously held out two lemonades for them to sip.

Mike got right to the point. "Our company has purchased some land on Juruba Beach and we're here to take a look at it. We can't locate it on our GPS and we were wondering if you might be able to point us in the right direction."

She chuckled. Her nametag identified her as Maria.

"Why are you laughing, Maria?"

Maria smiled pleasantly at him. "It's no wonder your GPS can't find it. Juruba Beach is on the island of *Gipoia*, about a thirty-minute ferry ride from the *Santa Luzia* docks."

Mike and Troy just stared at her with their mouths agape. Mike composed himself quickly. "An island?"

"Yes, and oh, it's so beautiful. You'll love it. You're so lucky if you've bought land there. I'd heard that a large tract was purchased, but hadn't seen the new owners yet. The tenants there are so excited."

"Tenants?" Mike felt his stomach starting to heave again. Gerry was surely torturing him from the grave, grabbing his stomach and trying to turn it inside out.

"You don't know?" Maria frowned at him.

"No, we were under the impression that the land was undeveloped."

"Well, it is, mostly. There should be no problem building something else there, if that's what you want to do."

Mike relaxed a bit. An island resort had some appeal in his mind, so maybe this wasn't so bad after all. "So we can take a ferry right to Juruba Beach?"

Maria laughed again. "Oh, no. That would be impossible. Juruba can only be reached by canoe. The waters are far too shallow. You can reach the island itself by ferry, but you must use canoes from that point on."

Mike thought he was going to pass out. He glanced sideways at Troy and could see that his face had gone completely white. Almost afraid to ask, he decided to hit Maria with one last question. "Who...are the tenants?"

"They are known as 'The Nature Colony.' It's *Angra's* most famous nudist colony. You'll love them when you meet them—but you'll have to take your clothes off!" She chuckled again, giving Mike a naughty little wink. "The colony was so relieved when they heard about the sale of the property. They were afraid that their lease wasn't going to be renewed. But as soon as the sale looked like a sure thing, the old landowners went ahead and renewed the lease for an additional one hundred years!

"The colony attracts people from all over the world, you know. Even I like to toddle on over there once a month or so. Maybe I'll see you there sometime?" Maria winked again.

Chapter *11*

Breakfast consisted of rice and black beans, according to the waiter spiced with onions and cilantro, a crusty roll that could best be described as a jawbreaker, and Brazilian jet fuel coffee. It was going to be another scorcher; already ninety degrees according to the weather tower in the center of the square, and it was only 9:00 in the morning. Mike and Troy were seated on the outdoor patio of a restaurant down the street from their hotel in *Centro* Rio. Mike had retrieved the two files from his knapsack for the properties they had driven to yesterday and Troy was leafing through them, sharing his observations.

"There are no aerial photos, geological surveys, or market value assessments on either of those locations. There are no appraisals either. These files are two of the thinnest I've ever seen. Considering how much we spent for each property, I would have expected considerably more due diligence."

Mike was shaking his head in disgust. "Doesn't sound like Gerry's work. He was always a detail guy. What the hell happened?"

"Oh, here's the name and address of the lawyer he used: Juan Paradis at *Paradis and Associates* at *207 Av. Rio Branco*. Looks like it's easy walking distance from here, near that beautiful cathedral we saw driving in—*Our Lady of the Candelaria*."

Mike took the files back from Troy. "Okay, finish your java and we'll walk down there and pay a visit to Mr. Paradis. I'm wondering why Gerry didn't use our corporate lawyers, who have an affiliate down here. It doesn't make any sense for us to use someone else. Gerry himself was a lawyer. He should have known better."

Troy tried to change the subject. "If we have time, I'd like to drop in on that Candelaria Cathedral. I hear it's beautiful, about 300 years old—has an incredible white dome as a topper. That dome alone apparently took a hundred years to finish. Wendy loves old churches; she'd be thrilled if I could get some photos."

Mike looked up from his coffee cup and clenched his teeth. "Troy, what planet are you on right now? Do you actually think we have time for sightseeing? And I can't believe you're in the mood to run around taking touristy photos, after what we discovered yesterday. Geez."

Troy had known Mike for so long that getting dressed-down by him nowadays had little effect on him. He knew Mike was on edge, but he was trying his best to keep things light. "Mike, calm down. Let's get all the facts before getting our nuts in a wringer. Chill out. Like, you should have let us go visit that nudist colony down in *Angra dos Reis* yesterday. I mean, we were already so close—it wouldn't have hurt to just paddle over there for a few laughs."

Mike glared at him. " I can't believe you wanted to do that. Why would we want to see a bunch of fat, ugly old men and women naked? And hear them gloat about how they have us locked into a hundred year lease on our new property!"

"It would have taken the edge off, Mike, that's all."

"I want to keep my edge, thank you. And there was no point looking at that useless property. We can never build on it, with only water access by canoe for Christ's sake. Not to mention a nudist colony that we can't evict!"

Troy knew that there was nothing he could do to calm Mike down. He finished his coffee and stood. "Okay, let's go then, Mike. We'll see the lawyer and do whatever else we have to do today to pin this all down. Our flight to Acapulco leaves at 6:05 a.m. tomorrow. I think both of us could use a hearty meal tonight, some wine, and a good night's sleep. Right?"

*****

"Gentlemen, it's a pleasure. Welcome to Rio de Janeiro! I hope you're enjoying the city." Juan Paradis spoke excellent English. Mike thought he looked like Julio Iglesias and seemed to be almost as suave. His office was on the third floor of a beautiful old historical building, and seemed to be spacious enough to house several associates. Juan ushered Mike and Troy back to his bright corner office with a view of the harbor.

"You'll have to excuse how we're dressed," said Troy.

Juan held up his hand. "No apologies needed. Hey, even I wouldn't want to kidnap you guys with clothes like that!" He clearly knew the score.

Mike leaned forward in his chair. "Sorry to pop in on you like this unannounced, Mr. Paradis. We need some information on a couple of transactions that our company hired you to complete for us a couple of years ago. You would have dealt with a Gerry Upton."

"Gerry, Gerry...what company are you with?"

Mike and Troy handed him their business cards.

"Of course, of course, I remember now—Baxter Development. A couple of properties; Rio and Angra, correct?"

Mike flashed him a friendly smile. "Yes, that's right. We'd like you to pull your files so we can ask some questions if you don't mind."

"No problem at all. I'll go get them right now." He got up from his chair and headed toward a back hallway. Turning his head back in Mike's direction, he said, "I'm glad to see you've healed up nicely from that accident, Mr. Baxter."

Juan disappeared down the hall and was back in less than five minutes with two files in his hand.

As soon as he reappeared Mike asked, "Mr. Paradis, how did you hear about my accident?"

"Please, call me Juan. Well, of course, you told me all about it when you were here two years ago—you and Mr. Upton. Don't you remember? You came in here all bandaged from your neck to the top of your head." Juan chuckled. "We laughed about the slits for your eyes, nose and mouth. It was a vehicle fire, if I recall correctly."

Mike's mouth hung open as he glanced at Troy, who just shrugged and showed the same confused look on his face.

"No, Mr. Paradis...sorry, Juan...you must be mistaken. I've never even met you before today. I was most certainly not here with Mr. Upton two years ago."

Juan frowned, and Mike sensed from his body language that he had gone instantly defensive. "I don't know what kind of game you two are playing here, but I know what I'm saying. And the file documents back me up. Do you think you can deny being party to buying your own properties? Is that what's going on here?"

Troy jumped in. "Exactly what documents are you talking about?"

Juan flipped open one file folder with a flourish, and spun it around so they wouldn't have to look at it upside down. "Here are copies of the passport and Ontario driver's license for Gerald Upton." He turned over a few papers. "And here are copies of your passport and driver's license, Mr. Baxter. These look like you, don't they? For legal reasons I always have to take copies of such documents at the time of real estate transactions as a prevention against fraud. I'm very careful about my work. You gave me these documents to photocopy—two years ago, and you were sitting in that very chair you are sitting in now."

Mike looked at the copies and there was no doubt that they were his. "What legal proof is this? These documents could be fakes! You couldn't even see the person's face if it was all bandaged up. What kind of fucking scam have you pulled here?" Mike knew he was losing control, and he could see out of the corner of his eye Troy leaning over toward him in a bid to calm him down. It wasn't going to work.

Juan sat back in his chair and gave Mike a steely courtroom glare. This was a man who clearly was used to confrontation, and probably thrived on it.

"My job is to assure myself to the best of my judgment at the time, that the principals to a transaction are who they say they are. No court would expect me to pry off someone's bandages to make sure their face matches their photo. Don't be ridiculous, Mr. Baxter. And don't try to tell me you weren't here. I met you. The voice is the same, the height and build are the same, and I have copies of two of your photo identifications. If you were a judge, a Brazilian judge, who would you believe—you, or me?"

Mike jumped from his chair, leaned over Juan's desk, and slammed his right fist down on top of the file. "You should have done more than you did! Someone was clearly impersonating me. And that couldn't have been Gerry Upton with this man, because he would have known the man wasn't me."

Mike could see the slightest hint of a smile turn the corners of Juan's mouth.

"Well it just so happens I did do one more thing. I had Mr. Upton swear out an affidavit attesting to the fact that you were who you were representing yourself to be. The document is right here in the file. And it was indeed Mr. Upton who was with you— unlike you, he wasn't wearing bandages all over his face so I could clearly see that his face matched his photos."

"I wasn't wearing…" Troy put his hands on Mike's shoulders and stopped him from yelling any further. Mike could feel the blood rushing to his face, could feel the heat.

"Mike, let me handle this, okay? You're too distraught right now. Calm down."

Troy gently pushed Mike back down into his chair, and then he turned to face Juan. "Can you advise us as to why there was so little documentation verifying the value of these real estate purchases? We have discovered that these are both fairly useless lots for our purposes, and we had to physically go to each one to discover that. Weren't you being paid to look out for our interests?"

Juan began leafing through both files again, pulling out papers and putting them aside. "I beg to differ Mr. Askew. You'll see that all appropriate documentation is here in both files: geological surveys, appraisals on fair market value, and copies of letters sent by me to Mr. Upton in Toronto—by registered mail—advising him of my opinion and warning of the restrictions to value enjoyment."

"Let me see." Troy reached over and took the papers. He studied both sets of documents. Then he saw something that made his stomach do flip-flops. He lurched forward in his chair. "What's this? For the Rio property it says fair market value is five million, and for the Angra property, three million. We paid twenty-five million for Rio and fifteen million for Angra!"

Mike reacted to this, leaning forward and grabbing the documents out of Troy's hands. He took out his glasses and started reading. The more he read, the more violently his hands shook.

"Mr. Askew, the two of you seem to be pretending you had no knowledge of anything that transpired. So, okay, I'll play your little game with you. Yes, you paid a total of forty million for two properties that had a sale price of only eight million. But, at the direction of Mr. Baxter and Mr. Upton, development monies were invested in a Brazilian bank account covering both properties. It would appear as a dual property purchase for forty million on your balance sheet, but in fact you only paid eight million to the vendors. The remaining thirty-two million was diverted to an account that would disperse funds as the development of the two properties commenced.

"I assumed at the time that it was done in this fashion to allocate all of the capital costs in advance, that would be needed to prepare these properties for your projects; for example: dredging, filling, etc. And of course, your balance sheet would look better by capitalizing the full forty million as real estate. In any event, all legal by Brazilian law."

Mike felt bile rise up into his throat from his stomach. "Do…you have a record of the bank account that the remaining thirty-two million was deposited to?"

"Yes, I do." Juan wrote out the number. "This account is in the *Banco Vargas* here in *Centro.* And before you ask the question, I want to show you the signed authorization from both Mr. Baxter and Mr. Upton, giving us permission to deposit these funds in that joint account."

Mike and Troy looked at the signatures. They were, without a doubt, Mike's and Gerry's. Mike's hands were shaking very fast now, and he clenched his fists attempting to hide it. But then his forearms just started trembling. There was nothing he could do to stop it.

Troy stepped in front of his friend and asked, "Juan, what name is this joint account in?"

"Let's see…yes, here it is… 'Baxter/Upton Reclamation Ltd.' And the signatories to the account are Michael Baxter and Gerald Upton."

Mike lost it. He pushed Troy out of the way and grabbed the frame of Juan's desk with both hands, heaving it over onto its side, knocking Juan backwards. He leaped over the desk and yanked the handsome little man up by his collar, slamming him back against the wall. "You tell me what's going on here, or I swear I'll…"

Suddenly the door to the office swung open and a young lady ran in. She stopped dead in her tracks when she saw the chaos, put her hands to her mouth and screamed, loudly. Following her in was a muscular young man in a suit, well over six feet tall. He yelled out, "Let go of him, right now!" He rushed toward them and met up with Troy first. Troy stretched out his hands trying to slow the young man down, but he was thrust aside with ease.

Mike let go of Juan and turned around just as the big guy reached their corner of the office. The man swung his monster fist at Mike's head. He easily dodged it and lashed back with a solid fist to the younger man's mid-section. He groaned and doubled over in pain. Mike finished him off with an uppercut to the jaw that sent him decisively to the floor.

He turned back to face Juan, who was busy dusting himself off, seemingly unconcerned with his dazed associate lying on the floor.

"Mr. Baxter, this is the last time we will meet. Leave this office now before I phone the police. Believe me, you do not want to spend a night in our jails. I will overlook this violence on the condition that you never return here again. Go to the bank and get your money, then leave this country." A sarcastic smile crept across Juan's face. "Oh, and make sure you have photo identification with you. The bank will want to see it. You do have it, don't you?"

Troy was at Mike's side now, and spun him around toward the door. "Let's get out of here, Mike. This is not a good situation."

Mike nodded and they both headed for the door to make their escape. But Mike turned around to address Juan one last time. "We'll sue you, you slimy bastard. I don't know what kind of scheme you've pulled here, but I promise you we'll get to the bottom of this."

Juan just smiled his best smile, displaying brilliant white crowns sparkling against his dark complexion. "You can try to sue me. Sure you can. But remember, this is Brazil."

*****

They were sitting in an office in *Banco Vargas*, waiting for the busty Financial Services Manager to call up the bank account on the screen. She was fiddling with the key entries, leaning forward over her desk, squirming in the most creative ways imaginable to properly display her breasts. Troy had to keep looking away, and of course kept looking back. He felt a stiffening in his crotch and wondered how on earth he could have imagined visiting that nudist colony. He would have been tarred and feathered in the town square.

Mike had calmed down now, but he was quiet, deadly quiet. They hadn't said a word to each other as they made the walk through Centro to the ornate stone edifice occupied by *Banco Vargas*.

Troy looked closely at him as they sat there waiting for big boobs to find their account. Mike's right leg was bouncing up and down underneath his chair, in perfect cadence on the balls of his foot. He had his hands clasped together in his lap, but Troy could tell that it was more like a death grip, the whites of his knuckles being a dead giveaway.

What was the deal with that anger back at Paradis' office? Troy had never seen such an outburst from Mike before, and he had known him since their university days. Mike was not a violent man. But the anger and fighting skills he had unleashed were a shock to Troy. What was going on with his friend? Sure, these were shocking developments that they had uncovered, but Mike's outburst seemed like overkill.

Big boobs shifted her head from the screen, and turned toward them. "I've located your account, Mr. Baxter, but I have to advise you that it shows a zero balance. I called up the history, and it looks like you and Mr. Upton authorized a bank transfer of the entire thirty-two million dollars to a numbered bank account in Panama—two years ago, shortly after this account was opened. I have your signatures on file authorizing it, and also copies of your photo identification on file. You should know also that due to privacy protections in Panama, I am barred from disclosing the name of the accountholder."

"Can you at least tell us the name of the bank?" Troy had his pen and paper poised ready to write down her answer.

"Yes, of course I can do that. It's *Banco Liberacion Nacional*, in Panama City, Panama.

Mike tilted forward as if he was going to say something, then just leaned back in his chair again and sighed, a look of defeat written on his face.

"Would you like to see your signatures and photo identifications?" Big boobs looked concerned.

Troy glanced at Mike, waiting for a reaction, an outburst…anything.

Mike just laughed and shook his head. "What's the point?"

Suddenly he tilted forward again, this time with a loud gasp escaping from his mouth. He clutched frantically at his chest, then just keeled over onto the floor.

Chapter 12

"What time did you say our flight is to Acapulco tomorrow?" Mike was sipping his second scotch, nicely washing down the steak and potatoes he had just devoured.

"It's at 6:05 a.m., and you had better go easy on the booze, Mike. You scared the shit out of me this afternoon." Troy was watching his friend closely, on the lookout for any troubling signs.

Mike was starting to feel uncomfortable with the mother hen glares that Troy was casting him. "Look, Troy, I've been given a clean bill of health. You were there—the doctor said I was fine. Just a stress collapse, kind of like exhaustion, he said. And let's face it, I've had enough stress the last couple of days to last me a lifetime."

"Well, I'm sharing that stress with you too, Mikey. You're not in this alone."

"Thanks. I appreciate your saying that but let's face it—it looks like I'm the one who diverted funds, not you. I'm the one who's been set up."

"Mike, quit being so self-centered. The entire company has been put at risk with this, not just you. The Board and shareholders will have some serious questions, as will the Ontario Securities Commission. We've made disclosures that are no longer true, and a balance sheet that needs restating. We have tens of millions of dollars missing, apparently sitting in some tinpot tax haven in Central America."

Troy paused for effect, then continued. "This is bigger than just you. I'm a senior officer of this company too, so I share your stress. And we'll deal with it together."

Mike reached out and squeezed his friend's arm. "Thanks for the kick in the ass, buddy. I needed that. And thanks for looking out for me and being a good friend."

According to Troy, Mike had only been unconscious for a few minutes. He came around, lying on the floor of the bank office with several frantic ladies hovering over him, Ms. Big Boobs about to give him CPR. The next thing he knew, he was in an ambulance on the way to the hospital. They hooked him up to monitors, and carried out several tests until he was finally given the 'thumbs up.' Of course they had insisted on keeping him overnight, but Mike flatly refused.

"Are you sure you're up to flying to Mexico? We could just head right home instead and go back there some other time."

"No, we're going to get this over with. I want to see the complete picture. We've owned the Mexican properties longer than the Brazilian ones; four years if I recall. So, who knows, we may be okay there. But we need to find out."

"Fair enough." Troy paused and scratched the back of his head, which Mike recognized as his usual signal that something was troubling him.

Mike raised his glass, and gestured in Troy's direction. "Fire away. What do you want to ask me?"

"You know me too well. Okay, what was going on in Paradis' office with all that anger and fighting stuff? You don't do that sort of thing. Sure, you have a shorter fuse than me, but I've never ever seen you behave like that. Forgive me for saying this, but you were totally out of control. That's not you."

"I agree, it's not. I'll be honest with you—that's been happening a lot lately: the subway thing, some blackouts, saying things that don't sound like they're coming from my mouth. Our family doctor said that these all might be side effects from the lightning accident, but he can't say for sure. All I know is, I don't seem to be myself at certain times, and I seem to have these behaviors, skills and knowledge that I didn't have before."

Troy's eyes betrayed his shock. "Geez, this all sounds kind of creepy, Mike. I don't want to scare you but it reminds me of one of those multiple personality things. Is your doctor looking into this for you?"

"Yeah, he is. But I'm not holding my breath. There's not a lot of data they have to go on, so the effect of lightning on humans is apparently mostly guesswork at the present time. It's still a relatively uncommon occurrence, particularly for two people to bash their heads together at the same instant they're zapped. He'll probably just prescribe drugs or have me lie on a couch and talk to him a few times, for all the good that's going to do."

"Those punches you landed—good god, you looked like a pro boxer! I don't recall you ever having boxed before. Did Gerry teach you a few things back when we were in university?"

"No, I've never boxed in my life. I can't even recall getting into any fights in grade school. I kind of kept under the radar and managed to keep a full set of teeth." Mike chuckled. "I was your basic wimp."

"Is there anything I can do to help?"

Mike drained his glass of scotch and signaled to the waiter to bring some more. "Maybe. I'll let you know when things become clearer to me." He didn't want to confide in Troy just yet, his theory about the lightning bolt connecting his and Gerry's brains at that last second of Gerry's life. It was too bizarre to talk about, and he was starting to feel like a freak. He didn't want his friend thinking of him that way.

Troy scratched the back of his head again, and blurted out the thing neither of them had talked about yet. "Gerry was embezzling. I would never have thought he was capable of such a thing. He was a straight-up guy and a great friend. Are you as stunned as I am?"

"Yes, and no. Now that I look back I realize that he had turned somewhat distant the last few years. Sure, he joked around and we all traveled and golfed together, but the serious conversations we used to have just kind of stopped. He seemed to put up some sort of shell, and this embezzlement was probably the reason why. I always assumed it was because of the tragic deaths in his family that caused him to cocoon.

"The embezzlement must have been the thing he was carrying around. What a huge guilt trip, and burden—wondering when he would get caught, and knowing that he had been betraying the company and his friends. Not to mention the risk of going to prison."

Troy finished off his scotch, and signaled to the waiter to bring them the check. "Who do you think that guy was with Gerry, all bandaged up pretending to be you? Gerry obviously had a partner, and together they pulled off a pretty slick crime. They had your identification forged, they were careful to make these land purchases outside our normal scope of operations to reduce scrutiny. Also, they knew that the controls would not be as stringent in Brazil. I wonder also if that lawyer was in on the scheme."

"I've been wondering about the exact same things, Troy. And they knew the shit would hit the fan one day, so they created a diversion to make it look like the CEO, me, planned this embezzlement. I've been royally set up. I do look pretty guilty if someone wanted to follow the trail. Interesting that this could have continued for quite some time if Gerry hadn't died. And I wonder when it all started. What other surprises might we discover?"

Troy paid the check, leaving a typically generous Canadian-style tip, and they headed out into the street. It was a humid night and both were looking forward to getting back to their air-conditioned rooms and peeling off their clothes.

Once they reached the hotel Mike lit a cigarette. Troy waited outside with him until he finished his smoke. "Troy, did you notice Gerry living differently at all? Any expensive purchases out of the norm?"

"No. Mind you, none of us are poor. This is what I don't get. Gerry certainly didn't need the money so why would he do it? Why would he take such a risk?"

"I don't get it either. It doesn't make any sense to me, and it seems totally out of character for Gerry—at least the Gerry we knew."

The two friends would carry that thought to sleep—"the Gerry we knew."

*****

Two days later, Mike and Troy were in the air on their way back to Toronto from Acapulco's Alvarez International Airport. It was going to be the longest flight of their lives as they pondered how they would explain to the Board of Directors, the shareholders, and the Ontario Securities Commission, that in both Acapulco and Huatulco they had discovered the exact same plot of deceits as they had uncovered in Brazil.

They would have to explain that in Mexico someone pretending to be Mike, as was the case in Brazil, had been a man with a bandaged face and with impeccable documents of identification. That he and Gerry had spent twenty-five million dollars of the company's money for two properties in Mexico that were really only worth five million. That the twenty million extra had been diverted to a Mexican bank account under the name of Baxter/Upton Reclamation Ltd., and that same money had been transferred almost instantaneously to a numbered bank account at the Banco Liberacion Nacional in Panama City, Panama.

After the initial shock wore off, the flustered Board members would understand that the company had been scammed in both Brazil and Mexico by virtually identical schemes—the only difference between the two countries being that Mexico happened four years ago, and Brazil, two. And the CEO was saying he knew nothing about it, nor did he know how useless the four properties were. What kind of CEO was he?

Mike knew that the Board would be busy counting in their minds the missing dollars, while he talked in the most soothing terms to them. And he knew that some smart-ass director trying to make a name for himself, would probably pipe up and remind the Board what a genius he was at math, and state that his calculation between Brazil and Mexico came to sixty-five million dollars for four properties that were worth only thirteen million. This grandstanding director would then remind everyone that fifty-two million dollars was unaccounted for and possibly sitting in a tax haven that Mike Baxter may or may not have access to. He would make the suggestion that perhaps Mike's travel itineraries and expense accounts should be audited for at least the last four years. The director would then close his tirade by suggesting strenuously that the matter be referred to the OSC and the RCMP.

Mike knew it would go something like that, and he also knew that in a few minutes time he would be rushing into the tiny little toilet three rows ahead, and barfing his guts out.

After that he would take the time to ponder how curious it was that the Rio law firm of *Paradis and Associates* also had a branch in Acapulco.

Chapter *13*

"Would you like me to make some coffee?"

"No, I would like you to just get dressed and scram."

She danced her beautiful naked body over to him in her usual provocative manner, and wrapped her arms around his neck. "Now, that's no way to talk to your favorite companion."

He smiled and kissed her on the lips, slipping his tongue inside her eager mouth. Then he quickly withdrew it and bit her lower lip. This wee bit of teasing got her excited again, he could tell. She responded predictably by grabbing his buttocks and squeezing as hard as she could. She knew he liked it rough. She dug her nails into his skin and slid one finger up his anus. Just as she was getting ready to ram a second one in, he picked her up and threw her onto the bed.

He jumped on top of her and put his hands around her throat, squeezing until her face turned red and her eyes began to bulge. He let go and watched in amusement as she coughed herself back to life, gasping desperately for air.

He laughed, but just as suddenly transformed his face into a look of rage. "When I tell you to get dressed, you get dressed! Understand, you cunt?"

She nodded her head quickly, and started to cry. He grabbed her long bleach- blonde tresses and dragged her off the bed, tossing her like a bag of garbage onto the floor. Snatching her clothes off the nightstand, he flung them in disgust on top of her quivering tits.

"Now, get dressed and get the fuck out! You had better be gone in five minutes or you will feel the power of my hands once again."

She struggled to her feet and pulled on her undergarments, then wiggled into her dress. Reaching for her bling purse, she looked at him one last time before leaving the apartment. Speaking as if nothing at all had just happened, she asked, "David, do you need me to come here again tomorrow night?"

"Sure, come by around 9:00 and you can spend the night again." His voice was calm now.

She pleaded, "Can't we just go out sometime—somewhere, anywhere?"

"We will go out when I say. And right now, I do not say."

She nodded, and hurried out into the hallway, slamming the door behind her.

David Samson chuckled as he strode into the adjoining room, which he had expertly decked out into a home gymnasium. He started his usual routine of weights, treadmill, rowing machine. He was still naked; he liked to exercise in the buff so he could watch and admire himself in the floor-to-ceiling mirrors in the gym. Yeah, he was still an Adonis—he knew it. In his mid-forties, muscular, just over six feet tall, and around 200 lbs. His skin was lightly tanned, kind of an olive look, but not from the sun. His hair was dark and moderately long with a wavy texture that most women would kill to have. He was blessed with a face that looked like it could have graced the front cover of a Mediterranean travel magazine.

David was a lawyer, but he didn't use his law degree much anymore, not in practice anyway. It was still handy for credibility and of course gave him the knowledge to find his way around the bureaucratic corridors. But the last five years of his life had earned him more money than he could have ever dreamed of earning as a lawyer. In fact, in just the past month alone he had earned more than all of his years practicing law.

He got dressed and walked down the hall to the kitchen. Time for some breakfast. Now he would make coffee, and he would enjoy it much more than if he had to sip it in the company of that whore. The last thing he wanted was to pretend to enjoy idle romantic chit-chat with a woman who was, in his eyes, good for only one thing. In fact, that's all any woman was good for. He preferred his own company instead.

He took his mug out to the oversized balcony of his twenty-fifth floor condominium on Toronto's trendy Bloor St. West. He had purchased the unit about four years ago for $500,000. It was now worth well over a million. He smiled at his genius. David stretched out on his chaise lounger and looked down at the lines of cars snaking their way down Bloor St., all the little people stressed out trying to get to their pathetic little jobs. He smiled again, then spit up a large green gob and sent it flying down twenty-five floors to the roof of someone's car. They'll just think it's bird shit, David thought, chuckling to himself.

He knew that his lifestyle was frowned upon by his compatriots overseas, but he didn't give a shit. They could frown all they wanted; he knew that he also brought smiles to their stupid bearded faces more often than frowns. He liked western ways, he liked the decadence, money, good food and fine wines.

He absolutely loved his seven-room penthouse condo, and enjoyed cruising around in his silver Mercedes CLK. If his friends in the homeland wanted to sleep in tents and hovels to underscore their beliefs, they were welcome to it. He didn't mind supporting the cause; in fact he felt an obligation to do so, but he also wanted to live life to its fullest, the western way. Those clowns back home could pin all their hopes on Allah giving them seventy-two virgins in paradise if that's all they aspired to. But as far as he was concerned, he could have as many as he wanted right here on earth. Why pin his hopes on a mystical promise, when he could reach out and grab the real thing, right here, right now? Well, his pickings didn't include virgins of course, but what was so great about a virgin anyway? Too messy and emotional. David also kept an apartment and offices in an old decrepit rooming house, located three blocks away from his condo. That was for his visitors from across the pond, and when he had to meet with any of his "contacts" here in Toronto. Only the whores were invited to his penthouse because he knew they were impressed by that stuff, and he never wanted to have to work too hard at getting fucked.

One of the rooms in his condo was outfitted with five separate computers, as well as a mobile satellite phone, which was the only phone he used. So far, it had proven itself to be very secure, with state of the art encryption devices, coupled with the inherent security of the digital environment of satellite transmission.

David considered himself first and foremost a "banker." Not the type one would normally think of, but the word "banker" best described what he did. It was the civilized term to describe what he did. Quite simply, he obtained and controlled money, then diverted it to worthy projects. He was one of many bankers across North America that were hiding in plain sight. Right now, at current count, he had his fingers into ten separate corporations. Ah, the thrill of reaching out and taking what he wanted from capitalism. It was the ultimate irony, he thought, considering who he really was and who he was working for.

He also considered himself a "controller," because he had numerous contacts that he had to keep under control until he finally abandoned them. Eventually, everyone had to be abandoned and it was important for him to recognize when it was time to move on to fresh meat. Kind of like the whores in his life. Each corporation and contact had saturation points. He didn't abandon them easily, however. He squeezed as tight as he could for as long as he could, because it was very labor-intensive to get new contacts going.

David took advantage of the inherent greed and carelessness of capitalism. The system was easily picked, because virtually everyone in that system wanted the next "big deal," the next opportunistic manipulation. Corporations were so easy to compromise, and it was a brilliant strategy for that very reason. Rich executives would do almost anything to cover their butts in the quest to preserve their narcissistic egos and reputations. And when they resisted—and inevitably the ones with consciences did— there were other methods to get them to comply. There were lots of geniuses like him across the continent. They would even meet at their own little "conventions" just like capitalists, although their meetings were a little more discreet. But they did insist on meeting at the best hotels in the best cities. All of the other bankers enjoyed western ways too.

The continent was divided up into "franchise" territories, copied again after capitalist methods. David's franchise territory was all of Canada, because the country was so sparsely populated that it didn't need more than one banker. He had, however, an extensive team of operatives across the country dispersing the money as needed. Good plans required patience, many painstaking steps, and lots of money.

He also coordinated regularly with his banker colleague in New York City. Together, project planning was productive and could be organized in unison. There were several projects on the drawing board, and unfortunately a few that had failed.

The two cities were similar. Toronto egotistically thought of itself as the "Big Apple" of Canada, and New York was the undisputed "Big Apple" of the World. Well, as far as he was concerned, if Toronto wanted to be admired as being in the big leagues like New York, he might just do his part to make the city feel like it had finally made it. David's roster of ten companies had been extremely successful in his banking activities. But one had recently gone sour due to an unexpected turn of events. He wasn't ready to give up on it yet though, because he had a few cards to play first. But he was ready and willing to abandon it if he couldn't draw an ace.

It was time for a follow-up. He picked up his satellite phone and dialed a number in Rio de Janeiro. It rang twice and a familiar voice answered.

"Hello?"

"It is me. Just checking to see how it went."

"Not well. It was nice that you warned me he might show up, but I didn't expect a madman. He's violent. I don't like violence, David. You know that."

"You are being paid well, so quit your whining. And, how did you really expect him to react? I am sure it was a teeny bit of a shock to the poor man. Anyway, I do not think you have anything more to worry about. He probably just exploded, that is all." David didn't care to hear the details of what Baxter had done to scare the little Brazilian. If he made the mistake of showing any real concern, that would only cater to Juan's need for comfort—and more money. He also didn't intend to admit to Juan that he, personally, had some ancient history with Baxter's dark side.

"Well, for a few minutes I was worried. Then they went on to Mexico from here. From what Alejandro told me, he was a lot calmer there—kind of resigned."

"Just what I wanted to hear. He is ripe for the picking, then. Juan, keep me posted on anything else that happens, or any more contact with him or his colleagues. Okay?"

"Will do. By the way, when will I receive my next installment?"

David chuckled. "You are such a little sleaze. Not only did I have to go to great lengths to make sure you and your Mexican partner would have plausible deniability if the roof caved in, but you have the nerve to remind me of my end of the bargain? You will get your money when I feel generous enough to send it to you."

David slammed down the phone, then quickly changed gears and began browsing through his file on Baxter Development Corporation. He had a couple of ideas up his sleeve and would probably make contact again soon. He looked over the newspaper clippings of Mike Baxter; articles that had appeared over the last few weeks. David chuckled when he saw the cartoon of The Briefcase Braveheart, all decked out in animal skins. He certainly had never expected that the man would garner such publicity, but thought that it might be a fortunate coincidence that Baxter had encountered those subway thugs. Mr. Baxter now had a modicum of stature, a good-guy hero reputation that David could exploit to his advantage.

However, it was indeed a puzzle that this clean-cut executive had exploded with violence twice now, in a very short time frame. He figured that there might be some brain damage from the man's lightning accident. While David wasn't afraid, he made a mental note that he would have to be on his guard.

He poured himself another cup of coffee and stretched out on his custom leather couch. He thought back to many years ago when his organization was able to raise money so easily and without interference through their front charity, The Benevolence International Foundation. Millions of their hard-earned dollars had been frozen when the FBI, in conjunction with the RCMP, finally discovered the charity's connection to the Abu Nidal Organization. Funds could no longer be raised in the traditional ways ever since the United Nations Suppression of Terrorism Regulations, or UNSTR, came about. Did those fools really think that other avenues would not be found? Did those arrogant capitalists believe that they were the only entrepreneurs in the world?

The ring of the phone disturbed David's thoughts. He glanced at the call display and smiled. It was his mother.

"Hello, Mama."

"Oh, my Dawud. How are you?"

David winced at her use of his birth name. Even though the Zamir family had been Canadianized for a couple of generations now, the old folks still made use of homeland names whenever they could. It made them feel comfortable, he guessed. When he had finally changed his name to a western version, it made his mother sad but she seemed to understand that he needed to do it to fit into this world. *More than she knew.*

"I am just wonderful, Mama. How about you?"

"Oh, I have these aches and pains that just will not go away. I think it is because I do not see my boys enough."

David laughed—her same old gentle coercion. "Mama, I will be there on Sunday for dinner, okay?"

"Now, do not forget—it is always nice when we all get together."

"I will not forget. Family means everything to me, you know that." David could almost see her smiling at the other end, and it warmed his heart.

Chapter *14*

Cindy rushed around the house, doing some last minute preparations. The helium balloons were floating up at the ceiling, the streamers were hanging just perfectly, and the 'Happy Birthday Mike!' sign was tacked over the front entry. The caterers would be arriving shortly, followed by the guests. At last count, she was expecting about forty people; only their closest friends and the few neighbors they actually liked. She was grateful that her three best friends, Amanda, Wendy, and Carol, had volunteered to help out. All three were busy in the kitchen, putting out plates and making coffee.

Diana and Kristy were due home from school at any moment. They were so excited this morning when they left the house, knowing their dad was getting a surprise party tonight.

Cindy was hoping this party would cheer Mike up. It had been several days since he had returned from his trip down to Brazil and Mexico, and he had seemed so despondent. He hadn't told her anything about the trip, but he didn't normally discuss his business with her anyway. Cindy figured that it must just be his mood swings again, which had become frequent since the accident in Florida.

She had asked him to come home from work on time tonight, which for Mike meant before 6:00. He promised he would—Cindy said that the girls wanted to enjoy a nice dinner with him on his birthday, and watch him open presents before they went to bed. She knew he suspected nothing. The party would be a wonderful surprise; at least she *hoped* he'd enjoy it. Not much seemed to give him joy over the last few months, and Cindy was cautiously optimistic that spending an evening with his friends and family would be a nice new beginning.

Mike was usually a funny and charming man, the life of the party. Those qualities had seemed to disappear after the lightning accident and Gerry's death, only occasionally making their reappearance. She wanted to see those qualities again tonight, the qualities of the man she had fallen in love with so many years ago.

Cindy strolled into the kitchen and smiled as she saw her three friends fussing around with the decorations and the dishes. Everything was looking so nice. She liked things a certain way, and her long-time friends were the only ones, aside from Mike, who knew how things had to be to satisfy her exquisite taste.

She went up to Amanda and gave her a warm hug. Amanda returned the embrace and they lifted their heads back and smiled at each other. Amanda gently squeezed Cindy's shoulder. "I'm so happy that you invited me. This is the first party I've been to since…" She trailed off.

"I know. It is good for your soul to finally get out again. I'm glad you agreed to come. I hope you'll make a habit of this and also start joining me for coffee once in a while like you used to."

"I will, and maybe even later on this week, Cindy. I've been meaning to talk to you about something and I wasn't sure how to say it or even if I'm ready to say it."

Cindy frowned. "Is everything okay? You know you can talk to me about anything."

"I know I can. And I'm okay, considering my Gerry's gone." Amanda stopped to wipe away a tear, then continued. "But it's not about me. Anyway, could we perhaps get together on Friday morning? You can come over to my house if you want."

"Of course. Count on it—Friday morning."

Amanda smiled and hugged Cindy again. "I'm probably making a mountain out of a molehill—you know me, the big worrier. But I'll feel better if I share my thoughts with you."

Wendy piped up, hoping to break the tension. "Cindy, how has Mike been since he got back? Troy has been a bit of a mess—doesn't sleep, his mind's off in space somewhere, and he doesn't talk much. Did Mike tell you how their trip went? Troy has been pretty tight-lipped."

"No, I don't know a thing, except that Mike has been kind of down in the dumps as well. Something went wrong, I think, but you know our guys—they'll probably just sort through it, fix it, and we'll hear nothing about it." Cindy hadn't yet confided in her friends about the strange symptoms Mike had been experiencing.

"True. I guess they just don't want to worry us. Maybe that's a good thing." Wendy laughed. "Anyhoo, I'd rather just think about where our next vacation is going to be." As soon as the words left her mouth, Wendy glanced over at Amanda realizing in an instant how insensitive they must have sounded. What a stupid thing to say—she could have kicked herself.

Amanda dropped her eyes to the floor, and walked off toward the bathroom. Wendy was painfully aware that she had just reminded Amanda that their next group vacation would have one less participant.

*****

"At the Board meeting next week, I have to come clean. I can't wait any longer, Troy."

"We could just delay until the meeting after that one, Mike. That would give us time to do our own investigations, see if we can recover some of the money, flush out some more details."

"We could, but I don't know about you, this is killing me. The deception is huge to all of our stakeholders. The balance sheet needs some provisions to restate those four assets, and perhaps an arbitrary provision for possible other impairment of assets that we don't even know about yet. We know about these four, but what if there are others?"

"Yeah, it's killing me too. I can't sleep as you can probably tell by the black rings under my eyes. But I would prefer we buy a little more time."

Mike got up and paced his office. "I haven't told Jim yet, have you?"

"No, not yet. I'll leave that to you. Being the CFO, he'll have a shit-fit. He cut the checks that Gerry authorized—well, and someone pretending to be you authorized too."

"Thanks for reminding me of that, Troy."

"I'm sorry, but you know you'll have to tell the Board about that as well."

Mike poured himself another coffee. "Yes, I'm well aware of that. They have to know everything and I'm not going to sweep this thing under the rug."

"Didn't expect you would, but at least consider the fact that it doesn't have to be disclosed this soon. We're a couple of months away from the close of the third quarter, so that does buy us some time. You'd still be disclosing properly if you waited until then."

Mike shook his head. "Nope—sorry, Troy. I'll face the music now. I'll sleep better knowing that I've told the truth. And you know what bothers me even more?"

"What?"

"I should have known about these properties before now. I should have done some oversight, some due diligence of my own. I left Gerry to his own designs. And I should have reacted to the red flags that were waving at me about Gerry's behavior. He wasn't the same man—I knew that, but I let our friendship cloud my judgment. If Gerry had been any other executive who I didn't know so well, didn't vacation with, hang out with, I would have been on top of this. I didn't allow myself to remain objective. Bottom line—I have no one to blame but myself."

Troy stood up and patted Mike on the back. "Blaming yourself accomplishes nothing. And you trusted Gerry; you let him do his job. He was a senior executive and a shareholder. How can anyone expect you to run a company with your most senior people on leashes? No one can run a company that way, and no CEO can know everything that's going on. It's impossible."

Mike looked at his friend and allowed a slight smile. "Thanks for trying to make me feel better. But it's not working."

*****

Cindy heard the familiar squeal of the school bus brakes. Her girls were home. She ran to the front door to greet them. She wanted to see the looks on their faces when they saw all the balloons and streamers.

Cindy opened the door and walked out onto the front porch. She saw the bus, saw the other four kids who always got off at this same spot, but did not see her girls. Cindy felt a knot in her stomach as she saw the bus driver get out and walk up her driveway. The palms of her hands started to sweat.

"Hi, Mrs. Baxter. Did you pick up your daughters yourself today?"

Cindy opened her mouth but couldn't find the words. She just shook her head, and wrapped her arms around her chest fighting off the chill that had suddenly enveloped her.

A worried look came over the driver's face. "They didn't board the bus at school, and I checked with the principal. She said they didn't stay behind for any projects." He paused and took a deep breath. "I don't want to alarm you, but just to be safe I think you had better call the police."

Cindy just nodded and could feel the tears well up in her eyes, experiencing for the first time a mother's worst nightmare. She struggled back inside, her knees feeling like rubber, and then collapsed onto the floor. Amanda and Carol ran to her side. The driver came into the house and told them what he had just told Cindy.

"Get me the phone—quick!" Cindy wailed, as she lay on the floor.

*****

Mike had just finished up with Troy when he got the call.

"Mike…the girls are…missing. They…didn't get on the bus." He could hear the tears in his wife's voice.

"What! Have you called the police?"

"Yes, I...just called them. They're...coming over."

"Okay, I'm on my way home now, hon. Try to calm down. I'm sure they're okay. Maybe they went to a friend's house."

"They...would have called me, Mike. Plus...tonight was your surprise birthday party. They were so excited."

Mike felt a lump in his throat. "I'm leaving right now!"

He grabbed his jacket and car keys and ran out of his office, not bothering to lock it behind him as he usually did. Mike dashed down the hall toward his secretary's desk.

"Oh, Mr. Baxter. I was just ringing your office."

"Not now, Stephanie. I have an emergency," Mike yelled back as he rushed past her desk.

She called after him. "I just wanted to tell you that your girls are at the front desk."

Mike whirled around. "What?"

"They're waiting for you at reception."

Mike ran down to the reception desk, and saw his two little darlings sitting in the big leather chairs, looking intimidated. It was the loveliest sight he had ever laid eyes on. "Daddy!" They both yelped in unison and ran into his arms.

Mike picked them up and swung them around just the way they liked it. "How did you get here? Your mother is worried sick that you weren't on the bus!"

Diana, being the elder, assumed the role of spokeswoman. "But Daddy, the lady said you sent the car for us and that your party had been changed to your office and that it wasn't a surprise party anymore."

"What lady?"

"The one in the uniform and hat, driving the big limousine."

Mike didn't want to scare them with any more questions. "Look, I have to phone your mother and let her know that you're here and you're okay. Then I'll drive you girls home and we can talk about it more there. The party's at home, not here."

"Oh, I almost forgot, Daddy." Mike looked down at Diana as she reached into her pocket and pulled out an envelope. "The nice lady said to give you this birthday card."

Mike took the envelope and slowly broke the seal. It was indeed a birthday card, but unsigned. He read the typed words:

"Happy Birthday, Michael! Many happy returns! What lovely daughters you have, and they are so cooperative and trusting! If I were you, I would take some extra time to make them a little more street-smart. You never know what can happen these days—lots of weird characters out there.

"I hope that you reflect on the many good years behind you, and try to forget the sad moments and discoveries that have caused you pain. Some things are just best left alone, do you not agree?

"Your birthday each year must be an especially sad time, because if my memory serves me correctly, your good friend Amanda Upton lost her parents in that armed robbery around this time many years ago. Is my memory accurate?

"And good luck at your Board meeting next week. It is always such a difficult balance for an executive like you, is it not? Knowing how much to tell your Board and how much to just keep close to your vest. Sometimes, 'less is more,' as the saying goes. 'Many happy returns!"

Chapter *15*

Thoughts were swirling around in Mike's head faster than he could process them. He stuffed the card in his pocket, grabbed his two little girls by their hands, and led them back to his office. He sat them down on the leather couch and instructed them not to move.

He had to phone Cindy, but first he had something else to do. Removing the birthday card from his pocket, he reached into a desk drawer and dropped it inside, hiding it from view underneath some papers and files. Then he opened another drawer and removed a blank birthday card, one of a stash he kept for those of his senior staff who were celebrating birthdays. They always enjoyed getting a card from the boss.

He wrote nothing at all in the new card, and simply stuffed it inside the same envelope. Mike knew that the police would ask to see it, because once the police questioned his daughters they would volunteer that the driver had given them a card. And he wasn't prepared to ask his daughters to lie. But he also wasn't prepared to involve the police in this extra piece of the puzzle—not yet anyway. So, he had to produce a birthday card. And only he, and the writer, knew what was written inside the real card.

The brazen kidnapping of his girls in broad daylight, and the sarcastic veiled threats contained in the card's message, made Mike's blood run cold. Fear and anger were ganging up in crushing his chest and he was finding it hard to breathe. He plunked down in his desk chair while Kristy and Diana gazed at him through puzzled eyes.

"It's okay girls. You're not in any trouble. I'm just going to phone your mom, okay?" The girls nodded in unison.

Mike picked up the phone and dialed his home number. Cindy answered it on the first ring.

"The girls are here at the office, dear. Everything's okay." He could hear Cindy gasp with relief, and then start to sob. "We're leaving now. I'll tell you all about it when we get home, but for now just have a stiff drink and maybe close your eyes for a while."

Mike couldn't see her nodding but in his mind's eye he could picture her, skin white as a ghost, eyes red from crying, holding a tissue to her nose. She had just experienced a mother's worst imaginable hell.

*****

It was a quiet dinner table. Mike and Cindy sat alone; the girls were sleeping over at their grandparents' home. It had been several days since the kidnapping and there were more questions than answers. Mike had his own set of questions, but Cindy had a separate set entirely, hers created mainly by Mike's duplicity.

The police had tracked down the limousine that had picked up the girls, and it turned out to be the same limousine service that Baxter Development Corporation had under retainer. And the woman driver was the regular driver that Baxter executives always asked for. This answered the question as to why the Baxter daughters would have gone with this driver—because they had been picked up by this woman many times before upon the request of Mike or Cindy. The girls knew the driver.

The driver had been questioned and the birthday card that Mike had substituted had been dusted for prints. No surprise to Mike that they had found only his. The driver said that the card had been left for her at the dispatch office to bring along when she picked up the girls. No one at the office saw who left the card with the instructions.

When the dispatcher himself had been questioned, he showed the officers an email from Mike Baxter himself, instructing the limo company to pick up his daughters at 4:00 p.m. sharp that day. The driver knew what the girls looked like, and they knew who she was, but she took along her large sign anyway that she always used for the Baxter girls so that they wouldn't miss her and take the school bus by mistake.

The police showed Mike and Cindy a printed copy of the email, and sure enough it was from Mike's personal email address at the office. The officers had started to take the matter less seriously after that. So had Cindy. The police made a visit to Mike's office and together they looked at his email 'sent' file. The message was sitting there clear as day. Without a doubt, it looked as if Mike had sent the message. The police certainly thought he had, and Cindy was now leaning in that direction as well. They also surmised that he was the one who had arranged to have the birthday card left with the dispatch office to be delivered to…himself.

The matter was now dropped with the police promising not to press 'mischief' charges if Mike promised to seek psychiatric help. Mike promised. Considering the crazy things that had been happening to him since the lightning bolt accident, Mike felt that even he might believe he was responsible for this if it wasn't for the fact that he had the real birthday card. Funny enough, that card, sinister as it was, was preserving his belief in his own sanity. And he wasn't about to produce the card just to convince his wife and the officers that he wasn't crazy.

He was scared for his family and he had taken to heart the not-so-subtle hint in the birthday card that he should keep things close to the vest, or…

He needed to do some investigation of his own, keep the police out of it. The warning in the card was clear. And he didn't want to worry Cindy and the girls needlessly.

Mike felt the soft touch of Cindy's hand. He looked up from the table into her beautiful eyes. They were sad beyond anything he had ever seen before.

"You have to leave for a while, Mike." Her voice was almost a whisper. "Just while you get some help. I'm afraid for the girls."

Mike felt a lump in his throat. "I would never hurt you or the girls, Cindy. You know that."

"Not knowingly—I know. But you're doing things that you're not even aware of, sending emails that you can't remember, sending yourself a birthday card. It scares me, Mike. The fact that you could have the girls picked up from school and brought to your office, with no consideration of the heartache that would cause me…that's just not you."

For a split second Mike wanted to tell her the truth—tell her about the fraudulent land purchases he discovered, tell her about the threats in the real birthday card, tell her his suspicion that someone was manipulating him and even hacking into his email system. But he stopped himself. She would want to involve the police, and a nagging thought in Mike's brain told him that that would be even more dangerous. It was safer for Cindy and the girls, at least for now, that they just think that he was losing his mind. It hurt Mike to know that they would be thinking that of him, but he knew he had no choice. His thoughts were interrupted by the realization that Cindy was still talking.

"…that the lightning bolt has caused some damage deeper than we feared. Dr. Fenton warned us about some possible weird symptoms, but I don't think either of us could have imagined what's been happening. I'll be sending him an update on the latest, and you should get in to see Bob Teskey again as soon as possible. I think this is just going to take some time, and some treatment. But I think you should live elsewhere for a while until things settle down a bit."

Mike nodded and got up from the table. He leaned over and kissed Cindy on the cheek, detecting the familiar salty taste of tears.

He knew without a doubt that she was right.

*****

The apartment was spacious enough, and luxurious enough, but it was missing life—the voices, laughter and smells of a family that always made a house a home. It would have to do for now, Mike knew, but he wasn't going to like it. He would tolerate it until he could solve this problem and prove to Cindy that he was normal enough to return.

The apartment was one of those fully-furnished executive suites that were just perfect for business folks who were visiting Toronto for an extended period of time and didn't want to suffer in hotel rooms. That was a big market in a business-friendly city like Toronto, and Mike guessed that guys and girls like him were another big market—the newly separated or divorced. The apartment building was thirty stories high, located on Queen St. West, downtown. Mike chose it because it was near the subway line, and it was close to his office. On nice days he could walk. On other days he could make the short drive or even dare to ride the subway again if he felt so inclined.

It had been heartbreaking to pack his bag and leave his family. The girls didn't understand, and Cindy was classy enough not to admit to them that she had asked him to leave because he scared the shit out of her. They both just explained to the girls that Daddy had a couple of months of lengthy meetings coming up at work that would require some all-nighters. So he had to take an apartment close to the office. He would see the girls on weekends. Mike didn't think serious little Diana believed that story at all.

Cindy had walked him out to the car and gave him the tightest hug he had ever had in his life. He was surprised at her strength. In between sobs she said over and over again that she was sorry, and Mike had said over and over again that it was okay. Then he drove away, looking back, wondering for just the briefest instant whether or not he would ever live in that beautiful house again.

After taking a walk around his new neighborhood, Mike settled in at the desk in his suite. He opened his briefcase and took out the strange birthday card that he had hidden in his office. He read it over again, very slowly, making notes in the margins.

The first paragraph was clearly a warning to him about his girls, emphasizing how easily they could be taken. The second paragraph was, in his view, a hint that he should forget the "discoveries" he had made. The discoveries referred to had to be the embezzlements that he and Troy had uncovered down in Brazil and Mexico. The writer wanted Mike to believe that it was safer if "some things are just best left alone."

The third paragraph was just as chilling as the first. The writer referenced the deaths of Amanda Upton's parents in the armed robbery several years ago. In fact it was four years ago this week. The writer had known that, but of course that was an easy detail to obtain. The point was why was it mentioned in the card? What was the purpose?

The last paragraph in the card was pretty blatant in Mike's view. It was written to make Mike decide that he shouldn't be telling his Board what he had discovered.

Mike was convinced that both this birthday card and the kidnapping of his girls was the work of Gerry's accomplice. He and Troy knew that Gerry had to have had an accomplice to do what he had done. The guy in the bandages was the accomplice. And this man did not want Mike disclosing the embezzlement to his Board. He was to keep it "close to his vest." And he wanted Mike to think that ignoring this advice would bring harm to his daughters. He shuddered at the thought and stared out intently at the lights of the city through his floor to ceiling windows.

And the whisky glass he was holding shattered in his hand, as Mike Baxter imagined squeezing the last breath of air out of the scum's throat.

Chapter *16*

Cindy headed north on Yonge St. She was behind the wheel of her Mini Cooper, a ride that always gave her a rush. It handled like a go-kart with a bit of sports car zoom. She was always amazed at the agility of her little monster, and despite the fact that there were lots of Minis on the road now, it still caused heads to turn. The racing-green color contrasting with a white roof was certainly pleasing on the eyes.

She had hesitated however before choosing the Mini this morning. As she was standing in the garage, she gazed longingly at Mike's Maserati GranTurismo. It just sat there looking impatient, its aggressive stance seemingly just begging for someone to turn on the engine. For a second she almost did it, but stopped herself just in time. She knew if she heard the growl of the powerful V8, there'd be no turning back. Cindy had only driven the car once before, but Mike had been sitting in the passenger seat guiding her through the movements of the slick manual transmission. He had warned her that the acceleration was sixty mph in five seconds, and she hadn't believed it until she put her foot to the floor. The thing was crazy. She'd never before experienced having her head thrust back into the headrest.

So, despite the temptation, Cindy decided to take her Mini and leave the Maserati at rest. She was intimidated by the thought of that huge engine generating over 400 horses. But, she was even more intimidated by the thought that if she caused any damage to Mike's prized toy, she'd never forgive herself and probably neither would Mike. The ride wouldn't be enjoyable with that thought swirling around in her head. At least she felt comfortable and confident in her Mini.

When Mike moved out he had taken the BMW; no slouch of a car in its own right, but less of a target to vandals and car thieves than the Maserati. Mike was afraid that not having his own secure garage to park his car in would be dangerous for the Maz. So, there it remained, lonely and anxious for exercise.

Cindy hoped Mike would come by sometime soon and take it for a spin—

not that she cared about the car's feelings, but she wanted to see him. It had been several days now since he'd left, and while they'd talked on the phone every day, it wasn't the same as seeing each other, touching each other. She missed him desperately.

Cindy slipped the Mini into sixth gear and picked up speed as she wheeled the car onto Hwy. 401, heading east towards the north exit to the 404.

She had second-guessed herself countless times since asking Mike to leave. Here he was, going through the most difficult time of his life, and she wasn't there for him. But the last stunt he had pulled—having the girls picked up at school without telling her, sending an email that he didn't remember doing, and having a birthday card delivered to himself—was too much for her. She had every right to be worried for both herself and their girls, she had convinced herself. And she didn't blame Mike—she knew that wasn't him, the real Mike, who had been doing all these strange things. It was the lightning bolt after-effects, and they seemed to be getting progressively stronger. She didn't understand them, and neither did he. She wondered if the side-effects would eventually just peak and disappear completely. Or, would he be this way for the rest of his life? She didn't want to think about that—it was too scary, and too…final.

However, she'd missed him terribly and was now leaning toward inviting him to come back home.

She turned off the 404 onto Aurora Sideroad. Today she was having coffee with Amanda Upton. They had set this up the day of Mike's upended birthday party, and despite what had happened she wanted to keep this visit. It sounded like Amanda needed to talk to her and Cindy wanted to be there for her. She also thought she might unburden some of her own worries today. It would be good to finally share these things with a close friend. She hadn't shared anything yet with anyone, other than Dr. Teskey, and Cindy rationalized that it might be good for her own mental health to finally find the courage to do that.

She pulled into Amanda's driveway, struggled out of the compact Mini with the usual difficulty, and walked up to the front door. She didn't even have to knock. Amanda must have been watching for her because the door opened the instant Cindy had her knuckles poised. The two friends embraced each other as if it had been years instead of just a few days.

"Coffee's on and it's strong, just the way you like it," Amanda said as she took Cindy's coat and hung it in the front closet.

Cindy took a moment to admire the expansiveness of the house—the huge foyer and grand curving oak staircase up to the second floor. It was truly a luscious home, not as large as Cindy's, but much newer and more of an open concept.

"I still get blown away every time I set foot in this house, Amanda," she said as she swung her arms around in recognition of the spaciousness.

"Thanks, Cindy, but somehow it seems kind of empty now without Gerry here. I'm thinking about downsizing—the boys and I perhaps moving back into Toronto again. I'd like to be closer to friends like you. It gets kinda lonely up here. Being a widow is bad enough but worse when your friends are such a long drive away. I like Aurora, but it's not Toronto."

"You know, I think that might be a smart decision. We would love it if you were back closer to us." Cindy then smiled in her customary sly way. "It would also give me an excuse to snoop at houses again. I hope you'll let me go with you when you start exploring. There's no pastime I like better!"

Amanda laughed. "You bet. That's just one of the many things we have in common—looking at houses and drooling!"

The two friends sat down in the large kitchen sunroom, and enjoyed their coffee and pastries. They talked about cooking, shopping, and children. Three hours passed quickly, and they had yet to discuss anything sensitive. Cindy knew they were just dancing around the inevitable, so she decided to finally break the ice. She told Amanda about her asking Mike to leave for a while, told her about the results of the investigation into the kidnapping of the girls where it was discovered that Mike had, apparently unconsciously, ordered the limo to pick up the girls. The email that he didn't remember, the birthday card he had sent to himself.

Amanda had finally seen the media reports about Mike being the famous 'Briefcase Braveheart,' so she just nodded, not seeming too surprised about these new revelations. "What was that subway thing all about, Cindy? It was a brave thing for Mike to do, but I never knew him to be a fighter—not like my Gerry."

"Exactly—totally out of character for Mike. We were all proud of him, but he didn't even remember doing it! Not until he saw a video of the news coverage. So, Mike went through that entire ordeal in the subway on autopilot! And he's had other blackouts too—one time in the office for about seven hours! It's...pretty scary."

Cindy then blurted out the disturbing incident with Mike being in an almost hypnotic state that one night in bed, when he had called her "Mandy," and had admitted that he had actually seen Amanda sitting beside him on the bed instead of his own wife.

At this revelation Amanda put a hand up to her mouth and gasped.

"What's wrong? Are you okay?" Cindy asked, alarmed.

"Y…Yes. But I have to tell you something. That's really why I wanted to see you today, aside from just wanting to see you as a friend again. What you just told me ties in a bit to what I want to tell you—have to tell you. That's why I'm kind of shocked."

"Okay, go ahead, Amanda. You have my undivided attention." Cindy got up and poured each of them more coffee.

"After you hear what I have to say, you may want to pour yourself something stronger than coffee," Amanda said wryly.

Cindy braced herself. A slight feeling of nausea came over her along with a sense of dread.

Amanda took a deep breath and began. "I'm just going to spit it out. Mike came to see me a few weeks ago. I was surprised because he hadn't called first—he just showed up. I was glad to see him though. I thought it was nice of him to drop by."

Amanda took a sip of her coffee and another deep breath. "We talked for a while, but then I started to get a bit spooked. He called me 'Mandy,' which was Gerry's name for me. He knew about the gift that Gerry had bought Sam before he died. He knew about our alarm system, and about the security patrol that we've had in place for the last few years."

Amanda folded her arms across her chest and shivered. "Those things alone could not be a huge concern, but when he hugged me from behind and nestled his cheek into my hair like Gerry used to do, I got really spooked. Then it got even more weird—he mentioned something about how he used to calm me down before exams at university. I was speechless—I just wanted him to leave at that point because I was so stunned. Calming me down before exams was what Gerry used to do, not Mike. I was in Law school with Gerry—that's how we met. We were in almost all the same classes. Mike was in Engineering. We never saw Mike on campus until after classes, usually at the pub."

Amanda paused and held Cindy's hand. Cindy was breathing heavily now, and her hands were shaking. "I'm sorry, Cindy. Maybe I shouldn't have told you these things."

"No…No, I'm…glad you did. Believe me. All of this is…relevant, and you're being a good friend by telling me."

"Well then, I have one more thing to tell you—if you're up to it." Amanda said with worry in her eyes.

"I'm up to it. Go ahead—don't hold back."

"Well, when Mike was leaving, he told me I could probably cancel the security patrol now—that I wouldn't need it anymore. I was shocked that he said that. I asked him if we were in danger when Gerry was alive. He didn't answer me. He just said something to the effect that I didn't have to worry anymore—then he drove away. Before he left though, he called me 'Mandy' one more time. I swear, he sounded like Gerry; the same affectionate tone. It was spooky."

Cindy lurched from her chair knocking it over in the process, ran straight to the bathroom and threw up.

Chapter 17

Mike picked up the files from his desk along with the CD burned with his Power Point presentation, and worked his way down the hall toward the boardroom. Stephanie leaned over her desk and handed him some papers as he passed—last minute insertions to the board packages.

Entering the boardroom he noticed that none of the directors had arrived yet— only Troy Askew and Jim Belton, his colleagues and two best buddies. They were standing over at the buffet table chowing down on danishes and fruit. Mike joined them and poured himself a cup of coffee.

Troy grabbed him by the arm and pulled him over to a corner of the room. In a whisper, he asked, "Have you filled Jim in yet on what we discovered?"

"No, not yet. I should have, I know, but for now I think it's best to keep it between the two of us."

"Okay, but we shouldn't wait too long. He's in the inner circle, and he's our friend."

Mike winced. "Yeah, I feel a bit guilty, but you know how frantic Jim can get. Maybe that's typical of most financial folks, but no need to add more stress than he can handle."

Troy nodded. "Are you still going to proceed the way we discussed yesterday? You haven't changed your mind?"

"No. I'm choosing to go with your advice. We'll keep it on the 'down low' for now, and see what else we can dig up."

"Good—I think that's the right move. It'll buy us some time."

They both turned at the same time to the sound of chatter. Several directors had just arrived and Jim was greeting them at the entrance. Mike and Troy sauntered over and expanded the receiving line.

Peter Botswait, the Chairman of the Board, greeted Mike with a hearty handshake, along with his congratulations on another successful month of financial results. Mike put on a good face, but he felt strange knowing that there was deception in the numbers and that the deception would have to continue for a while longer yet.

Guy Wilkins came through the door—Mike liked Guy. He was a director who asked good questions and was never prone to grandstanding. Unlike one of the other directors, Christine Masden, who had jumped all over him at the last board meeting. She was already pouring her coffee so Mike forced himself to go over and say hello. Christine shook his hand coldly, and said, "I hope we get some clarification today on those foreign properties."

"You will, Christine. It's the last item on the agenda."

She glared at him. "It should be the first item."

Mike controlled the urge to slap her across the face. "Nice seeing you again, Christine." He walked away, and took his seat opposite the end of the table where Peter would be sitting. He loaded his CD into the computer and turned on the integrated projector. At this sign, all took their seats. The moment of truth. Would they buy it?

*****

"...so we'll record that motion as carried. Now, this brings us to the last item on the agenda and the one most of us are most anxious to hear an update on. Mike, the floor is yours." Peter crossed his arms and leaned back in his chair, readying himself for Mike's presentation.

"Thank you Mr. Chairman. Just to summarize, we own two large tracts of land in Mexico with a book value of twenty-five million dollars. One is in Acapulco, and the other is in the south of Mexico in an area called Huatulco. These properties were purchased over four years ago, and are intended for resort use.

"The other non-North American investment we have is in Brazil, acquired about two years ago. Our book value investment there is forty million dollars, and consists of potential subdivision property just outside of Rio de Janeiro, as well as a resort property in Angra dos Reis.

"As we agreed at the last Board meeting, Baxter Development would commence a new strategic study to either confirm or reject our existing plans for those plots of land. We would basically be second-guessing ourselves, in light of the crippling recession and emerging trends in these hot zones.

"Troy Askew, our Senior Vice President of Construction and Completion, and I, made a recent trip down to both of these areas of the world. We wanted to get this process started by at least seeing the properties ourselves first. Up until now, only Gerry Upton, our now-deceased executive in charge of Development and Legal, had visited these sites.

"Making a long story short, while we still remain somewhat optimistic about the long-term prospects in Mexico and Brazil, we feel less confident now than we did years ago before the economic collapse that is still impacting most parts of the world. In addition, each week the drug wars in Mexico seem to be gaining momentum and will no doubt begin to have an effect on the tourist potential. It may, in fact, result in many existing resort properties and more still under construction, becoming 'white elephants.'

"Surprisingly, Brazil, one of the most promising economies in the world right now, is beginning to have its own set of drug problems. The *favelas*, or slums surrounding Rio de Janeiro, have begun to burst with violence. Drug lords have always been present in Brazil, but now are becoming more brazen and resistant to law enforcement. Perhaps they are emboldened by seeing what the drug lords are achieving in Mexico. In any event, it's beginning to simmer, and we see a similarity there to the Mexico of ten years ago.

"To conclude, we do not feel we are invested wisely in Mexico or Brazil. The current economic conditions coupled with invasive and expanding organized crime in those regions, make our investments down there extremely risky. It is therefore our recommendation to the Board that we put all four properties up for sale as soon as possible. We believe that local investors would be the more likely purchasers, consequently our marketing efforts will be concentrated in those countries as opposed to being directed at foreign commercial interests. With the Board's approval, we will proceed to list these properties for sale immediately."

He paused for effect. "I now invite any questions that directors might have pertaining to this item." Mike looked around the table—faces looked surprised, but not angry. That was a good thing.

Christine Masden crossed her legs and made some notes on her pad. Then she spoke. "Michael, I suggested this at the last Board meeting and it was rejected at that time. However, in light of your report and what you are recommending, perhaps this is the time to make a provision against the book value of these properties, as a precaution. The proceeds of sale may not equal or exceed book value, so until we know, I am uncomfortable with having overstated assets on the books."

Guy Wilkins jumped in. "With all due respect, Christine, that may be premature and an overreaction. Mike is recommending we put the properties up for sale—at this point there is no indication that we will realize less than book value. I would suggest that we await activity and offers, to test the water.

Based on that, we can decide at the next Board meeting if provisions to the financials are needed. Let's not jump the gun in a negative fashion here. It will just make investors nervous needlessly."

A few other directors addressed questions, mostly of a minor nature, and finally the Chairman, Peter Botswait, spoke up. " In my opinion, we have witnessed exactly what a Board should expect from their CEO. Mr. Baxter has been honest and above- board in his assessment, and has swallowed some serious crow in admitting to us that the investments in these properties were a mistake. He is now recommending a course of action that is the right one in my judgment, rather than spending more money on development in increasingly unstable areas of the world. I applaud Mr. Baxter for his candor and accountability. I would like a motion from the Board that we proceed along the course that he has recommended. Also, I agree with Guy that it is premature to administer provisions against book values. A motion, please?"

Guy made the motion, and Bill Henson seconded.

"Motion carried," announced Peter.

With that, the meeting was adjourned. Mike glanced over at his friends; Troy nodded his approval and Jim just looked puzzled. The directors began filing out of the room, and Christine made a point of glancing back at him with a look that betrayed her disgust.

Mike didn't need Christine's glare to make him feel bad. He hadn't lied to the Board but he had committed the sin of omission. He had not made full disclosure, which was in violation of his fiduciary duty as an officer of the company. And Christine was right—they should have put a provision in the financials. The path he had chosen to take was to do the wrong thing for the right reasons. What he had started in motion would now undoubtedly lead to one lie after another.

Despite this, Mike breathed a sigh of relief. He now had some time to figure things out on his own. He began his walk back to the relative safety of his office. Missing was the usual bounce in his step, with eyes uncharacteristically looking down burning an invisible path in the carpet.

Chapter *18*

Colin Spence sat forlornly in his office, looking out over University Avenue. It was 8:00 at night, already getting dark, and once again he had missed dinner with his family. Usually he wasn't this late getting home, but every couple of months when he had no choice but to attend one of these special evening appointments he would tell his wife, Karen, that he had a late dinner meeting. She always bought the story.

With Colin's position as Senior Vice President of Underwriting and Claims with the Ontario Life Insurance Company, his wife had gotten used to the travel and the long hours. She didn't like it but she knew it came with the territory. Karen was always supportive, although leaving her alone in the evenings didn't sit well with Colin.

Whenever he had these late evenings, he would urge her to get one of the neighbors or her sister to keep her company. Karen never argued with him—not after what happened to her three years ago.

He hated these secret meetings, and the fact that he couldn't tell anyone about them to reach out for help. He detested what he had been doing to his company for the last few years. His dream job had turned into a nightmare. He knew he was protecting his family, but he wondered what his little boys would think of the lie he'd been living. He reached into his desk drawer and withdrew some paperwork and two bank drafts; one in the amount of $2,000,000 and the other for $500,000. He stuffed the documents and drafts into his briefcase and snapped it shut. Then from another drawer he took out a large hunting knife in a sheath. He pulled back his suit jacket and slipped the sheath over his belt, sliding it back just enough so it wouldn't be easily visible. He felt better having this weapon with him whenever he met with David, or whatever the fuck his real name was. However, the man was so arrogant and confident, that 'David' probably *was* his real name.

Colin left his office and walked down the long empty corridor to the elevators. Everyone was gone by this time and the office had a lonely, forbidding feel to it; kind of the way his life felt like right now. He exited on the main floor and headed north to the subway station. He could do this route blindfolded by now. He would ride the subway north to the Bloor/Bay station, then walk west to Avenue Rd., then north two blocks to his final turn onto sleazy Lowther Avenue. To the third house on the left—a run-down rooming house. He would enter on the main floor where David had an office. Colin was pretty sure David owned or rented the entire house, but he was only allowed to see the main floor office. He would buzz first—two quick buzzes and one long one. Then the door would be unlocked from inside by remote control.

As he rode the subway, Colin thought back to how he had gotten into this mess in the first place. It was three long years ago, and he had been drinking in a bar near his office with some of his colleagues after a business dinner. They had a few laughs, drank far too much, then staggered on down to a strip club; the first time he had been to one of these since he was a teen. One of his business friends was quite insistent that they go—he said it was more of an executive hangout rather than the typical junky strip joint.

A few hours passed but Colin decided to linger a little bit longer due to the affectionate attentions of an exotic Middle Eastern stripper. His friends had already left, but the girl was still working—at thirty dollars a pop for one lap dance after another. Two hundred and ten dollars later, she suggested he accompany her to the private room—the so-called VIP room—down at the back of the strip joint. At that point, he was a bit smitten, drunk, and hardly in any condition to refuse. In all honesty though, he knew he had thrown away the willpower to refuse.

As she escorted him back to the room, with the knowing eyes of all the other men glaring at him as he passed, she told him her name was 'Fadiyah.' Colin told her that was a pretty name, and she laughed. She said her parents must have wanted her to be a suicide bomber, because the Arab name meant 'self-sacrificing.' Colin didn't think that was funny, but at that point he didn't care.

Once in the room Fadiyah got closer and more naked than in the main hall. Colin thought he was going to blow his load. Then, remarkably, she suddenly wanted to talk business. A couple of hours before he had told her he was a life insurance executive and even gave her his business card for some stupid reason. Perhaps he thought that a stripper would be impressed by his title. Sure.

In the sweetest voice and with her boobs in his face, she asked him if he could arrange for a million dollar policy on her oil-rich father. Colin replied,

"Sure," and then she asked, "Can we avoid a medical exam?" Colin briefly snapped out of his alcoholic haze and replied through the 36Ds pressed against his mouth, "No, sweetie, not for that amount."

Then she popped the big question. "If I paid you $50,000 under the table, would you accept a fake medical, and not fact-check?" She giggled. Colin giggled too, and said in a drunken slur, "Honey, for $50,000, I won't even read his file!" She giggled again, and quickly pulled herself off him.

"Come back tomorrow night and we can talk some more, yes? Maybe I will let you get naked too." She reached down and gently guided his hand between her legs, and up against her G-stringed crotch. Then she squeezed her legs tightly together and swiveled seductively from side to side with his hand locked in place. That was more than Colin could take. He felt a sudden explosion in his own crotch and the stickiness began spreading across the front of his Saville Row dress pants.

Fadiyah smiled knowingly and then she was gone. He was left alone on the tacky red leather couch in a room barely illuminated by three broken tiffany lamps. Colin sat there like an idiot and wondered how long it would take for him to sober up, while thanking his lucky stars that he had decided to wear a dark suit today.

He got off the subway at the Bloor/Bay station and worked his way along Bloor Street, hanging a quick right at Avenue Road. As he walked along, Colin remembered back to the day after his encounter with Fadiyah. At the office that morning, he got a call from one of his friends, Bill, who had left the strip joint early. The guy made a few smarmy jokes about the luscious body that Fadiyah was blessed with, and asked Colin in typical guy fashion if he had gotten lucky.

Colin played it down.

Then Bill said, "I feel guilty about not sharing something with you. I was approached on the street a couple of nights ago by a promoter of the strip joint. He offered me $1,000 if I brought my friends over to the joint. Well, I mentioned we would be having dinner the next night, so I promised I'd steer us over there. He paid me $500 up front and then a girl slipped me another $500 once we arrived. He seemed to know you by name. He wanted an important executive like you to come; good for business."

Colin tapped his pen on the desk. "That's pretty strange. Why didn't you tell me about that?"

"Ah, greed I guess. I wanted to keep the money. But now I feel bad and would like to split it with you, especially since you're the one he really wanted to be there."

"No, don't worry about it. We all had a good time, so you earned your money. I'm surprised, though, that these places are promoting themselves like that. And I'm really concerned that he had my name. I never go to places like that."

"Recession, I guess. Businesses these days will stoop to any tactic that works. And they do their research, I guess, just like we do in our businesses. And this tactic worked. We spent far more than $1,000 dollars last night, and we'll probably all be back there again sometime."

Sooner than you think, Colin mused to himself. They said their goodbyes and Colin turned back to the files that he had piling up around him. But he couldn't stop thinking of that exotic Arab body gyrating in front of him. He got excited thinking that if he wanted to, he could go back there tonight. After all, she had specifically invited him. Him! How many strippers would invite a man back like that? Can't happen too often. She must have liked him. However, if he did go back, he would have to shut off any conversation about the large policy she wanted on her father. He was sure she had been joking with him, but if she wasn't, what she was asking was unethical and illegal and he couldn't do it. However, maybe he could just string her along for a while, make her think that he'd do it—just so he could have some more fun.

Colin got up and paced the room. What was he thinking? He was acting like a schoolboy with hormones racing. He had a lovely wife and two boys—a family he loved deeply. He had to stop this before it got out of hand. Colin picked up the family portrait from the credenza, and stared at it. Tears came to his eyes. How could he think of betraying them? Was he going through a mid-life crisis?

He shook his head and decided in that instant that he would not go back to that strip joint. He would put Fadiyah out of his head, and be home for dinner tonight—on time for a change.

Colin sat down at his desk, satisfied with his decision. He spent the next couple of hours on the computer, working up volume and expense projections for the next quarter. He was fully absorbed in his work when the phone rang.

"Hello?"

"Hi handsome. It is Fadiyah. Are you coming back to see me tonight?"

Her voice—seductive, visual. He could practically see her bejeweled belly button, green eyes, and long, black hair hanging down past her beautiful breasts. Colin shuddered with excitement.

He struggled with conflict but heard himself saying, "Hi Fadiyah. Thanks for spending time with me last night, but I won't be coming back again. It's not for me."

"Oh—I am so sorry to hear that. Can I say anything at all to change your mind? A promise, perhaps?"

Colin shuddered again at the sound of her voice and the meaning of her words. But he held fast. "No, Fadiyah. Thanks again. I'm rather busy and have to hang up now, okay?"

Suddenly the tone of her voice changed. "No, not okay. Listen to this—perhaps it will change your mind." Colin heard a click, and then a slurry version of his own voice:

He felt bile coming up from his stomach, stinging his throat. Colin swallowed hard. "Fadiyah, what's the meaning of this?"

"You are a big smart executive. I am sure you can figure it out. Be here at the club tonight, 7:00 sharp." Then she hung up.

Colin sat back in his chair and put his feet up on the desk. He could feel his heart pounding in his throat. Then his quick brain started to rationalize. Sure, she wanted something from him—probably that fraudulent life insurance policy on her father. After that, she probably planned to have her father killed. He'd seen it before. His job was to make the funds happen. However, what did she really have on him—a tape of his voice making an incriminating statement while intoxicated was hardly something that would hold up, he didn't think. It was just a tape, and his voice could be impersonated.

Maybe he could just give her some money and she'd go away. Yes, that's what he'd do tonight.

At 6:00 p.m., he phoned Karen to let her know he'd be late getting home. No answer—that was strange. She was always home at this time, preparing dinner for the kids. And if she were busy in the kitchen, one of the boys would usually answer. Maybe they all went to the store, or out for a walk with the dog. Yes, that was it. Nothing to worry about.

Colin turned off his computer and left the office around 6:45 p.m., for the short walk to the Big Shots Club—a play on words? He had phoned Karen one more time before he left, but still no answer.

He arrived at the club, which was mostly empty at this time, taking a seat near the stage where a buxom blonde was doing her thing. Colin was disinterested—a naked woman was the last thing on his mind right now. This time the thought that he was sitting in this sleazy place made him feel sick to his stomach.

He couldn't see Fadiyah anywhere in the room. Several half-naked women were hanging around in groups talking, but none of them looked like her. Then one girl caught him looking; she sashayed over to his table.

"Hi there. Would you like me to dance for you?"

"No. Actually, I'm looking for a girl named 'Fadiyah.' Could you ask her to join me, please?"

She looked hurt. "No one here by that name, honey. I know all the girls. She may be a part-timer. We get some of those for a night or two, then they're gone." She walked off in a huff. Colin was puzzled, but also a little bit relieved. Maybe Fadiyah was a transient, and had just moved on. Maybe she had just been having a little fun with him.

Colin got up and started for the door, anxious to make a beeline out of there and put this whole episode behind him.

Suddenly he felt a heavy hand on his shoulder and he whirled around to see a tall, well-dressed, Middle Eastern man. He had a movie star air about him, a gold chain around his neck, and expensive rings on several fingers.

The man smiled at him, and said in an authoritative voice, "Colin Spence—follow me, please."

Colin sputtered something, but the man simply grabbed him by the arm and ushered him back to the same sleazy room he had been in the night before. Once inside, the man shoved him onto the couch and said, "We have some business to discuss."

The man introduced himself as David. He then told Colin to shut up and listen.

The 'business' was that Colin had been selected. He had been selected because he was an executive in charge of both Underwriting and Claims at a life insurance company that was privately owned. As that kind of executive, he had absolute power over both the acceptance of risk and the payment of claims. It was rare to have one executive in charge of both, so that's why he was perfect for his assignment. In addition, due to Ontario Life Insurance Company being privately owned, there were far less oversight regulations and far fewer audits. And less detailed. So, the combination was perfect.

Colin was told that he was expected to enter into an arrangement with David, whereby Colin would approve life insurance applications for people who didn't exist, and pay claims based on phony death certificates. All proper documentation would be provided by David as to phony birth certificates, driver's licenses, profiles, fake medicals, background checks, death certificates. All Colin had to do was process the applications and pay the claims. Simple.

For Colin's agreement to participate, he would receive absolutely nothing in return. Colin got up from the couch and was promptly shoved back down again.

"You will agree to this, yes?"

"This is preposterous! I won't agree to this. Why would I? I'm going to the police."

David pulled out a recorder and played Colin's voice and his slurry statement that Fadiyah had made him listen to over the phone.

Colin glared into the Arab's black eyes, and said, "That proves nothing."

David smiled. "There are cameras in this room." He pointed. "Up there in the ventilation ducts. So, be patient while I show you what else we have." He pulled out a camera phone and shoved it in front of Colin's face. He could clearly see and hear himself and watched in horror the entire encounter with Fadiyah. This film could go to his wife, his employer, or perish the thought—the internet.

"Fadiyah is beautiful, no? She is my associate and she does wonderful work." The Arab displayed his perfectly crowned teeth as he smiled at Colin, evil oozing from his eyes.

Colin felt as if he was going to pass out. But he mustered enough anger and bravado to say, "Fuck off, you prick. I'm not going to be blackmailed. Do what you need to do with that film and I'll take my chances. I will not—repeat, *not*—do what you want me to do."

At that, Colin got up again and this time David didn't shove him back down. Instead, he noticed him speed dial a number on his phone, and heard him say two words, "Do it."

Then David put his arm around Colin's shoulders as if he were his best friend. "Go home and think about it. Come here tomorrow night and let me know your decision. Right now I think your wife, Karen, needs you." Then David shoved him through the door and slammed it behind him.

When Colin arrived home an hour later, the police and an ambulance were already there. Karen had been brutally raped and beaten. His boys had been tied up and gagged in another room. At least whoever did this hadn't made the boys watch. And he couldn't deny that he knew who was behind this.

A broken man, Colin went back to the Big Shots Club the next night and agreed to the terms of the 'partnership.' While there he kept his anger in check and thought only of his lovely wife lying in a hospital bed, and his anguished sons waiting for him at their grandma's house.

The partnership had now lasted three years. And this partnership had seen the life insurance proceeds of twenty-five "deaths" totaling thirty million dollars on people who didn't exist, being paid out to a myriad of David's iron-clad aliases.

Colin turned left on Lowther and headed to the familiar tenement house where he had spent many an evening. At their last meeting he had advised David that an external audit was coming at his company within the next six months. The owners planned to go public, and the audit was the first step in the submission to the TSX. David had just smiled calmly and said, "We'll talk about that at our next meeting."

Colin buzzed the doorbell using the agreed-upon cadence, and he heard the click of the lock opening. He entered and walked down the hallway to the office. David sat behind the desk, smug as usual, with his two usual henchman sitting expressionless in the corner.

He sat down in the guest chair in front of David's desk, opened his briefcase, and withdrew the two bank drafts and associated paperwork. He handed them over to David, who just smiled. He was good at smiling.

"Colin, you will be glad to know that I am ending our partnership. It has gone as far as we can take it and it is time to set you free."

Colin felt his shoulders sag with relief. The tension suddenly lifted—three long years were coming to an end.

David grinned at him. "Fadiyah is upstairs. Would you like a charity fuck before you go?"

Colin grinned back at him. "Fuck off."

"Okay, then. I was just trying to be nice." He nodded towards his henchmen in the corner. "My friends here will drive you back to your office. It is the least I can do."

"I can make my own way back, thank you."

"No, I insist." The two goons suddenly came behind Colin and grabbed him under the arms. Colin felt an adrenaline rush of fear run through his veins. He flung his right hand to the left side of his belt, and yanked out the hunting knife. David reacted with lightning speed, diving over the desk and wrenching the knife free from Colin's hand. He handed the knife to one of his men, "Use this later."

Colin noticed one of the men had a needle in his hand, bringing it up towards his neck. Suddenly David yelled, "No, you idiot! In the wrist, in the wrist!" Colin was aware now of one man holding his wrist still, while the other one inserted the needle. He felt nothing, but he knew that the nothingness wouldn't last.

David was talking again. "We will just wait a few minutes until the 'juice kicks in'—is that how you westerners say it? Hah! I will talk to you in the meantime. You were one easy target, Colin. You made a stand early in the game, resulting in your wife being raped, and then you backed down." Colin was aware of his breathing becoming shallow, and his efforts to move his legs were fruitless. But he could still hear David's voice.

"Usually it takes a murder or two of a family member to keep you depraved executives on track. But you just gave up and did my bidding. I did not have to kill anyone. You never balked. Most of the others balk, and I have to kill someone to remind them who is in charge—sometimes they balk many times and I have to kill many. But not you. You coward. You weakling. If I respected you, I might let you live. But instead I am going to humiliate you and your family. You are going to be found in a most disgraceful state, I can assure you. You hypocrite Christians and Jews hate to have your perversions displayed to the world. You prefer to keep them hidden and pretend to be better than Muslims. Hah! I will paint a picture of you that would horrify you—if you were to live."

Colin could still hear him, but now he couldn't even move his lips to reply. He watched David walk around the desk, put his fingers on his wrist and feel his pulse. He nodded to the two guards. "It is time."

Colin felt himself being lifted off the chair, and carried down the hallway toward the back door. The last thing he heard before he passed out was a chant from back in the office, "Allah Akbar! Allah Akbar!" followed by a derisive cackle.

Chapter *19*

Monday morning was busier than usual at the office. Up first was a conference with the head office staff in the company auditorium, presenting the previous quarter's financial results. There was always a delay in being able to provide these to staff, as they couldn't hear the results until disclosure was first made to the public at large. With the worries and regulations regarding insider trading, executives of public companies had to be careful. So, it was usually old news by the time the staff finally heard from their CEO.

It was usually a tag-team approach. Mike, Troy and Jim would each speak and display power point presentations covering all aspects of the company's operations, giving updates from the previous quarter. Then the staff would ask questions. Microphones fixed to stands were situated throughout the auditorium to enable employees to easily express what was on their minds.

The most important question asked this morning was pertaining to Gerry's role and whether or not a decision had been made yet as to his replacement. Mike answered that one, and told the audience that he was not rushing into the decision. In the interim, he had appointed one of the VPs in Gerry's department, Ross Fielding, as acting department head. Ross would report directly to Mike until a final decision was made. In Mike's mind it just wasn't a priority, particularly since he was trying to keep hidden what Gerry had been involved in. He wanted to retain hands-on control himself over that department for the foreseeable future. In fact, considering the size of the company now, they were too lean in the top executive ranks to begin with. The entire structure needed to be reviewed. For now, he, Troy and Jim were overseeing the entire operation, with the help of VPs underneath of course. But they did indeed need several more Senior VPs. For now though Mike was having a trust problem, understandable after what he and Troy had discovered.

The conference had taken about three hours away from his morning, so Mike was glad to be back in his office frantically trying to deal with some time-sensitive issues. He had just ended a phone call with an irate vendor who had wanted Baxter Development to buy his large tract of land in Muskoka. Mike had declined due to the inflated price. He was replaying the phone conversation in his mind, when Jim Belton burst into his office with a newspaper in hand.

"Have you seen this?"

"No—haven't had the chance to read anything this morning yet."

Jim dropped the newspaper onto Mike's lap. "You'll be shocked."

Mike picked up the paper, and immediately saw the photo of a familiar face underneath the headline: **Apparent Suicide of Prominent Executive**

Mike caught his breath and began to read the article:

The Toronto business community is shocked to hear of the death of an influential and popular executive. The body of Colin Spence, Senior Vice President of The Ontario Life Insurance Company, was discovered last night in an apartment on Pembroke Street, in the Dundas/Jarvis area of Toronto. The police have refused to disclose any information regarding the death, pending completion of their investigation.

However, this reporter has determined from sources that Mr. Spence was discovered in the bathtub of an apartment, naked, his wrist slashed, a hunting knife lying beside him in the tub. There were signs in the room that he had had one or more visitors during the evening.

In addition, the apartment was littered with condoms and pornographic magazines. All of the magazines depicted gay men in graphic sexual scenarios. Most disturbing, however, was what was found on Mr. Spence's laptop—hundreds of photos of boys as young as possibly five years old, engaged in sexual acts with men.

Mr. Spence leaves behind a wife and two young sons. Discussions with colleagues at The Ontario Life Insurance Company revealed no pertinent details other than that Mr. Spence was touted as being the next CEO once the company's IPO was completed within the next six months.

Mike let out a whistle and looked up at Jim. "Christ, this is unbelievable!"

"I know. And to think that we just met with Colin a couple of months ago."

Mike remembered the meeting. He hadn't known Colin well; it was just a casual business relationship. But he had respected him and never would have guessed in a million years that he could have met his end like this. The suicide itself was shocking but what stuck in his mind was the image created by the magazines and kiddie porn photos. Sickening. Mike was also aware of the sordid reputation of the Dundas/Jarvis area— known as a street hooker stroll, populated with drug addicts and sleazy prostitutes of both genders. Mike had a difficult time picturing a guy like Colin in that section of the city.

He and Jim knew Colin from their dealings with him on their employee life/benefit plan. Ontario Life had held their account for at least a decade, and Colin was their key corporate contact over there. He gave Baxter Corp. his personal attention as the account was one of the largest Ontario Life had. They usually met once a year to review the plan for the next term. Mike also saw Colin occasionally at Chamber of Commerce meetings plus the usual corporate and charitable functions held throughout the city. Most of the more prominent executives in the city knew each other, at least casually. Toronto was a tight business community.

Mike looked over at Jim, who had now collapsed into one of the guest chairs. "Find out when the funeral is. You and I should attend. And send some flowers to the funeral home."

*****

St. Stephen's Cathedral on Church Street was crowded to overflowing. It was lucky for Mike and Jim that they had gotten there an hour before the service, otherwise they'd be standing out on the street for the duration. And Catholic funerals were not short.

As far as funerals went, it was a nice one. There were several eulogies at the end, and each speaker respectfully avoided any reference to how Colin had died. The focus of each speech was on good memories, humorous moments, and Colin's reputation as a protective husband and father. Mike thought to himself that there was a major disconnect. The reports in the newspapers had painted Colin as a twisted pervert and possible pedophile, yet what he was hearing at the funeral were depictions of a totally different person. A Jekyll and Hyde? He could see many people turning to each other and whispering during the service. He could only guess what they were saying; recounting what they had heard and read and probably snickering at that stark contrast with the eulogies. Human beings were predictably shallow and cruel whenever the mighty fell from grace.

Mike and Jim made their way through the crowd to the promenade outside the cathedral. They hoped to be able to pass along their respects to Karen. They knew her only slightly, from some business dinners that she had attended with Colin. However, they still wanted to let her know how highly they had thought of her husband, despite the reports that were circulating in the aftermath of his death.

Mike stood up on his tiptoes, straining to look at the people coming out of the church. He saw her standing over with a group of people outside the door, leaning against an older woman's shoulder. He tugged on Jim's sleeve and pointed. They gently pushed their way through the crowd and politely eased their way into the group of people surrounding Karen. Mike and Jim took turns holding her hand and saying their regrets. She smiled wearily. Mike wasn't sure whether she recognized them or not, but it didn't matter. She seemed to appreciate the attention and the gestures. Mike noticed two little boys standing off to the side with two other ladies. He figured they must be Colin's sons.

He was thinking about how they would extricate themselves from this little circle surrounding Karen without appearing rude, but the timing wasn't good. She had continued talking after greeting Mike and Jim, and the little group of people was transfixed. She talked about how Colin had changed in the last few years, more protective, more worried. He had installed an alarm system after she was attacked, and had wanted to hire a security guard at nighttime—which she had resisted. Instead, she always had a relative or friend sit with her in the evenings if Colin was out. This had seemed to reassure Colin.

She figured his obsession with precautions had to do with her attack, but lately she had begun to think it was something else. She suspected—from things that he had said, from his behavior, and the fact that he had purchased a gun and trained her how to use it—that there was some other danger he was worried about. An even more serious danger than the attack she had suffered.

Karen was sobbing as she talked. Through her tears, she talked about how impossible it was that Colin was the person portrayed in the media. Something was terribly wrong; that person found dead in the apartment was not even close to the Colin she knew, and who everyone else knew. Gay sex, little boys, suicide? She just didn't believe it. Mike figured that it was only natural that she would be in denial. The evidence was overwhelming—and what else could explain how they found him? A set-up? Why?

The two of them finally managed to move away from the group. Mike turned to Jim and asked, "What attack was Karen referring to?"

"Oh, I thought you knew. Must have been about three years ago now—she was raped and beaten in their home while Colin was out."

Mike whistled. "Geez, I had no idea. That poor woman. And now Colin's dead. Makes you wonder how people survive these back-to-back shocks. Did they catch the guy?"

Jim shook his head. "No, not a clue. No DNA left—he used a condom. Wore a mask. Bound and gagged the two little boys, and kept them in another room."

"God, I can't believe this. Colin sure hid his grief well."

"Well, he was always the consummate professional. Mike, this guy had everything going for him—had the world by the tail. Something went horribly wrong along the way, or he managed to hide one hell of a secret life."

They walked down to the bottom of the promenade, heading toward Jim's car parked on the street. Suddenly Mike heard his name being called. He turned around to face the church. A tall man, Middle Eastern looking, was working his way through the crowd toward them, waving his hand.

Jim shielded his eyes from the sun, and whispered. "Who the fuck is that?

"I haven't a clue." Mike lied—he did have a clue, a stirring in his gut that he didn't understand.

"Hello, Mike. Long time no see." The handsome Arab held out his hand. Mike shook it and nodded, apprehensive. "Do we know each other?"

"David Samson. You do not remember me?"

Suddenly a light went off in Mike's brain—something else was going on in his brain too, but he couldn't make any sense of it. Like a million little thoughts churning, none of them seemingly connected with each other.

"Yes, I think I do. You used to work for us, didn't you?"

David nodded. "I was in the legal department. I left your company about five years ago. Some new opportunities came along."

Jim tilted his head sideways, squinting. "You were fired, if I recall correctly."

David chuckled. "Just a little misunderstanding between Gerry and I, God rest his soul."

Mike was feeling lightheaded. "What are you doing here? Did you know Colin?"

"I have done some legal work for him in the past. A wonderful guy, despite the news reports."

Mike clenched his teeth. "Did you say 'legal work,' or did you really mean to say 'illegal work?'"

The Arab smiled at the jab. "Very funny, Michael. Not very polite, though."

"I wasn't trying to be funny, or polite." Mike took a step toward David. "Apparently we have some unfinished business with you. I understand that a criminal complaint was closed that should have stayed open."

David smiled again and rubbed his knuckles, probably to draw attention to the massive rings on his fingers. "Sometimes, what has been closed should stay closed. It is much more pleasant that way. Speaking of being pleasant, did you receive the sympathy card I sent to you after Gerry's death?"

"I might have. I don't remember." Mike lied.

"Oh, I am certain that you do remember. I even suggested that we have lunch sometime and reminisce about Gerry. I was disappointed that I never heard back from you."

Mike felt the blood rushing to his head. Why was this creep getting to him so much? For a split second, he saw images flashing across his mind: a parking lot and a football field, a gymnasium with a naked boy banging on the door, lockers, pushing, shoving, laughing, mocking, chasing someone down the hall of his old high school. He shook his head and the images disappeared.

But then just as suddenly a new image appeared—a rundown old house and a door that seemed to unlock itself. He was entering the house, but it felt like it wasn't him entering. He walked into an office and saw David Samson sitting at a desk, laughing at him.

Mike shook his head again and this image also disappeared. But what remained was an overwhelming feeling of anger and hatred—building to a rage like nothing he had ever experienced before. He could feel his fists clenching, and blood rushing to his face. Muscles tensing, coiling. Jim must have noticed something because Mike could feel him grabbing him by the arm and attempting to pull him away from the smiling devil standing in front of him.

But Mike could not be swayed now, too far into the zone. He yanked his arm free, and in the same move rammed his fist into the gut of David Samson. The man grunted and doubled over, a combination of pain and surprise written on his face. Mike took advantage of the moment and swung his right fist in an uppercut to the Arab's chin. The helpless man fell backwards to the cement, hitting his head with a thud. Mike straddled the prone figure and grabbed him by the collar, yanking his head up until their eyes met. He could faintly hear Jim in the background pleading with him to stop, feeling him pulling him back by his jacket tail. But Mike ignored him and easily shook him off. Instead, he burned a stare like laser beams into the evil black eyes of his victim.

"You're a fucking animal, Samson—a cold-blooded murderous son of a bitch. I swear, I'll kill you myself before allowing you to kill anyone else."

Chapter *20*

"What in God's name were you thinking? You acted like a madman!" Jim was pacing the floor in Mike's office and Mike was sitting on the couch with his feet up on the coffee table, rubbing his forehead.

"I don't know—I can't explain it. It's like something came over me. I'm just as puzzled as you are." Mike could tell that Jim was very tense, more than he was at the worst of times.

"Not good, Mikey. This day and age, as you well know from that subway incident, you can expect that somebody recorded that. And you're famous, or I should say infamous right now as the 'Briefcase Braveheart.' You'd be a financial bonanza for someone if they ran straight to the media."

He banged his fist on the credenza for emphasis. "We don't need the publicity, Mikey! You have to control yourself! What's gotten into you?"

Mike looked up at his friend. "Settle down, Jim. We need to talk about a lot of things—not just this. It's about time I brought you up to speed."

Jim stopped pacing, stood in front of Mike and put his hands on his hips. "Okay, what's the deal here? Is there stuff you've been holding back from us?"

"Troy's in the loop—you're not. Give Troy a ring and get him down here. We need to tell him about this latest thing anyway, and we'll both bring you in on the rest of the story."

*****

Two hours later the air had been cleared between the three friends. Troy and Mike told Jim about what they had discovered in Brazil and Mexico. Mike told them about the blackouts since the lightning bolt accident, and the other strange symptoms he'd been having. He confessed that due to the so-called kidnapping of his kids, Cindy had kicked him out of the house. He showed them the birthday card that his daughters had been given. He even told them about his mistaking Cindy for Amanda and his suspicions about absorbing some of Gerry's thoughts and skills from the lightning bolt. To wit, how had he suddenly become a skilled boxer? There was no logical explanation for that.

When he'd finished sharing his feelings with both of them, there were a few minutes of eerie silence in the room. Then Jim broke the spell.

"Whew. I wish I had known about all of this. Why didn't you guys tell me?"

Troy put his arm around Jim's shoulder. "Because we were afraid you would react exactly the way you are reacting now. I can see the stress all over your face, Jim."

"Sure, I'm stressed. I'm in one hell of a position of conflict here. I'm the Chief Financial Officer. We have impaired assets. The Balance Sheet needs some provisions, just as Christine suggested. You've lied to the Board."

Mike glared at him. "Fuck off, Jim. Don't go 'official' on me. Remember, I'm the CEO. My own responsibility is much larger than yours."

Jim lowered his head. "True, but I feel guilty now and I haven't even done anything…yet."

Mike grimaced. "I understand that, but we're just trying to buy time right now. What's done is done, and hopefully the foreign properties will just sell quickly and we'll be rid of this problem without anyone knowing. Remember, I've been set up here. It looks like I inflated assets and diverted funds. I need your support. And your silence."

Jim looked at Troy, who simply nodded in agreement. With a look of resignation, Jim replied, "Okay, I'll play it your way. You can count on me. But don't you guys leave me out of anything again. Sure, I'm not as cool as you two but I'm your friend and if I keep quiet about this like you're asking me to, it means we're all in this soup together. Agreed?"

"Agreed."

Jim continued. "We have some damage control now to think about. This incident at the funeral—we won't know for a day or two whether someone captured it on video. So, we shouldn't worry about that for now. I think, however, that our immediate concern has to be this David Samson character. What if he presses charges against you? We don't want you going to jail but even worse we don't want the company to have that kind of publicity. Think what that would do to stock prices."

Mike lowered his head and shook it from side to side. "I know, I know. It's a worry." Snapping his fingers, he looked up. "Why don't you contact Samson on my behalf and offer him some compensation to shut him up. We'll need a signed release of course, but he may be satisfied with some kind of payment—say, start at $25,000 and go as high as $50,000? And tell him we will agree not to re-open the criminal investigation of his embezzlement five years ago. You should have his phone number in your personnel file."

Troy spoke up. "I think that's a good idea. Let's try it. We have to be proactive to fend this off at the pass."

Jim nodded in agreement. "Yes, let's put one fire out at a time. Okay, I'll call him and see what he says. I can easily classify the expense under 'Legal Fees.' He's a lawyer after all, so we can hide it that way."

Mike got up from the couch. "I don't give a shit how you classify it. Those things are just mechanics. Make it happen."

Troy rose from his chair as well. "Tell me, Mike. What was going through your mind just before you beat this asshole up? You said there were images? It might be helpful if we understood what set you off like that. You'll remember that pretty much the same thing happened with you and that lawyer, Juan, in Rio. Maybe it's lawyers you have a hard-on for?" Troy chuckled.

Mike frowned, not appreciating the joke. "Well, suddenly I saw images of being back in high school—you know: school pranks, football, and places I used to hang around. It was all so familiar to me, but I have no idea why those visions popped into my head. Then in an instant it was like the movie reel changed, and I was seeing myself going through a door into a tenement house—but it didn't really feel like me at all. And this Samson character was sitting at a desk, laughing, mocking me. Don't ask. I haven't got a clue as to what that all means. But I remember feeling that he was a killer, feeling the danger, and I experienced this incredible rush of hatred for the guy."

Mike ran his fingers through his hair. "Then I just slugged him. And it felt right."

Jim rested both hands on Mike's shoulders, leaned forward and stared straight into his eyes. "Mikey, I heard you tell him that you were going to kill him to keep him from killing anyone else. What possessed you to say something like that?"

"Jim, that's the weird crux of everything that's been happening so far. What in God's name is possessing me?"

*****

After lunch the next day, Mike sat in his office contemplating the events since the accident in Florida. And he thought of David Samson and the man's reference to the sympathy card he had sent him. Mike yanked open the lower drawer to his credenza and pulled out the cards he had received and hadn't yet acknowledged. He felt a bit guilty looking at the pile, but quickly forgave himself. He had been busy, to say the least.

He flipped through the various cards until he came to the one that Samson had sent. He read it over again to refresh his memory. Suddenly, he felt a jolt in his gut. He jumped up and hurried over to a cabinet next to the door, unlocked it and took out the birthday card that was given to him on the day his girls were taken. He went back to his desk, laid the two cards side by side, and examined them. No doubt about it, the distinct handwriting in each card was identical!

*****

David Samson looked in the mirror and wasn't pleased by what he saw. His chin was still swollen and had colored to an ugly shade of purple. He admonished himself for being so unprepared for Mike's sudden outburst. He couldn't understand what had caused him to react like that. And he wasn't even aware that Mike knew how to fight. It brought back memories of what Juan down in Brazil had reported to him.

There was more than just anger going on—the man had a genuine ability to box. David didn't like being unprepared. He had vowed after his high school years that no one would ever pick on him again. In school he had been scrawny, nerdy—and worse than that, he had been a visible minority: the only Arab boy in a Toronto school of 3,000 students.

Those had been the worst years of his life. He had wanted so much to fit in, to be accepted, but due to the efforts of a few "leaders" he had been subjected to unbearable and unrelenting humiliation. There were a lot of other kids who had also been weak and nerdy, but most of them had been left alone. He knew that because he was dark-skinned, and probably because he was an Arab, he became the favored target. He dreaded going to school each day; had even contemplated suicide several times.

The jocks were the worst, one jock in particular. He had been captain of the football team, hockey team, and generally just the 'Big Man On Campus.' Everyone followed him, did his bidding, wanted to be his friend. No one wanted to be the victim of his bullying.

Back then David Samson had been Dawud Zamir. That foreign name made things even worse. Just going from class to class had become a fearful adventure. He would get yelled at, have his books knocked from his arms, pushed to the ground, spit on, called a faggot. There were usually girls around; the jocks usually picked the times when girls were watching. He could always hear their cruel giggles and cackles, and could still hear them ringing in his ears to this day. Vividly.

At the end of the day, Dawud would usually sit on the floor near his locker until all of the kids had left. Then he would begin the walk home. No way did he want to come out the front door of the school and end his day with another barrage of insults and mocking jokes that the school "leaders" would hurl at him.

He wanted peace, but could never enjoy it. He tried to keep a low profile, but they always found him. The worst humiliation came when he had been stripped in the locker room and tossed through the door of the gymnasium right in the middle of a basketball game. At least two hundred students were in the gallery watching the game, when his naked body flew through the door onto the court. The game instantly came to a stop. There was a collective gasp and then utter silence in the crowd. Well, almost silence— the one and only sound being Dawud's banging on the door begging to be let back into the locker room. The only other sound was a flurry of giggles coming from some girls in the gallery.

His banging on the door went unanswered. The gym door to the locker room had been locked from the inside and the perpetrators had fled. It took a full ten minutes for the coach of the basketball team to wind his way from the gallery through the school to the inside of the locker room to unlock the door and let him back in to the relative safety of the smelly room. They were ten of the most humiliating minutes of his young life— everyone staring at his naked torso, snickering, probably talking about what a loser he was. No one offered him a jacket or towel or anything else to cover up with. None of the teachers in the audience even approached him. It was like he had a disease.

Since high school, David vowed to never be a loser again. He embarked on a regimen of anabolic steroids and spent years obtaining his sixth degree black belt in Tae Kwon Do. No one would make fun of him again. He became committed to his Muslim heritage and, in a strange paradox, committed himself also to enjoy all of the sins of the western way of life. It was one form of revenge. He wanted their world too, but protecting his world had become an obsession. If he had to wear "sheep's clothing" to blend in, he was prepared to do that—plus at the same time enjoy the decadent pleasures that these infidels enjoyed. In some small way, he relished the irony of it.

He looked different now than he did in high school—heavily muscled, his face had filled out, he had a confident air about him. None of his old enemies would recognize him now. He knew he looked like a totally transformed person but deep down inside he was still Dawud Zamir. He was a proud Palestinian. He understood the endless persecution and second-class citizen status that his ancestors and countrymen had endured for generations—and still endured. He understood it so well. Their living conditions in Gaza and the West Bank were no better than what zoo animals enjoyed. The Israelis, supported by Jews and Christians around the world, would never allow the Palestinians to have their own state.

Israel pretending to want peace merely extended the slow genocide while the rest of the world watched and pretended right along with them.

David also understood hate now. A hate so deep and entrenched he knew that only his death would cause it to leave his spirit. Because of that hate, he had been an easy recruit for the Abu Nidal Organization. He wondered sometimes whether it would have been different if he had enjoyed a happier life as a youth; not ridiculed and humiliated so badly by his peers. Would he have been so easy to recruit?

No matter. When they had come for him from Beirut, he listened and signed in blood.

He wondered also—did Mike Baxter now understand hate as well? And why had he accused him of being a murderer? What did he know? How did he know?

And did Mike Baxter, 'Big Man On Campus,' ever think back—way back—and remember a skinny little naked Palestinian boy named Dawud, frantically banging on the gymnasium door?

Chapter 21

Mike could see Stephanie out of the corner of his eye, jerking her head up as he dashed past her desk. She was so startled she almost spilled her coffee. Stephanie yelled after him, "Is something wrong?" He almost answered, "You bet your ass!" but wisely decided against it. Instead, he just waved her off and continued his breakneck pace.

Skidding to a stop in front of Jim's office and bursting through the doorway, Mike shouted, "Don't phone him!"

Jim looked up, eyebrows raised in surprise at the sudden intrusion by his friend.

"Don't phone who?"

Mike leaned against the doorway, attempting to catch his breath. "Samson."

"Sorry, too late. We already talked about an hour ago. Surprisingly, he actually seems like a nice chap. He'll take $35,000 to keep his mouth shut. Why the panic?"

Mike slammed his fist against the doorframe. "Damn! I discovered something. Come down to my office right away and bring Troy with you."

*****

It couldn't become personal. The Nidal officials who David met with in Toronto had made that very clear. They said that if emotion got in the way, a terrorist couldn't function and would make mistakes. He knew they were right, but he also knew that his own personal experience with discrimination and bullying had scarred his soul. So he had a secret agenda in accepting their generous offer. He had decided right away that some of what he would use his newfound power for would definitely be personal. David figured that he could easily kill two birds with one stone. He would take care of their business while at the same time exact revenge on those who had ruined his teenage life, and who in his mind were typical of the infidels who the Nidal cells were attempting to terrorize anyway. It was just a slight sidetrack, buried in with all of the other activities— but it was indeed personal.

David had been recruited while he was a student in university. He chuckled to himself as he thought of all the newspaper articles that wrote of impressionable young Arabs being lured to jihad while they attended mosques. Typical western naivety. They liked to think of terrorists wearing robes and head garbs, praying and talking death in the same breath. That was the stereotype they painted in the minds of the world, however westerners were too ignorant to know that it would be an insult against the Qur'an to conduct conspiracies in holy places.

The recruiting was done in a sophisticated fashion. Nidal operatives approached bright young men and women who were identified after extensive research, and who were almost always propositioned on university campuses. In his case they offered to pay for his education but made it a requirement that he continue on to law school. Funds were also provided to buy his mother a house, and David himself was paid a substantial "signing bonus."

They wanted him educated and easily equipped to blend in with western society. After all, he was to become one of their "bankers," so he had to be respectable. David had no problem with that—he wanted all the riches and decadence he could get his hands on. Of course he didn't tell his recruiters that.

As a banker, he was told he would be the central figure in the Nidal terrorist network in Canada. His job would be to infiltrate businesses by coercion. He would raise money by capitalizing on the fear, greed, or lust of business executives. He would threaten, extort, and kill as deemed necessary to get that money. And he would have a large team of operatives right across Canada.

With the monies obtained he would be expected to plan and execute strategic attacks. Occasionally he would be told by his controllers who or what to attack, but mostly he would be left to his own designs. However, a specified percentage of all funds would have to be transferred by David each month to Beirut for the use of the "mother" organization. David saw this as comparable to the usual obligation of regional company operations in the business world. This was simply the terrorist version of capitalism.

David had made many trips over the years to Beirut, Lebanon as well as Tripoli, Libya. Sometimes for weeks at a time. He received extensive training in electronic hacking, firearms, sabotage tactics, assassination techniques, explosives, and biological weapons. He blended in as just one of many other recruits enlisted from around the world. David had met many wonderful comrades, people that he would be able to network with.

It was made clear to all recruits that at no time would the Abu Nidal Organization claim public credit for terrorist attacks. As far as the world was concerned, the Nidal group had been inactive for at least two decades. It was to remain that way. Claiming credit was just egotistical and silly, not to mention suicidal to the organization. Who the hell cared who was responsible? The key objectives were to terrify and to bring attention to the plight of Palestinians. Only fake organizations like Al-Qaeda claimed credit, and they usually did so for every Nidal attack. Nidal wanted to stay under the radar and do their work without scrutiny. Arabs around the world were well aware that Al-Qaeda was simply a creation of the CIA, and it served a useful purpose for the U.S.A. to have an "enemy" that would justify perpetual war, an excuse to attack innocent countries, steal their oil and their sovereign rights. One day the truth would come out, but in the meantime Al-Qaeda served a purpose for everyone. All attention was focused on a ghost instead of the real perpetrators.

Raising money was key. All former sources that had been available prior to 9/11 were now cut off, so funds could no longer be raised through charity front organizations. Whoever had knocked down the Twin Towers—and it certainly wasn't the ghost Al-Qaeda—had planned in advance for the movement of money to be strangled. This caught groups like Abu Nidal by surprise. Now as a result, money had to be stolen. David thought that the extortion of business executives was an excellent strategy; the Nidal people were brilliant to have thought that one up. And the irony was titillating.

Terrorist attacks were expensive. Operatives had to be paid, officials had to be bribed, and materials had to be imported or created from scratch. The black market supply of explosives, biologics and weapons was opportunistic—prices were outrageous. And shipping costs and the expertise in disguising those shipments? Very expensive. So David had to have many sources of income. The ten companies that he presently had his hooks into—correction, only nine now after the untimely death of Colin Spence—had to be squeezed and squeezed until the juice was drained or until it became obvious that they could be drained no more.

David chuckled at the irony of Baxter's CFO phoning to *offer* him money. How ridiculous was that, considering how much he had already stolen? Yes, Baxter Development Corporation had been one of his more lucrative corporate providers. And there was probably still more that he could take.

David would assess the risks and decide. But even if the well was now dry, the revenge was sweet. But it was not finished. Far from finished. This was where it got personal. His controllers in Beirut did not need to know that. As far as they were concerned, Baxter Development was just a profitable pigeon. To David it was much more than that.

He would look forward to his meeting with Mike Baxter, to see him grovel while handing David an envelope containing $35,000, begging David's forgiveness for his violent outburst. Hah! Begging him for mercy, as if any mercy had ever been offered to sixteen year old Dawud Zamir.

*****

"The handwriting does look the same. But, we're not experts. Perhaps we should get someone who specializes in this sort of thing to look at it." Troy was holding the two cards up to the light over Mike's desk.

"What do you think, Jim?" Mike glanced at his other friend, knowing that committing to decisions was not Jim's strong suit.

This time he didn't waffle. "We don't need a specialist. The same person wrote out both of those cards—no doubt about it."

Mike plunked himself down in one of his guest chairs. "Well, if the handwriting is the same, then I think we know what this means. This Samson dude arranged to have my girls taken from school. And the implicit threats in the birthday card were made to stop me from disclosing the Brazil and Mexico frauds to the Board. Which means that he was Gerry's accomplice in this entire scheme. He was the guy in the bandages."

Mike's buddies nodded solemnly. The truth was settling in.

Jim sat on the edge of the desk. "Mike, he intends to call you directly to set up a meeting, for some time next week. He wants you to bring the payment in cash, and he'll decide on the place to meet. He wants you to come alone."

Mike grasped his hands together and cracked his knuckles. "I have to decide how I'm going to handle this. Giving him more money, knowing the millions that he's already raked in from us on those phony land deals, makes me sick to my stomach."

Jim nodded. "Yes, and remember also that you accused him of being a murderer. Do you think there could have been some psychic truth in that episode you had? If so, you could be in danger."

"Well, who knows if there was anything to that? It could have just been another one of my brain farts. God knows I've had enough of them since the lightning bolt hit. Or it could have been an irrational temper-fueled outburst."

Mike shrugged. "I have nothing at all to go on, guys."

Troy walked over to the window and began talking slowly, with his back to his friends. "Why don't we get our tech boys to wire you up—see if you can trick or provoke him into admitting that he was Gerry's accomplice. Then we just go to the police with the tape and end this shit. Once he's off the street, his threats will be moot."

Mike scratched his chin and smiled. "I like that idea, Troy. Let's do it. Get your best people on this and tell them that we want to test out new technology to protect ourselves in disputed transactions—some bullshit like that. Maybe we can trap this prick after all."

*****

It was late in the day, and Mike was sitting at his desk gazing out the window at Lake Ontario. It shimmered in the setting sun, generating a magnetism that made him imagine being out there on a sailboat forgetting all of his troubles.

However, he did feel good about the day's developments. It was heartwarming to have his two old friends in on this mystery with him and watching his back. He no longer felt so alone. It was bad enough not having Cindy and the girls with him right now, but if he didn't have his friends he wasn't sure he could survive the stress.

And being wired up for his meeting with Samson was a great idea. It felt as if he was now taking over some control of a nightmarish film that was being directed by someone else. At least he was finally going to be *doing* something—and knowing now who Gerry's likely accomplice was could only be a step in the right direction.

His thoughts were interrupted by a knock against his open door. Standing there was his Vice President of Information Technology, Simon Hawthorne. "Come on in, Simon. I see you're burning the midnight oil too, eh?"

"Yeah, Mike. Just a few things I'm trying to keep on top of. Nice and quiet this time of the day. I like it."

"I'm with you on that. So, how can I help you?"

"Well, I've finally finished the detailed tracking to pin down the source of the hacking of your computer. Remember that e-mail that went out to the limo company instructing them to pick up your daughters? The one that went out from your computer?"

"How could I forget? What did you find out?"

"I wish I didn't have to be the one to tell you this, Mike, but the source that accessed your computer to send that e-mail was Jim Belton's computer."

Chapter 22

Mike jumped up from his desk. "Are you certain?"

"Yes. One of my senior analysts ran the trace, and I double-checked it. It's definitely Jim's IP address." Simon took a step toward him. "I'm sorry, Mike. I'm sure this comes as a big shock."

"That's an understatement." Mike walked to his credenza and poured a glass of water. He took a long sip then slammed the glass down. "Simon, I don't know a hell of a lot about computer technology but if it's possible for Jim's computer to hack into mine, isn't it also possible that his computer could have been hacked from another IP address and then used to access mine?"

Simon scratched the back of his head. "I suppose it is possible—yes, absolutely. I don't know if my guy checked that far. He may have stopped as soon as he found the apparent source."

Mike hitched his thumb towards his office door. "Go check that out—quickly. Make this your number one priority. I need to know for sure whether or not Jim's computer was really the villain here. I want an answer by tomorrow, Simon."

Simon sheepishly headed for the door, saying on his way out, "Okay, Mike. Be back to you tomorrow."

Mike went over to his couch and stretched out. A million things were running through his mind, not the least of which was the possibility that not one, but two, of his best friends may have betrayed him. But his instinct told him that was impossible—he couldn't believe it. Aside from just how well he knew his friend, he also knew that this just wasn't in Jim's character or personality. Jim was a decent-living guy, honest to a fault and as conservative as they come. Taking risks was just not in his nature. Most people drawn to the accounting field had that in common—they generally weren't risk-takers.

However, he wouldn't have predicted Gerry doing what he had done either, but at least Gerry was in the risk-taker category. He could at least see that Gerry would be capable of it, even though it was hard for Mike to believe that with Gerry's strong character that he would have been sucked into such a scheme.

Bottom line, was there anybody he really knew, or could really trust?

*****

David Samson pulled out his calendar and looked at the month ahead. He had a hectic schedule, but he would make sure to squeeze in time over the next few days to meet with Mike Baxter—for the money drop. David chuckled to himself. The stooge, the big tough guy, who was accustomed to winning all the time. Mike was in for a surprise.

Yes, David would phone him shortly, but first he had to go over plans for the event that was coming up in two weeks. The five men he had selected were already briefed, the timeline had been studied by all of them. Under his direction disguises were dress-rehearsed, the sites had been reconnoitered. David was happy. It was going to be a rewarding evening and the only regret he had was that he wouldn't be there to enjoy it in person. But he would read all about it in the news, and see it online of course. This time around that would have to suffice.

*****

"Jim, I want to ask you a question. Have you ever let someone else use your computer?"

Jim looked puzzled by the question. "No, of course not. Naturally, my secretary has proxy from her computer, but only to read my e-mails. Why are you asking this?"

Mike answered Jim's question with another of his own. "Have you ever given out your password to anyone?"

"Never. Mike, what's this all about? These questions are making me uneasy."

Mike shook his head. "I'll tell you once I know more."

They were sitting in Mike's office. It was the day after the shocking discovery that Mike's computer had been accessed by Jim's. Mike still couldn't believe that Jim had done this, but he wasn't going to allow himself to be naïve either.

Jim stood up. "Hey, what happened to our agreement that there would be no secrets? I demand to know what you're getting at with these questions—now!"

Suddenly Simon Hawthorne appeared in the doorway. "Mike, can I disturb you for a second?"

"Sure." Mike nodded his head in Jim's direction and Simon caught the cue.

"Jim can stay, Mike. He'll want to hear this too."

Mike motioned him in. Simon sat down in the guest chair beside Jim. "I've got good news and bad news."

"Give us the good news first."

"Jim's computer was indeed hacked from an outside party."

Jim opened his mouth in shock. Mike explained, "Simon's department discovered that my computer had been accessed by your computer to send that e-mail to the limo company ordering them to pick up my girls from school."

Jim gasped. " Oh my God, now I understand your questions."

Mike nodded, then turned his head toward Simon. "The bad news?"

"We can only trace the location of the IP address which did the hacking. The RIR, or Regional Internet Registry for the location, typically assigns IP addresses in blocks to their local Internet Service Providers, or ISPs. The RIR involved in the hacking of Jim's computer handles the Africa region—the internet name of the RIR is 'AfriNIC.' The location is as far as we can go. The IP address, or the owner's name, will not be disclosed by the RIR or the ISP without a subpoena. And there is a zero chance of getting a subpoena served or recognized in that area of the world."

Mike and Jim were speechless for a few seconds. Then Mike broke the silence. "Africa? What the fuck? Jim's computer was hacked from Africa?"

Simon just nodded solemnly. He wasn't used to hearing the CEO use the 'F' bomb.

Jim jumped in. "Africa's a big continent. Do you know whereabouts in Africa?"

"Yes, I do. Brace yourselves. The IP address is based in Tripoli, Libya."

*****

David Samson picked up his phone and dialed, finding it hard to wipe the smile of satisfaction off his face.

"Mike Baxter here."

"Good afternoon, Michael Baxter. This is David Samson. I am surprised an important man like you still answers his own phone."

"Skip the crap, Samson. When and where do you want to meet?"

"As usual, you are very impolite, no? Fine then. Have it your way. We will meet next Wednesday, 1:00 p.m. at the Metro*Cafe* on Queen Street West, corner of Spadina. You will buy me lunch and of course you will bring me my gift, no?"

He could hear Mike leafing through the pages of his calendar. "That works for me."

"Good. I will see you then. You know of course what I look like, but I do now have a swollen, purple chin. It might still be present next Wednesday, so you can enjoy the vision of your work."

David heard the click of the phone. He guessed that Michael Baxter was not too delighted with him right now. He chuckled to himself.

Okay, that step was done. And two weeks after that, there would be the other event that David could look forward to. He opened his desk drawer and took out the printout of his e-mail invitation. He had given his regrets as he usually did when he got these invitations—they came every five years and he had never attended one of these yet. What would be the point? No one would care if he was there, and probably wouldn't even remember him. He had been the faceless geek, a toy to play with, just a tool to make others look cool and tough.

He knew however who all would be attending. His skill at hacking enabled him to know virtually anything he wanted to know. Nothing could be hidden from him.

And his men were ready. David had already assigned them new names for that night—the names of men long dead, but who were still on the list of invitees. It was amazing how records were never updated properly. Made his job easy. He had decided on the number of men he would need based on how many dead men he discovered had been invited in error. This way they would have free access when they registered as they would already be on the guest list.

One man would be dressed as Al Capone, wearing a long coat and a sinister 'Big Al' mask. Another would be going as "the man with no name" from the famous western—again with a long coat. The other three men would be hauntingly real as 'Grim Reapers' with long capes and horrifying masks.

The timing for this year's event was wonderful as it was close to Halloween—the affair would be a costume party. The costumes of his men would be perfect for concealing their olive-brown skin—and their weapons.

Chapter 23

It was Wednesday morning. Mike, Jim and Troy were behind closed doors. Mike had his shirt off, while his friends examined the small microphone and transmitter, the wires of which were taped around Mike's chest. They had to make certain they were tight—any slackness would be visible under his shirt. The microphone and transmitter were fastened up where his shirt collar would be so that the thicker material of the collar would conceal the subtle bulge. Everything had been applied expertly by Simon Hawthorne's senior tech staff, who were under the impression this was simply an experiment to test the covertness and effectiveness of the device for future business transactions.

The tech girls also gave Troy and Jim their marching orders—they weren't getting off scot-free in this exercise. Due to the limited range of the transmitter, the two of them would have to be parked in a car no further than one hundred meters from the café, with the receiver up on the dashboard. Mike was advised to try to get a table on the outdoor patio of the café. The weather was still warm even though it was mid-October, so the patio would be open. Outdoor reception would be far better for this device at that distance.

Mike started buttoning his shirt. Troy cracked, "I saw Melissa eyeing those sissy little nipples of yours. I think she wanted to tweak them—God knows why." Troy and Jim both laughed.

"Not funny guys. Just be glad she didn't have to look at your big gut, Troy, or your ugly little outtie belly button, Jim."

"Hey, no need to be nasty, now. You're about to pull off a 007 and you need us to watch your back."

"You're right—just shows you how low I'm stooping, to be relying on Frick and Frack to protect me!"

The three friends laughed—it had been quite a while since they had trash-talked each other, and it felt good. Only real friends could get away with that.

Mike sat down and looked at his watch—12:00 noon. "We should head out in a few minutes. Traffic on Queen West at lunchtime can be a bitch. We don't want to keep our friend waiting."

"No, he might get spooked." Jim picked up the briefcase containing the $35,000 in cash. "Don't forget to take this. And Mike, for God's sake please don't lose your temper. We need to get this asshole on tape admitting that he and Gerry embezzled us."

Troy smacked a fist into his palm. "We're going to outsmart this prick. We end this nonsense today. This is going to feel good."

"Damn right, Troy. I'm looking forward to getting this over with once and for all." Mike got up from his chair and put on his jacket.

Jim jangled his car keys. "We'll take my car, Troy. Mike, you take your own. We obviously can't be seen together—just in case this guy is watching when we get there."

"Right. I'm a novice at this espionage game!"

Troy held out his hand in a stop sign. "Before we go, I'm curious—what are your thoughts about that Libya connection, Mike?"

Mike grimaced in reaction to the question. "I don't know what to say about that. It's weird. Why would Libya be involved in something like this? It's a real puzzle to me, and kind of makes me worry that there's something bigger involved here. Libya's been a hotbed for terrorism going back decades, but it seems to have cooled off since the U.S. brokered an agreement with them to destroy their nuclear arms projects. They seem to have an almost friendly relationship with America now; probably due to the billions of dollars the U.S. paid them to be good ole boys. But a 'tiger doesn't change its stripes' that easily. I don't feel good about the Libya connection at all. I hope we're not getting in over our heads here."

Troy frowned. "You're not getting one of your visions are you? Is this you talking, or Gerry?"

Mike laughed, shaking his head. "No—no visions. This is me talking. By the way, I don't just get those feelings at will, Troy. They just appear at random and I can't predict when they're coming." Mike poked his finger into Troy's chest. "And buddy, quit making me feel like a freak."

"Sorry, I'm not trying to be a smartass. I just get a little concerned when you express fears. You're usually the fearless one."

Jim jumped in to break the tension. "Nah, we're dealing with simple embezzlement here—large dollars, but still just embezzlement. The way I understand it from what Simon told me yesterday, geeks can route their hacking throughout the world via numerous IP addresses. This makes it almost impossible to track down the original source sometimes. So there may be no significance at all with the Libyan IP." Jim patted Mike on the back. "We're going to be fine—and this is going to be kinda fun. Just like hazing way back in our university days!"

Mike smiled and squeezed the shoulders of his two friends. "You're right. Let's roll."

*****

Fazal and Hamat walked confidently along Queen St. West, dressed in their Toronto Police Service uniforms. They were walking the beat, passing by the Metro*Cafe*. They nodded at the Middle Eastern man sitting at a table on the patio with his Caucasian lunch partner. They continued on to the end of the block and turned right. They had already walked the other beat at the opposite end of the block and everything was in order there. This would be their last checkpoint.

Then they saw it—a black BMW with two men sitting in the front seat. They appeared to match the photos. Fazal and Hamat exchanged knowing glances and, without a word, crossed the street and headed straight toward the shiny black Bimmer.

*****

Troy and Jim sat in Jim's car, parked a block away from the Metro*Cafe*. The receiver was sitting on the dashboard and working like a charm. The conversation between their boss and Samson was coming through loud and clear.

Troy was giving the thumbs up sign. "It's going well so far. Samson seems anxious to talk. This might be a breeze."

Jim nodded. "Yeah, we may not have to hang around here too long. If Mikey can just control himself this may be over soon."

Troy suddenly nudged Jim in the arm and pointed. "Shit, we have cops coming our way. Grab that receiver and stick it on the floor!"

Jim pulled the machine off the dash and put it on the floor beneath his feet. He hoped the cops hadn't seen him do it. He watched as they strode purposefully toward his car, two dark-skinned uniformed officers. Affirmative Action at work, he thought wryly.

Troy and Jim tried to look nonchalant as the officers approached. They were definitely coming to their car and looked as if they were on a mission. One came over to the driver's side window and the other to the passenger side.

*****

In their most official fashion, Fazal and Hamat rapped their knuckles on the windows just as they'd seen done in American movies at least a hundred times.

The stooges inside immediately cooperated, and hit the power window buttons.

The skinny guy in the driver's seat asked, "What's the problem, officer?"

Fazal smiled. Then he lifted his right hand and fired a small pistol at the man's neck. The big guy in the other seat yelled in protest for half a second until he was cut off with a shot from Hamat's gun. Both men slumped forward instantly. The assailants pulled them back against their seats, and pushed the power seat buttons to lower them into prone positions. Fazal opened the driver's door and lifted the receiver off the floor, sticking it under his arm.

Before leaving, they pulled the darts out of the necks of the two men and closed their eyelids. Fazal left a note in the lap of the driver. Then the power windows were rolled up again, and the doors locked.

Fazal and Hamat looked back as they walked away. The two stooges looked just like a couple of fags having a peaceful autumn nap together, which was of course exactly what they were doing.

*****

Mike sipped his coffee and looked into the black eyes of the embezzler sitting across from him. Samson was smiling as he picked away at his salmon salad.

"Are you certain that you do not want something to eat, Michael? As I said, I changed my mind and decided to treat today, so choose anything you want."

Mike sucked up the willpower to be polite. "No. Thanks for your kind offer, but I'll just stick with coffee."

David shook his head and reached into his pocket, pulled out a twenty-dollar bill and stuffed it under the salt shaker. "Okay, suit yourself. The food is very good, though."

Mike reached down at his side and pulled the briefcase up onto his lap. He opened it a crack and showed David the bills inside. "Let's get this over with. This is yours. We have an agreement, I believe?"

David's face showed no reaction. "And what is that agreement we have, Michael, and how much money is in that case?"

Mike started seething inside. "Christ, are you stupid? The agreement is that you will not press charges against me for the unfortunate incident in front of the church. And the case contains $35,000 per your agreement with Jim Belton."

"Oh, so this is a bribe, no?"

"Let's just call it a business deal. To promote harmony between us." The word 'harmony' dripped from Mike's mouth with undeniable sarcasm. He emphasized the word further by cracking his knuckles in frustration.

"Are you truly sorry? I have not heard you say that yet?"

With great willpower Mike stopped himself from diving across the table and punching the man again. "I'm not going to apologize to you. I still think you're a crook. You deserve more than that beating. I'm well aware of the stunt you pulled with my daughters. The handwriting on the birthday card matches the condolence card you sent me. You kidnapped my girls you piece of shit! Why did you do that?" Mike moved his hand up to his collar and felt ever so casually to satisfy himself that the microphone was still in its place.

"That is a strong accusation, Michael. Are you a handwriting expert now in addition to all of the other talents you think you possess?"

Mike leaned forward and smacked both palms down on David's side of the table. "Quit the bullshit, Samson! You've done more than just kidnap my girls. You also embezzled my company in cahoots with Gerry Upton. Admit it!"

Mike did a quick check to make sure they were still the only people sitting on the patio. He realized with some alarm that he was losing his temper again. He tried harder to focus on Jim's warnings—stay cool.

"Are you not full of crazy accusations today?" David smiled at him in that evil way that made Mike's skin crawl. "And when you beat me up in front of the church, you called me a murderer. What caused you to say such a thing?"

"That was just a burst of anger. I had no idea what I was saying." Mike looked away from the table and noticed two police officers walk by; one was carrying a black box. He felt like calling out to them and asking them to arrest this man right now. But for what, and what real proof did he have of anything? Samson seemed to be too smart to say something that would be useful in the recording. It was like he knew. Or, was Mike wrong? Was it possible that Samson was not Gerry's accomplice after all?

"So I will ask you again—before you hand over the money, are you going to apologize for hitting me?"

"No, I'm not. Just take the money, shut up, and stay the fuck away from me."

David smiled, and patted himself on his left shirt pocket. "Feel my chest, Michael."

Mike sat up straight in his chair, and sneered, "What are you, queer now? I'm not going to touch you!"

Suddenly, before Mike could react, David's left hand shot out and grabbed his right hand in an iron grip. At almost the same instant, Mike realized that his left wrist was immobilized by David's right hand. David was squeezing the wrist with his thumb, ever so slowly, ever so painfully.

David yanked the right hand back toward him and onto his chest. Mike tried to pull his hand back, but it wouldn't budge. The pressure on the hand was extreme. This man was strong. And his left hand was starting to throb as the blood flow was being cut off by the man's superhuman thumb.

"Now, Michael. Concentrate on what your right hand is feeling. What do you feel?"

Mike decided there was nothing he could do but answer. "A...pulse of some... kind," he said through gritting teeth.

"Very good, Michael. A vibration, no? That is a little detection device I have in my shirt pocket—very tiny, just like the device you're wearing, no? It tells me by vibration if I am near any type of radio transmitter. Clever, yes?"

Mike gulped. What was going to happen now?

"You should know that I too have a recording device, just a simple one in my jacket pocket—not as highly technical as yours. But it works. I now have a recording of you trying to bribe me to not press charges—which of course is 'obstruction of justice.' Remember, smart man, I am a lawyer."

David then forced Mike's hand down onto the table and gripped it on the wrist in the same way as he had his left hand. Then he applied pressure with his thumbs on both wrists. Mike was afraid he was going to have to scream out, the pain was so bad.

"Where is your boxing ability now, Michael? It is considerably different when you are not the one taking the cheap shots, no?"

Mike could feel tears starting to well up in his eyes. The pain was bad, but his worst fear was letting this maniac see him cry.

"I will release the pressure if I hear you apologize to me. Apologize now, or I will squeeze even harder. I am skilled at putting my thumbs through wooden boards or wrists—both are of equal ease to me."

Mike believed him. "I'm...sorry...David."

The pressure was released almost immediately. Mike breathed easier. Then

David let his hands free. Mike pulled them back on to his lap and rubbed his wrists. He could feel the comforting warmth of blood flowing back into his hands.

"Do you know what you are apologizing for, Michael?"

"Hitting you."

"You are too arrogant and superior in your elitist mind to realize that you have a lot more in your life to apologize for than just that. But, no matter, we will leave here now. Bend over please and look under the table."

Mike did as he was told. To his shock, he saw a gun with a silencer pointed at his crotch. He looked up. "What's that for? There's no need for this! Take your money and go!"

"I have no intention of taking that money. Get up from the table and walk down the street to your right, then turn right at the next street. And remember, this gun will be pointed right at your back. Take your fancy alligator leather briefcase with you."

Mike's legs felt like rubber as he made his way down the street, hearing the footsteps of Samson directly behind him. They turned right at the corner and he immediately saw Jim's black BMW parked across the street. He felt a rush of hope—his friends would see right away that he was in trouble, and they would have also heard the conversation over the receiver.

Samson instructed him to cross the street, right at the point where the BMW was. Mike thought—this was perfect. But then in the next thought he realized that neither of his friends was armed. He hoped now that they would just stay in the car and remain safe. There was nothing they could do to help him now.

As he got closer he noticed that something was wrong. Troy and Jim were reclined in their seats and appeared to be asleep—or dead.

"Look at your two incompetent friends. Sleeping on the job. It is so comforting to have friends who are concerned about you, no?"

They passed by the car and Mike could see that neither of them was moving. And based on what Samson had just said, he had known all along that they were there. He prayed to God that they were alive, and admonished the amateurish plan they had devised. What had they been thinking? They were in way over their heads with this guy. They had underestimated him by a country mile.

"Turn here." It was an alley with a barricade in front to block off traffic.

Mike did as he was told, and his stomach did a flip as he noticed two police officers standing just inside the barricade. They looked like the same officers who had walked past the Metro*Cafe* a few minutes ago. His hopes rose. David didn't seem to be the least bit concerned as Mike stared at the officers with his most convincing look of fear. He didn't have to act, he was indeed afraid. They looked back at him, expressionless. Mike then dove to the ground in front of the officers and yelled out, "He has a gun!"

To Mike's horror, both officers just laughed. Samson joined them. He then motioned with his gun for him to get up and keep walking. Mike thought, and hoped, that he was in a bad dream and would awaken at any second.

He got to his feet and continued walking until David told him to stop. He looked around. The alley was completely shrouded in tall trees on both sides. Through the trees he could see fences on both sides of the alley, separating it from the backyards of houses. They were stopped about halfway down the alley. There was nothing else there except for a metal dumpster up close to the trees. He could see the police officers at the end of the alley looking towards the street as if they were standing sentry. Mike was horrified—the police were within shouting distance. They had seen that he was in trouble, and had simply laughed at him.

"Take your clothes off."

"What?"

David yelled now. "Take your fucking clothes off!"

"No, I will not do that, you pervert!"

David took one step towards him and lashed out with a lightning kick to his groin. Down Mike went, grabbing at his crotch and screaming in pain. He looked up at Samson who now had the gun pointed at his head. "Take your clothes off now or you will have a hole in your head to match your ass."

Mike struggled to his feet and did as he was ordered. Slowly taking off each piece of clothing when what he really wanted to do was just wretch. His balls and groin area were throbbing as he lifted his legs up to remove his pants and underwear.

Now naked with the exception of wires and a device taped to his chest, and shivering more from fear than the temperature, he pleadingly looked one more time toward the two police officers at the end of the alley. One of them waved to him and laughed again.

Mike turned his head back toward Samson just in time to see a blur of movement, the spinning of a human figure in midair, and felt the impact of a powerful blow to his temple. He crumpled to the ground.

Mike slowly turned his head sideways and through his fading eyesight gazed helplessly down the length of his publicly naked body. For just an instant he experienced two unfamiliar and equally horrifying sensations: vulnerability and submissiveness.

His weary eyes glanced up and he saw the blurry figure of David Samson walking away from him, back in the direction of the police officers. Then Mike just closed his eyes, thinking that the blackness was more comforting than the light of day.

Chapter 24

Troy opened his eyes, yawned, and stretched his arms out, promptly hitting the lid of the glove compartment. It took him a couple of seconds to realize that he was lying in a recline position in a car. He looked to his left and saw Jim in the same state. Troy flicked the power button and raised himself into a seating position, trying to recall what he was doing here. Then it hit him—Mike!

He shook Jim hard until his eyes opened. Jim jerked upright and looked over at Troy, mumbling, "What the fuck?"

"Yes, 'what the fuck' exactly. How did we both fall asleep?" Then Troy's eyes widened as his memory started returning. "The cops! I saw one of them shoot you!"

Jim opened his door and stumbled out. A little unsteady, he began walking back and forth on the road, rubbing the left side of his neck. Troy got out on his side of the car and began stretching his rubbery legs.

Leaning over the hood of the car and shaking the cobwebs from his head, Jim finally started recalling. "It's coming back to me now. There were two of them. I rolled down the window and asked him what was wrong, and...I remember seeing a pistol." Jim scratched at his neck again. "Jesus, there's a welt coming up. I think this is where the bastard shot me!"

Troy walked over to Jim and examined his neck. "Yep, it's a welt alright—but luckily no bullet hole." He reached up and felt the right side of his own neck. "I've got one too. Look."

Jim nodded. "They must have tranquilized us." He opened the car door again and looked inside. "Shit! They took the receiver!"

Suddenly Troy took off, ran to the end of the block and looked down Queen Street towards the Metro*Cafe*, then rushed back to the car out of breath. "Mike's...gone! They're not...on the...patio!"

"We had better just get back to the office. Hopefully he's already there, waiting for us." Jim pulled out his car keys and slid in behind the wheel. Troy ran around to the other side and jumped in. Then he noticed something on the floor.

"Jim, what's that?" He pointed down at a piece of paper on the floor beneath Jim's feet.

Jim leaned down and picked it up, brushing off the dirt that his shoes had left. "It's a note." He read it aloud:

"Gentlemen. I hope you have enjoyed your nice nap. So sad that you had to miss all the excitement, but I do prefer to work without bystanders and eavesdroppers. Your boss will probably now need your assistance. You will find him down in the alley just off the street where you have been catching some shut-eye."

Jim and Troy glanced up at each other for just a second, then bolted from the car at the same time and ran toward the alley just to the rear of the car. They ran around the barricade and skidded to a stop. About fifty yards down the alley a naked body could be seen lying on the ground near a dumpster.

Troy grabbed Jim's arm and pulled. "Let's go! That must be Mike!"

They ran down the alley looking from side to side as they went, wondering if anyone was lurking, waiting for them to come to Mike's rescue. Troy got there first, and immediately knelt down beside his friend. Jim joined him and together they lifted Mike's body and moved him over to the side of the alley, stuffing Troy's jacket underneath him. Jim rolled his own jacket up and used it as a pillow for Mike's head. They noticed a large bruise on his left temple, but otherwise he looked unharmed. No blood, pulse was strong, he was breathing fine.

Gently, Troy started slapping Mike's face. "Mike! Mike! Wake up, you're okay!"

After a few seconds he started to come around. His eyelids opened and he made eye contact with his two friends, glancing from one to the other. He looked puzzled. With a loud grunt, he slowly pushed himself up into a sitting position. Then he noticed he was naked. "Shit, give me some clothes!" Troy could see the embarrassment written all over Mike's face—an expression he couldn't ever remember seeing before.

Jim picked up his jacket that had been serving as a makeshift pillow, and draped it over Mike's front. "It's okay, Mike. It's just us. Are you okay? Where does it hurt?"

Mike put his hand up to his temple. "I'm fine—my head hurts where the prick kicked me, and my wrists are aching. I remember him doing some mumbo jumbo thing with his thumbs on them—God, did that hurt." Troy could tell that Mike was alert now, and aside from his embarrassment about being naked, no worse for the wear.

Mike struggled to his feet, and tied Jim's jacket around his waist. Troy picked up his own suit jacket and put it around Mike's shoulders. He could see Mike instantly relax now that he was pretty much covered up. Then he started looking around. "Where the fuck are my clothes? He must have taken them!"

Suddenly they all heard a feeble little voice. "They's over the fence." The three of them whirled around in all directions, trying to figure out where the voice was coming from. Troy yelled out, "Say again?"

"They's over the fence there." It was a child's voice, coming from the direction of the dumpster. Troy could see a rusted hole in the side of the old metal structure, with two eyes peeking out. He ran over and lifted the lid. There he was—a young boy about eight years old, crouched inside with toy guns and cars surrounding him.

"Hi there. Do you want some help getting out?"

"No, I's okay here." The filthy little boy cowered in the corner of the dumpster. "This my fort. Kees me safe."

Troy could tell that this dumpster hadn't been used for what it was intended in a long time. There was no garbage inside, and none of the usual sickening odors. Each corner of the container had different toys set up. It was clearly this boy's little makeshift playhouse.

"Do you live around here, son?"

The boy nodded. "Jus down street there."

"And did you see what happened here today?"

He nodded again. "Mean man, flew through th'air and hit that man with no cloz. Then threw cloz and case over this fence behind here. I's scared. Dint move."

Troy was joined by Jim and Mike who were also now peering into the dumpster, clearly perplexed at seeing the paradox of a little boy in such a decrepit bin with all his shiny toys. His clothes were tattered and his shoes were missing half of their soles. Strangely, his toys looked brand new and Troy suspected that the kid stole them from backyards and kept them in this dumpster so his mother wouldn't know.

Mike turned to Jim. "Could you check that yard for my clothes? I'm in no condition to be vaulting fences."

Jim nodded and took a run at the fence and pulled himself up to the top edge. "Yep, they're in here." He yanked himself up and over. The first thing he threw back was the briefcase, followed by a bundle of clothes and a pair of shoes.

Suddenly a woman was screaming, and they could hear the sound of footsteps thrashing through the bushes. "Get out, you pervert! Get out of my yard! I'll call the cops!" There was the thud of something metallic banging against something not so metallic. Then Jim's panicked voice: "Shit, take it easy, lady! I'm leaving, I'm leaving!"

Jim came flying over the top of the fence, crashing to the ground onto his back. He slowly got to his feet while holding one hand to the side of his face—blood was dripping from his jaw. "Let's get the fuck out of here—this is nuts!" He rubbed his back with his other hand. "There's a maniac in that yard. She hit me with a shovel!"

Troy couldn't help but chuckle at the image, but he made sure he turned away so that Jim wouldn't see the insensitive grin on his face.

Mike heeded Jim's warning and quickly donned his dirty clothes. Then he stopped and took a look inside the briefcase. "Look, guys—he didn't take any of it. That money apparently wasn't even on his agenda."

"No, he was several steps ahead of us on this. We were set up. Troy and I were drug-darted by two fake police officers—plus, they took our receiver. Looks like this lunch meeting was intended to be an altercation, with the bribe as the cover story. He sure came prepared and seemed to know exactly what we were planning to do."

Troy motioned to his friends. "Let's move our butts before that woman really does call the cops—and this time the *real* ones will come." They started walking back down the alley towards Jim's car.

*****

A weird feeling came over Mike, and he stopped. He felt he just couldn't run off like this, not after what he had seen in the dumpster. "Wait for me a second!" He ran back to the dumpster, and opened the lid.

"Hi again, little friend." Mike was favored with a shy but friendly smile from the tiny face looking up from the depths of the bin. "Tell you what, if I give you some money, will you take it to your mummy and ask her to buy you some new clothes?"

The boy gave Mike a big toothless grin. "Yes, Mister—thas real nice o you."

"Okay, here you go." Mike snapped open the case and took out two five-hundred dollar bills. He reached down and stuffed the bills into the boy's pocket. "That's a lot of money, son. You go home right now and give it to your mom, okay?" The boy nodded. Mike reached down into the dumpster and lifted him out. He felt so light.

"What's your name?"

"Do want nickname…or real one?" The boy clearly had trouble putting his words together, but he tried hard. His pronunciation at his age should be much better though, which made Mike wonder.

"Your real name."

"Is Jonas, Mister."

"Would you prefer me to call you by your nickname?"

"Oh, no. I don like it. Mos of the kis call me that and I wish they stop."

Mike braced himself. "What do they call you?"

Jonas looked down at the ground. "Cuntface. I don even know what that means, but it duznt soun nice."

Mike felt a sinking in his stomach as he looked down at the sad little face. "Jonas is a nice name, and I'm going to call you that. Don't worry about other names kids call you; you know what your real name is."

Jonas looked up and flashed one of his charming grins. Mike could tell that he was a cute little guy underneath all the grime. His hair looked like it could be blonde if it was clean, and his eyes were a beautiful shade of blue. Sadly, he could also see several bruises on his arms and legs. "Who made those bruises, Jonas?"

"Jus some kis who make fun—they jus kiddin."

"Is that why you hide in the dumpster?"

"I's safe in there. When they see me, they chase. I keep this place secret."

Mike frowned. "What happens if they catch you?"

"They each jus hit me and laugh—duznt hurt anymore. I use to it now. But my mom won let me go school anymore." Jonas politely held out his tiny hand, inviting Mike to shake it. Mike obliged, with tears in his eyes. "I's sorry I coont help you, Mister. I's scared when I saw that man spinnin. I dint want him to know I's watchin."

Mike ruffled Jonas' curly hair. "That's okay, son. You did the right thing. He was a bad man and he might have hurt you just like he hurt me. By the way, call me Mike, okay?"

"Okay, Mike." Having been forgiven, Jonas gave a final smile and ran down the alley, no doubt excited to show his mummy their newfound wealth.

Mike called after him. "Hey Jonas! Which house do you live in?"

He pointed over the fence at a red clapboard bungalow.

*****

The three amigos made it back to their Harbor Square office complex in record time. Their clothes were dirty and rumpled, and Mike and Jim looked considerably banged up—so they decided to take the service elevator up to the fortieth floor to avoid the enquiring eyes of the usually full passenger elevators.

Once they reached their floor, Mike ordered, "Get changed, cleaned up, and come to my office in twenty minutes." They each had private washrooms along with a change of clothes that they always kept on hand—never imagining that it would be for something like this.

Mike managed to sneak by Stephanie with a quick "hello", covering his forehead with his hand

She called after him, "Coffee, Mike?"

"Sure, bring three cups—black today."

He closed his door and went into the bathroom. He took a good look at his forehead in the mirror. A bruise had formed already, and his temple was swollen down over his eyebrow. Geez, Samson had kicked him hard. And what a kick—he remembered the blur of him spinning in the air, just as Jonas had witnessed. The man was skilled, no doubt about it.

He got changed, washed his face and hands and went back into his office. His friends were already there, as were the three mugs of steaming coffee. Mike took a long sip and sighed with relief. He looked at his buddies. "God, I'm glad to be back. Never thought I would ever be so relieved to see my own office."

He stretched out on the couch; Troy and Jim were sitting across from him in the easy chairs.

Jim spoke first. "I think we need to call the police about this. I've been thinking and I don't know how we can keep this quiet. This is serious business now."

Mike nodded. "Yes, it is serious. This man is more than we ever imagined. He clearly knows martial arts, with the things he did to me. And he has a team behind him, probably more than just those fake police you guys encountered...by the way, I saw them too. I asked them for help and they just laughed at me. They were guarding that alley so no one would come down and interfere with what Samson was doing to me." Mike took another long sip of his coffee. "Samson had a bug detector in his shirt pocket—he knew I was transmitting. Pretty sophisticated stuff—police uniforms, transmission detection, tranquilizer darts, karate."

Troy interrupted. "What did you two talk about?"

"He pretended not to know what the payoff was for—he didn't want to talk about it. He just wanted me to apologize, and intimated that I had more to apologize for than just the beating at the church. He wasn't satisfied when I did apologize. He wanted more." Mike shook his head. "I got the feeling he wanted to just intimidate me, humiliate me, which of course he did. Why, I don't know." Mike leaned forward over the coffee table. "He didn't even flinch when I tried to trap him into saying he was Gerry's accomplice. Calm as a cucumber."

Jim stood up and started walking the room as he usually did when he was stressed. "Mike, this is getting dangerous. As I said before, I think you need to report this."

Mike stood up too, and rested his hands on his hips. "And what would I say? It would open up a Pandora's Box. The company would be dragged into this. My apparent complicity in the fraudulent property purchases. My deception to the Board. We can't prove anything; Samson's hands are clean. It's my word against his—and all the evidence points to me. But my biggest fear, especially now knowing that he has other people working for him, is the safety of my family. He's already proven that he can reach my children. He wanted me to know that. He could do it again. And if somehow we managed to get the police to pick him up and actually hold him—which is unlikely—what would stop his thugs from continuing to carry out his orders? He wants to hurt me for some reason. It's like a vendetta. I wasn't even the one who fired him—it was Gerry. And Gerry's the one he's been working with the last few years."

Troy rose from his chair and headed toward the door. He motioned for Jim to follow. "This is too emotional a time for us to discuss this. We've been through a hair- raising experience today. Let's talk again later when we're more rational. Right now, we have jobs to do and those jobs have been suffering with all this covert nonsense. Okay?"

Mike nodded. As his two best friends left his office, he plunked down on the couch again. He didn't know what to do. He'd never felt this powerless before in all his years as an executive. He was usually decisive, and never had hesitations about the right actions to take. But this time was different.

This time he didn't feel so confident. He had tried to put on a good face for his friends, but the truth was he felt humiliated and...well, subservient, useless. He felt naked in both the literal and symbolic sense. It was not a good feeling. He felt stripped of his façade, his shell, his image. If this is what Samson had been trying to accomplish, he succeeded today.

Mike got up and walked over to his bar. He poured himself a stiff scotch and took a slow sip. The strong liquid felt good as it slid down his throat. He sat on the edge of his desk and looked out at Lake Ontario. Then he turned his gaze to the portrait of Cindy and the girls on his credenza. They looked so healthy, so happy. So unlike Jonas.

He pictured the little guy, crouched in the corner of his dumpster, his fort, helpless and scared. Wondering if one or more of the bullies would find him, chase him, punch him, call him 'Cuntface.'

Jonas had said that it didn't hurt anymore, that he was used to it now. Mike wondered how many times something so disturbing had to happen before it 'didn't hurt anymore.' He shuddered. It had apparently gotten so bad for Jonas that his mother wouldn't let him attend school.

Jonas had said those things so matter-of-factly. That was his pathetic little life and he had grown to accept it. And he couldn't be more than eight years old! What kind of person would Jonas be at sixteen, twenty-five, forty? It was bound to have a long-term negative effect on him.

Mike wiped a tear from his eye, and took another sip—a longer one this time.

Chapter 25

Mike was driving north on University Avenue, winding his way through rush hour traffic. Tonight was one of his nights at home—his real home—with Cindy, Diana and Kristy. Things had been going well whenever they got together, and Mike was hoping that one of these nights Cindy would invite him home permanently. For the first time since he left, he finally had some things to share with her that might help her see the world more in his favor.

It had been a few days now since the terrible incident in the alley, and the swelling on his forehead had come down considerably. Should Cindy notice it, he would explain it away as just a fall caused by one of his little blackouts. He wasn't certain she'd buy it, but he sure wasn't going to worry her by telling the truth. Sometimes 'the truth' was overrated anyway.

He pulled into his driveway, and honked the horn at his two girls who were sitting on their bikes. They hopped off and gleefully ran over to the car. Mike could barely open the car door with the girls dancing around beside it, giddy to see him.

Squeezing out of the car he grabbed both of them, and swung them around like he always did before he was banished from the house. Kristy gushed, "Daddy, are you going to stay tonight?"

"You bet I am. I need to catch up on lecturing you two about all the bad things your mom has been telling me about!"

"No way! You're kidding, right?"

Diana rolled her eyes and glared at her younger sister. "Well, duh. Do you think?"

Kristy ignored Diana; instead she just grabbed her dad's hand and led him up to the front door.

"So, Daddy, when is your special project going to be finished so you can live at home with us again for good?"

Diana couldn't resist another jab. "Kristy, you're so naïve. Don't you know anything?"

Mike whirled around and gave Diana a look that made her stop in her tracks. He held up his finger in admonishment. Sheepishly, she nodded her head.

"What does she mean, Daddy?"

"Nothing Kristy. She's just teasing you."

"She does that a lot." Kristy opened the front door and skipped into the front hallway.

Mike and Diana followed; Mike allowed his nose to lead him directly to the kitchen where he knew he would find his gourmet chef of a wife working hard at her craft.

Cindy was in front of the range stirring some concoction that was blessed with a magnificent fragrance. She looked up with a wide smile on her face, dropped her wooden spoon into the pot, and ran over to him. They hugged for a few seconds, and then Cindy leaned her head back and planted a big kiss on Mike's lips. Mike returned the gesture and held it, vaguely aware of the two girls watching them.

Kristy yelled, "Yay!" Diana mumbled, "Yuck."

Mike and Cindy turned around and laughed at the starkly different, but predictable reactions of the girls. Sometimes they found it hard to believe that these two were created from the same gene pool.

"I'm sooo happy to see you, Mike! We talk everyday on the phone, but it's so exciting when I actually see your handsome face again!"

"Same for me. I miss waking up to your gorgeous smile every morning."

Cindy blushed at the compliment. Then she gently touched his forehead, concern in her eyes. "What happened here?"

"Oh, just fell against the doorway. One of my little lightning blackouts."

She leaned up on her tiptoes and kissed the spot. "There, all better." Then she hugged him again. "Isn't it nice that we have all weekend together? It will seem like normal again for a little while."

Mike gave her another squeeze. "Let's have a drink and we can talk for a bit before dinner."

*****

The dirty martinis were great—Cindy always made them perfectly, with just the right amount of olive juice. They were sitting side by side on the cozy leather couch in the family room. It was cool for October, so they had the gas fireplace on. It was a perfect Friday evening. And the best was yet to come—Cindy's superb lamb stew. Talk about comfort food!

Mike had decided that he was going to share with Cindy as much information as he could, without alarming her too much. He would just omit the violent stuff from the conversation, but he felt she had a right to know the rest.

The next hour or so was spent going over what he and Troy had discovered down in Brazil and Mexico, the embezzlement of Baxter funds and their diversion down to a bank in Panama, and their suspicion that Gerry along with an ex-employee had committed the frauds together. Cindy's crestfallen face lost all color, as the shocking revelation about Gerry was dropped in her lap.

Mike skipped the parts about beating up the Brazilian lawyer and his associate, as well as the slugging of David Samson at the church. He also wisely left out Samson's subsequent revenge against Mike in the alley. He found it humiliating just remembering that incident himself, let alone sharing it with someone else—even if that someone else was his wife.

The most important parts that he wanted Cindy to know about were the matching handwriting on both the condolence and birthday cards, and the tracing of the e-mail that ordered the limousine—back to, first, Jim's computer and then further back to Libya.

After disclosing those particular discoveries to her he could see relief wash over her pretty face. Up until now he knew that she had been convinced that Mike had sent the birthday card to himself, and that he had unknowingly, in a daze, sent the e-mail to the limousine company. Those were the two main reasons she had asked him to leave the house. Mike was now quietly praying for a reprieve.

Cindy made another couple of martinis for them and sat back down next to him again on the couch. She leaned in and tenderly kissed his cheek.

"I forgot to tell you. Bob phoned and wants to see you again. I agreed that we would meet him at his office tomorrow. He seemed quite anxious to see you."

Mike grimaced. He wasn't sure he wanted to see Dr. Teskey again, especially with so much still up in the air. But for Cindy's sake he would. "Okay, we'll go."

"Good." She rubbed his arm. "You must be feeling a lot of stress. Are you sure it's too dangerous to report all of this to the police? And lying to the Board must be a huge weight on your shoulders."

"Yeah, it is. And as for the danger, I may be overreacting on that," Mike lied. She didn't know the other parts and that's how it would remain. "I didn't like the words used in the birthday card message, and I know it was Samson's writing. He was demonstrating to me that he could very easily have our kids picked up. He didn't hurt them, but I know he meant it as a warning. He doesn't want me to disclose the fraud to my Board—or the police—pure and simple. I'm worried that if I do, something bad will happen to us, either by him or one of his cronies. I can't take that chance and if I'm breaking the law by keeping this quiet from the police and deceiving the Board, well, so be it. I've had to decide which is the worst danger and I've decided that it's Samson."

Cindy shivered and folded her arms across her chest. Mike took a long sip of his martini. "Hon, I'm hoping we can just sell those properties and bury this whole thing. That way, Samson will be out of my life, and I can just allow things to slide back to normal. He'll have walked off with millions of the company's dollars, but that's the least of my concerns."

"What are your chances of selling those properties soon?"

"Probably not good, at least not close to the price we paid for them. They were inflated by millions. And now with the recent floods north of Rio, and the public display of beheadings down in Acapulco, our chances are even worse. However, the one positive thing about the publicity from those two events is that the Board will probably accept a recommendation from me that we drastically lower our prices to sell those turkeys. At 'fire sale' prices, they may just go."

Cindy laid her head against Mike's shoulder. "Things were going so well for us. We shouldn't have these stresses at this point in our lives. And Gerry—Christ, I'm so disheartened to think that a close friend would do that to us. Why didn't we see any signs? Do you think Amanda knows? And what did he do with his share of the money? Surely Amanda would have noticed large amounts going into their account."

Mike shook his head. "He probably buried the money in an offshore account. And I don't think she suspected anything, I really don't."

Cindy sat up straight, and looked directly into Mike's eyes. "Amanda told me about your visit to her house. You never told me about that. Why?"

Mike lowered his eyes. "I just kind of went there on automatic pilot without understanding why. In hindsight, I know I was in 'Gerry mode.' I wasn't myself at all."

"I was alarmed when I heard about the things you said to her—you knew things that probably only Gerry would have known; and about your supposed university days together when she attended in a totally different campus section than you. She was in classes with Gerry, not you. She also said that you were affectionate towards her in the same way that Gerry used to be. It freaked her out. And it freaks me out!"

Mike cracked his knuckles. "Nothing happened between us, Cindy. Be assured of that. But I know I said some things that were strange to me. I'm sorry. I had no control over that. Just like when I called you 'Mandy' while we were in bed together."

Cindy continued. "You knew about the security patrol Gerry had arranged for. Do you think that was related to all of this embezzlement stuff? Was he afraid for his family for that reason?

"I don't know."

"These thoughts of Gerry's that you get—you can't just think hard and summon them?"

Mike chuckled. "No, I wish I could. I'd be able to figure things out about all of this much quicker. The thoughts, and skills like the boxing, seem to come without warning."

Cindy shook her head. "Too weird—maybe we should arrange some security ourselves until you get clear of this mess."

Mike nodded. "I was thinking the same thing. We already have a good alarm system so I'll arrange for a night patrol as well—the same company that we use for security at the office. They offer armed patrols."

Cindy put her arms around Mike's neck. "I appreciate your telling me all of this. It takes some of the uncertainty away, but I have to admit, it's all pretty alarming. I always thought shit like this only happened in the movies." Mike could see that she was swallowing hard, fighting a dry mouth. Then he heard her speak, with difficulty, the words he didn't want to hear. "It's still…too soon for you to…move back in. I don't feel…right about it yet. I think there are…some things…you're not telling me. Just a gut feeling I have. I'm sorry."

Mike could feel his heart sink in his chest. Cindy was as perceptive as usual. He sucked up his disappointment. "Okay, I understand." He kissed her cheek. "But will you at least accompany me to my high school reunion next week? I know it's probably boring for you, but it only comes around every five years. I'd like you to be with me."

"Oh God, I hate those things! All you old jocks getting together and reminding yourselves about what big shots you were in your wild youth years. It's nauseating."

Mike laughed. "I know, I know. We just give ourselves an ego boost every few years. Keeps us going."

Cindy shook her head. "I guess 'boys will be boys.' Alright, I'll go with you, but you owe me one, Mister Baxter!"

Mike smiled lovingly at her. He owed her more than just one.

Chapter 26

Mike was enjoying the view of busy Yonge Street from Bob Teskey's office. There was always something to look at on Yonge, Canada's longest street. It was the hub of Toronto, with some sections also unfortunately being the shame of Toronto. The main subway line ran beneath this street, and not too far from here was the stretch of track where Mike had beaten up the punks who were tormenting that pregnant lady. That seemed so long ago now, but in reality it was only about four months.

He turned from the window and smiled at Cindy. She was sitting on the couch sipping her coffee and watching him with a curious look on her face. She was probably still trying to figure out her husband, the enigma. The poor girl, she had a lot to be puzzled over and she'd only heard the half of it.

Mike sat down beside her and glanced at his watch. "In all the years we've known Bob, he's never been on time. We're always kept waiting. What's the deal with that?"

In answer to Mike's question, the door opened and in walked Bob, resplendent in a black linen suit, white shirt with gold cufflinks, all accented by a red silk tie. "Hello Baxters! Nice to see you again." He gave Cindy an extra-long hug, which made Mike flinch just a bit. Then he grabbed Mike's hand in a hearty handshake and Mike could feel that the squeeze was a little on the aggressive side. It took a couple of seconds for Bob to let his hand go but strangely it seemed as if he was trying to squeeze as hard as he could. Mike winced.

"Let's sit down, shall we?" Bob pulled one of the guest chairs closer to the couch and motioned for Mike and Cindy to resume their seats.

"So, Mike, we'll skip the small talk and get straight to it. This is Saturday after all, and I'm sure we'd all rather be doing something else, right?"

"Agreed. I'm willing to leave right now if this is an inconvenience."

"No, no. I wanted to see you. It's been quite a while since we last talked and I've been worried about you. Cindy's been keeping me posted, but I was hoping you would pop in once in a while yourself."

"Too busy—and you've known me long enough to also know that I'm not a big believer in head-shrinking. I'm here because Cindy asked me to be here. I'd rather just meet you out on the golf course."

Bob crossed his legs, and put on his most serious psychiatrist face. "You have to realize that you've had a serious accident that may have long-term implications for you. Already, you're out of your own home because of some of the symptoms."

Mike turned to Cindy and gave her a look. Cindy shrugged. "I've been keeping Bob up to date, Mike—for your own good. We don't exactly have a normal life right now, and I want it to get back to normal, quickly. Don't you?"

"Sure, but every aspect of our private lives doesn't need to be shared."

Bob quickly changed gears to break the tension. "Tell me about any new symptoms you've been having."

Mike stirred his coffee, and answered him while staring into the swirling liquid. "Nothing other than what you know already. We talked about this last time—my adoption of some of Gerry's characteristics. I still think there's something weird going on with that."

Bob was writing some notes on his pad. "So, you've had some more incidents like the one on the subway?"

Mike squirmed. He took a quick look at Cindy. "I don't want to go into details, but there have been a couple of other cases where I became a boxer. Quite a good one too."

Cindy leaned forward to catch his eye. "You didn't tell me about those."

"No, I didn't want to worry you. They were just minor incidents anyway, nothing sensational like the subway thing."

Mike could hear Bob's pen furiously scratching away at his pad. "Cindy told me about your visit to Mrs. Upton's house, and the things you said to her there. What are your thoughts on that?"

Mike glared at Cindy again. "No thoughts at all. I got caught up once more in a Gerry memory, and it didn't seem as if I had any control over it."

"Mike, I told you I would be keeping in touch with Dr. Fenton down in Sarasota. We've been talking quite a bit, and you agreed before you left Florida that it would be okay if we shared information with each other. Do you remember that?"

Mike shrugged his shoulders. "Sure, I have no problem with that. If it helps the scientific cause, and could possibly help me too, no sweat."

"Good. Well, he's as intrigued by your case as I am. You're the only known subject of a lightning bolt accident who seems to have adopted the characteristics of another person. This is quite extraordinary."

"I'm thrilled to be such good entertainment for the two of you." Mike didn't hide the sarcasm. Cindy nudged him with her elbow, clearly annoyed.

Bob laughed. "I'll ignore that crack. I'm learning a lot from Fenton and his Keraunopathy specialists. There is still much to learn, especially from a case such as yours." Bob got up from his chair and sat on the edge of his desk. "Mike, can you remember how you were feeling each time, just before these changes came over you?"

Mike sighed. "For the fighting—and I'm not a fighter by nature—it was anger that seemed to trigger it. But not every time I got angry, only those few times that I've mentioned. So it seems to be a bit selective."

"How about fear? Did you go into fighting mode when you've been afraid?"

Mike remembered back to when he was standing naked in the alley in front of a madman with a gun pointed at his head. "No, I would have to say that when fear was predominant, the fighting stance was not triggered."

Bob wrote some more notes. "How about when you started thinking of Mrs. Upton as your wife—when you called her Mandy, when you said things to her that could only have come from Gerry's memory, when you got affectionate with her. Also, when you were in a tender moment with Cindy and you called her 'Mandy' by mistake. What were you feeling at those times?"

Mike ran his fingers through his thick hair. "That's a good question, Bob." He paused for a couple of seconds. "I would have to say I was peaceful, melancholy, not really thinking of anything too deep."

Bob nodded and scribbled again on his notepad. "You usually have a temper, don't you Mike?"

"No, I wouldn't say 'usually.' I can lose my temper at certain times, but I'm never out of control. I'm demanding, sure, anybody who has ever worked for me will tell you that. But there's a big difference between being demanding and assertive, versus having out of control temper fits."

Bob nodded, wrote a couple of notes, then put his pad down and strode directly to Mike's side of the couch. Then, out of nowhere, he slapped him hard across the face. Mike felt the blow but didn't really comprehend the source. He thought he was dreaming. Did Bob really just slap him across the face? He jumped to his feet, and in the background he could hear Cindy shouting, "Bob, what are you doing!"

Mike could feel his muscles tensing, and a rage building inside of him, right down in his gut. He was now standing toe to toe with Bob. Through clenched teeth he seethed, "Don't fucking touch me again!"

Bob laughed in his face, then took his glasses off and set them on the coffee table.

"I'll bet you use that temper on Cindy and the girls, don't you? I'm guessing you're an abuser, a control freak! Aren't you?" Mike saw too late Bob's other hand swooping up from his side and striking him on the other side of the face. He turned his cheek to soften the blow, and could feel his fists clenching, then rising quickly to a now familiar position. He had no control anymore. Cindy was crying, coming around the coffee table.

Bob demanded, "Answer me!" This time Mike was ready. He saw the hand coming up again. He blocked it with his left forearm, and delivered a crushing blow with his right to Bob's mid-section. Bob grunted and doubled over. Then Mike followed up with a left cross to Bob's jaw, sending him flying back against his desk and crumbling to the floor.

Mike watched as Cindy ran over to Bob and knelt down beside him, cradling his head. Bob groaned, rubbed his chin, and struggled to his feet. "I'm okay. I can take a punch—used to do a little boxing myself a long time ago. I must say that was one amazing combination you laid on me."

Cindy glared at Bob like an angry schoolmarm. "Why did you do that? You provoked him!" Then she turned to Mike. "Did you have to hit him so hard? I've never seen you like that before!" She wiped the tears from her eyes. "Are you sure you're okay, Bob?"

"I'm fine. More than you realize."

Mike's muscles were starting to relax. He started seeing flashbacks of the last few moments, and couldn't believe what had just happened. Why did Bob slap him? What was the purpose of that? Bob was a professional, and they were friends. This was just so out of line for someone of Bob's caliber that it was hard for Mike to believe it.

Bob was still rubbing his chin as he came back over to his chair and sat down. He calmly put on his glasses, picked up his pad, and wrote some more notes as if nothing at all had happened. Mike and Cindy didn't say a word. They were both in a state of shock.

Finally Bob spoke. His jaw was starting to show signs of swelling, but he didn't seem to notice, or care. "I'm sorry I had to do that, Mike. Believe me, it was a hard thing to do to someone I care about so much. But I had to see for myself. I had to see what it would take to provoke you into the boxing mode. I was watching your physiological reactions very closely. It was amazing how quickly you changed right in front of my eyes. It was real—and, well, eerie."

"So you deliberately baited me? Quite frankly, that pisses me off."

"I don't blame you for being upset. But let's get things into perspective here. We just did a controlled experiment, and it worked. You demonstrated an incredible transformation. I had to see it first hand, in order to be able to understand it and help you."

Mike shifted uncomfortably in his seat. "What the fuck did you learn from slapping my face that could possibly help me?"

"I used that provocation technique at the suggestion of Fenton. It's a technique that's used sometimes in the States to ascertain degrees of latent aggression. I'd never heard of it before, but it makes sense. How can I help you? First of all, I can prescribe pills that can keep this reaction of yours in check. Secondly, I'd like to take you to Florida for further testing with a team of Keraunopathy specialists that Fenton will assemble. You've created quite a stir amongst the medical community that has heard of your case. Further study will teach us a lot, and will probably help you as well."

Mike stood up. "So, I'm a curiosity now, am I? A guinea pig? Someone you doctors can all poke, squeeze, provoke, videotape—and slap—then put in a straitjacket?"

"Come on now, Mike. It wouldn't be like that at all. It would be a professional study that would probably culminate in your attendance at a medical convention where your case would be studied and presented."

Mike shook his head in disgust. Cindy grabbed his arm. "Mike, maybe you should at least listen."

Mike sat down again and Bob grabbed the opportunity. "What I'm hearing from my colleagues in Florida is that what may have happened to you is indeed scientifically possible. Think of your brain as a hard drive—in fact the most sophisticated hard drive imaginable. You're familiar with how we can easily transfer data from one computer hard drive to another, or to a flash drive. No problem. It's feasible under the right circumstances—such as when the lightning bolt hit at the exact moment your head and Gerry's were in contact—that some data along with motor skill memory could be transferred just like with computers."

Bob paused to let that sink in. Mike was listening, but he also had an uncontrollable urge to just get up and leave. Bob continued. "Mike, it's apparent that when anger is the predominant emotion, the fighting mode is triggered. From what you told me, when fear is predominant, no such change takes place. When you are at peace or feeling content and romantic, the memories of Amanda Upton and her children creep into your brain. So it seems that changes take place when it's one extreme or the other, and certain triggers cause certain changes. This is quite remarkable. The best comparison for the fighting mode would be the story of, don't laugh, 'The Incredible Hulk.' But further study may discover that other emotions could also cause other aspects of Gerry to emerge. Right now we know that fear doesn't cause the fighting mode, but it could under the right situation cause an entirely different skill of Gerry's to emerge. Same thing for joy, sadness, etc. It might all depend on what skill is needed at the time, for whatever. Example: fear—if you were in danger of drowning—might turn you into an expert swimmer if that's a skill that Gerry had. Or joy might turn you into a comedian if that was one of Gerry's skills. Do you get my point?"

Mike snorted, then put his arm around Cindy's waist, gently nudging her up out of her seat. Together, they walked to the door and Mike opened it with a flourish. With his back to Bob he said, "I want no part of your experiments. I refuse to be a lab rat, allowing you and your colleagues to become rich and famous by making a spectacle out of me at your conventions and in your medical journals."

Before following Cindy through the door, Mike turned to face the highly educated slapper. "I won't be seeing you again."

Chapter 27

Mike browsed around inside a popular sportswear store on Front Street near the *Rogers Centre*, formerly known as the *Skydome*. The stadium was the home field for the *Toronto Blue Jays* of the AL East division, and where Mike had seen two World Series championships won by his beloved home team back in the early nineties. But, that was then, this was now. They weren't winning too often anymore but he still enjoyed the sport, the ballpark atmosphere, and of course the great hot dogs. Ah...the "boys of summer."

Rogers Centre was famous for its retractable roof and had been one of only a handful of domed stadiums in the world when it was first built. There were several more now, but in Mike's biased opinion none that stood up to the engineering marvel of Toronto's entry.

The stadium was located next to the *CN Tower*—considered by the *Guinness Book of World Records* to be the world's largest tower. It was the equivalent of 147 stories, built in 1976 for what would be considered today to be a paltry cost of sixty-three million dollars. It took three and a half years to build, and in Mike's view was one of the most hypnotic structures he'd ever seen—particularly so if viewed when standing on the sidewalk looking up. This magnificent tower received worldwide recognition when it was designated as one of the "The Seven Wonders of the Modern World."

When Mike was at work, he could see both the *Rogers Centre* and the *CN Tower* from one of his corner office windows. If he was in a pensive mood, he gazed dreamily out over Lake Ontario; but when he was in the mood for being inspired to achieve the near impossible, he looked out at these two impressive buildings.

Today, as Mike had been driving down Front Street and gazing at the buildings, he felt inspired. Inspired enough to stop at a sports shop and buy something for his new little friend.

He chose a *Blue Jays* game sweater and cap, along with a fielder's glove and an authentic MLB baseball. Mike didn't know whether Jonas liked baseball or not but he figured, hey, what little boy wouldn't? He paid for the merchandise, jumped back in his car and headed north on Spadina.

Once intersecting with Queen Street West he continued along Spadina until he reached the infamous alley where he had made his naked debut. This time there were no barricades so he turned left into the alley and drove on down as far as the garbage bin that had housed Jonas. Mike got out and walked over to the bin, opened the lid and looked inside. The toys were in their usual spots, but no Jonas.

Mike got back into his car and sat for a few minutes, thinking. He knew which house was Jonas,' but did he dare knock on the front door? What would the boy's mother think? Mike prided himself on being a personable guy, but would she think he was some kind of pervert, a pedophile? And had Jonas told his mom yet that some strange man had given him 1,000 dollars in cash? Or did he say he just found the money?

Mike didn't even know what had possessed him to be here. Why was this important to him? He barely knew the child—but he did know that something powerful was tugging at his heartstrings, and that certain something was telling him that he needed to help the young boy. He felt sorry for him, and for some strange reason he felt responsible for him.

Mike had been thinking hard lately about his own early years, and about the trials and tribulations of growing up—the things a guy had to do to fit in, to be admired, to have friends. He was glad he'd survived that cruel world. He sure wouldn't want to be young in this day and age, and have to go through all that again. He had been popular in school but it had been stressful maneuvering to reach a pinnacle where he had finally become one of the "untouchables." He knew that life had been hell for some of the kids who hadn't reached that pinnacle.

Mike's eyes teared up and he rubbed them with his knuckles. Then he cracked those same knuckles while he continued going back, way back. It was a hard thing to accept, but now that he was a man with the insecurities and brashness of youth left in the dust, he could honestly admit that he no longer liked who he'd been back then. In fact he was ashamed of who he'd been. Deep in the recesses of his mind, he knew he'd always felt this shame, but had never really faced it head on. He had, in a nutshell, become popular on the backs of some of the weaker kids. As a boy, he had viewed it as just 'survival of the fittest,' and all in good fun. They would get over it. They would suck it up—or so he had convinced himself.

Now he wondered if they ever really got over it. How had they turned out? Were there any lasting effects? Being so self-centered back then, he had never seen those kids through the same sympathetic eyes that he viewed Jonas. And he knew in his heart that Jonas would not survive intact from what he was going through if it was allowed to continue. Jonas couldn't live his childhood hiding in a dumpster, stealing toys, not being able to show his face at school. And this made Mike recall the many nameless faces from his own school—the sad eyes, the weak bodies, the clumsy geeks—the ones they called 'losers.'

But why now? Why all of a sudden was he feeling guilty about events thirty or so years ago? And why did this little boy matter to him so much?

He rubbed his forehead—a headache was coming on. He couldn't make the images go away. The images of kids whom he and his friends had tormented in high school, seeing the pain in their eyes as they were displayed as losers in front of the other "cool" kids. Mike had never hurt anybody—not physically anyway. That wasn't his style. But making fun of the weaker ones was considered innocent fun. It was innocent, wasn't it? People recover from such things, don't they?

Then he remembered his own helplessness and humiliation in this very alley. He didn't want to think that it was the same thing thirty years ago, that those kids were really hurt by what he and his buddies had done. They were just having fun, surely those kids knew that. Was David Samson just having fun?

Then he thought of Jonas again. Cute little Jonas being called "Cuntface." Did Jonas know that those kids were just having fun?

The throbbing in his head was getting worse. Mike rolled his neck around a bit, then put the car in gear and drove to the end of the alley. He hung a right towards the next street where Jonas' house would be, the red clapboard that he could see from the alley. Reaching the street, he turned right again and parked in front of the little red house. He noticed that none of the houses had driveways, and they were all in desperate need of some TLC.

There was an old pickup truck parked in front of him. Mike got out of the car, grabbed his bag of gifts for Jonas, and slowly walked up to the front door. He paused for a second before knocking, once again challenging his actions. Then, satisfied that he was doing the right thing, he quickly pulled his hand out of his pocket and raised his fist up to the old wooden door.

His fist froze in mid-air as he heard a crash from inside the house, followed by the sound of whimpering. A man's voice was yelling; words that were difficult to make out. A child screamed. And the sound of smacking, loud and repetitive.

Mike felt the muscles in his arms tightening, becoming rigid, and his face getting warm, then hot. He tried the door handle. It was locked. From the way the door wiggled he could tell that the lock was flimsy. Mike put his shoulder to the door and sure enough the lock easily gave way. He stepped cautiously into the front hallway and his eyes took in the scene. A large burly man wearing an undershirt and jeans was bending over a woman lying on the floor of the living room. One hairy hand held her by the hair, and the other one was swinging a belt down at her bare back, over and over again. She was covering her face with her hands and her blouse had been torn exposing her bare back Mike looked to the end of the room and could see Jonas kneeling under the dining room table, eyes closed, hands covering his ears, rocking back and forth on his knees and elbows.

The stomach-churning sight of the woman being beaten caused Mike to gasp in shock, unfortunately loud enough for the thug to hear. He let go of the woman's hair, turned around and swung the belt around in Mike's direction. They were about twelve feet apart.

"Who the fuck are you? Get the hell out of here, you motherfucker!"

Mike stood his ground and said, "Just put the belt down, sir. Leave her alone." He said it as calmly as he could, belying the eruption of anger building in his gut. The woman on the floor was looking up at him now, a puzzled look on her face. Blood was dripping from her nose, and Mike could see streaks of blood across her back as well.

Then out of the corner of his eye he saw movement from under the dining room table. Jonas was now on his feet. "Mike! Mister Mike!" Mike held out his hand toward him, signaling to stay where he was.

The man shouted again. "I'll shove this belt up your ass, you faggot!" Now that he was no longer bending over the helpless woman, Mike could see that the guy was bigger than he thought. At least six and a half feet tall, and probably weighing around three hundred pounds. The man was a slob: long greasy black hair hanging over a severely pockmarked face, heavy unkempt brows framing bloodshot eyes, and an overpowering body odor that Mike could smell from where he was standing. But despite the man's bulk, Mike didn't feel any fear—only a boiling rage.

He knew which mode was taking over, but this time he was fully conscious of the change. He was still who he was, not in one of those trances that he'd had in the past. He was Mike, not Gerry. But he knew that Gerry's skill was going to show itself, in a matter of seconds. And for the first time he relished the thought.

The brute was advancing towards him now, swinging the belt, buckle end first. Mike dropped his bag of gifts and quickly slipped out of his suit jacket. He twisted it and held it up in front of him, firmly grasping both ends of the jacket in hopes it would function as a guard. The man swung the belt and Mike deflected it with his rolled-up jacket. Then it came again, this time glancing off his neck. The buckle had done its work; Mike could feel the warm blood dripping down under the collar of his shirt.

The man sensed an opening and was on him in a flash—pawing, grunting, grabbing his hair and then swinging him around by the scalp. He slammed Mike's head into the doorframe and the room started to spin. Mike managed to wrench free from his grasp and move several feet away. He shook his head to clear the fog, and went into a boxer's stance. The man laughed. "Who are you, Muhammad Ali?" The giant rushed him. Mike slammed his right fist into his gut, and it felt like hitting a brick wall. The punch had no effect at all; it didn't even slow him down. He grabbed Mike by the neck and shoved his back up against the wall, squeezing tightly on his throat with both hands.

The room was starting to spin again, and with the power this man had, Mike realized that boxing skills alone were not going to save his life. The man seemed intent on killing him and Mike had to do something, fast. Despite gasping for breath and feeling faint from the guy's body odor, he summoned enough strength to ram his knee up into the brute's crotch. He heard him grunt in pain, and instantly felt the release of pressure on his throat. Mike shoved him backward and punched him square in the nose. He felt the crunch of the bones an instant before he heard it. A massive amount of blood was now spurting out over the man's face.

Mike knew he couldn't let up. He dove to the floor and grabbed the belt, then came up behind the bleeding beast and quickly pulled it around his neck, sliding the open end through the buckle.

The rage was surreal. Mike had never before experienced such a cocktail of strength, hate, and adrenaline. He swung the beast around by the belt, slamming him into the wall face first. Then, planting his feet firmly on the hardwood floor and bending at the knees, Mike yanked him back and started pulling the shocked giant around in a circle, around and around, slowly at first, then faster and faster. He let go of the belt at just the right moment, sending the dizzy man flying straight down the basement stairs.

Mike leapt after him, hitting the light switch and taking the stairs down three at a time. He found the guy crumpled on the floor, groaning and struggling to get back on his feet. Mike would have none of it. He grabbed the belt that was still around his neck and pulled the free end until he could feel the tension on the man's throat. Mike lay down on the floor behind him, positioned his feet up against the massive shoulders and leaned backwards as if he were fighting a tug of war—pushing with his feet, pulling with his arms. The animal on the floor began coughing and twisting, clawing helplessly at his throat with his hands. For a sickening second, Mike was afraid that the head was going to tear right off the top of his neck.

Mike prayed that he was still himself, Mike Baxter, pulling on the belt—but he couldn't help but wonder. Something inside of him wouldn't allow his hands to let go, and that scared the shit out of him. This cruel bastard choking to death on the floor was not going to walk out of here alive, and it felt like there was nothing that could change Mike's mind on that.

That was, until he heard a frantic little voice from the top of the stairs. "Don kill my Daddy! Please, Mister Mike!"

Chapter *28*

Mike lifted his eyes from his victim for just a second; enough time to catch a glimpse of his little friend at the top of the stairs, and also just enough time for the man on the floor to detect that Mike's grip on the belt had weakened slightly. Before Mike could react, the guy had flipped himself over into a kneeling position facing him.

A massive fist came next, then blackness.

****

David Samson didn't want to kill Mike Baxter. That was the last thing he wanted to do. Instead, he wanted to ruin him—in every way possible—his life, marriage, career, dignity, and confidence. Gerry Upton's death had moved up the schedule. David would have been content to suck the company dry for as long as he could; he had been willing to wait for his revenge. However, life—and death—work in funny ways sometimes, and there was no reason to wait any longer. The process had already started. Mike was already hurting now, not necessarily physically, but mentally. This is the kind of pain David wanted Mike to have. He wanted him to feel it—to know what it felt like to be humiliated, alone, helpless, living in fear. He wanted him to feel like a loser.

Following Mike's career over the years had become an obsession for David. He had never lost sight of him. He hated him more than he could ever imagine hating any man. David had discovered that the feeling of hate didn't require knowing someone—it just required knowing of him. He had never really known Mike in high school. They had never talked, never hung out together or even in a group. They were in some of the same classes but David, or more correctly Dawud back then, had been invisible to guys like Mike.

Mike probably hadn't even known his name, or if he had, he had dismissed it as being foreign so not worth remembering. Dawud hadn't served a useful purpose to the "cool" kids, except of course when they needed someone to jostle around, or humiliate. Then he wasn't so invisible.

Mike and Dawud had even graduated in the same year, walked on the same stage. When Mike had gone up to receive his diploma, there had been a standing ovation for the hero who had broken every school athletic record imaginable. The quarterback with the arm of steel. The track star whose record for the one hundred meter dash was probably still standing after all these years. The jock who had dated half the cheerleading squad. Yes, Mike had been the whole package and the audience had let him know just how they felt about him. They loved him.

The audience also let Dawud know how they felt about him when he went up on stage to receive his diploma. First, someone in the front row tripped him before he reached the stairway to the stage. Lying flat on his stomach in his gown he could hear the jeers and the laughter. Then, when he finally made it up the stairs he heard catcalls of "Loser," "Camel Jockey," "Faggot." Then more laughter. The principal went to the microphone and politely asked them to stop, but he wasn't too assertive. Dawud thought he detected the man snickering a bit himself.

Dawud had decided that he would never set foot in that gym or on that stage again. There would be no reunions for him.

David had just held the last meeting with his five associates—the last meeting before the event. They were well prepared and they knew their orders. They also had their weapons—in fact, the most frightening small arms weapons ever manufactured. David chuckled at the irony of Arab terrorists brandishing machine guns made by the Israelis.

At a pre-set time one of his men would cut the telephone and fire alarm lines on the outside of the building, while two others would be pretending to mingle inside the gym. The last two would wait in the hallway until the lines were cut, then, joined by their associate from outside, they would firmly usher any hallway stragglers into the gym. From cut phone lines to the end of their assignment, they would be there no longer than thirty minutes. David's operatives had to commit to memory the names of eight men who would be attending the party—all of them former football stars, all of them now successful and wealthy. Each of the eight had always enjoyed the spotlight and David was going to give them that spotlight once again, this time in a way they had never experienced before.

*****

Cindy rushed into the house, carrying two garment bags over her shoulder. She'd just spent the last two hours choosing costumes for her and Mike. Mike had left that task to her. He would be going as Abraham Lincoln, and she as Annie Oakley. Her costume was simple—western garb, cowboy hat, and boots. Mike's was a little more elaborate—long black jacket with matching pants, white frilled shirt with tie, legendary stove pipe hat, and a full head mask of 'Honest Abe.'

Cindy really didn't want to go to this stupid reunion, but it was important to Mike so it was important to her. She would endure it, smile, listen to all the old stories as well as the usual accolades dished out to her husband, and then sweetly talk him into leaving early. It was the same routine every five years. She thanked her lucky stars that it wasn't an annual event. And she always reminded Mike that she never dragged him to her school reunions. She didn't believe in re-visiting the past. She thought reunions were unproductive and egocentric. Everybody was always trying to show each other up—bragging about how far they had come since high school. Her attitude was—who cares?

The benefit to going, however, was being able to spend some time with Mike—out in the world as a real couple. They hadn't done much of that since he had moved out. She knew that his absence was only temporary. She desperately wanted him back home again, back in their bed, and hugging his daughters goodnight. But she was afraid to rush it. Cindy wanted these symptoms of his to settle down. She was disappointed that he refused to see Dr. Teskey again, but she really couldn't blame him after their last visit. That unorthodox method of Bob's, slapping Mike until he fought back, was ridiculous. She could understand why Mike felt used and provoked. And she certainly didn't agree with Bob's plan to use Mike as a lab rat down in Florida.

But she was really shocked to see, first-hand, the violence that erupted from Mike's fists when he was provoked. She never expected to see him react like that and towards a friend at that. She knew he was entitled to defend himself but his reaction was way over the top.

That altercation in the doctor's office simply reaffirmed her decision not to let Mike move back in yet. She hoped that once he simmered down she could convince him to visit Teskey again, or at least another psychiatrist. He needed help, and if he didn't get that help she wasn't sure she could let him live with her again.

That was a heart-wrenching thought. Cindy put it out of her head and started pulling on her cowboy duds, just for fun.

*****

Mike awoke to the sensation of moisture on his forehead and something soft and fluffy under his head. He opened his eyes and looked up into the kind face of Jonas' mother. He reached behind his head and realized that he was lying on a pillow. There was a single light bulb hanging from the ceiling over his head, and as he squinted through heavy eyes he realized he was in the basement. Now he remembered. He had lost his concentration and the giant had punched him, hard.

"How...long have I been out?"

"Oh, only about twenty minutes. You'll be fine. It looks like your nose may be broken, though. Don't worry. He's far away from here by now. We're safe."

Mike reached up to touch his nose, and it felt like it had been expertly bandaged. His forehead was aching as well, and he remembered being slammed into the doorframe. Then he realized that this was the second time in a couple of weeks that he had been knocked unconscious. Not a good thing.

The young mother smiled at him. "Your forehead is a little red, and so is your throat. But those marks will go away soon."

Mike smiled back at her and felt a jarring pain in his nose. He made a mental note not to smile for a while. "Thanks for patching me up. You should let me take a look at your back. You took quite the beating." He noticed she was wearing a robe now.

"That's alright. I've already taken care of it with Jonas' help. I'm a nurse down at St. Mike's—Intensive Care. I've seen a lot worse."

The robe covered most of her body except for her forearms and lower legs. The black and blue bruises betrayed her nonchalance. "Those sores look painful," Mike said, pointing at her arms.

"Oh, they're nothing, really—I bruise very easily. Someone just has to squeeze me a little too hard and I'll bruise."

Mike didn't believe her one bit; he figured she was just trying to be brave. Battered wives got a lot of practice being brave. He held out his hand. "My name's Mike. Yours...?"

"Pleased to meet you, Mike. I'm Alison. Alison Jenner."

Mike pushed himself to his feet, and Alison held him under the arm to steady him.

"Jonas told me about you. He said you were very nice to him. But...why did you come by today?"

"Oh, I brought him a couple of little presents. I hope you don't mind. I took a liking to your son—nothing weird, I promise you. He's just such a nice little boy, and he was kind to me when I had a bit of trouble."

"I don't mind at all. Jonas seemed thrilled to have met you. He said you were his new friend." Alison chuckled.

"Well, he's my new friend too." Mike frowned. "Who was that guy?"

Alison lowered her eyes. "My husband. We're kind of separated—he goes away for days at a time, then comes back angry."

Mike realized all of a sudden how pretty Alison was. She had cleaned herself up a bit while he was unconscious; long brown hair, hazel eyes, shapely figure, tall—about five foot seven. It made him furious all over again thinking how that giant, who outweighed Alison by about a hundred and seventy pounds at least, had been beating this sweet mother senseless. It was hardly a fair fight.

Alison raised her eyes and smiled at him again. Mike noticed that there were cute little crinkles around her eyes and mouth when she smiled, and she cocked her head in the cutest way as she talked. Her eyes danced with life. As she spoke, Mike found himself becoming mesmerized by the expressions she made. "We were high school sweethearts. He wasn't always this way. Wade became a professional wrestler and was doing very well. We lived up in Willowdale. After a while he started taking steroids, and he changed. He became addicted. Then an injury ruined his career and our lives went downhill fast." She lowered her head again. "I think he's still on steroids, and he comes here looking for money. When he doesn't find any, he beats me. All I can say is, thank God he never hurts Jonas."

Mike put his hand on her shoulder. "Listen, there are places you can go. My company donates a lot of money to one of the women's shelters. They're usually full, but I'm sure if I make a call I can get you and Jonas in there tonight."

Alison shook her head. "No, he'll find us."

"No, I promise you that he won't. These shelters are top secret. Their locations are not known to anyone who isn't staff or a resident. Even I don't know where this shelter is, and I'm a financial supporter."

Alison looked up and smiled with those cute little crinkles that melted Mike's heart. "No, Mike. Thank you for your help today, but this is our life here, such as it is. I don't want to make a change like that. I know Wade will get better. He's promised me. Sometimes he's very nice. I still love him. And he's Jonas' dad."

Mike wouldn't give up. "You could press charges. I could help you."

Alison shook her pretty head, pushing her long hair behind her left ear. "Thanks for caring. But you're a stranger. I'm sure you have your own life to worry about."

Mike nodded. *You don't know the half of it.* "Okay, Alison. But I'm going to come back and check on you guys once in a while. Is that alright with you?"

She nodded. "Yes. We have something in common now, don't we? We've both been beaten by the same man." She laughed at her attempt at gallows humor, and the little crinkles appeared again.

They walked up the stairs together, and Mike met Jonas standing at the top. He rustled the little guy's hair, then walked to the hallway and picked up the bag of gifts.

"These are for you, Jonas. Maybe I'll play some ball with you next time I visit."

Jonas smiled his big smile. "Are you coming gan, Mister Mike?"

"Yes...and just call me 'Mike', okay?"

"Okay, Mike."

Mike knelt down on one knee. "Jonas, did you give your mother that money I gave you?"

Jonas looked at the floor. "No, I dint."

"How come?"

"I's fraid she think you was strange."

Mike gave the little guy a hug. "Well, now she knows I'm not strange. So you can give it to her, okay?"

Jonas nodded eagerly. "Okay, Mike."

Mike stood up and held out his hand to Alison. "Thanks again for nursing me back to health." He pulled a business card out of his pocket and handed it to her. "In case you ever need help—whatever it is—please don't hesitate to call me."

Alison took the card, shook his hand and pulled him closer to her. She put her arms around his neck, then squeezed tightly and whispered, "You're a brave man, and a decent man. I can tell these things. Thank you for caring enough to help us today." She kissed him lightly on the cheek. "And you can call me 'Ali.' All my friends do and you're our new friend. So you qualify."

Mike could feel a tear in each eye as he walked out the door and down the pathway to his car. Jonas wasn't the only one being bullied. Ali was clearly suffering from 'battered wife syndrome.' She was hoping for a miracle; that everything would be back to the way it was when her and Wade were high school sweethearts. Miracles like that seldom happened. Redemption is a romantic thought, but usually a hopeless one. What kind of future did Ali and Jonas have? Mike shuddered.

Chapter 29

All Mike hoped for was that he would get through the day without too much grief. He was standing in front of the mirror in his private washroom, carefully removing the bandage from his nose. It was looking better now—a little crooked, but the swelling had come down and the cuts weren't as visible. He'd been applying ice for the last couple of days. It was amazing how effective that had been.

The last Board meeting of the year was this morning. It was always around this time, just before Halloween. His colleagues always joked that this October meeting was the most appropriate one of all, seeing as the directors who sat on the Board were scarier than goblins.

Once again Mike would have to make an excuse for another injury. Cindy had bought his last story—the one about one of his blackouts causing him to bump his head. He couldn't use that excuse this time because the Board didn't even know he had been having blackouts, and he sure wasn't going to raise alarm bells by telling them. So instead, he would explain it away by saying he'd picked up an elbow to the face in a game of touch football. That sounded very 'Kennedyesque,' and the Board would love the image.

Yes, once today's meeting was over, he could relax a bit. Today was Friday and he was spending the weekend back home with Cindy and the girls. And tomorrow night he and Cindy would be going to his high school reunion, which was always kind of fun. This year it would be even more fun than usual due to everyone being dressed up in Halloween costumes. Then Monday night was Halloween and he was looking forward to taking the girls out trick-or-treating.

It would seem like one of those old family weekends of togetherness that he'd been missing so badly.

*****

"So, in conclusion of the financial results reporting, we will have another record year. We think this is a great performance considering how severe this recession has been and the toll it has taken on commercial real estate. Our strategy has always been to ensure that we are reasonably recession-proof. Consequently, over the years we have positioned our largest commercial developments in the most economically diversified cities in North America. For example, we have no properties in Detroit, Windsor, Toledo, Los Angeles, Cincinnati, or Miami—just to name a few. Our chosen cities didn't see the loss of tenancy that other cities saw, and most of our leases were locked in to terms of five years or longer. This augured well for revenue stability."

Mike paused and gazed down the table at the directors. Most were nodding their approval. He felt more comfortable now, but still just a wee bit apprehensive. He'd been saving the worst news for last, and he hoped they were pumped up enough now on the good stuff to be able to handle it.

"Finally, I'd like to report on the attempts to sell our four properties in Brazil and Mexico. You will recall that we have been endeavoring to sell these at book value—in other words what we paid when they were purchased years ago. Unfortunately, while there have been a few enquiries, we have had no offers. Making matters worse, of course, are the headline-making events in both of those countries over the last few months. We have seen severe flooding in Brazil and…beheadings in Acapulco. The drug wars in Mexico seem to be spreading to the tourist areas which is something we had hoped would not happen, and the unprecedented floods in Brazil have caused deep-pocket buyers to be concerned."

Mike looked up from his notes and saw that several directors were frantically writing notes of their own. He continued. "Our investments in those countries are clearly now impaired. Christine had recommended at the last Board meeting that we put provisions against the balance sheet to reflect this impairment. It was the opinion of the majority of the Board that that might be premature. However, in light of recent events, I would have to now agree that Christine was correct and it is clear that her perception of the problem was uncannily accurate." Mike figured that a little sucking up to the most troublesome Board member couldn't hurt, and would actually cause her to probably shut up and not ask any more probing questions. She could smugly declare victory, which was all that she ever really cared about anyway—being proven right.

"Due to the record-breaking year for Baxter Development, we can easily afford to reflect the impairment without any tangible impact on earnings. This would be the year to do it, if we think the sale of the properties will drag on. Therefore I am recommending, due to the extreme geo-social emerging trends in Brazil and Mexico, that we write off these four properties during this fiscal year. Take the book values down to zero. This will enable us to lower the sale prices to rock bottom, and any eventual sale can be reflected in earnings in a future fiscal year. For this year, we would take the hit of sixty-five million, and in the future we can look forward to any positive proceeds that we are able to eventually obtain. Respectfully, I would ask for a motion and a second, to allow us to proceed in this direction."

There was silence around the table for a good minute. Then Christine Masden, with a self-righteous grin on her face, raised her hand. "I move to approve."

Guy Wilkins raised his hand too. "I second that." Peter Botswait finalized the item. "Motion carried."

Mike breathed a sigh of relief. Worked like a charm—a compelling case that no one could argue with. Now that these assets would be off the balance sheet, there would be no more questions at future meetings. These useless lots were buried deep now, only to be cheered if they got sold at a later date. Whatever leverage David Samson had on him was now nullified. He didn't have to disclose the fraud and an audit wouldn't bother commenting on the properties because they were deemed in the balance sheet to be worthless. No one would know. He was free.

*****

The six Muslims knelt together in meditation. David allowed Omar, chief of the team of five commandos, to lead them in prayer. Not because he was being respectful but instead due to the fact that David had forgotten the prayers.

David was not a devout Muslim, but he was a devout Arab. There was a big difference between the two. And there were a lot of Arabs just like him, although it wasn't something they generally shared with others. It was better to allow the religious fanatics to think they were just as fanatical. In truth, David thought religion was all a load of crap.

The six men rose from the floor and touched hands, bowing to each other. Then they embraced for a group hug. This hug wasn't a required part of the ritual—it was just a good old hug in acknowledgment that five of them would die tomorrow night. And proudly die. David used the religious shit whenever it suited his purposes—such as at times like this when he had to order men or women to sacrifice themselves. He had to play the game in order to get obedience.

They sat down on chairs in the main floor office of the old tenement house. This was the only place he ever met with his operatives. They had no idea that he actually lived in a luxury condominium a couple of blocks away. They'd be horrified if they knew. Fadiyah lived on the second floor of the house, and whenever David's men saw her coming or going they just assumed she was his woman. She wasn't home very much—Fadiyah spent most of her time at strip clubs, luring lecherous businessmen into David's traps. That was her job and she did it well. But David knew also that if he asked her to sacrifice herself, she would. She was a fanatic just like the others. Sex was her avenue to eternity, and she felt no guilt in using it to serve Allah.

David directed his attention to Omar, a tall and handsome Arab who no doubt hoped that his looks would help him secure the sexiest seventy-two virgins in paradise. He probably hoped they all looked like Fadiyah. David had noticed the way his eyes had wandered over her luscious body every time she walked through the house. David chuckled to himself—Omar would find out tomorrow night whether or not he was going to get lucky in paradise.

"Omar, my friend, do you have any last minute questions for me?"

Omar bowed his head. "No, Dawud, you have been very clear in your instructions. Everything is ready." All of David's associates used his given name. They understood that he had to have a western name to co-exist with the infidels, but they refused to use it. David didn't care.

"And the car is loaded?"

"Yes, all is secured."

"Then we are done here. I bid you all to go with Allah. Allah Akbar!"

In unison, the five men replied, "Allah Akbar!"

They left the house, on their way to eternity. David locked the door and walked back into his office muttering under his breath, "Allah Fuckbar, you fools."

Tomorrow night would be quite the night. He would lose five of his best men, but there were many more where they came from. David had no shortage of operatives. These five would not fail him. They were loyal, devoted to the cause, and had been expertly trained in some of the best camps in the Middle East.

Yes, tomorrow night would make a statement on behalf of all David's fellow Palestinians: 'Persist in denigrating the lives of people who were robbed of their homeland, and your lives will suffer denigration as well.'

And Mike Baxter and friends would be the sideshow to the main event, a role that a headliner like Mike was unfamiliar with.

Chapter *30*

Mike glanced over at his wife, sitting coquettishly with her sexy legs crossed in the passenger seat of the Bimmer. She looked 'hot' in her Annie Oakley outfit. Surprisingly, she suited a cowboy hat. Mike made a mental note to take her to Alberta some July to attend the Calgary Stampede. She would fit right in. His eyes wandered down her legs to her smooth calves that were adorned with a pair of snakeskin boots which rose almost to knee level. For a brief moment he pictured Cindy with nothing on except those boots, the hat, and a lasso in hand. It was a nice image. Some women looked downright sexy in cowboy attire, and his wife was definitely one of them.

"Hey, keep your eyes on the road, Mister. We want to get there in one piece."

He hadn't noticed her watching him as he scanned her body. Mike laughed.

"Well, you'll have to forgive me. You look so adorable in those duds that I have this sudden urge to just rip them right off you and drag you into the back seat."

Cindy smacked him playfully on the shoulder. "I can tell you're going to your high school reunion. You're already getting in the mood with all your trash talk and back seat memories—or should I say 'back seat fantasies.'"

"Ha, ha. If I had known you in high school, you would have been all over me. You would have been begging for that back seat."

Cindy hiked up her skirt to show a bit more thigh. "Oh, yeah? I think it would have been the other way around, buster. And I wouldn't have been easy, either. You would have had to work like a dog for it."

Mike chuckled. She was probably right.

They rode in silence for a while, both taking in the bustling activity of Yonge Street on a Saturday night. There was a lot of traffic—people out shopping for the weekend, heading to pre-Halloween parties, or just cruising around enjoying the city.

Mike drove north until he reached Sheppard Avenue. He turned left heading towards the residential area where his old high school was located. He marveled at how the Sheppard area of Toronto had changed over the years.

In 1974, the Sheppard/Yonge subway station was completed, opening up this vast area well north of Lake Ontario to the fast transit system direct to downtown Toronto—and all points in between. For him and his buddies back then, it was a godsend. It exposed their social lives to a whole new world. They were no longer stranded in the burbs—they could hop on the subway and head to where all the action was. Even in their later teen years when their parents bought them cars, they seldom used them to go downtown. It was so much easier, safer, and quicker to ride the "red rocket" as it was referred to back then when all the subway cars were red. Plus, they could drink and not worry about getting caught for impaired driving.

Then in 2002, the east-west corridor was opened up—the Sheppard subway line which connected to the north-south Yonge line, was greeted with ebullience by the people who lived in the northeast quadrant of the city. They could now ride underground along Sheppard, connect at the Sheppard/Yonge station, and then ride it all the way underground to Union station in the heart of the city's financial district. Commuting suddenly became a lot easier, which in turn opened up more housing districts, more shopping malls and an incredible array of amenities.

The subway brought North York out of the burbs and into being a self-contained city in its own right. The Sheppard/Yonge subway station was the centre of the universe for North York. It was a hub for commuters from east/west and north/south, and was connected to shopping, restaurants, bars, and apartment buildings. A person could live there, eat there, shop there, and ride to work from there—without ever stepping foot outside. Mike thought this was kind of neat but also, paradoxically, kind of twisted.

Mike graduated from his high school in 1984, and then went on from there to the University of Toronto to obtain his engineering degree. He and his classmates had actually attended one more year of high school than the students nowadays, since Grade 13 hadn't been eliminated until the late 90s. He was glad now that he had that extra year. High school had been fun, whereas university had been too serious…and impersonal. Plus, it was one extra year of playing football. He had played at university as well, but that was a different brand of ball, more intense, and without the school spirit and level of enthusiastic student support that high school typically brought to the sport.

He pulled into the parking lot. Once they were out of the car, Mike put on his long Abe Lincoln jacket, the Abe mask, and his stovepipe hat. Cindy laughed and clapped her hands. "You look fantastic—so authentic! Although, I think your shoulders are a lot wider than Abe's, going by the pictures I've seen of him. He never looked all that healthy."

"Well, I guess if I had to fight a Civil War, I probably wouldn't look too good either!"

Mike adjusted his tall hat, and they walked arm in arm up the front steps of the school. On the front of the building a banner was hanging: "Welcome Class of '84!" Mike smiled, and thought about how quickly those years had flown by. It was always bittersweet coming back to these reunions. People changed a lot during the intervening five years, and there were always a few who had died since the last reunions. The crowd got smaller every time. Some moved away, others just became apathetic and quit coming. There had been 400 kids in his graduating class—most of whom he never even knew— but Mike guessed that they would be lucky to have a hundred show up tonight.

At the registration desk they picked up their name tags and pinned them on each other. Mike quickly scanned the other tags on the table and noticed the names of quite a few of his old buddies. He also noticed names of several guys who he thought were dead. In fact, a couple of them he was sure had been dead for at least a decade. Mike scratched his head, puzzled, and tried to recall the faces in his mind.

"What's wrong, Mike?"

He put his arm around Cindy's waist and started leading her down the hall toward the gymnasium. "Nothing, hon. Just testing my memory with some of those names."

"By the way, you haven't noticed what I'm wearing." Cindy pulled a pendant out from under her cowgirl shirt.

"My God—you haven't worn that in years! It looks great, although I doubt that Annie Oakley could have afforded something like that."

Cindy kissed the diamond pendant and stuffed it back under her shirt. "No, you're probably right about that. However, I seldom get the chance to wear it so I decided to be wild and crazy tonight."

"That was your great-grandmother's, wasn't it?"

"Yes, it's very old but still so beautiful. I have no idea what it's worth now, but I don't care. I'll never sell it. It will be Diana's one day—and then her daughter's."

Mike kissed her forehead. "Don't go putting pressure on her now."

Cindy kissed him back. "I'm so happy to be out with you tonight, even if it's just this stupid reunion. It feels nice."

Mike smiled at his pretty cowgirl. "It sure does."

As they walked down the hall, Mike felt like he was still a student. Everything looked remarkably the same, and smelled the same. It took him right back. He could see himself hanging out with his buddies, flirting with the girls, making fun of the geeks. Just before turning into the gym, he saw his old locker. He pulled Cindy over to it and uttered the exciting revelation that this had been his. She whispered, "Tell someone who cares."

"Ah, you're no fun. If you knew how many girls leaned against this locker, chatting me up, you'd be furious."

Mike led the way into the gym, passing by several couples whose names he didn't recognize. One disadvantage of a costume reunion was that almost everyone had a mask on and the only way to identify them was to stare at their chests. He walked over to one guy whose build he recognized. He leaned over and read the nametag.

"Well, Bill Semen—are you still shooting? Pool, that is." He remembered poor Bill had always been given a hard time about his name. He was a good sport, though. And he had been a football player, so no one was able to push the kidding too far.

"Hello, Abe. Too bad you didn't attend school here. You could have helped a guy named Mike Baxter. He was never too honest."

The two old friends laughed, shook hands, and then went on to mingle some more. Mike checked from time to time to make sure that Cindy was keeping up with him. He knew she hated these things, but was being gracious about being introduced to everybody—people she really didn't care about.

After about an hour he had met six of his old teammates, and four ex-girlfriends. Cindy didn't seem to be too upset at the patronizing attention from his old flames, probably because they didn't look so flaming hot anymore. Mike thought that while cheerleaders were cool in high school, they sure didn't seem to age too well. He was darn glad he hadn't married one of them.

Several carts were now being wheeled in to the gym, stacked high with appetizers and pastries. The bar was open and a duo up on the stage had started singing soft background music, accompanied by an acoustic guitar player and a pianist. Mike looked around at the streamers hanging from the ceiling. He remembered being in this gym for games, dances, and assemblies. It seemed so long ago in some ways, and just like yesterday in others.

"Penny for your thoughts?" Cindy was pulling at his jacket sleeve.

"Oh, sorry, hon. I was just remembering."

"I could tell."

Then Mike saw the guy he'd been hoping to see. His best friend in high school, and the last of the old teammates who he'd heard would be here tonight—Steve Purcell. He wasn't wearing a mask; in fact he wasn't wearing much of a costume at all. Steve obviously hadn't changed a bit—always the non-conformist. Didn't take orders. Did things his way. That tendency had helped to make him rich, and had made him one hell of a football player in his day. He was the guy Mike had always counted on in the backfield. Mike had been the quarterback. Steve had been his fullback. Steve always had Mike's back. If he had to throw his body in front of a 300 lb. attacker to save Mike's hide, he would do it. Then bounce back up and do it again. The two of them had made a legendary combination on the field. They became the most famous of all of the players.

It was sad. They never kept in touch anymore. They had gone their separate ways and probably each of them recognized that high school was the only thing they had in common now. Those five magical years, those five carefree years. It seemed to happen that way with most people. The friends you kept for the rest of your life were the ones you met during the next two stages after high school—college and work. Seldom did high school connections remain. Mike wondered if sociologists had ever done a study on why that was.

Steve didn't recognize him because he looked like Abe Lincoln. Mike pulled off his hat and mask, walked over to Steve and spread his arms out wide. "Come to Papa!"

Steve's face said it all. He was beaming. He grabbed Mike around the shoulders and shook him. "How the hell have you been without me protecting your scrawny ass?"

"Could be better—but at least I don't have to apologize for your lousy attitude anymore!"

The two friends embraced and laughed almost as hard as they used to. At least back in high school they could break out into uncontrolled guffaws without having to worry about popping a hernia.

"And you brought your lovely wife again!" Steve reached for Cindy's hand.

"Cindy, you remember Steve Purcell? And if you don't, I think you've heard me talk about him before."

Cindy laughed. "Only about once a week! Nice to see you again, Steve."

"The pleasure's all mine." Steve bowed. Mike was about to ask about his wife and caught himself. He remembered that Steve had lost his wife to cancer about a decade ago.

Mike and Steve spent a few minutes catching up on the years, with Cindy politely listening in, nodding, and smiling at the appropriate times. Mike could tell she was trying hard to stifle a yawn.

Steve put his arm around Mike's shoulders. "Listen, old buddy. I think I'm getting old."

Mike turned to him. "I've got news for you, Steve—you're already old."

"I'm not kidding. Help me out here. I've seen a couple of 'dead guys walking.' Didn't Phil Wilson die several years ago? And Jason Wetlaufer too?"

Mike poked his finger into Steve's chest. "I thought the same thing. I saw their nametags out on the reception desk, and I thought I was going crazy. I mean, I didn't know either of them that well, but I could have sworn I'd heard that they'd died. And they weren't at the last reunion five years ago."

Steve pointed. "Well, Phil's over there—the tall guy wearing the gunslinger outfit, long coat and the Clint Eastwood mask. And Jason is that stocky guy near the bar—see him? He's dressed like Dillinger, or Capone, or some gangster like that."

Mike looked over at both guys and studied them for a few moments. "Funny thing, Phil was short and Jason was tall. These guys were the exact opposite. Maybe they switched nametags to have a little fun with people?"

Steve shook his head. "I don't know. I'm just glad I'm not the only one who thinks these guys are supposed to be dead. I feel better now." The two friends laughed. A half hour passed by quickly while the two old buddies reminisced about their glory years. They each enjoyed their scotches and the occasional little sandwiches that passed by on platters.

Finally, Mike could feel a tug on his jacket cuff—the tug that he knew would eventually come. Cindy whispered. "Would you mind if we went home soon? I'll make it worth your while."

That was all Mike needed to hear. He could be bribed. He'd had enough reminiscing anyway. Enough to hold him over for the next five years.

"Steve, we have to run. It's been great seeing you again. Don't be a stranger."

"Yeah, yeah, I know. We'll do lunch sometime, right?" He chuckled.

"Yeah, the famous old exit line. We always say that and then five years goes by. Maybe we should really do it this time." Mike handed Steve a business card. "Phone me when a day looks good for you. We can catch a bite downtown. We're only a few blocks away from each other."

"I will. I promise. Nice seeing you again, Cindy. Thanks for putting up with our old jock talk. It must be nauseating sometimes, eh?"

"Nice seeing you too. And yes, it does grate on me after a while. But it sure is nice to see the pride you guys have for each other, and for what you did together. So, that's a good thing!"

Steve held up her hand and kissed it. "Thanks. Mike's a lucky guy."

At that, Mike and Cindy made their way out of the gymnasium and headed back down the hallway. It was empty except for one man—at least Mike thought it was a man—dressed in a grim reaper costume. Mike nodded as he passed. "Good night." He caught a quick look at his nametag and his stomach did a flip-flop. Richard Saunders, another dead guy. This was too strange.

"Excuse me, sir. Are you leaving?" Richard was calling after him.

Mike turned around. "Yes, we are. And you know me, Richard. Mike Baxter, remember?"

"I do not think I remember you, Mike." The man bent forward and gazed at his nametag. "But if you are indeed Mike Baxter, you will please go back into the gym."

The man had an accent. So, aside from Richard being dead, the accent was another reason why this was not Richard Saunders. Mike couldn't see his face due to the mask, but he noticed that his hands were dark. He must be a party-crasher along with his other two friends, Capone and Eastwood.

All of a sudden, he could hear a commotion coming from the gym: shouting, heavy footsteps—like people running, a couple of screams. He figured some rowdy fun was just starting up, as it usually did at these reunions. He was a little disappointed that he was going to miss it. But, he had some rowdy fun of his own coming to him once they got home, so that was some consolation.

"We're leaving now, whoever you are. I don't know what you mean by telling me we have to go back into the gym." Mike grabbed Cindy's hand, turned, and headed toward the school's front door at a brisk pace. That guy was nuts.

Mike was looking to his side, trying to see if the reaper was following them, when he heard Cindy gasp and felt her stop dead in her tracks. He looked in the direction she was looking. Another reaper stood just inside the front door, holding a machine gun pointed right at them.

Mike whirled around. The other reaper behind them now had a gun out too. Mike recognized both guns as Uzis. These weapons could shred them to pieces in a matter of a second or two. He felt Cindy's hand trembling in his. Or was that his hand?

"What do you guys want?" Mike asked, feeling his mouth quickly turning to sandpaper.

The eerie-looking mask answered. "I have already told you." He nodded his head back down the hall. "The gym—now!"

Chapter *31*

David Samson loved the sound of creaking bed springs. He couldn't enjoy sex unless he pounded hard enough to hear the springs, or even just the banging of the headboard against the wall. Those sounds always reinforced his feeling of power, and of course the absence of power from the woman underneath.

Tonight the woman underneath was Fadiyah. She was always a convenient distraction when he needed to calm down. She wasn't *his* woman as the other men thought she was; she was just obedient, beautiful and available. David didn't have one woman of his own; he had many women and most of them were just white whores. Fadiyah was a whore too, but a whore for Allah. She had convinced herself as a young girl in the West Bank that she was performing his work. All by herself, using her whoring and killing skills, she had been directly responsible for the deaths of no less than fifteen Mossad agents before she left the Middle East to assume her new duties in Canada. She was a loyal and skillful soldier. David knew only too well that if she thought he was a threat, she was capable of killing him with her bare hands within mere seconds.

Normally David would be ashamed of himself for fucking an Arab woman—he considered that slumming. White women were more satisfying to him. Fucking a whitey gave him the same kind of pleasure that an act of revenge or retaliation brought. It was a feeling of accomplishment—something he had been denied during a large part of his life in Canada. Going all the way back to the days when he was seen as a loser and a dirty little Arab.

But Fadiyah could not be considered slumming by any stretch of the imagination. David gazed down at the goddess lying beneath him: her Cleopatra-like face, green eyes and long black hair. Her skin was silky smooth and her shoulders and thighs perfectly sculpted—a subtle hint of all the training and deadly abilities she possessed in the muscle memory of her body. David found it rather exhilarating having sexual control over a woman whose killing skills were as deadly as his. It made an orgasm much more ecstatic than he ever experienced with the white sluts.

And Fadiyah was respectful to a man—she knew what a man needed and was fully prepared to make him feel special. One thing that David liked about Arab women was their willingness to fake orgasms. White women never did that. David needed to know that the woman underneath him feared and respected him enough to give him that satisfaction. He didn't care whether they actually climaxed or not—what he cared about was them wanting him to think they were satisfied. That demonstrated the pinnacle of respect.

He rolled off to the side, and glanced at the clock on the side table. It wouldn't be long now—phase one would be finished and he would receive a text message, photos and video footage from Omar. Then the men would be on to the second and final phase—the main event.

David felt Fadiyah's soft hand rubbing his chest. He turned his head and smiled at her. She smiled back. She knew something big was going on tonight, but she knew none of the details. Each of David's operatives knew only what they needed to know for whatever operation they were involved in.

David felt the stiffness returning. He rolled back on top of her heavenly body, anxious to hear the sound of the bed springs again.

*****

Mike held his arms around Cindy as she buried her face in his chest. He could feel her trembling and the wetness of her tears was soaking through his shirt. He looked around at the group of aging alumni assembled in a large tight circle in front of the stage. Most of them still had their masks on, which added a surreal quality to the horrifying scene.

Clint Eastwood, Al Capone, and the grim reaper who had guided them back into the gym, were standing at strategic points around the group, each with their Uzis in hand. Then two more reapers walked into the gym, carrying the same weapons.

Mike glanced up at the band on the stage. The four of them looked petrified. For a split second Mike saw himself up on that same stage decades ago, receiving his diploma to a round of cheers from the audience. Back then the stage seemed to him like Carnegie Hall. Right now it just seemed like something evil.

Clint Eastwood signaled to the other four. They each removed their masks, and the grim reapers tore off their capes. Mike watched as they transformed the capes into satchels, tightening the drawstrings that were sewn into the fabric. One of the reapers had a machete attached to his hip.

Now that the masks were off Mike could tell that they were all Middle

Eastern. They moved with a precision that was military-like. Calm, organized and in control. Mike wrestled in his mind with the only possible question: 'What did they want?' This was a high school reunion, not exactly a terrorist target or a great choice for a robbery. Mike was also really concerned that they had removed their masks. That wasn't a good sign. They obviously weren't afraid of being identified or described to police. He dearly wished they had kept their masks on, as he feared now that these thugs intended to commit a slaughter. Mike leaned down to Cindy's ear and whispered, "It's going to be alright. Don't worry."

"You—shut up! You will only talk when I speak to you!" Clint Eastwood was pointing his gun in Mike's direction. "Do you understand?"

Mike kept his cool. "Yes, I understand." In fact, contrary to what he had whispered to Cindy, Mike was terrified. He wasn't at all sure things were going to be alright.

Clint Eastwood moved around closer to the stage and held his Uzi up high so everyone could see. "You will all do as you are told. My men will walk around with their satchels and you will deposit your cell phones and your jewelry. Do not disobey."

The three former reapers circulated through the crowd while Eastwood and Capone stood guard. The steady clink of cell phones, watches, and jewels banging against each other dominated for the next couple of minutes. No one resisted. No one said a word. Mike dropped his watch, wedding ring and cell phone into the satchel, and Cindy followed suit, with shaky hands removing her bracelet, wedding and engagement rings. Mike noticed that Cindy had somehow found the time to button her Annie Oakley blouse right up to her throat; she was clearly hiding the heritage necklace. He cursed to himself and prayed that none of the men had noticed.

When they were finished they pulled the drawstrings tight and stashed the three bags close to the gym door. "Now, we are going to have some special evening entertainment." Clint was the only one doing the talking—he was clearly the leader of the group. "I will walk around and tap some of you on the shoulder. Each of you who have been so honored will then walk up onto the stage. And we need some music." He pointed his gun at the foursome on the stage. "Nice soft music if you please?"

The band started playing a shaky rendition of 'Midnight Rhapsody' and Clint began his stroll. He walked around the cluster of people, carefully examining each one. It looked to Mike as if he was reading the nametags. A total of twelve people had been tapped by the time he arrived at Mike. "And you will be the last—you will be our lucky number thirteen, no?" Instead of tapping Mike on the shoulder he poked him hard in the chest.

Mike unwrapped his arms from Cindy. "No, Mike—don't go," she cried softly.

"It's okay, hon. We'll do as they say. Don't worry." Mike looked back at her as he began his walk to join the others up on the stage. She had her hands over her mouth and he could see that her knees were shaking. She looked so alone.

The group on stage consisted of all men. Mike's seven teammates from the football team had been chosen, along with five other athletic-looking guys that he remembered only vaguely. Mike stood beside Steve Purcell, who simply nodded to him. Steve didn't look scared at all—instead he had the determined look of a man who was planning something. Mike whispered, "Don't even think about it, Steve. They'll kill you for sure." Steve looked at him and nodded, lips pursed together in an angry pout.

Mike looked out over the audience and could see that all of the partiers had now removed their masks. Most faces were covered in sweat, probably more from the stress than the heat. Their eyes looking up at the group on the stage reflected the paralyzing fear that Mike was feeling. He could see that Cindy still had her hands over her mouth, trembling, fingers twitching. Mike also noticed that Capone now had a camera phone out aimed at the group on the stage, his other hand firmly gripping his Uzi.

Eastwood moved closer to the edge of the stage and pointed his Uzi up at the terrified musical foursome. "I want us to hear that song, 'Moon River'. It will be appropriate." The band immediately complied.

The big man then addressed the thirteen hapless alumni standing on stage. "You will each quickly remove all of your clothes—all of them—and throw them down here."

Mike and the other twelve just stood there stunned—as if they hadn't heard the command. No one made a move to obey. Eastwood glared at them for a second then calmly flicked a switch that changed his Uzi to single shot from automatic. He turned and fired a bullet into the head of one of the hostages standing near him. The man dropped like a sack of cement, most likely dead before he hit the floor. Blood was pouring out of the side of his head, pooling quickly around him. His eyes were wide open, staring ahead seemingly in bewilderment. There was a collective scream from the audience of partiers, with several scampering backwards from the dead man as if afraid of becoming infected.

Mike felt the blood drain from his face. He couldn't believe what he had just witnessed. He glanced down at Cindy and could see that she was now kneeling on the floor, head resting in her hands, rocking from side to side. He could tell that she was crying—probably approaching a state of shock.

Mike and the other twelve quickly and silently removed their clothes and tossed them down to the gym floor. Eastwood motioned to one of the reapers, who retrieved a garbage can from the corner of the gym. He stuffed the clothes into the can and carried it over to the door beside the three bags of jewelry and cell phones.

Eastwood spoke. "Now that you are all naked, we are going to do a re-creation of the degradation that you westerners inflicted on our brothers and sisters at Iraq's Abu Ghraib prison. You all remember those humorous photos, do you not? Yes, of course you do—the entire world remembers those photos. You all probably had a good laugh, no? So, just like in the photos, you will form a human pyramid of naked, sweating, squirming bodies. Start now please."

There was no hesitation. The biggest men voluntarily knelt forming the bottom layer of the pyramid, and the others followed forming layer upon layer, until Mike and Steve finally climbed their way to the top. Mike could hear the grunting and groaning of the men underneath him, particularly the four brave guys at the bottom.

The pyramid held for about a minute until the men below couldn't take the weight any longer. The structure collapsed and they all tumbled to the floor. Mike could hear Eastwood laughing. He struggled to his feet and noticed Capone still with the camera phone, holding it up high to catch the drama.

Cindy was still kneeling and sobbing loudly. The noise caused Eastwood to turn his attention to her. He grabbed her by the hair and yanked her to her feet. Mike's stomach felt like it was in his throat. Watching the brutal killer with Cindy's hair entwined in his fingers caused a now familiar feeling to creep back again. Mike's muscles started to tense and he could feel the usual rush of adrenaline surge through his veins. It was happening.

"Now little lady, what are you crying about?" Eastwood held Cindy's head upright by the hair, pulling her face to within a few inches of his. Then he looked down. "What is this? I see a suspicious glint just under those buttons." He put his hand at the top of Cindy's blouse and ripped it down, exposing the necklace and her breasts. Her bra was dangling to her waist after being torn along with the blouse.

"My dear, you were holding out on us, no?" He slipped his fingers under the necklace and yanked with a thrust so powerful that Cindy's head snapped forward and banged into Eastwood's chin. Eastwood threw the necklace to the floor in anger, and slapped Cindy so hard across the face that she flew backwards into several other stunned hostages.

Mike was in mid-air, his naked body flying off the stage feet first, aiming for Eastwood's head. The feet connected with their target just as the shocked Arab turned his face towards him. They both went down but Mike got up first, pummeling him with his fists. Eastwood staggered backward, and Mike could see him reaching to his waistband where his Uzi was tucked. The thug was so far back from him now that Mike knew he wouldn't have time to reach him before the gun was out. A sinking feeling came over him—but then something else came over him too. Steve Purcell.

He came soaring headfirst in a flying block just as Steve used to do in their football days—Steve to the rescue, protecting his quarterback. Eastwood went down again with Steve rolling off to the side. Mike advanced…then stopped dead in his tracks. One of the reapers jumped between him and his master, leveling his Uzi at Mike's chest.

"No! Do not shoot! He was just defending his lovely wife. I admire that." Clint came up to his man and put a hand on his shoulder, then whispered something in his ear. He nodded at one of the other reapers, the one with the machete dangling from his waist. The reaper turned away from Mike and walked over to Steve who was just starting to get to his knees. The reaper held him there and put the gun to his head.

"Go ahead and put a bullet in his little brain," commanded Eastwood. Mike could see Steve's eyes widen with fear as he looked up at his assassin, silently pleading for mercy. The other reaper, the one with the machete, was standing behind him now, out of Steve's view.

Suddenly Eastwood laughed. "We are kidding around with you, sir. Funny, no? How do you say—just fucking with you? Ha." The reaper with the gun lowered it from Steve's head and backed up. Steve looked up at Eastwood with relief in his eyes. He mouthed "Thank you" just as the blow came from behind.

To Mike, the nightmare was in slow motion: the machete drawn from the reaper's waist and swinging backward over his shoulder, the glint of the steel as it came down in a perfect arc striking Steve across the neck in a smooth fluid motion. So powerful a swipe that the neck seemed to offer no resistance at all.

Steve's head detached cleanly, flipping into the air like a basketball and rolling onto the floor beside Cindy, spraying her with its blood. The headless body continued to kneel for what seemed an eternity, spouting blood upward like a chocolate fountain. Then it just collapsed like a lifeless rag doll, mimicking a macabre scene straight out of a horror movie.

For some reason Mike forced his eyes to look down at his old friend's head, lying on the floor staring up at him. He thought that the brain must have still been alive for a few seconds, as the mouth moved and the eyes blinked. A sickening and mind-numbing sight.

To the deafening sound of the screams of terror from the crowd, Mike fell to the floor, his legs feeling like rubber. He'd heard screams in this gym before, but they were happy screams, cheering screams. Never screams of despair and agony.

Mike Baxter, former high school hero, naked to the world and now changed forever by the unspeakable horror of what he had just witnessed, lowered his head and retched.

Chapter 32

Omar and his team strode calmly to the gym door, gathering up the three satchels and the garbage can. His four comrades lugged the stuff out into the hallway, while Omar turned back to the stunned audience for one last message.

"You will please be smart and not attempt to leave. We will be connecting an explosive charge to this door. The door to the locker room is already rigged as is the door upstairs in the mezzanine. So, please just carry on with your party."

Omar turned and left the gym, chuckling to himself. He unwound a long chain from around his waist, and proceeded to wind it through the door handles making as much clanging noise as he could. Then he nodded to his men and the five of them walked down the hallway toward the front exit. They left the garbage can containing the clothes of the thirteen men on the floor outside the gym door.

As they were just about to exit the school, they heard a shout from behind them. "Hey, what's going on here? Did I hear a gunshot?"

Omar turned and saw an old man in a janitor's uniform walking towards them. He sighed, not having the time or patience for this distraction right now. He quickly slid the Uzi out from his belt, slipped the switch to automatic and ripped the hapless janitor to shreds in a matter of seconds.

Out in the parking lot, the five men quickly prepared for Phase Two. Omar opened up the hatch of the stolen, repainted, re-plated SUV and began handing out supplies to each of the men. First, they received remote detonators that resembled small garage door openers. The only discernible difference was that these units had safety switches. Omar double-checked to make sure that the safeties were all in the 'on' position. Each of the remote detonators also had the initials of each of the men written in felt markers on the back. It was important that they didn't get these detonators mixed up because they were each programmed to two separate explosive devices.

Omar realized that he still had his Clint Eastwood cowboy hat on—he pulled it off and flicked it like a Frisbee into the adjacent field.

Next he handed the men explosive belts that contained about two pounds of Semtex each, which was probably overkill since only about one pound had been needed to bring down Pan Am Flight 103 over Lockerbie, Scotland. Semtex was a very reliable form of plastic explosive, manufactured only in the Czech Republic. Omar's comrades in Libya were the largest purchasers in the world of this type of explosive. He thought it was ironic that the distinctive orange color of the material was identical to the color of life jackets.

Each belt also had the initials of each man marked on it, because every belt was programmed to a specific remote detonator.

Omar put his own belt on, clipped the remote to his buckle, and threw his Uzi machine gun into the trunk. The other men silently mimicked his moves. He then withdrew from the trunk small Uzi machine pistols, which could be hidden under their jackets much more easily than the submachine guns. He handed them out, with the caution, "Remember, only use if the mission will be otherwise compromised." Each man nodded his understanding. Omar motioned them to draw around him in a semi-circle. Together they synchronized their watches, then knelt in one last prayer.

Before getting into the car, the terrorist who had dressed as Al Capone pulled out his phone and forwarded a text message along with video attachments to their leader. Omar knew that Dawud would ensure that the images went viral on the internet immediately. Perhaps the events of tonight would make Canadians think twice next time before they foolishly supported the infidel Americans in cowardly attacks on Muslim nations like Afghanistan and Libya.

The bags containing cell phones and jewelry were thrown into the ample trunk, behind a massive package that was covered up with plastic. Omar withdrew one of the partier's cell phones, slammed the hatch shut and drove out of the school parking lot. Once he was three blocks away, he stopped the car and dialed 911.

When the dispatcher answered, Omar talked frantically in perfect everyday English without his usual accent. "We need help! A gang's attacked our party and killed two of our group. One had his head cut off!"

"Sir, calm down for a second. First, where are you?"

"Northern Reaches High School, west of Yonge just north of Sheppard. We're in the gymnasium. The bastards told us they've hooked up explosives to the doors!"

"We're on our way. Tell your group that no one is to touch the doors."

"Okay, hurry. Oh, they may still be in the building because we heard gunshots out in the hall. I think they killed someone else out there."

"Thanks for the warning, sir. I'll pass that along to the tactical squad."

"Some heart attacks amongst our group too—send as many ambulances as you can. There are about a hundred of us trapped in here."

Omar flipped the partier's cell phone shut and threw it out the window. He turned his head toward his comrades. "That should prove to be a major distraction. It will also nicely tie up emergency vehicles for a while, making Phase Two even more effective." The other four nodded silently to the sound of sirens that could already be heard in the distance.

Omar turned left on Sheppard and headed east towards Yonge Street. He talked as he drove, using the time to help organize the thoughts of his men.

"You each know that Yousef has secured ten pound Semtex bombs to the underside of five of the subway cars. The train has six cars in total. We will occupy cars one through four, and number six. Those are the cars that will have the bombs. You each know which car you are to be in." Omar looked at his watch. "We are going to be perfectly on time for our train. It comes through Sheppard/Yonge station heading south at 9:15."

He looked over his right shoulder to double-check that they were paying attention. Their unblinking eyes were locked on Omar's face.

"Exactly one minute after the subway doors close, you will each switch off the safety on your detonator and press the button. We will be in the tunnel at that time. You will make sure that you are standing in the subway car at its midpoint. When you press the button, two things will happen. First, your belts will explode instantly causing immense casualties in the cars. You will each be transported to Allah's arms as martyrs and heroes."

Omar stopped talking as he turned left on Yonge Street and watched for Spring Garden Avenue. At that street he made a right turn. Omar thought about Yousef, who was an explosives genius. It was too bad that he was now out of the country on his way back to Libya. He would have enjoyed seeing or even just hearing his handiwork. Until tonight Yousef had been employed by the TTC as one of their chief mechanics, which gave him easy access to the subway cars and the scheduling of trains coming back on line as well as those taken out of service for mechanical problems—problems that Yousef himself created as needed.

"The second thing that will happen with the press of your buttons is the activation of a fifteen minute delay detonation for the bombs under the subway cars. Your individual detonator is programmed to the bomb under your specific car. Fifteen minutes after you press the buttons all five bombs under the train cars will blow. The damage to the subway stations, the tunnels and the trains will be complete. As well, any emergency personnel responding to the first blasts will be incinerated." Omar paused a couple of seconds for effect, then calmly continued in his professorial tone.

"As soon as your belt bombs explode, the train will come to a stop and should be in the middle of the tunnel between Sheppard and York Mills stations at that time. The tunnels on this stretch of the subway are only six inches thick, constructed of pre-cast liners. They will be no match for our second bombs, and the streets and roads above will cave in."

Omar turned right onto Doris Avenue, then another right into the three-level underground parking garage of Sheppard Centre. He parked on the lowest level, about fifty yards from the door to the mall and subway access corridor. The lighting was poor in this area of the garage, which he was glad for.

He turned his head around and faced his crew. "When we get out of the car, I want four of us to stand at the back of the car to act as a shield, while Amjad arms the bomb in the trunk. It contains twenty pounds of Semtex and will catch people rushing from the mall and the station after the explosion. They will be seeking the safety of their cars and, God willing, they will not find that." Omar looked at Amjad. "I want the delay set at thirty minutes." Amjad nodded his understanding.

They got out of the car quickly, opened the hatch and Amjad crawled inside. Removing the plastic cover from the bomb, he went to work on the timer. Omar glanced at his watch. They still had plenty of time—the procedure should only take a couple of minutes.

The four of them were standing beside each other, shielding the work being done inside the car, when Omar suddenly heard the metallic echoing sound of a door opening down in the direction of the stairway to the subway. Then the clip-clop of heavy footsteps.

A few seconds later, a chubby security guard came around the corner making his rounds. Omar could hear the heavy breathing of the fat man as he got closer to their car. He stopped and stared at them. Omar had to admit to himself that it must have looked strange—four men standing at attention at the back of the car with the heels of another man sticking out of the trunk.

"What are you boys doing—waiting for a parade?" The man chuckled at his little joke.

"We are just waiting for our friend to change his shirt, then we are going drinking," Omar replied politely.

"I thought you types didn't drink. Can I look inside the trunk?"

Omar took a quick peek at his watch—9:05. He didn't have time for this. "Sure, take a look if you want." He stepped aside and the guard shuffled over. Once he brushed past him, Omar quickly flicked his wrist and a long thin knife snapped into the palm of his hand from under his shirt cuff. In one smooth motion, he buried the knife cleanly into the base of the guard's skull, severing his spinal cord. The man gasped and collapsed to the ground.

Omar addressed the other three men. "Quickly—drag him up to the front wall and shove him under the car!" He called in to Amjad. "Are you done?" Amjad crawled backwards out of the car. "Yes, all set for thirty minutes from now."

"Okay, let us go. We have not much time." He slammed the hatch door and locked the car. The others finished their dragging ritual, each gasping from the weight of the fat guard. Together they ran the length of the garage and took the stairs three at a time to the subway level. They slowed down as they reached the turnstiles, and inserted their tokens. Once on the southbound platform, they separated to points where they guesstimated their particular cars would stop. Omar went to the far end of the platform, as his assigned car was the front one. He took a quick glance at his Semtex belt and checked it to make sure it was on tight and that the receiver was not obscured.

His watch showed 9:13. The train would be at the station any time now. He glanced around the platform. It was moderately full. He knew that each car could hold 250 people including standing room. So, 1500 maximum per train. It wouldn't be that full tonight though. He guessed that there were perhaps 400 people on the platform. When the train arrived it would of course have passengers already on it, from the Finch station at the beginning of the southbound line. So, maybe a total death count of 600—not counting people standing on the platforms at Sheppard and York Mills stations, plus emergency responders, people in the parking garage and on the roads and sidewalks above. Omar thought that Allah would be happy with this.

He felt the whoosh of air through the tunnel before he actually saw the train. Then the sound became very loud as the subway rushed into the station.

The doors opened and some people got out. Omar looked down the platform and saw each of his men boarding their cars. He followed suit, satisfied that the plan was going to be successful. Nothing would stop them now.

He heard the warning chimes and two seconds later the doors closed. Omar marked the time on his watch. Exactly one minute to go. He was standing in the middle of the car, and he noticed he was close to the emergency door. There was a panel above the door encased in glass. Omar knew that the door could be opened by smashing the glass and pulling the lever. He hoped that no one would be left alive to be able to attempt that.

He glanced at his watch—ten seconds to go. Omar pulled the remote from his belt buckle, and flicked off the safety. When the countdown reached two seconds he leaned his head back and looked upwards, screaming at the top of his lungs, "Allah Akhbar!" Then, without hesitation, he pushed the button.

Chapter 33

The sound of several large explosions, microseconds apart, reverberated throughout the train. Then, almost simultaneously a violent rocking of the cars as they were derailed. The front car, Omar's car, scraped to a stop leaning on a forty-five degree angle against the side of the rounded tunnel wall. Random screams in the subway car degraded to shrieks of terror when the lights went out—then abruptly changed to muted sighs of relief when the dim emergency lights came on.

Omar opened his eyes hoping to see paradise. Instead he saw a nightmare. He was lying on his back against the far wall of the car that was tilted on its side in the tunnel. In fact, all of the passengers had been thrown against the same wall, and they were all looking up at the doors that were now on an angle above their heads.

Omar opened his coat to check what was obvious—his Semtex belt was still intact. He was still holding onto the remote detonator; he instinctively pressed it again. Nothing. It was faulty. Either that or the receiver connected to the plastic explosive was faulty. Not knowing which one had failed, he had to assume that the massive bomb attached to the underneath of the car was going to go off in about thirteen minutes.

It took a moment for it to sink in—he knew now that he wasn't going to die at the instant he commanded it. He would now have to wait to be blown to smithereens along with all these other pathetic souls. This was not the desired methodology of a suicide bomber. Omar raised his head and gazed down to the end of the car, through the glass and into the next car. It was utterly destroyed from what he could tell. It looked as if it had lifted upwards and landed on its side—the upward momentum of that car causing his relatively intact car to lurch over onto its side against the tunnel wall. At least one of his comrades had been successful, and perhaps all four of them. He had no way of knowing. And in about twelve minutes now, all five ten-pound bombs would explode. Omar was a brave man but he was terrified at the thought of waiting for that. He wished that right now he were with his comrades in Allah's presence, receiving his reward of beautiful virgins.

Then he began to rationalize. This was meant to happen. Allah had other plans for him. He was not supposed to die yet.

With that thought, Omar suddenly got his edge back. He was alert now with the realization that Allah had more work for him. It was Allah's wish that he survive. Omar's eyes flicked from side to side and upwards, planning his move. He looked down at his watch—ten minutes left. He had to get out fast if he was going to fulfill Allah's wish that he live.

He noticed that several pairs of eyes were glaring at him in the dim light. Then he remembered that he had drawn attention to himself by screaming at the moment he had pushed the button. This could be trouble. Two pairs of eyes were crawling toward him now. They belonged to two men wearing a rage that Omar recognized from many wars in the desert.

"Grab him—he did this!" Hands were pawing at him now, scraping at his face, fists pummeling him. Omar managed to reach his hand down to his belt and pull out the Uzi machine pistol. He switched it to single shot not wishing to waste ammunition, and fired at both men in a quick swivel motion. They slumped to the floor as the screams in the car resumed, even louder than when the lights went out. The people closest to him scampered away on their hands and knees while the door to the driver's cubicle suddenly swung open. Out came the driver raising a baseball bat above his head. Omar calmly leveled the gun in the man's direction and put a single bullet in his forehead.

He could feel the eyes of everyone upon him as he struggled to his feet and swung himself upwards towards the emergency door, using the poles as leverage. Omar shoved the gun back in his belt, held onto the doorframe with one hand and swung his free fist into the glass emergency panel. Then he pulled the lever and held his breath. There was a creaking sound and the double doors slowly parted and stopped. They allowed him only two feet of space. Omar sucked in his gut and squeezed upward through the narrow opening, then jumped to the ground. He took another look at his watch—eight minutes to go until five massive explosions rocked this tunnel.

Omar was in good shape and a very fast runner; a skill that was even more important to him now than when he had raced in the Olympics for his home country Egypt twelve years ago. He looked north up the tracks. Yes, the other bombs had done their jobs. The tracks were blocked the entire length of the train by the derailed cars. Omar could only imagine what would happen in eight minutes when five bombs that were five times as powerful went off.

He had no choice—the tracks were impassible heading north to Sheppard station, so he would have to run south to York Mills. A no-brainer decision anyway. There was another bomb scheduled to go off in about sixteen minutes back in the parking garage at Sheppard Centre.

Omar stripped off his Semtex belt and threw it onto the tracks. Then he ran full tilt down the tunnel towards York Mills, being careful to avoid the electrified third rail. It was covered with wood, but the side of the rail was open and if he slipped and his foot just touched it he would be barbecued. Allah would not be pleased at such a pitiful waste. He had given him a second chance and Omar intended to take it.

The tunnel was dark, but there was some lighting along the way. As he rounded a corner in his sprint, he could see the station platform of York Mills looming ahead. He stopped and pulled out his machine pistol. The magazine was still almost full and he had a spare one in his pocket. Omar switched the pistol back to automatic, put the safety into the 'on' position and shoved the gun under his belt. He knew that if he were hindered in any way in his escape, he would need the shock value of a dozen bullets per second. 'Automatic mode' was brutal, but effective.

He took another look at his watch. Six minutes to go. He resumed his run, settling into a steady powerful pace along the dirt and asphalt between the tracks. The light of the station was getting closer. He could now see the safety gate at the junction between the platform and the tunnel wall. Visible now were curious people who had no doubt heard the explosions down in the tunnel. Their heads were leaning out over the platform edge, trying to peek down into the cavernous darkness to see what the commotion was. Or perhaps, Omar thought, the silly people were just impatient wondering what was holding up their precious train.

He stretched his legs out in a sprinter's stride digging at the ground beneath him. He imagined in his mind other sprinters racing beside him, their elbows practically touching, breaths coming in short puffs, chests thrust forward to snag the finish line. He urged himself on and could hear the Olympic crowd cheering—not for him of course but for the American beside him who was inching ahead. Omar grunted and panted and somehow found the power to reach the finish line first.

This time however the finish line consisted of a metal gate that he had to throw himself over to reach the platform. He dove headfirst in his familiar high-jump style, adjusting cleanly on the other side into a somersault position. Out of the somersault he landed on his feet, but the gun went flying. The platform was crowded with people who started backing away from him quickly when they saw the gun. Several of the astonished people closest to him gasped and a small crowd started running for the exit.

His big problem now was the gun, and the fact that two men were advancing towards him with one of them scooping up the gun on their way. Omar could run for it but his chances of getting away would be slim without the gun, being pegged now by every witness as a perpetrator. And the police would soon be there. And if he surrendered to these 'Captain Americas' walking toward him, he would be held for the police and simply die along with the rest of them in the next explosion which was mere minutes away. There was only one option.

Omar raised his hands in response to one of the men shouting, "Citizen's arrest!" That man held the gun on him while the other went behind and held him by the arms

In a move so quick that neither of his arresters had a chance to even digest what was happening, Omar thrust himself forward and down, head-butting the guy with the gun while in the same move locking the arms of the man behind him and throwing him over his shoulders into his head-butted buddy. The two men lay stunned on the floor as the gun slid away. Omar dove to the floor to retrieve it but suddenly another hero appeared on the scene. A tall, athletic-looking guy with a shaven scalp confidently picked up the gun and pointed it down at Omar's head. "You stupid camel-fucker." He smiled and pulled the trigger…but nothing happened. In a panic he looked down at the gun and started fiddling with it.

To Omar's luck, safety switches weren't quick and easy to find on Uzis. From his lying position on the ground, he swung his right leg toward the skinhead's knee, snapping it instantly. The man went down screaming in pain. Omar quickly got to his feet and yanked the gun from his hand. "See, there is a safety here that you forgot about. I think you are the stupid camel-fucker, no?" Omar switched off the safety and fired three rounds into the man's face.

More screams and people running.

Omar turned now to the two men he had thrown to the ground. They were just starting to struggle to their feet. One of them held his hands up and pleaded, "Take it easy man, no sweat here." Omar fired the Uzi again, this time several rounds at the chest, bellies and crotches of the two would-be heroes, practically splitting them down the middle.

The platform was in a state of utter chaos now. Horrified people were scattering in all directions, dropping their parcels and covering their heads.

Some ran for the exits, but others actually jumped down onto the tracks. Fatefully, a few of them ran the wrong way into the tunnel, facing certain death in just a few minutes time.

Omar turned and ran toward the exit, glancing at his watch as he moved. He had three minutes to go. He popped the almost empty magazine out of the pistol, shoved a fresh one in, and slid the bolt on the top. This time he kept the gun in his hand because he was certain he would have to use it again.

He muscled his way through a crowd of people trying to make the stairs, then took those stairs three at a time. On his way up he saw the blur of two policemen in the adjacent stairway, on their way down. They stopped and began to pull their guns. Before they even had their straps unbuckled Omar cut them down. He continued on his breakneck pace toward the exit. He could see the doors now, and the darkness of night outside. He leaped over the turnstiles and came face to face with another police officer. He had his gun out but only at hip-height. Omar brought his Uzi up to the man's face but couldn't pull the trigger. The officer was Arab, and something passed between them. The officer's eyes seemed to convey understanding, and Omar thought he detected a slight nod of his head. Omar ripped the gun out of the officer's hand, and pushed past him.

He had finally reached the fresh air of the street, and Omar drank it in as he ran. He crossed on a red light, deftly dodging traffic, and sprinted down Wilson Avenue. After about fifty yards he stopped and turned around to face back towards Yonge Street. No one was following him. He could see people still streaming out of the York Mills station, but there was no attention being paid to him anymore. Instead, people were running from a danger they didn't yet understand.

He looked at his watch. They would understand it in about ten seconds. Omar counted down. Precisely at three seconds to go, he heard a loud rumble and felt a vibration under his feet as the shockwave traveled through the ground. At first there were no visible signs of the calamity that had just occurred underground. Then, slowly but surely, the signs appeared.

First there was a loud whoosh of the air and dust that pushed out of the open doors of the York Mills subway station. Some people that had still been inside came tumbling out with the pressure. Then the sound of glass breaking as the doors and windows of the station shattered. Omar moved his eyes now to Yonge Street, looking northbound—the exact path that the subway underneath took. He could see a trembling of the ground, then the road and sidewalk pavement heaving briefly before collapsing to the tunnel underneath, taking cars and people with it. Like a domino, the same effect was seen all the way up the street as far as Omar's eyes could see. He knew this destructive pattern would continue all the way to the Sheppard station, and in about eight minutes their final bomb hidden in the stolen car would detonate, causing death and chaos in the Sheppard Centre.

Omar smiled. It was a good night—a night to remember. He had lived to see it all, and had never expected to. Allah had allowed him to survive for what must be an even higher purpose. He would discover in good time what the plan was. Omar was ready to serve as long as he was needed.

He looked up to the stars and marveled at their beauty. Then, for the second time that night he screamed at the top of his lungs, "Allah Akhbar!"

Chapter 34

Halloween weekend was erased from the calendar. No one in Toronto could remember Halloween ever being ostensibly cancelled before. There was a slight drop-off in traffic the Halloween after 9/11, but aside from that, it always took place; rain or shine, recession or prosperity. Fear, in its most irrational form, had paralyzed the city this time.

In the days after the event, it was hard to find an article in the local and national newspapers about anything else. Television and radio broadcasts predictably discussed the terrorist attack ad nauseam, which simply exacerbated the fear level. People were afraid to leave their homes, take a bus, go to work, or go to school. And the subways, understandably, were empty for at least a week.

When the stock markets opened on the Monday after the attack, the TSX had lost 500 points by the close of the bell and when the downward trend continued on into Tuesday, the exchange was closed to all trading activities for the rest of the week. The NYSE also lost ground that first week due to the proximity and cultural similarities between Toronto and New York.

Toronto was flooded with counterterrorism experts from the FBI, CIA, CSIS, and the RCMP. The Mounties took the lead in the investigation, but a true team effort between all parties was developing that was even stronger than what the world had seen after 9/11. By the second week, officers from Britain's MI5 and MI6 had arrived, quickly followed by Germany's BND.

Initial death estimates quickly became redundant as more and more people were reported missing. After two weeks of rescue and recovery the death toll exceeded 1,500, making the Toronto subway bombing the world's second deadliest civilian terrorist attack ever. The dubious honor of being champion remained with 9/11 at 3,000 deaths.

The fact that now a second horrific attack had taken place on North American soil disturbed the feeling of relative security that Americans and Canadians had settled into in the years following 9/11. The huge amounts of money spent on security and the seemingly endless aggravating precautions at airports had not prevented this one. The attack was brazen and had flown right under the radar. It was a subway, and while being an obvious target to even the uninformed, for some reason subways had not yet been forced to endure the intense scrutiny airports had been put under. This, despite the 2004/2005 train bombings in Madrid and London.

The damage was extensive and mind-numbing. The southbound tunnel between York Mills and Sheppard was completely destroyed; the thin sections of concrete and the earth above had collapsed all along the one kilometer stretch of track. No one was found alive in the train cars underneath. If the riders hadn't been killed immediately by the multiple blasts, they smothered to death in the earthen tomb. Lying in the cavernous stretch of carnage were also about a hundred vehicles that had been innocently driving along Yonge Street when they tumbled down into the chasm that suddenly opened beneath them. The bodies of pedestrians who had been unlucky enough to be simply strolling along the sidewalk above, were also found strewn amidst the rubble below.

Both subway stations were severely damaged from the chain reaction of the tunnel concrete pulling down other structural members, not to mention the shock wave that had reverberated down the tunnel resulting in more collapses far from the stricken train. Only a handful of survivors were pulled out of the station platforms.

The cruelest cuts of all were the deaths of dozens of emergency responders who came racing into the tunnel after the first bombs exploded. As they went about the dangerous task of pulling survivors from the train, the massive bombs underneath the subway cars exploded, obliterating any living thing in and above the tunnel.

Then in similar flytrap fashion, shoppers and subway patrons who had raced in panic out of the Sheppard station into the Sheppard Centre mall and down to the safety of their vehicles in the garage, were all crushed to death as a massive car bomb exploded—pancaking the three parking levels.

No group had officially claimed credit for the attack, but the CIA announced that it bore the signature of an Al Qaeda operation, and that suspicious chatter had been picked up—which indicated it was indeed that mysterious and elusive group. The public was not surprised as Al Qaeda seemed to be responsible for everything bad that happened in the world. Most water cooler conversations after the event had eyes rolling and the sounds of sardonic chuckling whenever the words Al Qaeda were mentioned.

The investigation had quickly and painstakingly retraced the crucial aspects of the operation, and the news media reported on the chronology as it became known to them. The operation was reluctantly hailed as having been extremely well planned and executed, starting with a hostage-taking of attendees at a high school reunion near the Sheppard subway station. The RCMP deemed this to be a diversionary attack, to draw police and emergency personnel away from the main event. Three people had been summarily executed at the school, with one being decapitated. Some of the people at the reunion had been ordered to disrobe and form a naked pyramid in front of the others. A video of the school attack went viral over the internet that same night.

The terrorists then drove from the school to the Sheppard subway station, parked in the lowest level of the parking garage and armed their car bomb, pausing only long enough to stab to death a security guard who must have tried to intervene. They then boarded the 9:15 southbound train; timing was important—they had to be on that particular train. While in the tunnel, the attackers detonated their belt bombs, causing the train to derail and most of the passengers to perish. Investigators deduced that the same remote transmitters caused a delay detonation of the huge bombs mounted underneath the subway cars, as they didn't explode until fifteen minutes later. Authorities believed that those bombs had been installed by an Iranian national named Yousef Nasser, who was a chief mechanic with the TTC. It was discovered that he had fled Canada on a flight the very night of the attack; the flight's ultimate destination being Tripoli, Libya.

The signature of the explosive residue indicated that Semtex had been used. There were five bombs and five terrorists, but it was apparent that the terrorist in the front car had failed to detonate his belt bomb. His unexploded belt was found on the tracks under the rubble. Video footage that streamed into TTC headquarters caught this man diving up onto the York Mills station platform from the tunnel. This footage was shown extensively on the television news in hopes that members of the public might come forward with any tips as to his identity. He was now the most wanted man on the planet.

This one terrorist was also filmed shooting to death three men on the platform who had attempted to stop him. And on his escape from the station, the video feed showed him executing two police officers on the stairway.

Immediately after viewing the video the city police launched an aggressive street by street, door to door search for this man within the twenty mile radius around the York Mills station. This search would continue indefinitely.

To assist in their quest to capture the terrorist, the RCMP began conducting interviews with all of the people who had attended the Northern Reaches High School reunion. Despite their harrowing experience, the police felt that someone might remember something that could help. The terrorist attack had shaken Toronto to its core. In fact, it had shaken the entire country. Canada was not accustomed to being a terrorist target. Citizens were comfortable that their country's foreign policy had historically been benign at best. Not controversial, never a bully, proud of being peacemakers. Sure there had been terrorist threats before, most recently the amateurish 'Toronto 18' plot but that one was more like an episode of the 'Keystone Cops.' This subway attack however was in a different league—professional, creative, brutal, and militaristic in its execution.

But in the last few years something had changed with Canada's role on the world stage. More and more, Canada was being drawn into America's foreign adventures, and was being seen now by many nations in the Middle East as being an obedient little shadow of their mighty neighbor. No longer could Canada brag about being the North American equivalent of neutral Switzerland.

Afghanistan and Libya were questionable wars and Canada had been in the thick of both of them. Of course, NATO obligations were cited as the reason, but most people could see through that—Canada was too eager. There was a risk involved in interfering in other countries civil affairs, a risk that Canada perhaps was finally feeling first-hand. The risk was amplified by the universal recognition that friendly, peaceful, naïve Canada was a far easier target than its friend south of the 49th.

Chapter 35

"Quit babying me. I'm okay now. Go! Do something, anything!"

Mike let go of Cindy's arm and backed off, raising his palms up in surrender.

"Okay, okay. I'm just trying to help."

"I know, Mike. But I don't want you hovering over me."

Mike carried her duffle bag upstairs to the bedroom and Cindy followed. He went into the en suite and started running a bath.

"What are you doing that for?"

Mike looked back at her from his kneeling position in front of the bathtub. "Well, I thought that with just getting out of the hospital, you might like to take a warm bath."

Cindy knelt down beside him, cupping her hands around his neck. "You're so sweet, but this is what I meant when I said 'hovering.' I need you to give me some space for a while. Okay?"

Mike kissed her and surrendered again. "Alright. I'll be downstairs if you need me."

"I won't. I'm going to take a nice long nap in my own bed."

Mike went downstairs, poured himself an extra-long shot of scotch and stretched out on the sofa in the family room. He put on some soft classical music and laid his head back on the cushion. He thought about how good it felt to have Cindy home from the hospital. She seemed to have recovered her feisty spirit, which was encouraging. However, he was worried that she might be trying too hard to be her old independent self again. After the attack at the school Cindy had become completely unglued, swallowed up by a full-blown nervous breakdown. It had been two weeks now since she had been transported from the high school to St. Mike's Hospital by ambulance. On and off heavy sedation and daily sessions with Bob Teskey had brought her back fairly quickly from a near catatonic state.

Mike had moved back into the family home to look after the girls while Cindy was gone, and he intended to stay there now until Cindy gave him his marching orders. He prayed that after what happened, she would let him stay for good. He was afraid for her mental state even though she protested that she was all cured. Things like that didn't cure fast—they just got buried deep until something triggered them to come back to the surface again.

She hadn't talked at all about the horror they had endured at the school. Mike knew that seeing one man shot in the head and the other one beheaded—both right in front of her—must have been more than her sweet, kindly psyche could take. While she hadn't talked about the incident, Mike wondered if she thought about it—Steve Purcell's head, spraying her with blood as it rolled around like a macabre toy, coming to rest right beside her. A part of Mike hoped she was managing to block the image from her mind, but the other part of him wondered if that was a healthy thing for her to do.

He thought back to that night, how terrifying the whole ordeal had been for everyone. He even selfishly remembered the humiliation he had felt, being naked in front of all those people in the gym. He had been overwhelmed and self-obsessed with the memories of the ordeal right up until he and Cindy had arrived at the hospital from the high school. It wasn't until then that he heard of the horrific terrorist attack on the subway system that had happened just mere minutes after the terrorists fled the high school. He had listened to the news reports stating the obvious connection between the school incident and the terrorist attack. Once that reality had set in and he had digested the facts about the massive death and destruction in the subway, Mike had begun to feel guilty about the feelings he had been having about their own ordeal. Of course it was horrible in itself but it certainly paled in comparison. He knew he should have just been relieved that he, Cindy, and the others had been allowed to live. The school attack, luckily, had only been intended as a diversion for the 'center court' event.

The RCMP had been conducting interviews with most of the high school reunion attendees over the past two weeks. At Mike's request, they left him alone until Cindy was back from the hospital. They had agreed, since they had a ton of interviews to conduct anyway.

But they indeed wanted to talk to both of them eventually. Mike, however, was able to recruit Bob Teskey to intervene and help get a restraining order. So unless he, Mike, agreed to waive the restraining order and then only on Bob's advice, the RCMP would not be allowed to talk to Cindy. Revisiting the event could regress Cindy back into the throes of another complete breakdown. He couldn't afford to take that chance.

Mike had been watching news reports of the terrorist attack almost non-stop. He couldn't believe this had happened here—peaceful Toronto, non-confrontational Canada. But he had to admit things had changed a bit in the last few years. Canadian politicians had allowed the country to be dragged into adventures in Afghanistan and Libya, and was perhaps now being punished for those decisions.

Mike had scrutinized the videos of the lone surviving terrorist, running through the York Mills subway station killing several people along the way. While the videos did not give a completely clear view of the man's face, Mike knew without a doubt that it was the same guy who had posed as the Clint Eastwood character in the school gym. The same man who had shot the partier through the head, the same man who had sanctioned the beheading of Steve Purcell, and the same man who had either shot or ordered the shooting of the helpless janitor out in the school hallway. He was the same man. Tall, athletic, handsome…and Arab.

Mike got up from the sofa and poured himself another long scotch. He took a sip and savored the feel of the strong liquid as it burned its way down to his stomach. As he stood beside the window looking out at the backyard, he started thinking about his old friend, Steve Purcell. Their high school years were wonderful together—all the fights and scuffles they had gotten into, the illicit drinking of cheap wine in Mike's parents' garage, the parties, girls, exploits on the football field. They had been inseparable in those years, and Mike reflected on how sad it was that they had lost touch. The bittersweet memory of their promise to get together for lunch just before Steve had lost his life in such gory fashion, brought tears to Mike's eyes and tightened his throat in a vice grip.

He wandered over to the bookcase, selecting the high school yearbook for his graduating year. He realized that he hadn't even opened this book in at least ten years. Mike eased back onto the sofa, with his scotch and his yearbook. He began leafing through the pages until he got to the individual photos for the graduating class. There was Steve, looking ever so confident and ready to take on the world. And there was Mike in a photo right beneath him, looking even more confident.

He flipped to the next page. Suddenly his gaze was drawn to one photo. One that had a vaguely familiar quality to it—the eyes. He read the name underneath the photo, and for a second or two Mike stopped breathing, while being only slightly aware of the glass of scotch slipping from his hand and smashing to pieces on the floor.

Chapter *36*

While Mike crawled around on the carpet picking up broken glass particles, he had Jim Belton on the speakerphone.

"Jim, I need you to check something for me. Do you remember back several months ago when I got that condolence card from David Samson? You checked his file and told me that he had changed his name before being employed with us."

"Yeah, I remember that—but I don't remember the name.

"Can you check the file for me? I'll hold."

"Sure, give me a few minutes, okay?"

"Aw, Shit! Shit! Shit!"

"What? I told you it would only take a few minutes—hold your horses!"

"Naw, it's not that. I knelt on some broken glass—hurts like hell."

"Broken glass? I think you need to get back here to the office, Mike. You're not meant for this domestic stuff."

"No kidding. I'll be back in a couple of days. But right now, I need that name."

Mike waited while Jim clicked away on his keyboard at the other end of the line. Jim was right. He needed to get back to work—anything to take his mind off the horror. But he didn't want to leave Cindy alone until he knew she could handle it. And if he weren't here with her, she'd have to take care of the girls by herself as well. Might be too much for her right now. Maybe he'd hire a nurse.

Jim came back on the line. "Okay, his original name was 'Dawud Zamir.'"

"Shit..."

"More broken glass?"

"No...worse. I'll tell you and Troy about it when I'm back in the office."

Mike hung up the phone and slouched down on the couch. He pulled some tissues from the box on the end table and began dabbing away at his cut knee, now exposed by rolled up jeans. He stretched out and raised his right leg up onto the coffee table to slow down the bleeding. Then he started thinking back, way back…

Dawud Zamir—a name he'd forgotten completely, in fact a name he probably didn't even know at the time. Mike only made the connection with the eyes in the photo, bang-on the same eyes as David Samson. And a memory from months ago when Jim had told him the man's original name…that memory came back when he looked at the yearbook. He had just been this skinny Arab kid, a weakling, a nerd—different in so many ways from the rest of them. He became a target because of that, and only because of that. Mike couldn't think of any other single reason why he had been picked on. He was just 'the one,' the unlucky one. Every school had at least 'one.'

Mike remembered seeing the kid for the last time at graduation, when one of Mike's buddies stuck out his foot and tripped the poor guy on his way up to the stage. Mike laughed, as did everyone else in the audience. He hadn't given a single thought as to how humiliating it must have been for him. He was just a toy to be played with. After the graduation party, which Dawud did not attend, Mike did remember wondering if the kid would be okay. Did he know they were just kidding? Would he get over it? Over the decades since, he hadn't thought of him again.

The kid had been hassled for the full five years of high school, and he had never fought back—not even once. It was commonplace, and routine, to see guys smashing him into lockers, slapping him as he walked by, spitting on him in the halls, laughing at him in classes if he tried to answer a question. Mike hadn't participated in a lot of that stuff, but as one of the leaders in the school he had sanctioned it all by simply not intervening. He encouraged it, and laughed along with everyone else. He and Steve Purcell—two of the most respected guys in school, had organized an elite group of people who reveled in their individual and collective glory, and bullied other kids and particularly that one. No one cared, no one felt sorry for Dawud. He was just an Arab, after all. His feelings weren't considered—it was like, in Mike's mind, the kid didn't even have any feelings. He wasn't real—he was just a caricature.

Mike liked to fool himself into thinking that he personally hadn't done very much to him, but he knew that was his own way of letting himself off the hook. As the leader, he got it started, and could have easily stopped it. But he didn't because it was fun, and became a tradition, and it made him feel powerful. He remembered that his coup de grace prank was to strip the kid and throw him out into the gym during a basketball game full of spectators. What a hoot---they locked the door to the locker room and the kid was stranded, naked in front of half the school. He could still hear Dawud's voice, pleading for them to let him back in, his fists banging on the door, the kids laughing out there in the gym. Naked…

Mike snapped out of his trance and shook his head free of the cobwebs.

Christ, Samson had been sending him one hell of a message when he left him beaten and naked in that alley! And now this latest incident, naked in the gym, degraded in front of all of his old friends, old girlfriends, all the spouses. This was revenge, everything that had happened to him was revenge: the fake kidnapping of his girls, the embezzlement of his company, the incident in the alley. This Samson guy had sought him out and might have been following him for decades!

It was no coincidence that he had obtained a job with Mike's own company as one of their in-house lawyers. Working directly for Gerry and then being fired by Gerry. But somehow Samson had coerced Gerry, even after being fired, into cooperating with the purchases of the four worthless properties and funneling the money into a numbered bank account in Panama. What was the leverage? How could he possibly have forced Gerry to cooperate?

And Mike might never have discovered the deception, or at least not for a very long time, if Gerry had not been killed by the lightning strike. That's what caused Mike to get involved in investigating the properties in Brazil and Mexico.

Suddenly it hit him—like a ton of bricks! Mike grabbed the directory and looked up Amanda Upton's phone number. Apprehensively, he dialed her number.

"Hello?"

"Hi Amanda, it's Mike here."

"Oh, Mike. How is Cindy doing?"

"She's home now, and she thanks you for the flowers by the way. She'll probably call you later in the week."

"Will she be up for a visit? I popped in once at the hospital, but she wasn't in her right mind. I'd like to see her again now that she's home."

"I think she'd like that, Amanda. Wait until she calls you and you can set it up."

"I'll do that. And how are you doing? I'm just sick about what you guys went through, and what's happened to our city. It's very scary."

"It is, and I'm doing okay. Worrying about Cindy has probably taken my mind off the horror of it all. I'm sure it will all start sinking in soon. But… anyway, the reason I'm calling you—I need your help with some information. This might sound like a weird and insensitive request, but I'm hoping you'll help. It's really important."

"Just name it, Mike."

"Okay, brace yourself. Can you look up the dates of the deaths of your parents, your brother, and Gerry's two brothers?"

Silence.

"Amanda?"

"I heard you. I'm just...surprised, I guess. But, hold on. I'll get those dates for you."

In a couple of minutes Amanda returned and gave Mike the three dates. "Mike, whatever you're going to do with this information, I hope you'll respect the fact that I don't want to relive those times. Gerry's death is still so recent and I'm not over that yet. I sure don't want to add to it."

"Don't worry, Amanda. This is just for my own information—related to something I'm trying to figure out. Okay?"

"Okay, I'll take your word for it. Good luck. Give Cindy my best, and tell her I'll be calling her."

"I will. And Amanda, thanks so much for this."

Mike hung up the phone and went straight to his study. He opened the drawer of his desk and pulled out his duplicate file on the foreign land purchases. He sat down and began to examine the dates of the original offers on the land deals, and compared those with the dates of the deaths of Gerry's relatives. The first thing he noticed was that the shooting deaths of Amanda's parents happened one month after Samson was fired. He remembered that the police file had been closed, no one arrested, described as a botched robbery.

He looked at the next incident—Amanda's younger brother killed by a hit and run driver while crossing the street. No one had been arrested in that incident either. The paper in Mike's hand started to shake as he noticed that this death had occurred two months before the offer of purchase on the two Mexican properties.

Okay, on to the last two deaths—Gerry's two young brothers who were shot while on vacation in Puerto Vallarta, Mexico. They had been sitting at an outdoor patio on the main drag sipping their beers when a car came roaring past with a machine gun blazing. Four people were killed at the bar including Gerry's brothers. The other two victims were known drug dealers, so the file had been closed by the Mexican police as being just another drug shooting with two innocent bystanders taken down by accident. Mike's eyes started to well up as he noticed that these deaths were one month before the offer of purchase on the two Brazil properties.

He put down the files and leaned back in his leather chair. Rubbing his eyes, he let out a big sigh. The pieces were falling into place. This could have all been just an elaborate plan of revenge, using his company and his friend against him. If true, because of him the Uptons had lost several beloved relatives. Did Samson steal tens of millions of dollars and five lives—all because of a deep-seated hatred against him? In his gut, Mike knew that this was highly unlikely. Too elaborate, too slick. He was just a slice of the bigger pie.

Poor Gerry. He had no idea what this was all about. Samson's first act against him must have been killing Amanda's parents as punishment to Gerry for firing him. He needed to get Gerry's attention and that brutal act might have been the initiation. Then, once Gerry was sufficiently horrified at the implication, Samson would have then asked him to cooperate with overpaying for garbage properties and kicking the money back. Gerry most likely put up some resistance, and each time he did, more relatives were killed. So, under duress he went along with the scheme and kept quiet, knowing that his wife and kids could be next if he didn't. That was probably why he installed the elaborate security system and hired the armed security patrol. And Amanda never knew. Gerry kept it all bottled up inside.

So Mike wasn't imagining things when he had sensed a change in Gerry over the last few years. His friend had been feeling guilty and scared, with no one he could dare talk to. And no wonder he had resisted the company going public on the TSX—he had been afraid of more extensive audits possibly uncovering the embezzlement.

Mike's mind wandered back to the terrorists in the gym at the high school reunion. Making him and his fellow ex-football heroes strip naked—the very same gym where he had forced Samson/Zamir to do the same thing when he was a skinny teen. The reality was setting in on Mike's brain now. It was hard to believe that horrible incident at the reunion was just a coincidence, or just a diversion for the main attack. He knew Samson had a team. The two fake policemen who stood guard for Samson in the alley when Mike had been beaten were his men. Those same men had rendered Troy and Jim unconscious in Jim's car that day as well. Samson probably had a lot more men at his disposal; of course, four fewer today after the subway attack.

Was it possible that Samson was actually some kind of international terrorist? Had Mike and his football buddies unwittingly created a future monster back in high school? Could mere bullying have had that kind of extreme effect on a person? If so, what in God's name had they unleashed onto the world?

Mike remembered that the hacking of Jim's computer had been traced back to Libya. And the news reports said the chief mechanic who had planted the bombs under the subway trains had fled to Libya the night of the attack. Samson was Arab and the terrorists were Arab. It was all starting to fit in a bizarre sort of way. The money that was embezzled from Baxter Development Corporation may have been used as seed money to finance plots such as what Toronto had just suffered. Was Samson a terrorist who just happened to be using his occupation to also take out revenge against the people he blamed for his high school life? Or just coincidence? Mike closed his eyes. He had a headache that was getting worse by the minute. As he nodded off he saw the frantic face of a naked, dark-skinned boy banging on a door, begging to be let through back to safety and dignity…

Chapter 37

"So what are you saying, Mr. Baxter? That this man Samson is the master terrorist we're looking for?"

"Well…I think it's worth looking into. It's worrying me…a lot."

They were sitting in Mike's office—the two RCMP inspectors had been kind enough to agree to come to his office for the interview. They were both dressed in black suits with boring ties and shiny black shoes, topped off with bloodshot eyes that spoke volumes about what they had been through in the last few weeks. They seemed friendly enough, but didn't waste time on small talk. They probably still had a couple of hundred interviews to endure before they slept.

"So, we're to believe that the high school gym attack killed two birds with one stone? He got his revenge against you, but also used the occasion as a diversion from the main subway attack?" The one named Inspector Wilkinson seemed to be the leader, as he asked most of the questions.

"Sounds crazy, and I know I'm not that important in the grand scheme of things, but I think in his mind I was important, and he wanted to take his shot." Mike walked over to his credenza, retrieved the coffee pot and re-filled their three cups. The two agents naturally had theirs black—Mike added two sugars to his.

Inspector Jallen jumped in. "If you're so afraid of this guy, why did you meet with him several weeks ago at the…what's it called… MetroCafe for lunch? You said you phoned him, and he suggested that spot?"

"I wanted to confront him about the kidnapping of my daughters, and let him know face to face that I was aware that the writing on the condolence card and the birthday card matched. I wanted to basically put him on notice, and hopefully then he would leave us alone." Mike lied. He didn't want to tell them the real reason he had met Samson at that café, and sure wasn't going to disclose anything about the embezzlement, Samson's relationship with Gerry, or the murders in Gerry's family. He didn't want to open up a can of worms about the foreign properties and his own activity in covering that up. He wanted to disclose just enough to set them on Samson's trail without incriminating himself.

"And after that is when he led you out to the alley, made you strip naked, and beat you up?" Jallen wrote notes as Mike was talking.

"Yes, that's right."

"Why didn't you report that to the police?"

Mike hesitated. *That was a good question.* "Uh, I was hoping that would be the end of it. I didn't want to make matters worse—the guy's clearly dangerous."

"But at that point, you didn't even know who he really was—as far as you were concerned he was just a former employee, a lawyer who worked for, uh,...Gerry Upton...correct? You didn't make the connection of Samson to Dawud Zamir until after the terrorist attack, until after you looked in the yearbook when you were still mourning the death of your friend, Steve Purcell. Only then did you realize Samson was an old classmate whom you had bullied in school. Do I have that chronology right?"

Mike squirmed in his seat. "Yes, that's right, but...."

Jallen cut him off. "So what reason would you have to think he would leave you alone, when you didn't even know why he kidnapped your kids, or beat you up?"

"Uh, I don't know—I guess I just hoped the incidents were isolated, and once I met with him face to face, he would know that I was onto him and it would just end." Mike knew that answer was feeble. He could feel sweat starting to drip down his back, soaking his shirt.

Wilkinson took over again. "Tell me if I understand this correctly—you agreed to have lunch with a guy who kidnapped your kids, then he beats you up and makes you strip naked at gunpoint, and you felt there was no need to report any of this?"

"Yes, that's right. Sounds crazy, but I don't think I was in my right mind when I made that decision. I was still in shock over how easy it was for my girls to be taken from us."

Wilkinson shook his head in bewilderment. "Do you still have the condolence card and birthday card for us to examine?"

"No, I threw them out." Mike lied again. This interview wasn't going as well as he thought it would. He was angry with himself—he should have anticipated that the detectives would easily see through the holes in his story. Mike regretted that he had told them anything about this.

Both inspectors looked at each other, with puzzled looks on their faces.

Mike noticed Jallen nod, and Wilkinson then opened his briefcase and pulled out two files. He opened the first file, and glared at Mike. "You're the so-called 'Briefcase Braveheart,' I see from this file."

Mike nodded sheepishly.

"Why were you on the subway that day? You're a rich man, accustomed to riding in comfort and privacy. Why would you subject yourself to a ride on the subway?"

"Once in a while I just don't feel like driving."

"You were quite the hero on that train. Not criticizing that at all, but I just find it kind of curious that you've been involved now in two very high-profile subway incidents in just a few months' time. Don't you find that curious too?"

Mike paused, then slowly answered the question. "I agree it looks a little odd…but I guess it's just one of those coincidences." *Pretty lame*, Mike thought.

Jallen smiled, and took the other file off Wilkinson's lap. He opened it and took out a photograph. He held it up in front of Mike's face. "Do you recognize this man?"

Mike squinted at the photo, and nodded…wondering where this was going. "Yes, that's Colin Spence; an executive with Ontario Life. He committed suicide earlier this year."

"You knew him?"

"Yes, most top executives in Toronto know each other, even if we're from different industries. He actually handled my company's group life and benefits program for our employees. I didn't know him well, it was just a casual business relationship."

Jallen leaned forward in his chair. "I can tell you that Mr. Spence did *not* commit suicide. He was right-handed and the right wrist was the one that was slit. Even people out of their minds will still always use their dominant hand to slit their wrists. In addition, he had a tiny puncture wound on his left wrist—a needle mark. We found a powerful drug in his system that must have sent him into a state of paralysis—then his wrist was slit to make it look like suicide. We think the killers meant to slit the left wrist to destroy any evidence of the needle mark, but they blew it and slit the right wrist instead."

Mike crossed his arms, leaned back in his chair, and took a deep breath. "I thought it was strange…he didn't seem the type to kill himself. So, that means all that porno material was probably planted in the room and on his computer…to discredit and distract? But why would someone want to kill him? And what does that have to do with what we're talking about?"

Jallen nodded. "There's more. A forensic audit was completed of the files at Ontario Life that Spence personally handled. Over the course of three years, over thirty million dollars in payments were made for twenty-five deaths. All applicant documentation was on file, identifications, etc. There were proper death certificates. However, all medicals at the time the applications were made were faked. And for twenty-three of the applicants, they had already been dead for several years."

Mike couldn't believe what he was hearing—another embezzlement that went on for years, just like with Gerry at his own company. He suddenly remembered back to Colin's funeral, hearing Colin's wife, Karen, talking about security precautions Colin had taken…and then seeing Samson at the funeral. Beating the shit out of him in front of everyone, Jim trying to stop him. Samson had his hooks into Colin Spence too.

"Earth to Mike—are you still with us?"

Mike gave his head a shake and rubbed his eyes. "Yeah, I'm with you. I'm just a little shocked by all of this."

"We're not finished. There is no evidence that Colin Spence enjoyed any personal financial gain from these twenty-five transactions. So, we're wondering…where did the money go?"

Mike had the funny feeling that he was going to find out. Déjà vu.

"We can't trace most of the money, but we did find a clear trail for the last two deaths—one check for $2,000,000 and the other for $500,000. Both were instantly transferred to a numbered bank account in Panama."

Mike clenched his fists.

"The last two people who are supposed to have died were your wife, Cindy Baxter—payment of two million to one Michael Baxter as beneficiary; and your daughter, Diana Baxter—payment of five hundred thousand to, again, one Michael Baxter, beneficiary."

Chapter *38*

Mike could feel his stomach churning. A rush of acid suddenly rose from within causing him to choke and cough until he thought his throat had turned inside out.

He could hear off in the distance somewhere, "Mr. Baxter, are you alright?" He felt a strong hand patting him on the back. He was vaguely aware of being grabbed from behind and yanked to his feet, two burly arms wrapping around his chest and squeezing hard, pumping in and out until he thought his ribs were going to break. Then relief.

Mike could feel that his face was fire engine red, as he sucked in deep breaths. He saw the two detectives, blurry images in his watery eyes, their worried faces, Wilkinson holding him up by the waist. "Are you okay now?"

Nodding agreement, Mike guzzled the glass of water that Jallen had shoved into his hand. Both of their faces were now looming large in his view, and the walls of the office seemed to be closing in, making him dizzy. He plunked down in his chair and held his forehead in his hands. There was a strong bitter aftertaste in his mouth, and his throat felt like it had swallowed flames.

The detectives sat down as well, across from Mike's desk. "If you're okay now, we'd like to continue. Is that all right with you, Mike?" Jallen sounded concerned, but still very officious. They weren't finished with him yet, much to his chagrin.

Mike cleared his throat. "Yes, go ahead. I'm fine now, thanks." *Not really.*

Wilkinson leaned forward in his chair. "We used our consulate in Panama to find out about that numbered account. It's...in your name, and tens of millions of dollars have passed through that account over the last few years. It's empty right now, but still active. All the funds in that account were transferred systematically to an account in Beirut, Lebanon. That's where the trail ends."

Mike came alive and slammed his fist on the desk. "I never opened an account in Panama—hell, I've never even been to that country. And I never worked with Colin Spence on a life insurance fraud scheme. I think I need a lawyer."

"We're not charging you Mike—at least not yet. Let's just say we consider you a 'person of interest.'"

Mike was starting to experience a feeling of absolute impotence. He was set up every which way he turned. *That Samson bastard!* "Okay, did you check into the information I gave to your office before you came over here? Samson's phone number and post office box number?"

Wilkinson looked at him sadly. "Yes, we did. Both the phone number and post office box are inactive. But when they were active, they were registered in your name." Mike jumped to his feet. "That's fucking ridiculous! Can't you guys see I'm being set up by this prick? I mean, why would I give you two things to check that I knew were registered to me? Seriously, do you think I would be that stupid?"

Jallen got up from his chair and walked around to where Mike was standing. He glared, unblinking. "We're used to seeing all sorts of deceptive behaviors, always designed to make the guilty look innocent. So, we can't discount what we've discovered until we investigate further. Not saying you *haven't* been set up, but not saying you *have* been either. Even you would agree that everything about your story is very suspicious, and all the facts pointing to you are incriminating as hell."

Jallen walked back around the desk and motioned for Wilkinson. Mike decided that Jallen was really the one in charge here after all. They both headed for the door. Jallen turned around to face him one more time. "We're not going to ask for your passport just yet, Mr. Baxter, but please do us the courtesy of not leaving the country."

*****

Mike passed by his secretary Stephanie, in a daze. He vaguely saw her holding out some papers to him, but he just kept on going down the hall toward the elevators. She called after him. He ignored her.

He took the elevator down to the parking garage and hopped into his BMW. He drove along in an almost hypnotic state, making his way down Front Street, hanging a right at Spadina, then down the alley where he had first bared his naked torso. A right, then another right, stopping at the little red clapboard house.

It had been several weeks since Mike had seen Ali and Jonas. He felt the need to connect with them again right now; didn't know why, he just did.

He walked up the front steps and knocked on the door. Ali opened up with surprise on her face, but Mike could see that she was clearly pleased to see him.

"Mike, how nice to see you! Come in! Come in! Jonas will be so happy that you're here!"

Almost as if on cue, Jonas bounded from the back of the house, and stood in front of him as if at attention. "Hi, Mike. How have you been? It's been a long time, and we've missed you." He uttered the words carefully and deliberately, with a huge smile on his face.

Mike was shocked. Jonas was speaking so clearly, enunciating perfectly. And he could tell that Jonas was proud of himself too.

Ali wrapped her arm around Mike's waist. "You can see that the speech therapy has paid off. The therapist said that Jonas is a very bright little boy—catches on so quickly. I'm so happy for him." Ali leaned up on her tiptoes and kissed Mike on the cheek. "I can't thank you enough for arranging for the therapist. It's only been a few weeks, but the results are amazing!"

Mike kissed her back. He had decided weeks ago that the only way the little boy was going to have any chance at all was to pay for some private speech therapy sessions. If it were left for too much longer, he would have a permanent impediment. Ali had objected at first, but Mike's insistence wore her down. She felt guilty about not being able to afford to pay for the sessions herself, and promised Mike she would pay him back one day. He didn't care about seeing the money repaid. It was just so worthwhile seeing that it had paid off. Now there was one less reason for the other kids to make fun of him.

Mike went over to Jonas, picked him up and whirled him around. He felt so comfortable with Jonas, just as if he were his own son. He could feel that he and the little guy had developed some real chemistry.

Ali went into the kitchen to make some coffee for them, and Mike watched her go. She had a rhythm to her steps now, a confidence she didn't have the first time he met her. And she was stunning to look at—those hazel eyes that seemed to change color depending on the light in the room or brightness of the sun. Sometimes they were green, sometimes gray, but always reverting back to hazel as the day unfolded. Her hair was long, sometimes left to hang down past her shoulder blades and sometimes tied up stylishly, particularly when she was in the kitchen cooking. But it was her expressions that always caused Mike to catch his breath—the little pouts she would make with her lips, the twinkle of mischief in her eyes, the way she shook her head when she talked or cocked her head on an angle when she listened to him. She was captivating, and warm, and affectionate. Jonas was lucky to have her as his mom, and Mike could tell that they adored each other. He had to admit he was reaching that point himself.

They talked for a couple of hours, catching up on what had been going on in both of their lives. Ali knew all about the gym attack that had preceded the subway bombings. Mike's face had been in the newspapers again—it hadn't taken long for the press to make the connection between that and the Briefcase Braveheart incident. Mike didn't tell her any more than what she had read in the papers.

"Mike, there's something I need to tell you." She paused and swallowed hard. "I think Wade died in that bombing."

Mike noticed her eyes tearing up. "What makes you think that?"

Ali wiped at her eyes. "I haven't heard from him since the attack. And that's unusual. He panhandled on the subway platforms quite a lot, and I'm thinking he was at one of those two stations that night, or even maybe in the train cars."

"Have you asked the recovery teams about their search for victims?"

She nodded. "Yes, they have a hotline and I phoned it. Then someone came by to pick up a sample of his hair from a brush that they could use for DNA testing. But they told me that many of the bodies may never be recovered—buried under tons of concrete."

"Have you told Jonas yet?"

"No, I haven't."

"Would you like me to do it for you?"

Ali nodded again. "Yes, I would. He might take it better coming from a man, and I think you would be able to handle it better than me. I would probably cry, making things worse for him."

"No problem. I'll take him outside before I leave today, and tell him then."

Ali tucked her face under Mike's chin and kissed him on the neck. "I hardly know you, yet I feel so comfortable with you. And you're so nice to us. I don't know why, but it's comforting, and we appreciate having you in our lives, Mike."

Mike squeezed her tightly and he could feel her shiver ever so slightly. "You're a wonderful little family and I'm glad to help out however I can. And why I'm doing it, I don't really know myself to be perfectly honest—I'm just drawn to both of you, I guess. And one of these days I'll tell you why helping Jonas out has become a personal mission of mine—making up for something in my past. So, one of my reasons is selfish, if that makes you feel better." He hugged her tightly again and this time felt a tremble go through his own body. Mike didn't understand it, but for that brief moment he enjoyed it.

They said their goodbyes, and Mike ducked out into the backyard with Jonas to throw the baseball around. They did this every time Mike visited and the little boy was getting very good. And he always proudly wore the Blue Jays cap that Mike had given him.

When Jonas seemed to tire out a bit, Mike motioned for him to sit down beside him on the grass.

Mike put his arm around his slender shoulders, and squeezed him gently. "Bud, your mom asked me to talk to you about some sad news. She was afraid she would cry and make you feel worse, so I agreed with her that maybe I should tell you."

Jonas looked up at him, his eyes wide with worry. "What is it, Mike?"

Mike took a deep breath. "Your mom's afraid that your dad may have died in the subway explosions."

Jonas nodded.

Mike continued slowly, choosing his words carefully. "The search crews have been working hard trying to find everybody, but they haven't found your dad yet. Your mom thinks that since he hasn't been around here for quite a while, that he may have been one of the victims."

Jonas blinked a couple of times, then nodded again.

"They may never find him."

Jonas struggled free from Mike's arm, jumped to his feet and picked his baseball glove up off the grass. "Good."

Mike looked up at him from his seat on the grass, shocked at what he had just heard. "You don't really mean that, Jonas. I know you're just trying to be a strong little man. You don't have to do that—you can cry if you want."

"No, I meant it. I thought I loved him, but I was just s'posed to think that. He was mean. Then I met you. You're not mean. You're my father."

Leaving Mike sitting in the yard at a total loss for words, Jonas ran back into the house without saying goodbye.

*****

Mike was driving north on University Avenue, not knowing why. He was thinking about little Jonas and what he had said about Mike being his father. The poor little guy—working so hard at being tough. That was his way of handling the shock, Mike supposed, but it also could be exactly how he felt.

Jonas was looking for a father figure because his own had never been around, and when he was around he was violent. So he wanted Mike to be that father. That was his way of coping. Mike vowed to have another discussion with him on his next visit, to gently explain that he couldn't be his father, but could certainly be his friend. A friend to him and his mother. Jonas would have to understand that Mike had his own wife and family that he was committed to. He didn't want to break the little boy's heart, but he didn't want to lead him on either. He kept driving, continuing along as University changed to Avenue Road. He finally reached Bloor, and without hesitation continued through the lights two more blocks until he reached Lowther Avenue. Mike turned left and pulled over to the curb, put the BMW in Park and turned off the engine.

Then he sat and stared at the third house from the left. A run-down old house that he guessed at one time had been a majestic structure. Almost every house on the block had a 'rooms for rent' sign in front. This particular house didn't have a sign but it looked like the others so he assumed it was a rooming house too.

He had no idea why he was at this place, staring at this house. He had no idea what had brought him all the way from downtown along the route he had come. He had never been here before, never driven that route before. He was sure of it, at least part of him was sure of it. Once again, he was becoming aware that another part of his brain was at work. But not really his brain. He could feel it, the wheels turning, knowledge of something that was coming to the surface.

That part of his brain seemed to know that he had been on this very street, and inside that very house. Something was drawing him to it—to make him want to watch it, stare at it.

And something else was now telling him to move his car away from the line of sight of the house. Mike started the engine and pulled away from the curb, glancing furtively at the forbidding house as he passed by it. He drove to the end of the street, and parked on the opposite side of one perpendicular to it. Then he got out of the car, opened the trunk and took out a pair of powerful binoculars. Sitting back inside the car again, he trained the binoculars on that house, the sleazy rooming house—the third house from the left.

He watched, and waited. For what he had no idea. Except that he knew he had been inside that house before. In another time.

Chapter 39

Mike had been dozing with his seat set in the recline position, binoculars on his lap, when he was suddenly awakened by the sound of a car door slamming shut. He punched the memory button and slowly rose back upright.

Walking up the street toward the sinister house was someone familiar. The man had just exited a Mercedes CLK parked two cars up from Mike's BMW. Mike raised the binoculars, thanking himself at the same time that he had opted for the heavy tint on the windows when he had ordered his car. No one could see him, but he could easily see them.

Viewing the man from behind, Mike couldn't be sure, but the well-dressed figure walking up the front steps of the house looked an awful lot like Howard Dixon, an executive with a major national bank. Mike had spent many evenings over the years with Howard, at Chamber of Commerce functions and other business affairs. They both sat on a couple of non-profit boards together as well.

Howard's walk was very distinctive, unforgettable. Almost like a slow hop—the feet moved as normal but the body seemed to raise itself up about four inches with each step. And this particular man was walking exactly the same way.

Mike zoomed in with his binoculars and could see that the man was wearing a hat, which in itself would have been unusual for any man in Toronto. And he could see the frames of glasses around his ears—must have been sunglasses, because if it was Howard, he didn't wear glasses. Mike watched as the man raised his right hand up and pushed the doorbell—looked like two quick presses and then one long one. Within a few seconds the door opened and the man entered. It didn't appear as if anyone came to the door to open it—it just opened by itself.

Mike decided to wait until the man came out again, to verify for sure if it was Howard. He reclined his chair again, turned on the stereo and closed his eyes. *Why was he feeling so tired?*

Half an hour later he was awakened again by the beep of a car alarm being deactivated. Mike lurched up and looked towards the Mercedes. He didn't need the binoculars this time—it was clearly Howard Dixon opening the driver door of the Benz. On impulse, Mike opened his door and stepped out. "Howard?"

The man jerked his head in Mike's direction. "Mike?"

Mike walked towards him. "Long time no see, bud. What are you doing in this neck of the woods?" Mike could see that Howard looked fidgety, looking side to side, and not raising his eyes to meet his.

"Uh…I was just…dropping off an envelope to a house over there." He pointed. "It was mailed to my home by mistake."

"Oh, okay." Mike glanced quickly at his watch and realized it had been thirty minutes since he had seen Howard enter the house.

"What are you doing here, Mike?" Howard was nervously flipping his keys around in his hand.

"Just stopped to make a phone call. Don't like using my cell when I'm driving."

"Well…okay then, Mike. Be seeing you, eh?"

Mike could tell that Howard was very anxious to leave. "What's with the hat, Howard? You trying to be a dude, or what? You never wear a hat." Mike said, chuckling

"Sometimes I do wear one—depends how I feel." Howard quickly hopped into his front seat, giving Mike a backhanded wave. He pulled out from the curb and headed south at a rapid clip.

Mike got back into his car, and raised the binoculars to his eyes once again. He was wide awake now, and puzzled even more than before. He knew that Gerry's influence and memories were doing cartwheels in his brain, and he was determined to listen to them. They were trying to tell him something. At least now he wasn't in an unconscious state when Gerry returned to take over. He was aware now, always a bit tired, but aware. He could still be himself and be somewhat in control.

But the feeling about that house was overpowering, and seeing Howard Dixon enter and exit after half an hour did not sit right. A man of Howard's stature did not return envelopes to sleazy areas of town. The post office could do that, or he had people who would do that. And it wouldn't have taken thirty minutes to drop off an envelope. Something was going on in that house. Mike knew there was a reason he was here, why Gerry's memory wanted him to be here. And there was most certainly a reason Howard Dixon had been here, and it sure as hell wasn't to return an envelope.

*****

At around 8:00 p.m. Mike noticed the front door of the house opening, and a man walking out. He raised his binoculars and focused—then almost dropped them in shock. David Samson, in the flesh, was standing on the front walkway, looking around, stretching his arms out as if he were trying to work out some kinks. Sampson took out a cigarette and lit it. Mike got the urge and did the same while watching, unable to take his eyes off the monster.

It became apparent that Samson was waiting for someone. He paced back and forth on his walkway, puffing on his cigarette. Right at the moment when a black Suburban turned onto the street, Samson quickly dropped his cigarette and stubbed it out. The Suburban stopped in front of the house. A man got out from the front passenger seat and walked up the pathway to greet him.

Mike had the binoculars trained on the visitor. His mouth went instantly dry as he realized who he was—the tall Clint Eastwood character from the gym, whose face was engrained in his memory for the rest of his life. The man who had shot a partier right next to Cindy. The man who had ordered the decapitation of his friend. The man whose face had been plastered in video footage over the mass media for the last few weeks, who had killed hundreds in the subway carnage and then several more on camera as he made his escape. This was the terrorist that investigators from all over the world wanted to apprehend. And at this very moment, that terrorist was hugging David Samson, and kissing him on both cheeks. The deference to Samson was obvious—Samson was his boss. These were the men who had brazenly killed hundreds of innocents, and they were now framed in Mike's binocular lens kissing each other.

He now knew why Gerry's memory had brought him to this place in time. Mike watched as they jumped into the Suburban, which pulled out and headed down the street. Mike started his car and followed at a safe distance. The SUV hung a right at the corner and continued down to Bloor Street. It turned left and after a block or two it pulled over to the curb and stopped. Mike pulled in two cars back in a 'No Parking" zone and waited. After about five minutes, the passenger door opened and Samson stepped out, ran across the street and into the lobby of a luxury condominium building. The SUV pulled out and headed east down Bloor Street.

Mike waited in his car for about fifteen minutes until he was satisfied that Samson wasn't coming back out again. He deduced that this was where

Samson lived, and that the rooming house was where he conducted his sordid business. Mike wrote down the address of the condo, then put his car in gear.

He knew he would have to come back, but he also knew that he needed some help. Troy had no idea to what extent he would be asked to stretch to earn his exorbitant salary. Tomorrow Mike would tell him.

Chapter *40*

"You want to do what?" Troy was massaging his temples with his fingers, as if this conversation with his friend was giving him a headache.

"I want to break into that rooming house. It'll be a quick in and out, no big deal. I just need you to be my lookout."

"Mike, we'd be breaking the law—again. We'll be in enough trouble as it is if it ever comes out that we covered up embezzlement. This sort of thing will just make us common street criminals."

Mike got up and perched himself on the edge of the desk, staring down at Troy. "Hey, how much worse can it get? The RCMP already suspects me of being a financier for terrorism, and that I was engaged in a life insurance scam with Colin Spence. What's a measly 'break and enter' charge compared to all that?"

Troy was still rubbing his forehead. "With this latest information connecting Samson with the subway terrorist, why not just go to the police now?"

"Do you really think they'd believe me, Troy? What proof do I have? It's only my word that I saw those sickos kissing each other. And how would I explain how I knew what house Samson was working out of? Do you think the police would buy my story that I have a dead friend's brain fused with mine, and that he guided me to the house?"

Troy lowered his eyes to the floor, and shook his head. "No, I guess not."

"Of course they wouldn't. They would think I'm an even bigger danger to society than they already think I am." Mike held up his thumb and forefinger, and gestured. "I'm this far away from being locked up for the rest of my life."

Troy nodded his head slowly. "You're right. Okay, I've got your back. When do you want to do this?"

"How does tonight sound?"

"I can do that. Do you have a plan?"

"Sort of. I've got tools in my trunk. And we'll do it after dark. Samson left the house for his own apartment just after 8:00 last night. So, we'll leave here around 9:00?"

"And the objective?"

"Evidence. I want to find some evidence, anything, to tie him to these terrorist attacks at the school and subway, and hopefully to his extortion schemes against executives like Gerry, Colin, and Howard. Also, I'm pretty certain he had Gerry's family members killed to make him comply—how many more people were killed or hurt to make these other guys comply? And, geez, how many executives from how many other companies were being extorted? There could be a hell of a lot more than just these three guys. You know, we may not find anything at all that the police can use, but I feel so powerless right now, I have to do something, anything, to regain some control over my life. It's quickly spinning *out* of control and I can't seem to stop it."

Troy stood up and put his massive arm around Mike's shoulders. "We're gonna do this, Mikey. We'll find what we need. And when we do, the police will have no choice but to listen to you."

The two friends bumped fists in solidarity.

*****

It was 10:00 p.m. by the time they arrived in front of the house on Lowther Avenue. It was already dark, with no moon. The houses on the street showed no signs of life, with the exception of several homeless cats roaming from tree to tree looking for prey. Mike figured since most of these homes were rooming houses, its occupants were probably out on Yonge Street, panhandling, dealing drugs, or drinking cheap wine from paper bags. This was the perfect street and the perfect time for a break and enter.

He raised his binoculars and zoomed in on the side window on the east side of the house. The rear of the house did not seem easily accessible due to a high fence. Mike wanted a quick getaway and the side window seemed to offer the best chance of that. He could see that it was equipped with a set of old iron bars, but they were fastened to the outside of the window frame. It would be an easy matter to remove them with a couple of tools.

He put down his binoculars and glanced over at Troy. "Well, are we ready?"

"Ready if you are. Hey, last chance to back out, Mikey. I'm with you but geez, it's kind of eerie that we're gonna do this."

Mike nodded and laughed. "Hey, we didn't get dressed up in our commando outfits for nothing, you know." They were each dressed in black sweaters and pants, with black toques to round out the commando image. "The only thing missing is charcoal on our faces." They both chuckled nervously.

"Okay, you're the boss, Mike. As your underling I wouldn't agree to this, but as your friend I'm with you. What do you want me to do?"

"Come up with me to the window and help me remove those bars. Then I'll pry the window up—should be easy, looks like an old slider. Then, come here back to the car, pull it a little farther back down the street and keep watch. I should only be in there a few minutes…hopefully." Mike tested the flashlight, then reached back and grabbed his leather tool pouch from the back seat. "If anyone approaches the house, or if anything else looks threatening, phone my cell. I've got it on vibrate. I won't answer of course, I'll just get the hell out through the same window."

"Okay, gotcha buddy. Let's do this."

Exiting the car, they walked cautiously up the front pathway, and along to the side of the house where the one side window was. Mike handed Troy the flashlight and he flicked it on, aiming it up against the bars for him. Mike could see that they were held to the frame by only four large rusted screws. *This should be easy.* He pulled his Phillips screwdriver out of the pouch, and proceeded to remove each of the screws, then pulled hard on the bar structure. It groaned and came free after a couple of tugs. He set the frame down on the grass and examined the window frame. He had guessed right—an old slider. He pulled a flathead out of his pouch and jammed it in underneath the frame. Pounding down on the screwdriver's handle made the window rise about an inch. He slid his fingers under it and yanked. It slid up slowly, but surely.

Mike strapped the tool pouch around his waist, then took the flashlight out of Troy's hand. He whispered, "Okay, Troy. Move the car back and wait for me. Can't say how long I'll be, but just keep watch. I'm going to examine everything I can. We'll only get one shot at this."

Troy nodded and headed back to the car, while Mike yanked himself up by the windowsill, sliding himself through headfirst. He switched on the flashlight, and swung it in an arc around the room. He could see it was an office, with one desk and two guest chairs. There was a large closet behind the desk and he could see out the office doorway into a foyer, which the front door entered into. The office was spartan—nothing fancy: no computers, no phones, no papers. But it was all familiar. He remembered sitting in one of those guest chairs and staring around at this bare office. In another time.

He wandered out to the hallway and down to the back of the main floor past a staircase, which he assumed led up to the bedrooms. He passed a bathroom along the way and entered the kitchen. Again, spartan: old appliances, worn laminate counters. A door out to the garden. There was a small table with four chairs.

Mike decided to take a look upstairs before rifling the office. The flashlight lit the way as he maneuvered up the narrow stairwell. At the top there was a bathroom, and two bedrooms. The first one he entered had one king-size bed, a small dresser and a closet. He opened the closet—a few men's shirts and pants. He pulled open the drawers to the dresser: underwear, socks, and a rolled up prayer mat.

He made his way to the second bedroom and he was immediately struck by how luxurious it was in comparison to the other one. This was clearly a woman's room, queen-size bed with a designer quilt and matching throw pillows. The drapes matched the quilt and the pillows; the room seemed freshly painted. He opened the closet and was stunned to see the collection of clothing—mostly western style, but a few outfits that looked like traditional Middle Eastern garb. Very fancy, very stylish. About twelve pairs of shoes were lined up neatly on the floor.

Mike opened the dresser drawers to find a colorful collection of sexy lingerie and not much of anything else. He slid his fingers underneath the clothes to see if any papers or files were hidden. Nothing.

He made his way downstairs again, trying to form a picture in his mind about who lived upstairs. Was she Samson's wife or girlfriend? If so, why didn't she live with him in the Bloor Street apartment? Or was she a renter? Mike doubted that, due to the secrecy of the business that was probably conducted in this house. Was she one of Samson's team? That was more likely. What was her role in all of this?

Mike knew he had to be both careful and quick now. A woman clearly lived here—and he had mistakenly assumed that the house was just a front for extortion deals. *She could be home at any minute.*

Back in the front office, he pulled on the drawers of the desk. Locked. Mike yanked a screwdriver out of his pouch, and pried the first drawer open, hearing the lock snap with the force. At this point, he didn't care if Samson knew someone had been here—he was past that. He was getting desperate.

The first drawer held pencils, pens, a staple gun, and various pieces of paper with doodles and squiggles. He ignored the papers; looked like nothing more than the workings of an idle brain.

Mike pried the second drawer open—this one was completely empty. But the third and last drawer held something a little more interesting. There was one document with some attachments. A colorful brochure for the Gulfstream G650 Business Jet, and several official looking documents that Mike recognized in the dim light as a bill of sale, along with storage and maintenance agreements. He scanned the bill of sale with his flashlight and whistled under his breath. The sale price was shown at 51,000,000 dollars, and it looked as if the delivery date had been June 30th of this year. He flipped the page back and looked at the maintenance agreement with a firm called Skyspace Services based at Buttonville Airport in Markham, a city just north of Toronto. He saw that the jet was stored there permanently as well, in the Skyspace private hanger. Mike flipped back to the bill of sale; it showed the registered owner as Mayday Holdings. There were two signatures at the bottom of the page—one on the salesman's line that he couldn't make out, and another one on the purchaser's line that was signed in very neat, almost girlish handwriting—'David Samson.' Clearly, Samson was the principal of Mayday Holdings, probably one of many shell companies the man most likely owned just for money laundering. And he was the proud owner of a slick Gulfstream fifteen-passenger jet.

Mike took the documents over to a photocopier in the corner of the office and turned it on. He didn't want to take the documents, thinking it safer to just make copies. He didn't care if Samson knew someone was here, but he preferred that the man think this was just a normal burglary. And a burglar wouldn't bother to steal purchase documents for a jet.

While he was waiting for the machine to warm up, he looked around the office one more time. He opened up the closet door—it was a large walk-in type with virtually nothing inside. Except for a metal box about a foot square in size, sitting on a shelf. He pulled it down and opened the lid. A large pile of American dollars was inside. Mike fingered the bills and guessed at least five thousand dollars. He pocketed the bills and threw the metal box onto the floor of the closet, lid open. He figured that might convince Samson that this was just a simple burglary.

Mike walked back to the now warm photocopier and made copies of each of the documents, including the Gulfstream brochure. He put the originals back in the drawer, and folded the copies to join the thousands of Samson's dollars already in his pocket. Suddenly he felt his cell phone vibrating against his hip. *Panic.* He flicked off the flashlight, hoping the glare hadn't been seen from outside by whomever was approaching. He took two steps toward the window that he had entered through, but stopped dead in his tracks. *A key was being inserted into the front door lock.*

Mike instinctively stepped backward into the closet, closing it softly behind him. He took a swift peek through the door slats toward the window, sighing in relief at seeing that he had remembered to slide it closed behind him.

The front door opened and the lights came on, followed by the click-clack of high heels in the front hall. Mike peeked again through the slats and saw two shapely legs kicking each foot forward one at a time, sending a pair of stylish shoes flying down toward the kitchen. Then the rest of her appeared and Mike quietly caught his breath. Passing the office on her way to the kitchen was the most beautiful woman he had ever laid eyes on. Just a glimpse was all it took for the charisma of the Middle Eastern beauty to completely dazzle him. She had long, sleek black hair hanging down close to her shapely bottom and a green halter-top displaying a voluptuous bosom and shapely shoulders. Her exotic dark skin contrasted seductively with the green halter-top and a tight silver mini-skirt.

She danced down the hall out of view, humming an unidentifiable tune. Mike knew he had to make his move now while he had the chance.

He carefully opened the closet door—it made a squeak—he grimaced, stopped and listened. He could hear her humming in the kitchen. Mike walked on his tiptoes over to the window and slowly raised it up on its track. *He was going to make it!* He put one leg through the window and was just raising the other one when he felt a soft arm around his neck.

She squeezed hard causing him to choke, and yanked him backward through the air onto the top of the desk. Mike was stunned by the strength of the beautiful woman. She leaned over him, with her hands around his throat. Mike looked up into her hypnotic green eyes which were flaring with anger. She seethed at him. "I know who you are. You are Mr. Baxter. I recognize you from our photos." Her voice was soft, but threatening. She squeezed harder.

"What are you doing here, Mr. Baxter? Do you want to fuck me? All you pale men do." She pressed her thumbs into his Adam's apple, and Mike knew she was starting the process of strangulation.

He brought his fist up and slammed her in the temple. She released her grip just long enough for him to slide sideways off the desk, crashing to the floor. Mike realized that the old boxer feeling was not with him—it hadn't kicked in. Then it dawned on him that he was terrified. That particular skill of Gerry's only came to him when he was angry. Right now he was too scared to be angry.

He slithered across the floor to a floor lamp, grabbing hold of the base and swinging it just as she arrived behind him. It caught her square in her exotic face, and she staggered backward. Mike jumped to his feet still brandishing the floor lamp, bracing himself. She wiped the blood away from her face, and smiled in a way that made Mike's blood run cold.

Suddenly everything was a blur. All he saw in the fog was her flying into the air, spinning. The first foot knocked the lamp out of his hand, the second foot followed a millisecond later with a hammer blow to the side of his head. Mike went down. She came after him. Mike scrambled along the floor again, making his way to the area between the desk and the closet. Then out of the corner of his eye he saw Troy flinging himself headfirst through the open window. *Thank God!*

Troy jumped to his feet and landed a punch on the beauty's nose. The only sign that he had hit her was the blood streaming from her nostrils. Otherwise, her fighting stance hadn't moved an inch. Troy looked shocked. Her tiny hands now moved in rapid succession, pounding several times into Troy's face. His head snapped back, and she spun—both feet thudding into his gut. Troy went down. The sexy Arab had landed securely on her feet, not missing a beat. She turned her head and looked in Mike's direction. He was still on his knees peering over the desk, trying desperately to figure out how they would take this lethal machine down. She moved toward the desk, smiling in that sinister way, seemingly aware of what Mike was thinking.

Suddenly Mike remembered. He slid open the top drawer and pulled out the staple gun, praying to God it was loaded. She screamed in a shrill banshee way and leaped on top of the desk, staring down at him. Mike could see up her skirt—no panties. He was momentarily distracted, and she knew it—the way she opened her legs to display her charms. She moved her feet to the edge of the desk, and raised her right one up in preparation for a killer strike against the man crouching on the floor.

Mike brought up the staple gun, aimed at her left foot that was planted on the desk, and pulled the trigger twice. He felt the gun jerk in his hand and he knew his prayers had been answered. It was loaded.

She screamed in pain. Mike rose to his feet and shot two more large staples into her breast area. He could see she was confused, screaming in pain and looking at him in shock. He wasn't going to waste a second. She brought her hands down to her breasts in a reflex action that left her face exposed. Mike brought the gun up and shot a staple at each eye. She shrieked and fell backwards off the desk, blood streaming down her cheeks.

She was gasping for breath now and her hands were clawing at her face, scratching in panic at the metal missiles that were embedded in her eyeballs. To Mike's shock, she suddenly leaped back to her feet and moved in his direction once again, deadly hands extended back in fighting mode, leg muscles tensed and ready. She sensed exactly where he was despite being blind. Mike froze in shock.

But Troy didn't. He was now on his feet again too, behind her now, wrapping one big forearm around her neck, his other hand sliding strategically along her forehead. He made one swift move with his hand, her head moved… Mike heard the snap of her neck, and a second later witnessed the instant limpness of a dead person, flopping down in Troy's big forearm.

Chapter 41

"We have to talk about this. We really do...I do."

Mike rubbed his tired eyes and looked up at his friend. "I know, I know. I've been trying to forget what happened, but it's not working."

They were sitting in Mike's office trying hard to enjoy a coffee together, but one topic was standing in the way. The topic both of them had avoided for several days now. They had killed a woman.

"I killed her, Mike. With my bare hands. I feel kinda sick."

"She was going to kill us, Troy. You saw her—she was an animal, and a very well-trained one at that. If you hadn't arrived when you did, I don't think I would have made it out alive. I owe you my life, Troy."

"Hey, you've saved my butt on many occasions in the past. You owe me nothing."

Mike got up from his chair, leaned over and gave his friend a tight bear hug. Troy hugged him back and slapped him on the back. "Thanks, I needed that, and I needed for us to talk about this."

"I know, Troy. But I've just been in a kind of state of shock over this. That wasn't supposed to happen. No one was supposed to die. Taking a life, even an evil one, feels very weird to me. And hey, remember this—don't absorb all the guilt yourself. We did the deed together. It was one of our more sickening team efforts."

"Thanks for that, Mike."

"We have to look at it this way—these people are pure evil. They're terrorists— they definitely were responsible for the school attack and subway bombings. We know that; I've seen Samson with that terrorist, a monster I will never ever forget. We've done the world a favor by killing that woman. She was one of them."

"I'm going to try to look at it that way."

Mike leaned forward in his chair and stared into Troy's eyes. "So, where... did you learn to do that...you know...neck thing?" Mike asked in a whisper.

Troy shrugged and whispered back, a sheepish look on his face, "T.V."

The tension broke with Troy's answer. Mike tried to restrain himself, but he couldn't. The laugh started deep in his belly, then exploded through pursed lips. Once he started, he couldn't stop. His laugh was contagious, and Troy couldn't help but join in. They were both doubled over in their chairs holding their stomachs when Mike's secretary, Stephanie, opened the door and peeked in. "Everything okay in here?"

Mike waved her off. "No problem, Steph. We're just unwinding a bit here."

Stephanie nodded, a suspicious smile on her face, and closed the door.

Mike and Troy smiled at each other, still holding their stomachs. Just the look in each other's eyes started the guffaws once again.

*****

The boardroom seemed huge with just the three of them sitting around the opulent table. Mike, Troy and Jim decided to use this room for today's discussion, due to the extra soundproofing in the walls.

Each of them had steaming mugs of coffee, and prepared themselves for a long session. Mike started the meeting off by summarizing everything that had happened over the last few months, including the terrorist attacks, the killing of the Arab girl, and the irrefutable evidence now that Samson was the master terrorist and intimately knew the commando who was now the subject of a worldwide manhunt. They also discussed Mike's precarious position with the RCMP and that it might only be a matter of days until he was arrested.

As Mike sat at the table he thought how ironic it was that he was conducting this meeting in a format just like any other business meeting with his executives. *Old habits were hard to break.*

"I've checked the papers every day this week, and the internet, and the online police reports. There was nothing, nothing anywhere about that girl's death. Or the break- in."

"Yeah, Mike—did the same thing. I'm stunned. It's like it didn't even happen." Troy was doodling on his pad as he talked.

"Yup, a woman died and it's been completely erased!"

Jim jumped in. "Well, from what we know so far about this dude, it sounds like he'd have the resources to 'clean it up' so to speak, and with the business he's in he would have every reason to not draw attention to himself. No way he'd report it."

Mike nodded. "You're right but…"

"These people consider death to be a necessary part of their cause. This is a war they're engaged in. They're desensitized to it." Troy got up and poured himself some more coffee, then refilled the cups of his friends.

Mike held up the brochure and bill of sale for the Gulfstream jet, and waved it in the air. “I think this is the key, guys. This jet may be the only connection that we can use to get this guy. Where the money came from, tracing it back. Not something we can do, but the police certainly can. This is a large expenditure and the money trail should prove that it was a laundered purchase. It’s at least something that may indicate to the RCMP that something is terribly wrong. I mean, fifty-one million dollars for a plane is a lot of laundered money. They could track this Mayday Holdings company—what it does, where it does business, if it does any real business. Any related companies.”

Jim stood up and started pacing the room as he always did when he was thinking hard about something. “Okay, you’re right. It’s a monster-size purchase and it would certainly raise some major eyebrows. But, who’s going to listen to you? You’re a suspect!”

“Yes, I am. And I fear that I don’t have much time to clear myself. If this guy disappears, I’m doomed.”

The three friends sat quietly for a few minutes, absorbing that last ominous comment.

Mike looked up. “Ideas, guys? Ideas? I’m desperate here. This should not be happening to me and this prick is not going to get away with it. He’s killed hundreds of people and he wants to stick me with it just because I bullied him in high school. It’s sick beyond belief. At the very least, he’s going to make sure I’m nailed for insurance fraud. I look pretty guilty with that Colin Spence situation and that damn Panama bank account.”

Troy smacked his palm on the table. “As you said, Mikey, the plane is the key. If we can at least get the turd arrested for money laundering, that’s a good start. It will lead from there to other things—hell, they can torture the truth out of him. Wouldn’t be the first time.”

“Okay, I agree. But how?”

“I think, first off, we should impersonate Samson on the phone and find out more about the status of the plane. Where it goes, what if anything is owing on it, where the payments come from, tax write-off declarations, etc.”

“He has a distinct accent—how would we do that?”

“You know Mehmet, don’t you? One of my engineers? Even though he’s a Canadianized Arab, he does have that distinctive tone and perfect word formation that Samson has. I’m sure he would sound just like him over the phone."

Mike rubbed his chin, deep in thought. "Has some merit, Troy. But we couldn't tell him anything. What ruse would we use to get him to do this so he doesn't think we're nuts?"

"Let me handle that. I would just tell him we need his help to pretend to be someone else—a potential client that we're not sure of. Someone who owns several plots of land that he's offered to sell us, but we're not sure of his credentials or whether or not we can trust him. He'll be okay with that."

"Okay, so we'd have to write him some kind of script."

"Yes, we'll jot down a few things for him to say."

Mike was getting more enthusiastic now. "Who would he call first?"

"Well, I would suggest we start with where the plane is right now, and go on from there depending on what we learn. So, we should have him call that maintenance company, Skyspace, at Buttonville Airport."

Mike nodded his head slowly. "But what would we learn?"

"I don't know, Mike—but it's a start. We'll see where it leads. We have to start somewhere."

Mike tapped his pen on the table. "Okay, I'm with you." He looked over at Jim, who gave a thumbs-up sign. "We're unanimous then…let's do this… today."

*****

They were back in the boardroom again, speakerphone in the middle of the table, Mehmet looking a bit sheepish with the company's three top executives sitting there with him. Troy had briefed him well and he seemed to understand what was expected of him. If he seemed puzzled by it, it didn't show on his face. But he did look a bit intimidated, Mike thought.

"Mehmet, we're counting on you to be convincing. This guy you're going to be imitating is confident, well spoken, and authoritative. Are you clear on that ?"

"Yes, Mr. Baxter, I am. I have a good idea of what you need to know, and I will do my best."

Mike glanced down at the sales agreement for the jet, and read out the number for Skyspace Services. Troy began to punch in the number and before he hit the last digit, he glanced at Mehmet. "You ready?"

"I am ready."

Troy punched the last number and they all heard the phone ringing over the speaker.

"Hello, Skyspace Services at your service!" A perky female answered the phone and gave the friendly greeting.

Mehmet took it from there. "Hello, I would like to talk to the service manager about the status of my jet, please?"

"Of course—your name, sir?"

"David Samson."

"Oh, of course, Mr. Samson. I didn't recognize your voice. I apologize."

Grimaces around the table.

"That is quite all right. We have only talked a couple of times before."

"I know, I know. But I pride myself on being good with voices. Let me transfer you to Grant Myers. He's the manager in charge of your jet, and I know he has been arranging for everything you asked for."

Eyebrows raised around the table.

There was a moment of silence, then a strong booming voice.

"Mr. Samson, Grant here. Are you getting ready?"

Mehmet looked momentarily stunned, then replied, "Of course, I am always ready."

"Ha, ha—I like your attitude. A man on a mission, eh?"

"Yes, there is always another mission." Mehmet permitted himself to chuckle.

"Well, thanks for checking in. I was going to call you. But, we're pretty much all done here. Your pretty bird is fit and ready to fly."

"That is good. Can we go over the arrangements once again so that I know we are together on our plans?"

"No problem. Hey, I knew you were a 'detail guy' when we met. So, let's see now. Your jet will be fueled, serviced and ready to fly this Thursday. Your scheduled departure here from Buttonville is 2:00 p.m. Our understanding is that you will provide your own crew, and your estimated time of arrival in Panama City, Panama, will be 8:00 p.m. local time. Oh, and I have already arranged for the broker in Panama to take possession of your Gulfstream when you arrive. He has agreed to a ten percent commission, and the asking price for the jet will be no less than forty-eight million. But if you ask me, Mr. Samson, I think you'll get more than that—in my opinion. Too bad you won't be returning to Canada though. We've enjoyed having your business. Hope you'll keep us in mind if you ever come back?"

"Oh, you can be certain I will make use of your company again. I have interests all over the world, so there is a very good chance that you will see me again."

"Wonderful to hear. So, we'll see you on Thursday then. The plane will be on the tarmac and you can just board at will. Customs and Immigration will be handled of course in Panama, so there should be no delays in your departure."

"Thank you so much, Mr. Myers."

"Hey, call me Grant, buddy."

"Okay, Grant. You call me David, then. Goodbye. We will see you on Thursday."

Mehmet hung up the phone and let out a deep breath. Mike, Troy and Jim each jumped out of their chairs and patted him on the back. They could tell that Mehmet was relieved, but also darn pleased with himself.

Mike glanced up at his buddies, concern written all over his face. "In three days Samson will be gone—forever. We can't allow that to happen."

Chapter 42

It was Tuesday, middle of the afternoon. Forty-eight hours to go until Samson attempted his great escape. An escape that Mike was determined would never happen. The three friends had strategized until late in the evening on Monday. They knew they needed to be at the airport well before Samson's Gulfstream was scheduled to fly—so around 1:00 in the afternoon. And they were relieved knowing this was not going to be the giant Pearson International Airport that they would have to negotiate their way around. Buttonville was a small privately-owned municipal airport where security would not be quite as stringent, and access to all areas would be quick and more convenient for them.

They needed a plan, and also needed free and unencumbered access. Jim came up with an idea; his brilliantly structured accountant's brain was usually the one they counted on for the details and mechanics of any business idea they adopted. This time was no exception. Jim was also a genius at desktop graphics and printing. He would produce three authentic-looking 'Transport Canada' identification tags in phony names. These tags would have the Canadian flag with the iconic red maple leaf—that alone usually made people want to genuflect in reverence. He would have the tags laminated and equipped with metal clips that could easily be affixed to the pockets of their suit jackets.

The research they did on Buttonville airport gave them their opening. The Greater Toronto Airport Authority (GTAA) had cancelled subsidies over a year ago, and since that time the private owners of the airport struck a deal with a large developer to have the airport land developed for a residential community. The airport was no longer viable after the subsidy was cut, so the owners had sought out an alternative use for this prime land north of Toronto.

The economic recession had put the plans on hold, it seemed. The land was supposed to be developed within the next five years, but that deadline now looked weak. So the airport would have to continue to operate until economic conditions made the development more viable. Which meant they needed a subsidy, or funding, from somewhere. Since the federal government already funded several regional airports throughout the country, it was logical that they might consider Buttonville, to make up for what the GTAA would no longer do and keep the capacity of the airport functioning. Obviously this would be in the best interests of everyone.

Logically, a surprise visit from officials of Transport Canada to conduct a spot inspection would probably not be opposed by the airport management, nor would it be seen as intrusive. It would instead be most likely welcomed with open arms—the prospects of money always opened doors. A fact of life that the three executives at Baxter Development Corporation were more than intimate with.

They would wear their best suits—dark of course—and wear the usual sunglasses, cop fashion, that government employees liked to wear. They would look like "men in black."

The only one of the three who owned sort of a weapon was Troy—a replica 357 Magnum pellet gun, complete with hip holster. He would bring it along and to the untrained eye, and not up too close, it would look like the menacing real thing. They would have to make sure that Samson and his men didn't get too close a look at it, because their eyes were definitely trained. It wouldn't do much damage if he had to use it, depending of course on which part of the body he aimed it at, but it would come in handy for what they had in mind.

Their plan was simple—capture Samson and take him back with them to the police. What happened to him after that they could only hope for, but at least they would prevent the guy from leaving the country. Mike deduced that he had no chance whatsoever if the man escaped. His only chance of redemption was to grab the bastard, hold him, and deliver him. After that, whatever happened was up to fate.

*****

It was Wednesday, and Mike was a man on a mission. One day to go until their dangerous caper, and he was feeling a bit scared about what could happen to him and his buddies—actually a lot scared.

He was driving north from his rented apartment towards his house in Rosedale, using Yonge Street today because traffic was light. It had bogged down on most of the secondary roads and he figured most drivers had assumed Yonge Street would be even worse. So they avoided it, and Mike had basically a traffic-free drive because of their paranoia.

Traffic around Toronto had been chaotic since the subway attacks. A large portion of the northern line was destroyed, and the entire section of the east connector route would be closed until reconstruction was completed on the north route. This would take at least two years by all accounts, which meant Torontonians would have to become accustomed to finding more creative ways of getting to work.

After a few days of Mike hovering over Cindy following the attack, she had asked him to move out again. She said his presence reminded her too much of what had happened at the school gym, a horror she chose not to revisit in her mind. So, Mike reluctantly packed his bags once again and moved back to his apartment. He understood, of course. Post-Traumatic Stress was what Bob Teskey had diagnosed, and Bob would continue to treat Cindy until she was largely over the shock. Mike was comforted knowing that she would have the best of care from a doctor who was also a family friend.

So today, the day before the big takedown, Mike wanted to see his family—not to scare them by telling them what he was doing, but just to see them, kiss them, say a subtle goodbye…just in case. And after that, he had one more important visit to make today—to see Ali and Jonas. To say his goodbyes to them as well. They had become almost as important to him as his own family. He didn't completely understand why. Well, part of him had an inkling—the bullying of Jonas and the brutality that his mother had faced with her husband. Their vulnerability had touched him and brought back painful memories of how cruel he himself had been in high school, a past that had now returned to haunt him—and incredibly, an entire city as well—decades later.

Mike pulled into his circular driveway and noticed another car was already parked at the front entrance. He thought he recognized the car, then confirmed it when he saw the license plate with the block letters 'MD' preceding the numbers. Bob Teskey was here. Damn—he wanted to see Cindy and the girls alone. Bob must have dropped in to check on Cindy because she had been reluctant to go out on her own for appointments since the attack.

Mike used his key and opened the front door. Silence. Something stopped him from calling out. He walked around the main floor first. Then he headed up the stairs. The door to their bedroom was closed. Mike held onto the doorknob and paused to catch his breath for a brief moment. Summoning up the courage, he turned the knob and flung the door wide open.

Cindy was naked on their bed, face down, with a naked Bob kneeling over her massaging her back. Bob turned at the sound, but Cindy didn't seem to react at all; as if she hadn't even heard the door open.

Mike stood in the doorway, mouth open, arms trembling, fists clenching. He couldn't think of any words to shout that would suit the image that was assaulting him from their bed. It was like a bad dream.

Bob jumped from the bed and grabbed for his clothes that were draped over the night table. Cindy turned her head lazily and looked back at Mike. Her face suddenly mirrored the shock that was all over Mike's face. They stared at each other, their eyes reflecting the anguish that both of them felt at that moment.

Bob had his clothes on in mere seconds and cautiously made his way toward the doorway that Mike was standing sentry over. When he got within a few feet, he scratched the top of his head and with a squeak in his voice, said, "I know this doesn't look good, Mike. But it's not Cindy's fault—it's mine. Please don't blame her. It just happened."

Mike could feel his temples throbbing, and fists clenching so hard that the palms of his hands felt like a thousand knives were digging into them. He slowly raised his arms toward a boxing position, and Bob jumped backwards, stark fear on his face. Bob had been hit by Mike before, and must have remembered it as clearly as if it were yesterday.

Mike wanted to punch the shit out of the sleazy prick so badly, but then he realized with some surprise that for the first time he had some control over this. The focus of his sharp mind was causing the anger to subside and he could feel his fists slowly unclench.

"I'm not going to hit you, Bob. I don't want an assault charge complicating my presentation to the medical board to have your license revoked. You will never practice again. I'll be happy to see you disgraced."

Bob began sputtering. "Mike…there's no…need for that. We've been friends…forever."

"Yes, we have, Bob. That's exactly the point, isn't it? Now get the fuck out of my house before I change my mind and rip your cock off and ram it up your ass!"

Mike adjusted his stance to allow Bob to pass by him. The man wasted no time, racing through the door and taking the stairs down three at a time.

Mike turned his attention to Cindy. She was sitting up in bed now, a sheet wrapped around her, head in her hands, sobbing, sniffling.

He walked slowly over to the bed, and sat down on the edge. He put his hand on the back of her head and gently ruffled her hair just the way she always liked. She cried harder. Mike put his arm around her shoulders and hugged her. She looked up at him, enquiring, puzzled.

He gazed back at her. "It's okay. I think I understand. I'm sad, but I'm not angry."

Cindy's face was flushed a deep red, and her eyes were bloodshot from the crying. "Mike, I feel sick. It didn't mean…anything to me. I love you…and I'm so sorry. You've just been…different lately. I've been so confused."

"Shhh. Go to sleep, Cindy. I'm okay. Goodbye, and say goodbye to the girls for me."

*****

Mike pulled up in front of the little red clapboard house, still in a daze, but focused on his next goodbye. He was doing his best to shut out the image of his wife naked on the bed with their doctor. There was a pain somewhere in the area of his heart, but he ignored it.

He headed up the walkway and knocked on the door. Ali opened up within seconds, greeting him with a smile that lit up the street. She wrapped her arms around his neck and kissed him on the earlobe. "You love to surprise me, don't you? Jonas and I are so lucky to have you pop in on us like this. Always makes our day!"

Mike smiled and hugged her back. It felt right. It felt real. It felt like she had always been in his arms.

Jonas came running when he heard Mike's voice. They jostled a bit, then settled down into a kind of father/son discussion. Jonas told Mike all that had happened since the last time he visited. He was back at school and the big kids weren't making fun of him as much. He was now enjoying school again, which warmed Mike's heart to hear.

"And Jonas has just graduated into the third phase of his speech therapy," Ali chimed in eagerly. Mike ran his fingers through Jonas' hair and then hugged him tightly. Jonas hugged him back just as hard.

Ali made dinner for the three of them—lasagna, her specialty. It was delicious. They chatted at the table for an hour before she shooed Jonas off to bed. He protested, but to no avail. Ali was a good mother, kind and stern—the right combination of both. Ali took Mike by the hand and led him into the living room, guiding him onto the couch. She then went to the kitchen and came back seconds later with a bottle of champagne.

"What's that for?" Mike asked innocently.

"We have two things to celebrate tonight—Jonas's success in his speech therapy, and my graduation as a Nurse Practitioner. I'm no longer just a Registered Nurse. I can now perform some of the same functions that doctors can perform! My salary will go up dramatically, so we won't need your financial help anymore."

"Oh, that's so wonderful. I'm ecstatic for you, Ali. But now I no longer have an excuse to come visit you guys."

Ali moved closer to him and whispered, "Yes, you do. We need you, for just being you. How's that for a good excuse?"

Mike nodded his head. "Yep, that's a good one. I'll use that one." He smiled tenderly at her, entranced by the gleam in her eyes.

Then to his shock he just blurted it out. "I caught my wife in bed with our doctor tonight."

Ali just looked at him with sadness in her eyes and said nothing. Instead, she gently held him by the hand, her other hand grabbing the champagne ice bucket, and led him off the couch and into her bedroom. Mike felt his willpower begin to melt away.

He stood in the dark bedroom, knowing what was about to happen—conflicted, not knowing whether it should happen. But a part of him was saying that this was happening as it was intended to happen. It was intended that he catch his wife in bed with Teskey tonight, and it was intended that he would be here at Ali's tonight saying a goodbye. A goodbye that had now turned into something else, something wonderful, something…intended.

He continued to stand still, waiting for…something. He heard a rustling behind him, felt her arms wrapping around his chest, then the feel of gentle fingers undoing the buttons of his shirt, followed by his jeans dropping to the floor. Ali slid the shirt off his back and pressed against him. He could feel that she was already naked, her soft firm thighs rubbing against his, her nipples getting hard against his back. She swayed to and fro, rubbing her lovely breasts against him. Mike tried to turn around and exert some control, but she held him firm. She wasn't finished yet. She slid her tongue down the middle of his back and onto the flesh of his buttocks. Mike groaned.

He could smell her perfume, Chanel #5, wafting into his nostrils, could hear her heavy breathing as she licked his body. He felt helpless as she went to work, and was more than aware of the sweetly painful bulge in his tight underpants as she continued to make him wait. She wouldn't let him turn around and feel her and it was driving him crazy. A good kind of crazy.

She pushed him gently onto the bed and pressured her hand on one side to indicate that she wanted him face up. He obeyed—he was putty in her hands now. He looked up. In the darkness of the room she was just a silhouette, a beautiful ghost working wonders on his senses. Ali sat on his lap as he lay there helpless. She swayed back and forth, slowly, seductively. His penis was throbbing but she wouldn't let him penetrate. She left him wanting it, crying for it. Her beautiful body was like a mirage, a blurry image against the backdrop of the ceiling.

Suddenly she leaned toward the side of the bed and reached her hand into the champagne bucket, scooping a handful of ice and popping it into her sensuous mouth. She swirled it around and to Mike's glorious shock, spread her mouth across his right nipple. The freezing cold of the ice, contrasting with the heat that now enveloped his entire body, made him shudder.

She wasn't finished with him yet. He watched her move, reveled in the motion and touch of her tongue, and then gazed in fascination as she reached across the bed once again, grabbed the champagne bottle and took a swig. Once again, she swirled the contents around in her mouth.

She pulled her hair back with both hands, lowered her head and pounced on his erect penis, swallowing it, allowing the champagne bubbles to stimulate the tip. Mike at first fought the urge to scream, then decided to just let it out. Hearing the sound of his anguished cry reverberate around the room, he looked up at her pleadingly as she raised herself into position. He knew she was smiling but it was too dark to tell. Alison took him, all of him, and he knew at that moment the torture he had just endured had been the most exhilarating feeling of his entire life.

Chapter 43

It was Thursday, and the three friends were bracing themselves for whatever this day would bring. They were silent as Troy drove them eastward in his Chrysler 300 along the Gardiner Expressway. As they swerved north along the Don Valley Parkway, Mike could feel the butterflies start. He looked over at Troy, eyes focused on the road, a stern look of determination on his face. Glancing into the back seat at Jim, Mike caught his eyes for an instant. Jim quickly looked away. He had been biting his fingernails all morning and Mike noticed that one of Jim's fingers was bleeding a bit. He handed him back a tissue. Jim just nodded, wrapped it around his finger and looked out the window again.

Mike went over the plan in his mind. It wasn't all that sophisticated. They were really just going to wing it and hope for the element of surprise. None of them were experienced at this covert stuff, so they would have no choice but to just follow their instincts. They were each dressed in black: black suits, black ties, shiny black shoes, the look capped off with intimidating sunglasses. Well, Mike hoped they were intimidating, or at the very least official looking. Jim had made up the laminated Transport Canada identification badges, and they were clipped to their lapels. Mike was pleased. Jim had done a great job as usual, and these badges looked like the real thing. The red Canadian maple leaf should succeed at opening doors easily for them and keep the curious questions at bay.

"Troy, did you pack your gun?"

Troy patted his hip. "Yes, boss. Right here."

"Did you put a fresh cylinder in?"

Troy smirked. " Do you think I'm daft? Of course I did. It's locked and loaded."

"Good." Mike turned to look out the side window. He thought back to his exhilarating experience with Ali the night before, and tried to make some sense out of it. But he'd pretty much given up on that. It was too amazing and too unexpected to try to rationalize. Why it felt so right to him, he had no idea.

But he was going to enjoy re- living it because it had been the most exciting... and the most lingering...sexual experience of his entire life. He pictured her in his mind, a dark intoxicating shadow swigging champagne, then dive-bombing him, bubbles tickling his penis, stimulating it beyond belief. The daydream he was having was so realistic that he could feel a woody coming on. He quickly folded his hands over his lap in embarrassment. What would his friends think if they noticed he was having an erection at a time like this?

His thoughts were brought back to earth by the vibration of his cell phone. Mike pulled it out of his pocket and looked at the screen. Cindy. He hesitated for a couple of seconds, not sure whether or not he wanted to talk to her. Then he broke down and punched the button. "Hi, Cindy."

"Mike, I'm so glad I reached you. I know you probably don't want to talk to me, but I wanted to let you know that the RCMP are here right now. They had a search warrant so I couldn't stop them. They're looking for you too. I think they want to arrest you." She paused, and Mike could hear her crying. Then she came back on. "Mike, what is going on? How did we get to this point? I don't know what to do, don't know what to say to you. Why do they want you?"

Mike cringed. *A search warrant. It was happening.*

"Settle down, Cindy. And don't think about last night, okay? We'll talk about that later when we're both much calmer. As for the search warrant, just stay out of their way. I can't talk about why they may want to arrest me, not yet. Trust me, I'm the good guy but it may be hard to prove. I'm working on that."

"Mike...what can I do? I love you."

"Nothing you can do. Just don't tell them you talked to me."

"Where are you, Mike?"

"Can't tell you that, Cindy. I gotta go. Goodbye hon."

Mike felt tears start to roll down his cheeks as he clicked off. He put his phone back in his pocket only to feel it immediately start vibrating again. He pulled it out and looked at the screen. Stephanie. "Hello, Steph."

"Mike, it's chaos over here. The RCMP came in with a search warrant. They're tearing your office apart right now. Everyone here knows—they're panicking."

"Okay, Stephanie—just let them do their thing. Nothing we can do to stop them."

"Mike, what's going on? Why are they searching your office?"

"Can't tell you that, Stephanie. Just trust me when I say that what they're looking for I had nothing to do with. Gotta go."

Mike looked over at Troy and Jim. "It's goin down, guys. Right now—simultaneous search warrants at my house and our office."

*****

Troy was turning off Highway 404 onto 16th Avenue in Markham. He and Mike exchanged glances as signs appeared announcing Buttonville Municipal Airport. Mike looked at his watch—12:45 p.m. They had plenty of time to get to the plane before it was scheduled to leave at 2:00. It was probably being serviced right now in preparation. Troy turned onto the road leading to the airport terminal and made a sharp right onto a driveway that led to a parking lot for the private charters and flight training center. The Skyspace hangar with its dramatic blue and yellow logo signage was dead ahead. Mike motioned Troy to park at the far end of the parking lot, just in case Samson knew the make and color of Troy's car. Mike doubted it—Samson had already seen Jim's car near the alley that day when Mike was beaten up, and he most likely knew all of the cars Mike owned. But Troy's car had been invisible so far.

They exited the car and began their walk. Troy buttoned his suit jacket to make sure the gun wasn't visible. Mike led the way and whispered over to his two friends, "Walk tall and confident, guys. We need to show some government arrogance here to be believable."

They wanted to avoid the main terminal. Too much bureaucracy there and it wasn't necessary for them to visit the terminal anyway for what they had to do. The private hangar area was what they wanted, and there were several hangars. But Skyspace was the only one that interested them.

Mike opened the front office door to Skyspace, and held it for his friends. He approached the reception desk. The office looked professional and luxury-adorned. The large waiting area had leather chairs, module pods equipped with computers, a large buffet counter with appetizers and coffee, along with a well-stocked complimentary bar. Skyspace clearly catered to a wealthy and exclusive clientele.

The well-dressed girl at reception looked up as he approached. "Hello, sir. How can I help you?" Mike could see her eyes drop to the badge clipped to his jacket.

"Hi. I'm Paul Burnett from Transport Canada. These two gentlemen are my colleagues. We're here at the airport doing a review and assessment of the facilities. We may possibly revive the subject of subsidization of costs for this airport, but we need to update ourselves on the capabilities of public and private facilities here first."

She smiled and put her hand over the heart area of her chest. "Oh, that's wonderful. We've all been so worried that the airport would close. What can I do to help you? Just ask."

Mike had gotten the reaction he'd wanted. He knew the possible airport closure would be a sore point with the people that worked there. The residential development now being in limbo left the airport vulnerable to early closure. And with the recession still in full swing, there weren't many jobs around, particularly airport jobs.

"That's very nice of you. All we'd like to do is take a look at your hangar and examine the condition of it, do an assessment of the current state of your taxiways, and take a look at the type of planes that make use of your services. We'll try not to disturb anyone."

"Oh, that's easy, then. Just go through that door behind me. That will lead you down the hall past several offices, turn right at the end, then down that hall and go through the far door. That will take you into the hangar. And from there, you can simply walk out to the taxiways. We have three jets stored in the hangar right now, so that will give you a good idea. Oh, and we also have a large Gulfstream out on the taxiway. It's scheduled for takeoff in less than an hour. Feel free to walk out and talk to the pilots. Ask them how they like our services. The stairway is extended already—you can just mosey on in and chat until it has to take off."

Mike smiled through his official sunglasses. This was going to be easier than he thought. "That's wonderful. Thanks so much for your help. I'll make sure your name gets positive mention in our report. Great cooperation. What's your name, please?" Mike took a pad of paper and pen out of his pocket.

Her face was beaming. "Marilyn, and if anyone stops you just tell them you have my approval. I'm the office manager here."

"Okay, Marilyn. Nice chatting with you."

Mike nodded to his friends and they quickly made their way through the door and down the long hallway, following Marilyn's directions the rest of the way. Once in the hangar, as they had rehearsed beforehand, they walked around and pretended to study the facilities. Some workers looked up as they snooped around the jets, but just nodded when they saw the badges with the Canadian maple leaf. They were convincing. No one stopped them. No one seemed concerned.

After their faux inspection of the hangar, Mike led the way out onto the taxiway. They tried to look officious, like they knew what they were doing—looking back at the hangar, bending over to examine the asphalt surfaces of the taxiway. All the while subtly moving closer and closer to the majestic Gulfstream jet that was almost ready for takeoff.

When they were within several yards of the jet, Mike whispered to Troy and Jim. "It's time, guys. Follow me, and stay alert."

Mike led the way to the extended stairway of the private jet and started up, his two comrades following. He entered the plane and waited in the galley for his friends to join him, putting his finger to his lips to signal silence. He motioned to Troy to pull out his pellet gun.

Suddenly they heard a whirring noise and the stairway started rising, forcing Jim and Troy to leap forward into the galley. It closed with a solid 'thunk.' They were stranded, locked inside a plane that was about to take off for Panama.

Mike saw the panic in his friends' eyes. He quickly waved it off and signaled them to follow him around the corner of the galley into the main cabin. First he glanced left towards the cockpit—the door was closed and probably locked. He could hear a rustling noise inside. He ignored it and led his friends slowly down into the main cabin to see if there was anyone in the rear of the jet. If not, he knew they would have no choice but to try to storm the cockpit. He looked back. Troy had his gun in hand safely pointed up at the ceiling.

Suddenly Mike heard laughter, a mocking kind of laughter. He whirled around and saw that the cockpit door was now open and two men were exiting, doubled over chuckling.

The man whose face alone gave Mike nightmares abruptly stopped laughing. "Hello, Michael. And your two friends must be Troy and Jim. It is so nice of you all to join us. You must have heard that Panama is lovely this time of the year, no? We were watching you and wondered when you would finally find the courage to actually board the plane. Now you are here, and we are all together. Wonderful. It will be a smooth flight to Panama. Well, at least for me it will be smooth." He started laughing again.

Mike stared back in barely-masked rage at David Samson. And behind him the Clint Eastwood character; the one who had wreaked absolute havoc upon the city of Toronto. And indeed, upon Mike's very existence.

Chapter 44

The three friends stood frozen as Samson turned around and yelled into the cockpit. "Get this thing off the ground! Now!"

The smooth Rolls Royce engines began to whir, and they could hear the steady whoosh of the air system start to circulate within the cabin. Out of the corner of his eye, Mike could see Troy slide the pellet gun back into his belt underneath his jacket. Jim had been blocking a clear view of Troy, so hopefully Samson and Eastwood hadn't seen the weapon yet.

The jet began to taxi, and Samson motioned with his hand. "You know the drill. Please, you will sit down and fasten your seatbelts. Or maybe you will choose not to. I do not care either way."

Mike sat down on one of the couches and pulled his seatbelt around his waist, followed by his forlorn friends who plopped down on the couch opposite him. They exchanged glances; glances that were now empty of any optimism. Their plan had failed. How could they have been so stupid as to think they would have been able to take on these international terrorists? A plan born out of desperation—Mike's desperation. And his two friends were now into this up to their necks. Samson had always been a couple of steps ahead of them right from the beginning. And now, what kind of ending did he have planned for them? Mike shuddered at the thought. They had no control now over the outcome.

The jet reached the main runway and turned in a 180 degree spin, ready for takeoff. Samson sat down in the plush leather seat perpendicular to Mike's couch. He smiled, in his own crazy confident way. He was always in control; had been in control throughout this entire ordeal. Today was no different.

Mike felt the thrust of the plane as it rose into the sky. They were now on their way to Panama whether they liked it or not. What was going to happen down there, he didn't have a clue.

Samson unfastened his seat belt, stretched his long legs out and sighed. "Michael, you can get comfortable now. And relax. You are flying in one of the most technologically advanced aircraft in the entire world."

Mike turned his head and stared into Samson's black eyes. "Why would you think I could relax? What do you intend to do with us?"

Samson smiled. "By now you have figured out who I am, yes? You remember our wonderful high school years, yes? I never forgot you, Michael. You made quite the impression on me." He chuckled. "Yes, without you, I would never have become the man I am today. Perhaps I should actually thank you?" Another chuckle.

"That was decades ago, Samson. That's an awful long time to hold a grudge."

In the blink of an eye Samson jumped to his feet and slapped Mike hard across the face. "You and your football friends created my life, Michael. You created a Frankenstein. You are proud of your creation, no? Did you think I would live a normal life after what you put me through?"

Mike rubbed the side of his face. He could feel it burning—that was no normal slap. He could also feel a rage beginning to burn within his gut. He struggled to control it, knowing full well that fighting back now would lead to no good. Not at 35,000 feet in the air, and having to depend on these maniacs to get them back on the ground safely.

The cockpit door opened, and out walked an Arab man dressed in jeans and a sweatshirt. *One of the pilots. One of theirs.* He walked back to where they were sitting and said something in Arabic to Samson. Samson nodded and the man walked back to the cockpit, leaving the door open this time. He obviously wasn't concerned.

Samson got up from his seat and called to Eastwood sitting near the front. "Omar, watch these three while I use the washroom." Omar nodded and walked back to them, taking a seat next to Troy.

So now Eastwood had a name—'Omar.' Mike thought that he looked more like an Igor than an Omar. The man who had murdered hundreds of people in Toronto and who was now the subject of a worldwide manhunt, was sitting just mere feet away from him.

Samson came out of the washroom and took his seat again. "You want to know something, Michael? I decided to ruin your life just like you ruined mine. And I think I have succeeded, no?" He made a flourish with his hands. "And your two stooges here, well, it looks like I may have ruined their lives too. Ha, it is their fault for being friends with an egotistical bastard like you. Big man, eh? You were always the big man. How big do you feel now, Michael?"

Mike squirmed in his seat. "Does that justify killing hundreds? Why didn't you just concentrate on me? Why kill all those people?"

"Because, Michael. You made it easy for me to hate. It was easy for me to appreciate that all of you are the same. The plight of the Palestinians is an example of how you in the West feel about people who are different than you—the downtrodden, the different colors and cultures. You want us all to look and think like you. And if we do not, you humiliate us, demean us, and imprison us. It makes us want to just slaughter you all."

Mike looked over at his friends. Jim seemed to be in a state of shock. Troy, however, was sliding his hand down slowly towards his waist. Mike gave a slight shake of his head. Troy saw it and drew his hand back.

Samson was eager to talk again. "I have tracked you for years. Deliberately sought out a job with your company. Gerry was a very nice man, nice that he hired me. But then he fired me. I was not ready to be fired. I had not yet done what I had wanted to do with you.

"So, that is when I found a way back in. Gerry's weakness for a pretty woman did him in. You probably did not know that? No? I can tell by the look of surprise on your face. Yes, it appears the two of them had been carrying on for many years already before I discovered it. Your close friend Gerry had been living a double life. The two of them loved to meet at that same café, the Metro*Cafe*, where you and I met for lunch. You remember that day I am sure." Samson chuckled. "I had him watched, tracked, videotaped, photographed, and recorded. Then I blackmailed him. I had a lot of dirt on him. He was so afraid of his lovely wife and kids finding out, he was easy. I enlisted him for some…ah…purchases, which you already know about of course. I made a lot of money off your company thanks to poor Gerry. And I killed some of his family members to make him compliant each time he started getting…how do you say…cold feet? He was terrified that his wife and children would be next. Which of course they would have been—I was running out of more distant relatives to kill." Samson laughed.

Mike felt the rage rumbling stronger inside of him the longer that Samson talked. He was confirming everything that Mike had already figured out, but hearing it right from the horse's mouth made the rage even worse.

But he certainly hadn't known about Gerry's affair. That was a surprise. It was obvious that he really hadn't known Gerry as well as he thought he had. And this had been going on for years, according to Samson. Considering that Samson had been fired over five years ago, right after which he hatched his dirty blackmail scheme, that meant the affair could have been going on for at least seven or eight years…or even longer?

"Isn't it ironic, Michael, that you and I had lunch at the Metro*Cafe*, the same place where Gerry used to meet with his little whore?"

Mike flinched. "Did you plan it that way?"

"Oh, yes. There is something about us dirty little Arabs that you should know—we love symbolism. We really love it."

Mike unfastened his seatbelt and stretched his own legs out, to match the length of Samson's. "People will be looking for us. You should land at the nearest airport and let us go. You want a clean escape. Having us with you doesn't allow you that."

"Oh, I have a plan, Michael. Just relax for a while. Our flight plan takes us over the continental United States and then over the Gulf of Mexico. We may adjust our plan a little bit, but by and large you should have wonderful scenery to view. Or just take a nap. I do not care one way or the other." Samson rubbed his chin thoughtfully. "I've been wondering how you knew about this plane, and it occurs to me that you must have found the information in my office. At the time you killed Fadiyah. Yes? Was that you?"

Mike didn't answer. Instead he just glared at the handsome, twisted killer.

"Ah, your silence tells me so much, Michael. Well, you have earned some respect. She was one of the most highly trained assassins ever to come out of the Middle East. Or…hmm…perhaps you had some help?" Samson glanced over at Jim and Troy, who were sitting quietly across from Mike. He smiled at them. "Yes, you and your friends must have ambushed her like the cowards you are. You have just lost my respect, Michael. You had it for all of five seconds." Samson got up and walked towards the cockpit. Omar was still sitting next to Troy, eyes flitting from left to right, making sure that he didn't miss even the most miniscule of movements.

Mike sighed, laid his head back, and closed his eyes. He didn't think he was going to be able to sleep, but he needed to think. What was Samson's plan and what would his own move be and when? He knew he had to make a move, gain control somehow. Jim and Troy were waiting for him to lead, just like he always did…but Mike wasn't sure he could this time.

*****

Mike awoke with a start. There was a sudden change. It was very subtle but his senses picked up something. *What was it?* He glanced at his watch; they'd been in the air only three hours, so it was far too early to have reached

Panama. He turned his head and looked out the window. It was still light out, and all he could see was water. They must be over the Gulf of Mexico, he thought. The timing would be about right.

He looked around. Omar was still sitting across from him, staring at him with his unblinking eyes. Jim and Troy looked stricken. He knew they had detected the change as well and were as puzzled as he was. Mike listened, raising his senses to full alert. The engines had slowed and now he could see by the angle of the plane compared to the horizon outside that it was descending. *Why would they be descending over the vast Gulf of Mexico?*

The airframe started shaking as they continued to descend. Mike knew this was simple turbulence that would always be experienced at lower altitudes, just potholes in the sky. As the air became warmer, it was more active as compared with the generally calm, thin, and cold air of higher altitudes. *Where had that come from? What the fuck?* The shaking became worse and the powerful jet began to sway from side to side. Mike knew that the pilot would need to reduce the speed quite a bit in order to mitigate the stress on the airframe; but not by too much or it would stall. And at the altitude they were now at there wouldn't be much time to recover from a stall. *What?* Suddenly a windburst came from the starboard side of the jet, and it caused it to slip sideways. Mike knew the starboard side would be affected more as they flew south over the Gulf as the winds at this height generally moved from west to east quite aggressively. *Starboard?*

Mike stole another glance out the window. He could clearly see the whitecaps on the water now, but he estimated they were still about 9,000 feet above the water. *Estimated?*

Mike unfastened his seatbelt, and, holding onto the top of the chair frames for support, began working his way up the aisle toward the cockpit. Omar jumped up and in a flash there was a gun in his hand, a short-barreled pistol. "Sit down, Mr. Baxter. You do not need to go up there."

Mike stared at the gun pointed at his head. Omar's cold black eyes stared right back. The tall and confident terrorist's steady hand did not waver. Mike knew he would fire and knew also that at the altitude they were at, a gunshot into the frame or through the frame would not be catastrophic. At less than 10,000 feet, the cabin was depressurized. The pressure inside the plane was now the same as the outside. On the other hand, while in flight at high altitudes, the cabin of a plane would always be pressurized as if it was at an altitude of 10,000 feet, which was the altitude pressure deemed most comfortable for passengers. Now, the pressure was equal, so there would be no effect from Pressure Gradient Force, which was the behavior of air always flowing from higher pressure to lower pressure. Mike knew this was the reason that passengers had been sucked out of airplanes when holes tore open at high altitudes, or when an emergency door or baggage door broke open. *Pressure Gradient Force? What the fuck is that?*

Mike shook his head trying to clear the thoughts that were now racing through it. It was like a rush of knowledge, of clarity. He felt scared to the bone, but there was something else going on now. A sense of confidence and familiarity was entering his mind, and the strangest feeling of invincibility—strange for sure, especially considering the predicament they were in.

He had a sudden recall of words spoken to him during his last official psychological appointment with his now sworn enemy, Dr. Bob Teskey: *'But further study may discover that other emotions could also cause other aspects of Gerry to emerge. Right now we know that fear doesn't cause the fighting mode, but it could under the right situation cause an entirely different skill of Gerry's to emerge.'*

It was starting to become clear to Mike. Gerry had been a fighter pilot in the military. He had also been a commercial pilot for one of the large national airlines. He had flown most things that had wings. This knowledge that was now entering his brain under these stressful and fearful circumstances was Gerry's knowledge. It was appearing at the right time, and fear seemed to be the trigger for this particular skill. Bob Teskey had been right—other skills might emerge from other emotions. The fear of being trapped in an airplane that was clearly going to tear apart if it didn't reduce speed, was dragging out Gerry's knowledge of flying aircraft from the deep recesses of Mike's brain. Mike realized in astonishment that he had the advantage of two emotions happening simultaneously right now: anger bringing out the boxer, and fear bringing out the pilot. The more often this weird stuff happened to him, the easier he was finding it to understand, accept, and rationalize.

"Mr. Baxter—I said sit down! Now!"

Mike snapped out of his trance, but stood his ground. "Omar, or whatever the fuck your real name is, the pilot has to reduce speed. Now! There is far too much turbulence for the airframe to handle at the speed he's flying. It could start to tear apart."

Mike's two buddies, sitting behind where Omar was standing, looked up at him in astonishment; mouths open, eyes wide.

Omar didn't budge. "We do not care what you think. We do not need your advice. Our pilots know what they are doing. Now sit down!"

Mike reluctantly obeyed, but began wringing his hands in frustration. He knew what would happen if the jet continued at this speed in this turbulence. Almost as if in answer to his concern, the plane dropped suddenly, a violent force that Mike could feel from his feet right up to his stomach. He was airborne for just a moment, rising quickly towards the ceiling. Quick instincts saved his head from being smashed; he managed to grab onto the rail on top of the couch holding his body from rising more than the length of his arms. Omar wasn't as lucky. He hadn't had the chance to sit down and buckle up before the sudden drop came. He flew straight up like a rocket, head impacting with the floor when he came down.

This was their chance—perhaps the only one they'd get. Mike pounced on top of the giant body, and started pummeling the killer's face with his fists. Rapid punches, one after the other, drawing blood from the nose and each eye. Suddenly he felt the cold shock of steel against his temple. "I have a hard head, Mr. Baxter. Get off me before I kill you."

Mike rose slowly to his feet and watched the giant struggle to get up, gun still trained at his head. Once Omar was up, he took one step forward and smashed the butt of the pistol into Mike's temple, knocking him backwards against the bulkhead. Then he stepped forward and positioned the barrel of the gun up against Mike's forehead, just above his nose. "I think I will just kill you anyway."

Mike heard the unmistakable click of a seatbelt being unfastened, and caught a simultaneous blur of movement out of the corner of his eye. Troy was on the move, and his replica 357 Magnum pellet gun suddenly violated the airspace between Mike and the terrorist. Troy rammed the barrel of the gun into Omar's right eye, hammer cocked, hammer slamming—twice. A blood-curdling scream and a burst of blood, as two steel pellets in quick succession tore through Omar's eyeball. Mike ducked to get out of the way of Omar's gun, then spun around and wrenched the pistol from his hand. The killer went down but Troy wasn't finished. He jumped on top of the squirming man, shoved the gun up against his left eyeball and pulled the trigger again, twice.

Mike marveled at Troy's smarts as he watched him pull himself back off the now useless threat. Troy had known that the pellet gun was basically impotent unless it was used on the right part of the body. The eyes were the best part to target—soft and fleshy, guaranteed to be blind after being hit. Omar was basically now out of commission.

Jim was out of his seat as well. He grabbed a nearby meal cart and led the way toward the cockpit, pushing it in front of him. "C'mon guys, we don't have much time. I'll ram, you guys shoot. Just don't shoot me!"

The three friends made a mad dash toward the now closed cockpit. Samson had to be in there, or in the washroom. Since he hadn't been seen for quite a while now, Mike guessed he was in with the pilots.

Jim rammed the meal cart into the door and it opened instantly. It hadn't been locked. The three friends stared at what at first glance seemed like an empty cockpit. Mike smelled a trap. "Jim, get back! Quick, get…"

Too late. From out of view of the open door, a rope lasso swung out and over Jim's head, unseen hands pulled it tight around his neck. Jim's body was yanked over the cart, and slammed hard against the back of the empty captain's chair. Now three figures appeared from the sides of the cockpit. Samson himself held the lasso and pulled the semi-conscious Jim up to a standing position. Then he began to tighten the noose as he smiled in that evil way that only Samson could smile. Jim's face was red, his breathing labored and his eyes were bulging. His glasses had fallen off his face in the tussle, making him seem even more vulnerable.

"Now, Michael. Throw Omar's gun into the cockpit please. And your friend can also throw his little spitball gun in here too. If you do not do as I say, I will tear this fool's head off right in front of your eyes. And Michael, we both know how much you enjoy watching your friends being beheaded." Samson chuckled.

On either side of Samson stood the two pilots. None of them were holding weapons. But the noose was weapon enough. Mike and Troy didn't hesitate for a second. They threw their guns forward. Mike squinted as he gazed into the cockpit and noticed that one of the screens in front of the captain's chair had a live display of the entire cabin. The screen showed Omar's body writhing on the floor. Samson and his pilots had watched the entire ordeal that had just taken place in the cabin and had done absolutely nothing to stop it. Puzzling.

The two pilots picked up the pistols and aimed them in front of them, leading the way for Samson who was brutally dragging Jim along by the neck. They waved Mike and Troy back, gesturing with their weapons, saying nothing. Mike and Troy backed up past the galley, into the cabin again.

Mike knew that the jet was now on automatic pilot, and it seemed to have leveled off. A quick glance out the window told him they were at about 6,000 feet above the threatening Gulf waters. The turbulence had mercifully stopped.

He saw one of the pilots push a button in the galley, and then heard an instantaneous whir accompanied by a cool breeze through the cabin. The exit door with the retractable stairway was now open.

Samson motioned Mike to come forward. Mike took a step. Troy grabbed him by the shoulder. "Don't go, Mikey! Don't!" Mike squeezed his shoulder in return, then turned away and completed the remaining tentative steps to the front of the plane. He was very close to Jim now. His friend's eyes were wide open, bloodshot; he was clearly scared out of his mind. His hair was mussed up from the steady breeze that was now streaming into the cabin.

Then Mike noticed something else. Samson and the pilots each had parachute packs strapped to their backs.

Samson smiled at him. "Well, Michael, it looks like for now we are at the end of our road. But I am sure we will meet up again, yes? Perhaps in hell? Yes, we will both be going there. You sooner than me. Not too long from now, this beautiful but helpless jet will run out of fuel and crash into this god-forsaken Gulf of Mexico. A body of water that you westerners have destroyed by your obsession with oil. Yes, Michael, soon you will taste the oil slicks that you and your types have created by your greed. Fitting, no?" He pulled tighter on Jim's noose. Jim gasped, and a sickening gurgling sound came up from his throat. Drool dripped around the edges of his mouth. Mike winced at the sight of his long-time friend being methodically strangled to death, one noose tug at a time.

Samson glanced at the watch on his left wrist, and then examined what looked like a small GPS unit strapped to the other wrist. He gave a subtle nod and the first pilot jumped through the open door, disappearing quickly into the darkening atmosphere. Five seconds later the second pilot followed.

Samson now edged backward towards the open door, pulling Jim with him. Mike looked hard into Jim's eyes; eyes that were pleading, tears streaming down his cheeks. His hair was blown over his forehead, in a carefree way that Mike had never seen before on his straight-laced accountant buddy. At that very moment Mike had the strange ill-timed thought that it suited him much better that way.

Samson had reached the edge of the door now. "No funny business now, Michael. Or your friend comes with me."

Mike raised his hands in surrender. "Just let him go, Samson. I'm not going to stop your escape. Just let him go—please, please."

"Oh, do not worry, my friend. I will indeed let him go." And with that Samson leaped backwards. But he didn't let go of the lasso. To Mike's eyes it was all in slow motion. First Samson disappeared into the darkening sky. When the rope went taut, Jim's head wrenched backwards followed by his obedient body. Out the door he went before Mike could even react. He heard a bang against the side of the plane, and in desperation Mike dove forward onto his chest and eased his head out over the chasm. Miraculously, Jim had managed to grab onto one of the lower steps of the retractable stairway and he was swinging precariously, hanging on by one hand. Far below Mike could see Samson's parachute floating peacefully down to the dark waters below.

Mike yelled back into the cabin. "Troy, hold onto my ankles and brace yourself!" Mike inched forward on his chest and could feel Troy's strong hands grab his ankles. He eased forward a bit more until his stomach was over the edge of the doorway. He hung his right arm down toward the swinging body of his friend.

Jim's eyes were locked onto Mike's. His one free hand reached desperately upward, the other hand hung on for dear life. Mike squirmed forward a bit more until he was almost vertical, bending at the waist. The force of the wind rushing past the airframe was becoming impossible to fight. Their fingertips touched. Jim smiled. Then he was gone.

*****

Troy was sitting in the co-pilot's seat watching Mike work the controls. They'd had no time to grieve for Jim. They were now in a mad dash to save their own lives. Grieving would have to come later. If they didn't pull off a miracle, they would soon be joining Jim in the oily Gulf waters.

Mike was sitting in the captain's chair, and had already contacted Miami International on the slick jet's voice activated dashboard radio system. He had declared a 'Mayday.'

Troy was absolutely astounded by the calm control that Mike was exerting in the cockpit. He had already ascertained that they just had enough fuel to reach Miami. He had taken the plane off autopilot and assumed skillful control, making a slick turn to the northeast. The plane was performing beautifully in his capable hands.

Then Troy had to remind himself that Mike didn't have capable hands. Mike did not know how to fly a plane. Troy knew enough about the lightning phenomenon by now and all the changes that it had wrought on Mike, that he accepted this latest skill as just another of Gerry's magic wands. Troy rubbed his aching forehead, marveling at how far he had come in accepting this mumbo-jumbo about his best friend.

He watched Mike punch more buttons while his alert eyes expertly scanned the instruments one by one. Troy didn't interrupt, didn't offer any help. He knew that Mike would call on him if he needed him for anything. At this moment though he felt strangely reassured by this amazing friend of his sitting calmly in the captain's chair.

The only bit of frustration he had heard Mike express so far was some muttering—almost under his breath—that he had never flown such a high-tech jet like the Gulfstream before. Troy didn't think it was appropriate to remind Mike that he had never flown *any* kind of jet before. Why take a chance on breaking the spell?

He watched in fascination as Mike's hands worked at lightning speed, sliding his hands over the controls, punching buttons, easing back on the 'whatever it was called,' easing forward on the 'whatever it was called.'

Within an hour, Miami International was in sight. Mike arranged clearance for runway number seven, and Troy sat back and enjoyed the smoothest landing he had ever experienced in his life. There wasn't an ounce of fuel to spare either. They had glided in and landed on fumes, and on Mike's incredible magical confidence.

After rolling to a stop halfway down the runway, the two friends looked at each other and smiled in relief. Then they just broke down and cried.

Chapter 45

"...and while there are plenty of temptations in the business world to cloak the truth, emphasize the positives, and downplay the negatives, you can never allow yourselves to cross that line between full disclosure and deception. Publicly traded companies are a sacred trust placed within the hands of the executives who are hired to run them. If you want secrecy, go work for a private company."

Mike gazed around the lecture hall, and he could see that the twenty-something students were all held at rapt attention. He was their celebrity of the hour, a guest lecturer who had something to say, something really important to say. They had read about him in the newspapers, googled him online, and had seen him interviewed on TV. Mike wasn't just the usual guest lecturer—he was indeed a celebrity who had a story to tell, and real lessons to teach.

It had been six months since Mike had glided the Gulfstream jet down onto the runway at Miami International Airport, ending an ordeal that seemed for a while like it would never have an end, at least not one that left Mike alive. The plane landed on fumes, and over the last six months Mike himself had been running on fumes. He was now known internationally as the man who captured the world's most wanted man, did what the FBI, RCMP, CIA, MI5 and countless other acronyms had been incapable of doing.

Mike was an accidental celebrity. And now an unemployed accidental celebrity.

"What I did was wrong, and I'd love to be able to tell you that I did it to protect my family but that wasn't entirely the case. At the time I started the deception, I really had no idea that my family might be in danger or that this man Samson's intentions were as dangerous as they eventually turned out to be. I only discovered his true intent when I got more deeply embroiled in his diabolical scheme.

"I lied to our board of directors and to the shareholders because I wanted to buy time. I had been framed in an embezzlement scheme and I wanted to buy time to clear my name and figure it all out. I was confident enough in myself that I had no doubt I would be able to find a way out of the dilemma if I had more time. But it snowballed out of control. I underestimated the skill and brutality of the people I was dealing with. I was, quite simply,

in over my head. And I wasn't accustomed to being in over my head. I was always invincible, a legend in my own mind. And I endangered every single person I cared about. The death of my friend, Gerry Upton, started this whole incredible story— but only as it involved me. His death sped things up. I would have eventually had to deal with the danger that was coming my way. But the danger came earlier because of his death. And my silence with the authorities, my lies to the board and shareholders, led directly or indirectly to the deaths of two more close friends—Steve Purcell and Jim Belton. Could their lives have been spared if I hadn't kept everything I knew so close to the vest? I don't know. Possibly. That question will haunt me the rest of my life."

Mike paused to look around the audience again. The lecture hall was full, standing room only. There had to be at least 1,000 students in the auditorium, most of them second and third year Business students. Mike reflected that it was nice to have been invited by the University of Toronto, his old alma mater, where he had obtained his engineering degree so many years ago, to come and speak to their students. They didn't care about the controversy, didn't care that he had been fired by his board of directors, didn't care that he had been disgraced as a liar within the Toronto business community. All they cared about was that he had a message their students could learn from—a powerful message of corporate responsibility in an era of deception, fraud and greed.

Sure, Mike was now a disgraced executive, fired from the company that carried his name. But he was also in a different league than the Enron criminals, the Wall Street bullies, the Madoffs, and the Bay Street assholes. He had a reason for what he had done that had nothing to do with greed. He hadn't been trying to personally profit by lying. Sure, he had been trying to hang on and survive, to buy time. But his story was clear—he had been trying to solve it on his own and clear his name. He wasn't trying to steal money from shareholders. And that was a message that the venerable institution known as the University of Toronto wanted its students to hear. And many other institutions wanted people to hear it too. Over the last six months Mike had given speeches at the Chamber of Commerce, three community colleges, two other Ontario universities, business groups, and a criminology symposium. And the one that he found particularly intriguing was a speech he had been asked to give at Kingston Penitentiary.

So, while unemployed now, Mike was very busy. He charged fees for his speeches, but donated all of the money to charities—primarily charities that helped troubled youth, and also those that dedicated themselves to abused women.

"In closing, I would use three simple words, words that if put into practice would probably single-handedly save the global economy. Those three simple words are: "Tell the truth." One lie leads to another, and the hole becomes deeper and more desperate as each new lie mounts on top of the previous ones. Even if somehow you're able to justify in your brain, like I did, that your reasons for lying are honorable, don't listen to that part of your brain. Just don't listen to it."

*****

Mike was cruising south on University Avenue, heading toward a lunch date with Troy. They were meeting today at, of all places, the Metro*Cafe*. They saw each other several times a week—Troy was now unemployed as well. Their furious Board of Directors promptly fired both of them after the details of their lies and cover-ups became public.

Funny, neither of them cared. Being worth hundreds of millions of dollars apiece made it easier of course, but there had been far too much water under the bridge for either of them to be able to pour their hearts back into the company again. And they would never be trusted again.

Now there was just the two of them—down from the four close friends who had taken a risk years ago to execute a leveraged buyout of a company that needed their creativity and expertise. They had provided those talents and the company was very strong now as a result, and they were very rich. There was nothing more for the two of them to do, and the prospects of continuing on without Gerry and Jim didn't sit well with them. If they hadn't been fired, they probably would have just quit.

Mike had suggested that they meet at the Metro*Cafe* today, a suggestion that Troy thought was a little bit crazy. "Why would you want to do that?" he had asked. Mike replied, "Closure, Troy. That little restaurant was the turning point, where a bad situation turned a corner and turned disastrous. I want to have lunch at that same table on that same outside patio where Samson held a gun pointed at my crotch. I want to remember how that bastard finally lost his vendetta against me."

As Mike wound his way through traffic, he reflected on the investigations over the last six months. The FBI took Omar into custody at Miami International immediately after Mike landed the plane. But the killer certainly wasn't a flight risk—he could no longer see a thing, not even a single ray of light.

The FBI also searched the jet and made an interesting discovery—or rather a nondiscovery. No other parachute packs had been found, which meant that Samson had intended all along that Omar would go down with the plane. He was the sacrificial lamb, the incredibly hot and hunted sacrificial lamb, to be offered up drowned and shattered on a silver platter. Whether or not Mike and his friends had stormed the plane, Samson never intended the jet to make it to Panama. It was obviously the plan all along that it would be scuttled in the Gulf of Mexico along with the hapless Omar.

After a few days of interrogation by the FBI and CIA, Omar was returned to Canada where the RCMP took over. Under threats of being sent to Israel or Guantanamo Bay for questioning, the coward began to sing. And the Canadian and U.S. authorities loved the tune he was singing. In fact it didn't take much to make him sing once they disclosed to him that Samson had not brought an extra parachute onto the plane for him. So—in the name of Allah of course—he told them everything that he knew about the banker network "throughout North America." He had apparently done covert work for each network over the last few years, so he was more intimate with them than the typical suicide bomber would have been.

Arrests were made swiftly before they too had the opportunity to run. Billions of dollars in assets that hadn't yet moved to Panama or the Middle East were frozen. It was heralded as the largest terrorist network takedown in history.

As for Samson, there was no sign of him anywhere. He and his pilots had literally disappeared 'into thin air,'—more accurately described as the humid, putrid, petroleum-polluted air over the Gulf of Mexico. Once Mike told the FBI about the GPS device that he had seen on Samson's wrist, they were convinced that a boat, trawler, or even a submarine had been waiting down below at prearranged coordinates.

Interpol had issued arrest warrants within every country on the globe that agreed to cooperate. David Samson, AKA Dawud Zamir, was the current 'most wanted man in the world,' taking over the honor from Omar, his protégé.

*****

"So, Mike, how does it feel to be sitting here at this little restaurant again? Must be a bit weird for you, eh?"

Mike leaned in, elbows on the table, chin resting on his clenched fists. "Weird, for sure, but also a bit victorious. I'm here—he's not. I'm sitting at the same table on the same patio where he gained control over me. That was the day that I was supposed to take control over him, as you'll recall. As with everything, he was one step ahead."

They paused their conversation while the waiter served their smoked salmon and cream cheese on bagels. Mike took a long sip of beer out of his frosty mug and gazed out past the wrought iron fence to the street where people were peacefully strolling on this particularly warm spring day.

Troy raised his head up from his plate and stared at his friend. He didn't say anything. Mike stared back, intrigued. "What are you thinking, Troy? You have a very heavy look in your eyes."

"Do you ever think about Jim?"

Mike lowered his eyes. "All the time. In at least one dream a week, or more like one nightmare a week. I'm looking into his eyes, he's smiling, our fingers touch, and then all I see are the fingers of his other hand slipping off the rung. His body falling in slow motion, hand still reaching out to me in desperation. But, funny thing, he's still smiling even as he's falling. Same dream every time."

"We'll never forget that day, Mike. I can't believe Jim is gone. I'd just gotten used to the idea of Gerry being out of our lives, but now Jim. God, it's so sad. We'd all been together so long, been through so much over the years. We were inseparable. Don't die on me, Mike. Please."

Mike reached over the table and grabbed Troy's hand, squeezing it hard. "We'll be okay, buddy."

Troy licked the cream cheese off his fingers, and quickly changed the subject. "Mike, the food at this restaurant is excellent. Despite the sordid little history we and Gerry have with this place, I'm going to recommend it to everyone I know." Mike noticed there were tears in his eyes. A big, tough guy like Troy didn't like to show emotions, especially those of the teary kind. But Mike knew he had always had the biggest heart of all four of them.

"It's nice sitting here with you, Troy. It's peaceful here now. This is the same table, the same spot where months ago there was a gun pointed at my balls. It's still hard to believe. This gives me a little bit of closure, believe it or not. Sitting here at Samson's place, Metro*Cafe*, and feeling safe. I feel like I've invaded and taken over his turf."

Troy shook his head. "I'm still astonished at how you took control and flew that damn jet. We were in such trouble, I thought we were goners, and you just took over and landed that big sucker. How the fuck did you do that? Well, I know what happened in your brain of course, but still—how the fuck did you do that?"

Mike cracked his knuckles. "It's the same old puzzle, Troy. I still don't really understand it, but I embrace it now. I accept it. I was indeed aware of what I was doing in that plane, but didn't know why or how I was able to do what I did. I was as astonished as you. But I just went with it—didn't resist. I knew it would save our lives, I just knew it, just had to go with it."

"So, Gerry in fact saved our lives that night. He did, didn't he?"

"Yes, he did—well Gerry's brain, memory and skills did. I don't believe that there's any kind of ghostly presence. When that lightning bolt hit both of us at the same time, parts of him just downloaded into me. That's the only way I can look at it."

Troy nodded and changed the subject again. "Mikey, what's the story with you and Cindy now? And with that Teskey prick? I know you were going to pursue a complaint—did you do that?"

"Cindy and I are finished. I still love her, Troy, but there's far too much water under the bridge now. Her affair with Teskey is only part of it—we could get past that if that's all there was. She's just not comfortable with me anymore, and I'm not the same person she fell in love with. It would never be the same again. And with the trauma she suffered from the horror she witnessed in the gym that night, she'll never be the same again. My presence would keep reminding her and bring it all back. She's better off without me now."

Troy reached over and squeezed Mike's shoulder. "I guess I can understand that. You seem at peace with it."

"I am. And as for Teskey, I decided not to file a complaint. It would just drag Cindy through the mud. She'd have to testify at the hearing, it would be messy and embarrassing for her. I didn't want to do that to her. What happened just happened. I can't turn back the clock and my wish for vengeance against Teskey would only hurt Cindy and the girls."

"I think you made the right decision. Best to just move on."

Mike nodded. "Yeah, and I see the girls every week—as long as I can still be with them whenever I want, I'm happy. Cindy's been very cooperative that way. The girls don't understand what's going on, they don't know anything about what happened with Teskey and they never will, but they seem to be adapting as well as can be expected."

Mike took a deep breath and continued. "Speaking of moving on, you should know that there's a new woman in my life. I met her accidentally through that little boy who was hiding in the garbage dumpster. Remember him? She's his mother. Her name is Alison. They live just around the corner from here."

"Really? Mikey, you never told me! What's the deal?"

"I know. I should have told you. I've been keeping her kind of my little secret. But you'll meet her. She's pretty special to me; in fact there's no doubt in my mind that I'm in love with her. The four of us should double-date sometime, take in a hockey game or something?"

"Wow, I'm shocked. Okay, but I want to hear the whole story very soon. Promise me?"

"I promise, buddy." Mike glanced at his watch. "But right now, I gotta run. I'm supposed to be over at her house right now. I can't believe how the time has flown by today. Time slips past pretty fast when you're unemployed, eh?"

Mike and Troy stood up and shook hands. Suddenly Troy reached out and threw his arms around Mike in a strong bear hug. They embraced each other—two friends, the only ones left now out of the inseparable college foursome.

*****

Mike parked in front of the little red clapboard house, a familiar parking spot for him now. He walked up the front steps, and before he could knock the door swung open revealing his gorgeous new lover wearing the biggest smile he had ever seen in his life. Her eyes lit up the day or night when she smiled. Ali had a face that always had a lot going on—good stuff going on. Mike had lost track trying to count all of the different expressions, and the cute little moves she made with her mouth—pouts, puckers, the twinkling eyes, twists of her head causing her long hair to fly across her face. She was fascinating. He knew he could look at her, *just look at her*, for the rest of his life.

She threw her arms around his neck, and kissed him softly on the lips. She pulled her head back and gazed lovingly into his eyes. Mike felt as if he was going to melt away into a puddle right there on her front porch. He loved this girl. He knew it without a doubt.

"So, what did I do to deserve this public display of affection? You normally don't kiss me in bountiful splendor on your front porch!"

"Well, get inside then and I'll do even more!"

Ali led Mike by the hand into the living room. He noticed that the table was set in the dining room, candles lit, a bottle of red wine already breathing.

"Ali, it's about an hour too early for dinner, and I just finished lunch. It looks lovely though. But why is the table only set for two?"

"I knew you were having a late lunch, so we're just going to have a light pasta dinner. And we can just sip wine until you're hungry…or do other things, your call." She smiled seductively at him.

Mike drew her into his arms and kissed her warmly on the lips. He adored her affectionate nature, her warm innocent heart; two of the qualities that made her a special mom as well as a special lover. He drew back, cupping her pretty face in his hands. "But where's Jonas? Isn't he eating with us?"

"That's one of the reasons I'm so happy tonight. Jonas was invited to his first ever sleepover with friends! I'm so excited for him! And so was he—you should have seen his little face, Mike. I was so proud."

"That's really amazing. He's come such a long way, hasn't he? He has confidence now, and friends—and best of all, he's not being bullied any longer."

"A huge cloud has been lifted from me. My darling little boy's heart is not being hurt anymore. Mike, it's all due to you. You've had such a positive effect on him—the speech lessons, the sports you play with him, talks you both have together. My God, where did you come from? What did we do to deserve you?"

Mike squeezed her tightly again, and ran his fingers lovingly through her long hair. He loved her even more at moments when she was like this—exuberant, excited, effervescent. His heart was on fire.

Ali kissed his neck. "You're our hero, Mike. You came to save us."

"Not so much a hero, Ali, just someone who was at the wrong place at the right time. Funny how life works sometimes—destiny, whatever we want to call it." He twirled her hair in his fingers, and leaned forward to kiss the tip of her nose. "So, what you're saying is that we're alone tonight. We can make as much noise as we want?"

"As much as we want, sweetie. So, wait here while I get into something more comfortable. Boy, is that ever a cliché line, eh? But it still works!" She slid off the couch, and floated off to the bedroom, leaving Mike with an exhilarating sense of anticipation. He thought back to that first sexual experience they had had, with the ice cubes and the champagne. He trembled at the images in his mind.

They had been intimate many times since then and each time was a surprise. It wasn't that she always did different things—she didn't. It was more just the way she did them. Sex had never been so passionate or satisfying for him until Ali.

A few minutes later she glided out from the bedroom, a captivating smile lighting up her face like a thousand twinkling lights. Mike gasped. She was wearing a multi-colored silk dressing gown, deep cut in the front displaying the curve of her beautiful breasts. The sleeves of the gown were wide and flowing, like a kimono. But it was still just a dressing gown and he could never have imagined that a piece of clothing could take his breath away. But Mike knew it had a lot to do with who was wearing it. And on Ali, it looked stunning.

She went over to the dining table, poured two glasses of wine, and carried them and the bottle over to the couch where Mike was relaxing. She sat on his lap, and they toasted to Jonas, to each other. Half an hour later and two more glasses of wine each they were still toasting—to silly things, giggly things, anything.

Mike knew that Ali was naked under the dressing gown. The smooth texture of her bare skin was apparent underneath the silky dressing gown. Nothing got in the way as she slid back and forth on his lap. He was still fully clothed, but was quickly reaching the painful point where he needed to strip, badly. His penis was pushing so hard against his jeans that he felt as if it could drill its way right through the button fly.

Ali never liked it if he was naked too soon. She liked to tease him, make him sweat, make him cry out for relief. Mike always felt a bit frustrated when she did that to him. But when he did achieve orgasm after usually an hour or so of playing around, it was an explosion; a much more satisfying orgasm than if she had allowed him to hurry it in typical male fashion. Ali always knew what she was doing. And Mike always let her do it.

He reached for her but she pushed him back, making him watch her lap dance for just a little while longer. He groaned in pain, his jeans getting tighter and tighter by the second.

Then, mercifully, she slid off his lap and took him by the hand. He obeyed her silent command as she led him into the bedroom. She stopped him beside the bed and began gently disrobing him, not saying a word. The room was quiet except for the sound of Mike's labored breaths.

Once he was naked with his penis already extended somewhat in the direction of the ceiling, Ali gently pushed him back onto the bed. She went around to the night table and opened a drawer, withdrawing four multi-colored silk scarves. Quickly and playfully, she tied his wrists to the brass headboard and his ankles to the footboard. Mike had no urge to resist. He was always titillated with whatever ideas she came up with. And surprisingly, for a take-charge aggressive guy, he enjoyed being a mere bystander until it was his turn to play. This was like his private little peep show.

Ali crawled on top of him with the grace of a mountain lioness, robe now discarded, and reached her lips up to his, kissing him deeply, probing with her tongue right to what seemed like the very base of his. For a weirdly glorious second he was afraid he was going to gag. Her tongue slid, licked, probed, while at the same time she took his erect penis in her hand and squeezed it, worked it, teased it. When she seemed satisfied with what she had molded, she slid her body down in one fluid motion until her lips found their target. The tip of his penis was now in her mouth. She was circling it with her tongue, confusing it.

Mike stretched his muscular body against the restraints, hoping against hope that he could loosen them. But his efforts only made the knots grow tighter. He was breathing faster now and could feel the blood rushing through his veins. A warm sensation was taking over and he knew, could feel, that his face was very flushed now. His head seemed to be throbbing in cadence with his penis.

As if sensing he needed relief, she gently blew on the now soaked tip, the sensation of her breath bringing him instant relief, slowing him down, cooling him off. Then she crawled like a wild cat once again, bringing her pelvis up close to his face. Inserting her fingers between her legs, she began to rock. Mike was mesmerized as he watched her rub and stroke herself mere inches from his lips, her own breathing now irregular and gasping, eyes glazed over, seemingly oblivious to him.

He yearned to touch her, kiss her, lick her, but all he could do was watch and wait while stretching in futility against the sexy scarves holding him captive.

She then inched her body forward a few inches, still on her knees, and framed his face with her strong thighs allowing him to penetrate her with his tongue. He could feel and taste the incredible wetness; he knew she was ready and he knew he was ready, but she wasn't yet willing to give in. She straddled his face for a few more minutes. He gazed up at her beautiful sensual eyes in wonder, as his tongue did its work.

Suddenly she moved, inching back down the bed ever so smoothly until she met resistance from his erect penis. She leaned back, pressing her buttocks against the throbbing and pleading member. Mike groaned as the pressure on his penis intensified, being teased and forced in an unnatural direction by her shapely ass.

Without warning, she lifted herself up and onto him in one fluid motion. He felt her warmth and wetness and he wanted to scream out, 'thank you!' Mike felt the sudden need to reach out and grab her body tightly, and to pull his knees up into a bent position. But he couldn't move. He was her prisoner, and she was gently raping him. Ali leaned her head down, long hair falling forward covering most of her face, and whispered, "Fuck me."

Despite being restrained from doing the things that he was accustomed to being *able* to do in normal lovemaking, in that instant before he climaxed he knew that it was going to be the most intense explosion of his life.

*****

Exhausted, they were lying side by side in bed, still naked and glistening. Ali had mercifully removed the silk scarves from his wrists and ankles, allowing Mike the pleasure of rubbing her smooth, toned stomach. She was moaning appreciatively, eyes closed, the hint of a smile on her pretty face.

She turned her head towards him, and pulled her hands up to cup his face. "I love you, Michael. I really do."

Mike didn't hesitate. "I love you too, Alison. More than I can say." He kissed her luscious lips. "This has all been so unexpected, but when I think back now to when we first met and how we met, strangely enough it seems that it was inevitable."

She smiled warmly, and her eyes twinkled with happiness and tears. "You're a hero to so many people. What you did, landing that plane and bringing that terrorist back to justice, it's just unbelievable. You're such a celebrity now, in big demand from everyone. Yet, here you are with me. I feel so lucky."

Mike hadn't told her about any of the spooky stuff associated with the unique talents he now seemed to have on command. She didn't need to hear that, and he didn't want to talk about it. All she knew was that he had encountered these terrorists in conjunction with his company's international land holdings and that they had embezzled money from his firm, trying to frame him in the process.

"I just reacted on panic and instinct when I landed that plane, Ali. And it was really pretty easy—that type of jet basically flies itself. But, I had no choice anyway. It was either try to do something or we were going to crash into the Gulf of Mexico. With those options, anyone would have attempted what I did."

She smiled. "So modest. One of the things I love about you."

"Ali, I lost three close friends in this entire ordeal: Gerry Upton, who was at the center of the embezzlement, then Steve Purcell, and finally Jim Belton. It's hard to feel like a hero, or even a modest one, when I've lost so much."

Ali sat up in bed, shivered and drew the sheets around her. "I feel for you. You have indeed lost so much, not only your friends but also your family life. It must be so painful for you."

Mike sat up as well and stretched his arms around Ali's shapely shoulders. "It makes it all so much easier to deal with knowing I have you and Jonas in my life now. And Jonas lost his father in the terrorist attack that these killers pulled off. Talk about 'six degrees of separation!' It's weird isn't it, how all the dots seem to connect sometimes?"

Ali nodded and lowered her eyes. "I have a confession to make, Mike. Jonas didn't lose his father that night at the subway station. Wade thought he was the father, and Jonas thought Wade was his dad—but he wasn't."

Mike leaned on his elbow, resting his chin in his open palm. "Tell me."

Ali took a deep breath. "I had an affair with a married man that went on for years, almost a decade. I'm not proud of the deception, but my marriage was shot and it just happened. He was Jonas' biological father but I never told him. I didn't want him to be with me out of obligation, so I kept it to myself."

"So what happened? Where is he now?"

"He's gone. He just disappeared over a year ago. I never heard from him again. I don't know why, we were great together, inseparable. I was so much in love with him, and then he was just…gone."

Mike gently squeezed Ali's bare shoulder. "Did you try to locate him?"

"Oh, yes. He said he was a consulting lawyer for various corporations—on litigation matters. His name was Tom Balderson. When he disappeared, I checked with the Law Society and they had no record of him. I never even had a phone number for him—he always called me. I accepted that secrecy because I did know that he was married. He was honest about that.

"And you know what? I think he always knew that he was Jonas' father. I could tell by the look in his eyes and by the way he related to Jonas. I think he knew, and he understood my reasons for not telling him. He respected those reasons, I'm sure, and he wanted me to know that he was with me because he wanted to be with me. I'm sure he didn't want me wondering. But then one day he was just…gone."

"That must have just broken your heart, to have him just leave you like that, no closure."

"It did. And my marriage to Wade continued to be a nightmare. But then you came along and I have to tell you that I've never been in love like this before. You need to know that. I loved Tom, but you've taken me by storm. I'm complete again, but in a way that I've never been before."

Mike kissed her sweet lips. "Do you have a picture of you and Tom together? Did you hang onto some memories?"

"I do. Do you want to see?"

"Yes, absolutely. It's good that you've kept your memories, Ali. When you think of it, our memories are the only real enduring things we possess. Tom may be out of your life now, but he was obviously an important part of it for a very long time. And he gave you a wonderful son. I'll never destroy photos of Cindy. At one time I loved her very much, and I want to remember that."

Ali smiled warmly at him, and nodded. "I'll go and get the photo. Be right back." She jumped off the bed and headed into the adjoining study.

Mike called after her. "I'll get out the photos of my friends too."

He slid off the bed and walked over to his jeans that were draped over a chair. He fumbled his way through his wallet until he found what he was looking for. He took the photos back over to the bed and waited for Ali.

In a flash she was back, with a single photo in her hand. She jumped happily onto the bed just like a little girl, obviously proud and eager to share this part of her past with Mike.

"You first," she said.

Mike passed one photo over to her. "This was Steve Purcell. He's the one who was…beheaded in that school incident."

Ali shuddered, and whispered respectfully, "He was very young in this photo."

"Yes, he was. That was a senior high school picture. After graduation we never really did anything together except meet at those boring reunions. Such a shame we didn't find the time to do more."

Ali nodded pensively. "Who's next?"

"This is Jim Belton. He's the one who fell from the plane. We'd known each other since university."

She trembled again. "He was cute, but kinda delicate-looking, eh? With those glasses?"

Mike laughed. "Jim was an accountant—glasses were mandatory."

"And the last photo?"

"Yeah, well this was Gerry Upton. The one whose death from the lightning strike started this whole unbelievable spiral of events."

Ali picked up the photo and stared at it. Then she held it up to the light on the night table. Mike was surprised to see that tears were running quickly down her cheeks, and her face had flushed a bright red. She was starting to tremble again as well, but this time violently, almost like the start of a seizure. Mike reached out to her.

Suddenly she whirled towards him, fire in her eyes, and the slap came—hard and fast. Mike didn't see it coming and had no time to brace himself, or protect himself. It was a strong one; so hard that Mike bit down on his tongue with his teeth. He tasted blood.

Ali glared into his eyes, into his soul, a glare that could melt an iceberg. She seethed, "You sick bastard! What is this, some kind of twisted practical joke?" Then she jumped off the bed and was gone.

Mike was stunned. What had he done? He reached over the side of the bed and picked up the photo that Ali had dropped onto the floor when she fled the room.

He laid it down on the bed beside his own photos. Then he gasped, choked. He could feel the crushing voltage of the lightning bolt all over again, from the top of his head to the tip of his toes.

With the photos side by side, it was just like the cartoon—Tom and Gerry side by side.

But this wasn't a funny little cartoon, not even close.

Because Tom was Gerry and Gerry was Tom.

About The Authors

Peter Parkin was born in Toronto, Canada and after studying Business Administration at Ryerson University, he embarked on a thirty-four year career in the business world. He retired in 2007 and has written seven novels with co-author Alison Darby.

Alison Darby is a life-long resident of the West Midlands region of England. She studied psychology in college and when she's not juggling a busy work life and writing novels, she enjoys researching astronomy. Alison has two daughters who live and work in the vibrant cities of London and Birmingham.